LO

Tales of a Footloose Man

Rick Haggard

Copyright © 2023 *Rick Haggard*

All Rights Reserved

This book is dedicated to the greatest pair of parents anyone could ever ask for, Otis and Betty Haggard.

I miss you and assure you that whatever mistakes I made were not your fault.

Acknowledgment

The following people were inspirations as I wrote:

Mandi Croft, my writing partner and prime encourager when it came time to publishing.

Ginger Moran, aka The Professor. It was Ginger who convinced me that LOVEBLIND could become a reality.

Steve Moriarity, fellow new author, who spent countless hours on the phone with me honing the story.

John Matthews, author, was always willing to lend an ear when I had questions about the process.

Notes from the Author

LOVEBLIND: Tales of a Footloose Man is loosely based on real-life events with dramatic license taken. Any resemblance to actual events is purely coincidental. It's pretty factual about music though.

About the Author

Rick Haggard is a native of Charlottesville, Virginia, where much of LOVEBLIND is set. He actually worked in the Charlottesville music scene in the mid-1970s after graduating from the University of Virginia in 1974. A description of that scene is part of LOVEBLIND! After moving around the state of Virginia for most of the 80s, he resettled in Charlottesville in the 90s and, except for a brief two years in SE Florida in the early 2000s, he's been there ever since. He's run a successful DJ and Entertainment Company since 1989. LOVEBLIND is his first novel.

Contents

Acknowledgment i

Notes from the Author ii

About the Author iii

Prologue: Fanfare For The Common Man ix

Chapter 1 – Hotel California 1

    February 4, 2014: The Unceremonious Exit 1

    Interlude: The Lebowski Level 4

    January 10, 2014: Do It For Love 5

    Turn Up The Radio: Take It To The Limit 10

Chapter 2 – Groovin' 11

    Autumn 1970 11

    The Village Inn: We Gotta Get You A Woman 12

    Late October 1970 15

Chapter 3 – Sweeter Memories 18

    Late Summer: 1971 19

Chapter 4 – I Met A Little Girl 25

    Late January 2014: I Love LA 25

    Summer Of 1973 25

    September 1973: I Meet A Little Girl 27

    The Next Saturday: Come Get To This 30

    The Autumn of 1973 31

    Interlude: In My Hour Of Darkness 32

    Winter and Spring 1974 35

Summer 1974: Hot Fun In The Summertime 37

September 1974: My Old School 39

Chapter 5 – Big Yellow Taxi 42

August 1976: Be Young, Be Foolish, Be Happy 42

Paradise and a Parking Lot 44

Autumn 1976 and Winter 1977: Killer Queen 45

Spring 1977: Me and Mrs. Jones 49

Interlude: Bubba and the Cocaine 50

Chapter 6 – Family Affair 53

Early Summer 1977 53

Summer 1978 55

1978-1995: The Good Marriage, The Bad Husband 55

1995-1999: Papa Was A Rolling Stone 57

Daddy, Don't You Walk So Fast 59

My Family: Remember When 61

Chapter 7 – I'm A Believer 64

October 1999: A Reunion 64

The Second Coming Of Grace: Sweet Blindness 67

January-July 2000: Life In The Fast Lane 72

Eagles Interlude: A Not So Peaceful Uneasy Feeling 75

Chapter 8 – Life In The Fast Lane 76

August 2000: A Knot That Can't Be Broken 76

The Honeymoon: Destination Boca 77

September 2000- June 2002 79

My Folks: Two Lonely Old People 82

Summer 2002: In The Name Of Love 83

August 2002 to January 2003 84

The Long Road Home: February 2003 until September 2012 86

Chapter 9 – Lyin" Eyes 89

September 22, 2012 89

Sweet Blindness 91

A Bible Verse: For What It's Worth 92

January 2013: A Trip To Boca 97

The Club: Three Little Birds and A Monkey 98

Chapter – 10 At the Dark End of the Street 103

Late January 2013: Boca Raton 103

A Well Respected Man 105

Chapter 11 – Got My Mind Set On You 110

The Poor Side Of Boca 116

February 2013: Money Honey 118

The Big Gorilla: Monkey Man 123

The Guido Shuffle: I'll Tumble For Ya 124

Chapter 12 – Heartbreak Time 127

The Testimony: Power 127

December 2012- March 2-13: The Love Dare 131

August 2013: A Peace That Passes All Understanding 135

August 2013: Lila's Back 138

August 31, 2013: Another Game 150

Chapter 13 – Open Up My Window 158

Early September 2013: Back To LaLa Land 160

Sex Drive 161

Masterpiece 162

Chapter 14 – God Blessed Our Love 167
    September 28, 2013: Wake Up My Soul.. 170
    Power: Jesus Will Fix It 175
    September 30, 2013: Graceland.. 178
    October 1, 2013: Suspicious Minds 181
    October 2, 2013: Hello Mr. O'Grady 183

Chapter 15 – Thieves in The Temple 184
    Early October 2013: After The Thrill Is Gone 185
    Sunday October 27, 2013: California Feelin' 192
    Hermosa Beach: Don't Get Above Your Raising 195
    Palos Verde: Don't Think Twice (It's Alright) 198
    November 3, 2013: The First Breakup.. 202

Chapter 16 – Sitting In Limbo/The Late Show 204
    Early November 2013: Sitting In Limbo 205
    November 6, 2013: The Long Run... 208
    Late November 2013: Woman Comes And Goes.............................. 215

Chapter 17 – Flaw... 220
    December 2013: One Fatal Flaw.. 223
    December 30, 2013: Future.. 225
    January 1, 2014: The Last Ride 232

Chapter 18 – Waiting In Vain 234
    The Next Day: It Wouldn't Have Made Any Difference 236

Chapter 19 – She's So Mean... 245
    Sunday January 26, 2014: It Never Rains In Southern California .. 245
    Monday, January 27, 2014: Rich Girl... 248
    February 1-2, 2014: Super Bowl Weekend... 253

Monday February 3, 2014: The Last Day 256

Chapter – 20 Heartbreak Time 2 259

    March 2014: It Ain't Over 'Til It's Over 265

    Spring 2014: Sound Of Silence 268

Chapter 21 – The Heart Of The Matter 272

    August 2014: Another Reunion 275

    September 2014: Heartbreak Time 3 277

    October 2014: Woman Comes And Goes Again 280

    Forgiveness 287

Chapter 22 – All You Need Is Love 290

    December 2014 290

    All You Need Is Love 291

    Happy New Year: Love, Love, Love 294

Chapter 23 – Aftermath: The Return Of The Grievous Angel 296

    The Future 296

The Soundtrack 303

Prologue: Fanfare For The Common Man

Have you ever just googled "I hate the Eagles?" Go ahead, try right now. I'll wait. You'll see a few references to the Philadelphia Eagles, but the very first thing that shows up is the video from the Coen brother's classic comedy, *The Big Lebowski*. These 47 seconds moved the Eagles from a very respectable place to the very tip top of the most hated musician's pantheon. Of all the scenes in this eminently quotable Coen brothers film, this may be the most memorable in that it is mentioned and quoted whenever a negative Eagles article is spun in print or online, which is a lot. Jeff Bridges is in the back of a cab after a horrible day and "Peaceful Easy Feeling" comes on the radio. He immediately asks the driver to change the station. "Come on, man, I've had a rough night and I hate the fucking Eagles." The driver pulls over and extricates him from the cab, leaving him standing by the side of the road. I can top that story.

Chapter 1

Hotel California

You pay for your sins. God has a sense of irony, perhaps a warped sense of humor, but a sense of irony for sure. He'll let us have exactly what we want, every single thing we think our willful little human hearts desire, just before He drops the hammer dead on us and we see that it all makes us miserable. Before we discover that everything we've ever wanted is the absolute worst thing we ever got. That's how I ended up rediscovering lost love.....twice! That's how I ended up being a twice-divorced 62-year-old man with ailing parents, estranged children, and barely a penny to my name. And that's how I ended up sleeping in a strange bed in a California beach house, suffering from my second broken heart in less than a year. You pay for your sins.

February 4, 2014: The Unceremonious Exit

The homes in the most ritzy of LA beachside communities, the communities that seem a totally different world from the rest of that smog-ridden and traffic-jammed city, places like Manhattan Beach and Hermosa Beach, those homes seem like they're stacked on top of each other and crammed together like Ritz Crackers in a way too small lunchbox. Belittling their million dollar or more price tags with a minimum of three flights of steep steps that guarantee the Latino moving companies will never run out of work, these cracker box palaces give a workout trekking from the front door to the kitchen, often found on the top of the three floors.

At least a million things were running through my mind that February morning when I stumbled down the lowest of those three flights to drop my bag by the garage door. It was almost 6:00 am. As I walked back up and reached the top of the stairs, Lila's bedroom door was open for the first time that morning and she was sitting on the bed beckoning me.

"Come over here." As I walked in, she announced, "I can't take you to the airport and make it where I need to go...there's not enough time. I called a cab for you. I'm gonna pay for it."

Really? This woman had just made me sleep in a separate bedroom, a strange bed, a cold bedroom, alone for my final night of a nine-day visit to see her...after spending eight nights of near-perfect intimacy sleeping in a warm bed with her. Now she was going to add insult to that injury by refusing to drive me to LAX for what promised to be a miserable six-hour flight back to the East Coast.

As I approached Lila on the bed and sat down, I noted that she was wearing a silk Victoria's Secret nightgown that I had given her. She had worn long pajamas and slept so far to her side that I had to text her good morning the last night I actually slept in that bed with her. What's this? A final act of torture? What's next? Are the Eagles coming on the radio?

As I sat down beside her, Lila's voice was sweet and soft-spoken, her demeanor warm, and comforting. Her words would not be. She was as comforting as a doctor telling you the disease is fatal. The bad news? You only have two weeks to live. The good news? Eh, the good news...? Uh, you don't need to worry about your medical bills? You won't need that oil change?

"Did you get cold?" Uh-huh. I knew my head was still attached, and I could feel it nodding as she asked and then answered the question. "I thought of that around 4 AM... that you didn't have a blanket." OK, well, that would have been a really good time to come in with that Victoria's Secret nightie for a personal warming session, I thought.

"I'm really glad you came." Yeah, me too. Nothing like traveling 3,000 miles for seven great days and then having a nuclear bomb detonate on your already crushed heart on the final day. Glad I was here for that in person. Wouldn't have missed it, honey.

When I mentioned that it was a great trip except for the last day, a flash of what almost looked like anger came across Lila's face as she blurted, "Oh, so I have to take the blame for that."

Being the sad puppy that I am, I back down and mumble some lie about it being both of our faults. Pretty pitiful. She kicks me in the groan and I apologize for provoking her. Lila presses forward with her personal cleansing.

"I'm sorry it didn't work out." Didn't work out? Really? Three nights ago, you were telling me you loved me...and you would never do me wrong...OK, let's be blunt, you said you would never "fuck me over." Yesterday afternoon, under the full light of sobriety, you declared that it just "wasn't there for you," that we had no future that you could see. And you think that's it not working out? OK, I can buy that, Lila, and give me one of those Florida "lakeside" lots as well.

"I hope everything works out for you." Last night, you were toasting that we would be friends for life, even considering that we could be neighbors if I moved to LA, and this morning, after making me sleep alone in that cold, hard, unfamiliar bed, you're packing me away in a cab with a "hope everything works out for you!" Really? Then, in a truly spiritually comforting moment, Lila says, "I've got a good feeling about you." And I'm sitting here taking this like being nice is going to melt the wall of ice that was protecting her heart. Friends for life. Right!! What's a mere 10,000 miles or so between friends? Oh, excuse me, I guess I mean to a friend, as the fact is only one of us actually traveled that 10,000 miles. Oh well, I guess even a fool is at least still a member of the queen's court, he just has to wear a funny hat, right?

Now to you, my friends, the really funny part is when I tell you that after Lila broke up with me, made me sleep in a separate bedroom, and refused to drive me to the airport, it was me who called her after I got to the airport to apologize for being "pissy." Thinking about that retrospectively, even I cannot help but laugh at myself. Funny, but also very sad, I can see that now. But not then, not when I was reaching for any straw I could find that might possibly pull me out of the sticky mess I found myself in. Go ahead. Look up "whipped" in the Urban Dictionary right now. My picture will most certainly be there.

We walk down her steps to where my bag, expecting a trip in her BMW Land Cruiser, but now downgraded to an LA cab, is waiting. A silent, strong hug and a couple of quick kisses and I'm off out the door where the cab is....not there...a minute or so later he pulls up, loads my bag in the trunk and I get in back. Not in the mood to talk, I tell the driver my destination is LAX and sit silently. His signal is it's OK to turn the radio back on.

"By the rivers of Babylon, we sat and wept when we remembered Zion." **Psalms 137:1**

As we negotiate the darkened streets and stacked up neighborhoods of Hermosa and Manhattan Beach, I lean back on the seat and close my eyes, thoughts racing faster than Sea Biscuit on the final turn at Santa Anita.

Interlude: The Lebowski Level

Before everything happened, I already had legitimate reasons to hate the Eagles. In addition to being despised by some of my favorite musicians for their pandering pop treatment of the country rock idiom, including one of my most cherished personal musical heroes, the late Gram Parsons. Gram's vision was to merge real country music with real rock. He felt The Eagles had severely poisoned the water by introducing pop into the mix to make radio hits. Additionally, the Eagles had a nasty habit of raiding other bands for musicians by dangling that irresistible rock star combination of money, drugs, and women under their noses. Given the vociferous cocaine diet that was the Eagle standard in the 1970's and 1980's, under their noses is probably anatomically correct. That's my Eagles background. Pretty typical. A pompous rock fan thinks himself above hit making Eagles.

But the Eagles were slightly more than just hit makers. They were purveyors...purveyors of the rock star lifestyle. Cocaine, groupies, sex with different women every night. These boys got around. In fact, I'm wondering if the Eagles might not be responsible for herpes...it had to start somewhere.

Don't ask me how a really mixed up guy from a small town ended up with not one, but two women who had some, well, "personal time" with the Eagles, but that's exactly what happened. That's what moved me from being a standard garden variety Eagles hater into what I like to call the Lebowski level of Eagles hatred.

It's only when you truly, truly Lebowski hate the Eagles that you begin to notice the Eagles are everywhere. That's when you can't walk into a retail store, grocery store, or anything without hearing the dreaded opening chords to *Hotel California*, *Take It To The Limit* or even worse, *Peaceful Easy Feeling*, the national anthem of Eagles haters, Eagles haters who have moved beyond the public hate their pop persona into the rarified air of truly Lebowski level Eagles haters where it's more personal. You not only hate the vast majority of that commercialized crap they call Eagles music, but the faces of certain Eagles (OK, two Eagles) are forever imprinted on the dart board inside your mind, where you gleefully toss the sharpest darts you can get into their eyes just hoping to "kill the beast."

January 10, 2014: Do It For Love

In the cab, my thoughts sped to that night less than three weeks earlier when Lila had pleaded with me to visit her. "My heart misses you, Rick." Despite our three months apart, despite the fact that Lila had painfully broken our relationship off after my last visit to LA, this little puppy dog was online within 10 minutes of the invitation securing a late January flight.

As soon as the said ticket is purchased, Lila begins to talk about how the LA world is our oyster. What on earth will we do with it?

"We could go see the Eagles, but I know you don't like the Eagles."

"No, I actually like some of their songs. It's just that I can't stand Don Henley and Glenn Frey." Gram Parson's ghost is patting me on the back. That's right, you tell her, brother. Stand up for me against those plagiaristic dirtbags!

That's when the famous other shoe dropped, and the shoe should have been the largest red flag in the history of freakin' red flags, but not for me, not Ricky boy, not when it came to Lila Wylde.

"I've had sex with Glenn Frey." When I look down, my jaw has also dropped. It is virtually rolling around on the floor of my townhouse. Can a jaw possibly roll? It's not symmetrical, right? Whatever! Either way, I can't remember the next 25 or so things I said. From the recesses of my memory is dredged the conversation I had over 13 years before with my now ex-wife Grace when she revealed that SHE had spent an evening with the Eagles. Really? Is it possible revelations such as these have been revealed in small towns all over the country for the last 40 years? OK, raise your hand if you've been with the Eagles or know someone who has. How did it take me so long to figure this out?

GP's ghost is now shaking his head vociferously and smiling as he lights his ghost joint just before he takes a deep swig from his ghost Tequila bottle. As I momentarily survey this apparition more close while absorbing what Lila has just told me, I take note of the fact that it is the thin, handsome, coolly dressed pre-1973 Gram that haunts me, not the overweight, scraggly looking, t-shirt too tight, I'm a heroin addict and I'll be leaving the planet soon post-1972 Gram. I guess you get your choice, which leads me to wonder if the gold lame' suit, thin, hip shaking, incredibly handsome Elvis roams around the afterlife instead of the overweight, bloated. Can we expand this jumpsuit one more time Elvis?

Shaking my head in the realization that I am still on the phone with Lila, my thoughts return to the Eagles, a musical group so detestable as human beings that entire blogs have been dedicated to showing these country rock emperors, indeed, had no clothes. I mean, I knew the Eagles had gotten around, but man, the Eagles REALLY got around.

"You had sex with Glenn Frey?" That's my voice, right?

"Like three times," Lila shoots back.

Steady, Rick, you can make it through this. "Three times? When? Where?"

"Florida, Virginia...it was like a two year hookup."

"Three times in two years. Sounds more like a groupie thing."

"It's not good. Once in the 80's, our eyes met as we were leaving a Lakers game at the Forum."

"Are you saying he recognized you?"

"Oh yeah." GP laughs so hard the Tequila comes out of his nose! I guess he's thinking the same thing as me, wondering how Glenn could have recognized Lila given the fact that the Eagles ingested copious amounts of various substances on a daily basis during the time frame in question coupled with the likelihood that Frey likely had relations with an additional 700 or so females during that two year period.

Gram takes a fresh swig of tequila. Come on, brother, call her out! You know that's not true. When I let it pass, I see the apparition before me look at me with disgust and walk away into the bathroom shaking his head again. Why the bathroom? Do you mean heroin is available in the afterlife?

Once the Eagles are out of the bag, Lila begins delineating the details of her time as a bartender at the Newport Beach Resort Hotel during the "Cocaine Cowboy" Era of the late 1970s and early 1980s. Sure, a normal person would have been terrified, normal being a man with any semblance of self respect. In addition to the Eagles, there are a couple of other rock stars as well as a former golden era Miami Dolphin player (whom she noted had snorted cocaine off of her bare arm), a hit man, and various cocaine dealers. Along with these shady characters and semi-questionable celebrities, there were the 'normal' encounters....the parking lot attendant at the Newport, with whom she had a 4 pm between shifts "conference" every day in whichever parked car was available at the time, many of her "clients" at the bar, and one guy who slept with both she and her roommate, Pamela, who was the one person Lila claimed was responsible for guiding her down to this road of promiscuity and debauchery with the promise of 300 tax free dollars daily, a considerable amount of money during those days. She noted it was Pamela who first took up with the Eagles, the other rock stars, celebrities, and other victims the shady owners of the hotel suggested she spend some quality time with. Together, the two ladies apparently enjoyed copious amounts of cash, cocaine, and celebrity hookups in service of the mafioso like board which ran the property. Lila eventually ended up in jail and was invited to depart Florida post haste by her attorney after one of the drug dealers she got tied up with locked her in a room and tried to hang the rap on her for the coke that he was transporting in her car......whew! Exhausted by the conversation and, at a loss for words to say the least, I could only blurt out, "so does anybody else know all these stories?"

"Only Debbie". Debbie had been her best friend in LA for over 20 years. I'm in the usual Lila quandary. Is she telling me this crap because she trusts me immensely or am I just the most disrespected man on the planet? Lila eases my concerns. "Rock stars and pro football players...not a bad life for a young girl."

"Is there more?"

"Oh, these stories are just the tip of the iceberg." Not unsympathetic, Lila offers solace by assuring me that she would rather do ANYTHING with me than have sex with the Eagle in question. A comforting thought, which, sadly, was enough for me. Since then, I have come to a realization. When someone flat out tells you who they are, BELIEVE them! But not then, not at that moment. At that moment, Lila could have told me anything and I would have bought in. This was a woman I had carried a huge torch for, one that continued to burn brightly despite me not seeing her for 35 years. It was like God was dropping a huge gift on me after the hell that I had been through for almost a year when Lila and I met again. You're not gonna look a gift horse in the mouth, are you? It would work out. That was my thinking. Heck, she must really trust me...right? Right? Plus she and I had just an incredible sexual chemistry, a Song of Solomon chemistry biblically speaking! That comes from God, right? Right?

I know what you're thinking. What is wrong with this guy? What idiot travels almost 3,000 miles to visit a woman who tells him stories like that? Is he brain-dead? Well, one thing I have come to realize is that hope is a funny thing, especially false hope. For one thing, it wears the same outfit as real hope. Like beauty, it's an eye of the beholder concept, and it can get pretty confusing. Another thing about false hope is the longer it lives, the tougher it is to kill. My hope for Lila had been running on fumes for almost three months. Since her first (or was it second?) breakup with me. There was no way a few stories about sex with rock stars or even drug orgies was gonna kill that hope, We're talking Super Hope, ladies and gentleman. Hope that it is not gonna die until it's been bludgeoned over the head multiple times and even then, it may stumble around the room for hours, days, or weeks before finally going down.

Turn Up The Radio: Take It To The Limit

"Which terminal, sir?" The driver's voice snaps me back into reality.

"Terminal 3...Virgin America", I mutter, staggering back from the emotional abyss I had been drowning into the present moment. The radio is still on.

I hear the familiar high pitched voice of Randy Meisner coming through the rear speakers singing a lyric about open highways, road signs, and pushing oneself to the outer edges. Yep, it's the Eagles. In fact, it was the song that got poor Randy booted from Hotel California nearly as unceremoniously as I was, except in Randy's case, it was his refusal to sing his masterpiece, *Take It To The Limit*, every night.

I can't help but crack a smile as I take a deep breath and we enter LAX. God whispers in my ear, "I tried to tell you".

Chapter 2

Groovin'

So I guess you're wondering how this all happened. How did eight beautiful intimate days and one lousy night end up a failure? I wish I could answer that question. I wish I knew the answer. All I know is that when it turned around, it was unchangeable, like a train that was chugging up a mountain, chugging, trucking, oh so close, almost over the top... then the straining engine gives out and down she goes, rolling backwards down that same mountain, only at five times the speed it was going up at. The crash at the bottom is unavoidable. And devastating. That crashed engine would be my heart, my hope for a love I harbored for years crushed flat underneath it. Flat as a Pancake House breakfast. That's what it felt like. Or it could have been God collecting a debt on a broken promise. That's not for me to say. You can decide for yourself once you've heard the story. The whole story.

There's really no way to understand the story completely until you know who Lila is and why? And there's no way to understand who Lila is without first understanding about Grace Jones and who she is? And there is no way to understand who Grace is without understanding the Rascals, the first snowfall, and the pebble on the window.

Autumn 1970

Echols Dorm is one of the oldest dorms on the UVA campus and is right beside the graveyard. It was my first time living away from home. My roommate, Chase Felson, was from Coral Gables, Florida. His father owned a trucking company. That put old Chase in what I call the Redneck Riviera Nation. You couldn't completely take the redneck out of him, but the real rednecks wouldn't be caught dead in a room with Chase. I'd known a lot of guys who were entitled and thought they were better than everyone else. Chase wrote the book.

Down the hall was John Healey. John was from Memphis, the son of a wealthy DC-based attorney, and had been one of the sources of my music love due to possessing the coolest and latest sound system around in 1970, an eight track tape system plus a warehouse of cool music. Yep, I said eight track! It was 1975 before I even realized that Jimmy Page's solo on "Stairway To Heaven" didn't have a break in the middle.

Right across the way was southwest Virginia boy Sam David, AKA the provider of the marijuana. It was a serious position and Sam took it seriously. We did routine quality assurance inspections while partaking in John's incredibly diverse selections and the music of CSNY, Buffalo Springfield, Neil Young, the Doors, Cream, the Who, and the Beatles was as omnipresent as the towel at the bottom of the door.

The Village Inn: We Gotta Get You A Woman

The Village Inn, an old high school hangout, was right up the road and one night, I took a solo walk there from the dorm. I had a very distinct advantage over my buddies in the first couple of months. There were only 500 women in UVA's first coed class, but being a local as well as a first-year man, I knew where to find more information that I held so tightly to my chest that you would have thought I had the nuclear codes. Seemed fair to me. I knew where the women were, and they didn't. I wasn't going to be stingy, I just wanted the first choice.

Judy Martin had grown up right up the street from me. She had been a cheerleader and since I dated her friend Samantha Snead, another cheerleader, we had become friends the last couple of years in high school. Judy was there at the Village Inn on this particular night in late September of 1970, but she wasn't alone. At her table was this incredibly beautiful hip-looking girl with the then edgy shag haircut and a smile that threw a light over the heavens, oceans, and anything else that was around...a smile that lit up the sky, life-affirming, beautiful...with the deepest blue eyes I had ever had the pleasure of gazing into in my first 18 years on the planet.

This was Grace Jones. At 19, she was a year older than me. I couldn't take my eyes or my focus off of her. She was the most beautiful creature that I had ever seen. If there is such a thing as love at first sight, this was it. The amazing thing was the same lightning would strike again almost 30 years later when Grace strolled into our high school reunion. That's right, it turned out Grace and I had gone to high school together. Not only that, she had a locker next to mine.

This realization had me scratching my head to see if my brain was still there. How is it possible this incredibly beautiful girl was right beside me every morning and I missed her? I remember rubbing my eyes just to be sure that I am not blind. Then I began to look past the tasteful makeup and frosted (remember frosted?) stylish shag haircut, which was the latest thing in 1970. Light bulbs went on as I remembered a tall and slim "country" girl who had the locker by me. Long natural blond hair, thin as a rail, and virtually makeup-free, it passed through my head on a daily basis that this girl sure had a natural beauty. Alas, though, she wasn't one of the "cool" chicks back then. She was a worker bee, involved in all the job programs the working class kids were in. We didn't run in the same circles.

As time went on and I found out more about the lovely Grace Jones, it became clear that she didn't run in any circles. Instead, she was fully focused on learning her trade as a hairdresser as well as contemplating her dreams of being a top fashion model. Aha, that explains the anorexic Twiggyesque look. Grace's father passed away when she was 14. The father who spoiled her by giving her 100% of his attention 100% of the time. He cooked for her, took her with him everywhere, and made sure she always had a pony. Grace was with him one summer day when he suffered a severe stroke, a stroke that turned out got be fatal, a stroke that changed Grace's life forever when he passed away the next day at home. What a crushing blow that must have been at 14.

To add flame to the fire, her mother married the man who became her stepfather only six weeks after her real father departed the planet. Then Mom piled insult on the injuries by selling the family farm that Grace had spent her life on. The rug was completely pulled out under poor Grace within a year of losing the most important person in her life. She was living in boarding houses, raising herself, and hanging around adults who smoked, drank, and had random sex. Yet amazingly, Grace was so focused on becoming who she now thought she had to be that she not only survived with her virtue intact, but her innocence as well. Even now, even after all that has happened between us in the ensuing 44 years, even though some might say she betrayed and used me during the course of our 13-year marriage, I still admire Grace. So many others might have gone the route of drugs, promiscuity, debauchery, it would have been understandable, but not Grace. Grace sailed through the rough waters God had placed in front of her with her sails high, her integrity intact, and her focus sharply on the prize. Even now, I am conflicted about Grace, my often inexplicable love for her, what to do with it, what to do with her.

There was no such confusion that night at the Village Inn in 1970, no conflict, my heart melted so completely that I remember glancing down to be sure there was no puddle under me. Unbelievably, she seemed to actually like me too. We talked and talked, sat close together, and did lots of arm touching. Judy would later tell me how obvious it was that Grace and I had just gotten run over by the same freight train on that September night. Cell phones weren't exactly the norm in 1970. Did they even exist? When the time came for the evening to end, as the Village Inn started shutting down, I walked Grace to her car, but not before I asked her to consider going out on a date with me. We set it up for the following Saturday night. Pretty sure we went to a movie that first date, perhaps a pizza after, the normal small town first date in 1970. Over those first few dates, I deduced that in addition to being stunningly beautiful, Grace was incredibly naive and innocent.

I don't exactly remember our first kiss as much as the fact that Grace had absolutely no idea how to kiss. So I taught her. How to kiss, how to French kiss, how much to use your tongue. She was a quick study and still possesses the softest, most giving pair of lips I have ever kissed. Years later, as our marriage crumbled, one of my greatest regrets was the loss of true kisses from those lips, soft as rain, gentle, and the perfect match for my own lips. Ah, Grace at 19. She was truly something.

<u>Late October 1970</u>

Back to Echols dorm. As a specific day in late October approached, Grace told me with trepidation about a date she had with an old boyfriend, a date that had been set up a while. It was that date that had me uncomfortably laying in my dorm room bed that night, trying to sleep but awake with the tortured thought that after this beautiful girl went out with the old boyfriend, a wealthy preppy, Rick would be the horse that was put out to pasture. Out of the picture, past his expiration date. I mean, it wasn't like I deserved a beauty like that. So I lay there staring at the dark. Suddenly, there's a sound, something hit the window. Then it happens again. I get up and take a look...then I see...there she is...standing right under the window. I couldn't get dressed fast enough. Grace was waiting at the dorm door. We kissed. Did I want to go to her apartment? On the way, she explained that she told her date, Bobby, that she was seeing someone else. My heart jumped out of the car and I took a few turns around the block on its own before jumping for total joy.

When we arrived in the driveway to Grace's tiny upstairs apartment, actually more of just a room, a gentle snow started falling, the first snow of the season. We climbed the steps to that attic apartment, where I beheld a beautifully comfortable brass bed that had to be just like the one Dylan described in Lay Lady Lay. Across the room from the bed, a tiny attic window, one of those little square ones you had to bend down to even look out of.

"How about some music?" Grace had a tiny record player and a meager selection of LPs to choose from. I perused until I saw one that looked familiar. The Rascals. Truthfully, the Young Rascals. I presented Grace with my selection and she placed it on the turntable. Holding hands, we huddled at that tiny window as, over a musical bed of lilting keyboards, gentle drums, and bird sounds, Felix Cavaliere sang a song about taking it easy and *Groovin'* on a lazy summer afternoon as we watched the snow fall outside.

It was, and still is, the single most romantic moment of my over 60 years on this planet. I was, at that moment, immersed, captured, a willing prisoner to the love you read about in books, and saw in movies, a total believer. That night, we slept together in that big brass bed, holding each for dear life as if we didn't believe what was happening. It was the first time either of us spent the night with someone, awakened next to someone, someone you cared about. Deeply. There wasn't any sex or anything other than pure Erich Segal's "Love Story" romance. I had too much respect for Grace to even consider that. It wasn't like that. It was an incredible, unbelievable, wonderful, special night shared by a couple of kids who were falling in love for the first time.

The moment would remain inscribed forever in my memory. Years later, in the midst of crisis, when the "love of my life" had decided that I wasn't for her anymore, I would reach back for that moment and address it poetically in a vain attempt to rekindle Grace's affection.

A pebble hit a window on a night so long ago,
a chilly late October night with a hint of falling snow

Outside the window, she waited that night
'til he woke up to a beautiful sight

The smile he'd been waiting to see all day,
a tender kiss shared and they drove away

> A cozy place, a room just for two,
> that boy was me, and that girl, you
> In that small room, we cuddled by a tiny window,
> and stayed up almost all night, just watching it snow

The stereo played "Groovin" on a Sunday afternoon and as we watched it snow that night, that became OUR tune. It was epic, noble, and a failure. A noble failure. It would be years later before I would finally discern that the only real difference between a believer and a fool is the end result of their respective quests. I was and am a little of both, a realization that would strike me deep in my soul that February morning over 43 years later as I walked down the causeway to board a plane bound for DC from LAX with only my twice crushed and broken heart for companionship.

Chapter 3

Sweeter Memories

Take a few of these, the sweeter memories

Don't forget them, please, the sweeter memories

Truest remedies set your mind at ease

Are the sweeter memories

(Todd Rundgren)

"Sweeter Memories" as performed by Todd Rundgren

Grace and I floated through the winter of 1970 and the spring of 1971 on the romantic clouds and sentimental winds of that October night. There were memories, of kids playing in the snow on New Year's Eve of 1971, Grace's nephews, little kids we agreed to keep as sort of a trial run for a future that would never transpire. Even as we floated on those clouds, storm clouds gathered on the horizon of our bliss. Small things.

At first. First was the fact that I led two virtually distinct and different lives for the entire first year in school, a trait that would continue 25 years later when we finally became husband and wife. There was the me that went out to restaurants and local night clubs with Grace, adapting myself to her lifestyle and social milieu, but there was also me that laid around the dorm smoking pot with my buddies and drinking Boone's Farm chilled in trash cans filled with ice. It was the old life reining me in, but the new life, fully aware of the changes attendant to the freedom of college life and the ongoing societal evolution that the 1970s were bringing to everyone. If I could've looked into the future and seen where my path would take me versus where Grace's would take her, I might have potentially avoided the two years of crushed heartbreak that would follow. I would end up your basic long haired, plaid shirt and blue jean wearing pot head hippie, whereas Grace would end up in New York for the beginning of the disco era as a top model in the world of Twiggy and Iman, eventually landing in Milan, where she would leave her simple country girl roots in the dust.

Once classes were done for the year, Grace took ownership of my being or more appropriately, I handed her the reins. We took jobs at a restaurant called The Triple S on Pantops Mountain on the east side of Charlottesville. We had already talked about the getting married part, the giving of the ring was merely a way of declaring it official. In fact, when I told my parents of my plan to marry Grace, they were not even remotely surprised. My mother immediately handed over her own diamond to be reset for Grace. REALLY!! Sweet, innocent, virginal, beautiful. We were both virgins. AND she was going to wear the family diamond. It was just perfect. How could I be so lucky? I felt God smiling.

<u>Late Summer: 1971</u>

The dark clouds popped up, especially on a trip we took to Birmingham to see Grace's extended family. I was working the restaurant and another job that summer, Grace at the restaurant and her full-time beautician's job. Both of us were fairly exhausted for a fair amount of time. When we, or more appropriately, Grace planned that mid-August trip, I begged her to allow us to leave on an early Sunday morning, allowing us to sleep before taking on the 14-hour drive. Grace, always in a hurry to arrive, insisted we leave that Saturday night as soon as she finished her last client.

So we packed up our bags in her baby blue 1970 Camaro. I suggested we drive in shifts, but Grace wanted no part of that, flying into a mini-rage as she asserted how hard she had been working and how dare I even suggest that she drive. I say mini because that rage was barely worthy of being called a preview of the one I was about to see, like comparing the Sahara to a sandbox. So we, or rather I, drove through the night, progressing nicely until about 1:30 am when we were just past Bristol. That was the first time I nodded off a bit at the wheel, shaking Grace awake when I made the correction to keep us from running off the highway. She begrudgingly allowed me to pull off at the next rest stop to nap, yet exhausted as she was, she managed to be awake enough to wake me up after 15 blissful minutes of shut-eye, punching me in the arm while declaring, "Come ON, Rick, we have 10 hours to go! We'll never get there." Thus it went throughout the long night, Grace dozing, me dozing behind the wheel, me pulling into a rest stop, Grace wakes up, punches me, wakes me up, I pull back onto the highway, and the entire cycle starts again.

It was about 5:00 am right outside of Knoxville when the crap finally hit the fan full-blown. No sooner had I pulled out of a rest stop when I nodded again and actually ran off of the highway into a construction zone. This was the moment when I witnessed my once innocent and beautiful fiancé evolve into Predator, screaming and berating me at the top of her lungs, making odd references not to the possibility that my exhaustion might be putting us in jeopardy, but rather to the cost of her precious Camaro. "Do you have ANY idea how much this car costs, Rick?" Huh???

Despite my eventual threats to stop in Knoxville and take a bus back to Charlottesville if Grace didn't stop screaming, we somehow made it in one piece to Birmingham by late morning. I should have been taking notes because once Grace's volcanic temper made its first appearance, it was like a faulty Jack-in-the-Box whose springs could no longer contain it. Years later, when we were married, Grace exploded on an assistant who was a mutual friend, one who expressed pity for me by saying I had to live with THAT for the rest of my life. The TEMPER was calculated, controlling, but in no way controlled. It was literally like a volcano, it just exploded and unpredictably burned up everything in its path.

Grace and I stayed together until early December of 1971, 14 months being my longest relationship ever at the age of 20. We held off on sex until August of 1971, when we each gave up our virginity in what turned out to be the only time we had sex. Neither of us knew what we were doing, especially me, so when Grace started crying in the middle of the act, I was pretty much traumatized and the damage would not be undone until the seductress that was Lila came into my life almost three years later.

There was Grace's sister, Tonya. Tonya and Grace lived together from the time Tonya left her Southern Baptist preacher husband and became the talk of the town in Stanardsville, the seat of Greene County, Virginia. Tonya lived up to the reputation by socializing strictly with her divorce attorney, who was obviously in love with her, and his wife, who for all I know, may have been in love with her as well. The three of them were certainly bizarre enough in terms of behavior to support any theory I could come up with, especially when the copious amounts of alcohol they consumed nightly were involved. Tonya was the epitome of the dark sister. She eventually died at age 43, her health overtaken by a long-term addiction to prescription drugs, uppers, and downers. She had her nose in everything we did and her intentions were questionable at best. Tonya constantly queried me about the state of our sex life or, more appropriately, the lack of one thereof.

Things began to really unravel for Grace and I beginning in September of 1971. That was when suddenly in the middle of an evening together, she announced that she was giving me the ring back. What? Yes, she didn't feel right wearing it anymore. Why? Because she had gone out with someone else. It seems that the dark sister, Tonya, had taken it upon herself to find Grace an appropriate match at HER new boyfriend's place of employment. Turns out cheating on men was a family tradition. Since I am stupid, I made Grace promise she wouldn't go out with him anymore because it makes perfect sense to tell the girl who just cheated on you not to cheat on you anymore, especially now that she is no longer wearing your engagement ring. So much incentive. Don't think being this stupid doesn't require some effort. I have to work at it.

My relationship with Grace had its idiosyncrasies over the years, one of which was this ridiculous tendency. I had to want to believe Grace no matter what she was saying and how far it was removed from what was really happening. As soon as she proved untrustworthy, I was ready to put all my trust in her again. One night in early December, reality struck me in the face like a solid bat on a good fastball. I had become a little suspicious because of Grace's various excuses, so I had occasionally taken to the occasional drive-by of the duplex that Grace and Tonya lived in.

Grace's blue Camaro was usually there, but not on this one evening. I drove around for about an hour and a half waiting for that Camaro to show up, finally ending up parked outside Tonya's boyfriend's apartment, where I got the nerve to go up and ring the bell. When they let me in, I sat down in the kitchen and began to tell my story of waiting for the car. Thence, I turned and confronted Tonya, "Where's Grace? I know you know where she is..." Tonya finally sighed and shrugged her shoulders, "She's with.." And she said his name. The name Grace had told me. The name of the person I asked her not to go out with again. The name of the man she was sleeping with. My heart sank so fast it was like an elevator that dropped 10 floors. I was devastated, seriously devastated. The air was gone from me.

Even with my forgiving nature, I had a streak of common sense in me then and, hard as it was, I resolved not to talk with Grace. I took back Christmas presents, took the ring to have reset for my mother again, and did everything I could to move ahead. Finally, one night Grace got me on the phone and I agreed to sit in her car and talk. She broke down and cried that she just didn't want me to hate her. I didn't hate her, I just didn't want to be around her. I think somehow I felt like she had hijacked all of my high ideals. How would I ever believe it again? Less than six months later, she and the man from her sister's job would get married.

I was devastated when Grace was unfaithful, crushed completely. How could my sweet little virginal Grace, whom I had taught to kiss and guided through our first trip into our sexuality after waiting over a year...how could she sleep with another man, have sex with another man?

Despite the sexual revolution spinning around in the landscape, I had turned my gaze inward with the assistance of LSD, MDA, marijuana, its' big brother hashish, and whatever other mind-expanding, enhancing substances I could get my hands on. Women were there, I dated many, but no one, NO ONE, could erase that smile, those giant blue eyes, that corrupted sweetness that had been Grace from my heart, my soul, my essence. No one until Lila.

For the next two years, I would only hear about Grace a couple of times. Then, in the autumn of 1973, right after I met Lila, Grace called me. I agreed to go for a quick ride with her. She spent the first 15 minutes telling me how cool her car, an MG3, was and the last 15 minutes crying incessantly when I resisted her advances, telling her about the new girl that I loved, meaning Lila.

I can still hear Grace exclaiming through the tears, "How could you fall in love with someone else? How can you love somebody else?"

As for me, you're right. Inside, I was thinking, 'Excuse me, honey, but didn't you MARRY someone else?' That's my Grace. She also wanted to know all about Lila, but I thought it best not to share, given what I considered her borderline psychotic behavior.

My final word to Grace that day was to tell her to either fix or leave her marriage, words which she tossed back at me in the spring of 1974. "Well, I did it. I left my husband!" Holy, I don't know. Grace invited me over to eat with her, allegedly so we could talk about getting her out in the world. Eh, that wasn't the plan. My sweet Grace, whom I had waited almost a year to have sex with, sweet once virginal Grace took me back to the back bedroom where both of us demonstrated the experience that we had gained while we were apart. It was quite a delicious evening with only one problem. Couldn't get my mind off

Lila. That was all I thought about, all I cared about. I went over to Grace's apartment two days later and told her that it wasn't going to work. She listened incredulously and nodded her head, never really crying, though. She was smiling and waving as I pulled away, the last time that I would see her for 25 years!

Chapter 4

I Met A Little Girl

Late January 2014: I Love LA

Lila looked great when she picked me up at LAX that Sunday morning in January of 2014, absolutely stunning to me. I have since come to realize, however, that my level of objectivity when it comes to Lila may be slightly below zero. Okay, WAY below zero. Even as she nudged her way from her late 50's towards 60, Lila was in great shape. She definitely carried around a few more pounds than she did at 23.

Hey, who doesn't? But she just looked more voluptuous, at least to my love-blind eyes. Befitting the princess she had always been, and become perhaps even more so during her nearly 30 years of marriage, Lila was dressed to the nines, even when casual. Her bright yellow sundress was like a neon sign blatantly issuing invitations for me to slip my hand between her legs as we drove down Manhattan Beach Boulevard. Her tanned skin barely hinted at her age and her "natural" blonde hair, which had been naturally brown when she was younger, contrasted the golden color of her skin. The truth is it probably wouldn't have mattered what she looked like. It was Lila, the woman who had fully occupied the back room of my heart for the last 35 years, the woman I had turned every available stone up looking for before finally finding her in 2008 through the magic of what? Facebook.

Summer Of 1973

1974 was scheduled to be my last year of college. Scheduled, but schedules, you know, they are like rules. They require an occasional "adjustment." I would not actually finish school until the fall semester of 1975.

It's early September of 1973. I was always delighted when the school year started. Not because of the academics, I hated that crap. It meant my party pals would be coming back. I could now safely transition from the summer life of construction work, extended high school friendships, and way too much alcohol to the autumn life of crashing first-year parties, skipping classes, way too much alcohol AND way too many illegal drugs.

In 1973, it meant my four buddies would return from their summer hiatus and the party could begin at their brightly painted 1940s model two-story brick house at 139 Stribling Avenue. When I say brightly painted, we are talking about an orange room, a green room, and my personal favorite, the empty room with royal blue walls and ceilings. This was what happened when you mixed home improvements and LSD. The acid we continued to add like gin to a straight up martini. Regularly!

I have distinct, eh, "memories" of spending about a year in that blue room one night under the influence of way too much LSD. Two of the Stribling guys, John Healey and Sam David, had been close buddies since my first year in Echols dorm. John was from Memphis, the possessor of the cool system and equally cool music from my first year. By the fall of 1973, I was setting my own path in the influence of music on my life.

Sam was from the little southwest Virginia town of Marion. Over the three years, we'd been close friends, I had been to Marion many times with Sam, including one MDA laced trip to see an infamous Black Oak Arkansas concert at the high school gym, after which Sam's high school girlfriend and first love ran off with the equally infamous lead singer of the group. The scene in that gym was the definition of Marion's life. Southern Baptist parents lined the upper ring of the basketball stands, looking down in shocked terror at the drug induced debauchery that was taking place on what once was simply an All American basketball court, all being orchestrated by a shirtless long haired lead singer whose speed enhanced black eyes shone from the stage like Lucifer himself. Man! Please allow me to introduce myself indeed!!

Along with all the drugs on the underside of little goody two shoes Marion, there were the women. Not exactly country girls, their sweet Southern accents belittled the sexual and drug induced sophistication these young ladies possessed. It was a world where the bowling alley was still cruised, but the underside was those same cars cruising nostalgically down Main Street where the sight of drug orgies and sex. Lots of sex. Marion was the kind of place where being a bad girl was a good thing. It was an enticing treat for a young man of 21 who was just learning to enjoy the bad things in life. The edges, the drugs, and especially sweet Southern accents that hid a promiscuousness that was a completely new experience for me. It was like biting into a piece of my grandmother's Southern Pecan pie expecting the sweetness of sugared pecans only to find the inside filled with jalapeños and exotic flavors of all manner instead. It was a hell of a lot spicier than you expected, but irresistibly delicious. This was Lila's world.

Sam and John had both witnessed the stomping that Grace Jones had laid on my heart first hand. My first love, my first everything, a girl who represented virginity, goodness, all the things God had ordained for His true children. I mean, we were engaged, wasn't that what you were supposed to do? Make love with one person, marry them, and live happily after, right?

September 1973: I Meet A Little Girl

A group of us sat around on the large couch in the orange living room of 139 Stribling Avenue one early September evening in 1973, passing an extremely fat joint back and forth. Amongst the usual array of regular attendees was one of Sam's brother Kevin's friends from Marion, an 18-year-old girl with long brown hair, dark bedroom eyes with long lashes, and one of those sweet but sexy Southern accents.

A girl named Lila. As we passed the joint for about half an hour, our eyes met frequently and we exchanged the occasional smart-assed jabs. They were dark brown eyes, not the eyes of an 18-year-old, almost the eyes of a woman of the world. Seductive eyes. Eyes that were speaking louder to me louder than anything had since the beautiful blue eyes and bright smile of my once sweet Grace had spoken to me when we met in 1970. There was nothing sweet about these eyes, though. Even at 18, those eyes enticed me, much like that Pecan Pie with exotic flavors inside. Those eyes said, I may be sweet on the outside, but I'm hot and spicy inside. It was the first time in my life I remember looking at something, or someone, and thought, I HAVE to have that! Right then, the die of my 40 years of torching was cast.

After some brief socializing, Lila said she was still putting stuff away and getting her dorm room together and took off walking. I waited about two minutes and took off behind her. Every time she turned a little corner and I was out of her sight, I'd break into a brief sprint to catch up. By the time we got near the dorms, I called out ahead, "Hey, it looks like we're going the same way."

Lila turned and waited for me. "Are you following me?"

I shuffled the random cards in my mind quickly and pulled out an ace. "I'm headed to a party on campus. Why don't you come along?"

"I already told you I have to finish unpacking." Behind the disgust at my inability to take no for an answer. I noted a slight look of almost fearfulness in her eyes.

"Maybe I'll come along...maybe I can hang a picture or something". Who is this talking about? It doesn't sound like me.

"I don't have any pictures." The look of fear that Lila had now turned to apprehension. What the hell is this guy doing?

"You never know, you might need help with SOMETHING."

Lila turned around and started walking ahead. "Suit yourself, it's a free world." She heightened the pace, but I purposefully followed from a few yards behind, just watching that wonderfully inviting rear end of hers swing to and fro like a pendulum on a grandfather clock. The voice in my head was saying this is no Grace, buddy, you'd better get your game in high gear!

Once we got into Lila's room, I didn't do a bit of work. I just watched her put things away and asked questions, trying to find out more about her while simultaneously trying to figure out if there was any way I could get that dorm room door shut and maneuver her to the bed, hopefully naked. She already had a boyfriend, her high school sweetheart, Daniel. He was here at UVA too, only a couple of dorms over, a revelation was ignored by my volcanically erupting hormones completely.

My libido told my brain to take a powder and declared itself in charge of the situation. "Why don't you just dump him, then go out with me?"

Lila stopped putting clothes away and turned around. She smiled with a look of astonishment at my newly discovered brazenness, a look that seemed to resemble desire. The other person that had apparently inhabited my body next said, "I guarantee you that you will have fun. Go out with me."

That apparent desire on Lila's pretty face now officially announced itself into the room, with the sweetness of the Southern accent now replaced by the confidence of the beautiful seductress. "You guarantee it, huh? Really...well, we'll see about that."

My brain has now fallen asleep in the next room and my now raging libido is fully in charge of the situation. "There's a football game on Saturday, the first game of the season. I'll be here at noon to pick you up."

She didn't answer, no yes, but no no. She looked at me like I was crazy. Pretty sure she was right.

"I'll see you then," my mouth announced as my libido took its hand and led it out of the room, picking up my sleeping brain on the way out. School? Friends? Stribling Avenue? What's that?

I was fixed, fixed on Lila. My mind was set on that next Saturday.

The Next Saturday: Come Get To This

There was not another word between Lila and I before I showed up at her dorm that Saturday in 1973 with a bottle of bourbon and a flask. Yep, she was ready to go. And she looked stunning. Platform heels, hoop earrings, nails painted red...these were the things that stood out. I never even asked what she did with her boyfriend, but I sort of figured out that she didn't exactly officially break up with him. I'd say it's more like she allowed the breakup to...evolve. In the rearview, I probably should have paid attention to that, but there was only one thing on my mind. She was 18, wearing platform heels, and had my 22-year-old hormones raging like the Colorado River after a cloudburst.

The game was just the beginning of a day that evolved into an evening of dancing at a crashed frat party and then the night together in one of the spare bedrooms at 139 Stribling Ave. Lila, years later, would attribute her "loosening up" to the bourbon. All I know is that as I stripped her clothes off of her that night, she kept saying that her dorm mates had her practicing saying no before I showed up that day. Her lips were saying no, but they were betrayed by her hands, which were hurriedly ripping off my jeans and putting me inside her. Years later, Lila would say she didn't remember a thing about that night except that she woke up naked.

Of course, at the same time, she would reminisce that the first minute she laid eyes on me, she knew she was going to have sex with me, that the entire five months or so we dated were basically all about sex. She would say that I was only the second guy she ever had sex with. Yet the stories she tortured me with about every other man that she has ever been with (I mean, we wouldn't want to leave anybody out, would we?), those stories called that into question even.

I finally came to realize that when it came to Lila's stories about drugs, sex, and rock and roll, the truth wasn't purposefully hiding, it was just elusive, somewhat slippery, sort of like a water slide. You may think you know the way it's going, but sometimes the water has other ideas. The only thing you can be sure of is that you will end up wet and you damn well better know how to swim. Lila's ingestion of substances combined with the social milieu she aspired to and the sexual prowess she applied to move forward naturally reduced the absolute truth to an occasional hit-or-miss intersection with actual reality at best. When there is so much to review, it's pretty easy to occasionally forget a footnote.

The Autumn of 1973

Yet in that fall of 1973, none of these complicated calculations were anywhere near my 22-year-old radar screen. The rear-view mirror didn't even exist. All of life was in the front windshield. Thanks to Lila, I was emerging from a deep and dark tunnel that Grace's betrayal had led my life into. I was discovering my sexuality, but it was more than that. Lila brought the sunshine back into my life, the lightness, the ease of living. What I had no way of knowing in 1973 was that while that sun would never fade completely, the lightness would carry her away on breeze after breeze, and the ease would entice her into a life that I could never measure up to.

Those thoughts didn't even exist in the fall of 1973, though, not as September passed to October and finally into November, then kicked into the chilly air of early December. It was a beautiful fall that year. The sun-bathed leaves changed into works of art and hung around on the trees for what seemed like forever, giving us all one final burst of their color and brightness before gently bowing out as they turned brown and floated to the ground in late November. This was the background as Lila and I went to football games, concerts, and parties, building what seemed like a lifetime of memories in only three brief months.

I don't know, maybe it was just the time of life, but the fire that was built in my heart during those months never extinguished completely. As the trees stood bare and the chill of December fell, I felt the warmth of our closeness dissipate into the distance that visited Lila's eyes when we were together. By the beginning of Christmas break, not only was the distance increasing, but I was to meet, for the only time in my life, Lila's father. As much as I felt the slight chill between Lila and I, it was a virtual heat wave compared to the arctic stillness of this man's eyes when he looked at me. There are very few times in my life about which I can say someone clearly didn't like me, but this one qualifies, even though I really only met James Wylde for a total of about an hour. Actually, let me restate, it wasn't so much he didn't like me, it was just that I wasn't what he had in mind.

Interlude: In My Hour Of Darkness

There was another significant event that took place in the autumn of 1973. On September 19th, at the Joshua Tree Inn outside Joshua Tree National Park, approximately 130 miles from Los Angeles, Gram Parsons died of a drug overdose at the age of 26.

Gram never had anything even remotely close to a hit song during his lifetime, but he cut a huge swath across the rock scene of the late 1960's with his injection of real Nashville-based country music into rock. Cosmic American Music, as GP himself would call it, was real steel guitar and fiddle playing country infused with a rock sensibility both musically and lyrically, but also incorporated blues, rockabilly, and a healthy dose of Southern Soul.

As a testimony to Gram's musical and personal persuasiveness, when asked to join the great American band, The Byrds, as a piano player, he completely hijacked the group and talked them into recording a country album. Released in 1968, *Sweethearts of The Rodeo* is generally acknowledged as the first true country rock album, but in reality, Gram had recorded the first country and rock hybrid over a year earlier with *Safe At Home* by the International Submarine Band. Byrds leader Roger McGuinn would later state that when Parsons joined the group, they thought they were hiring a piano player but instead ended up with George Jones in a sequined suit.

That's where I intersected Gram's music when I discovered him in 1972 after reading a review of his first solo album, *GP*. I actually bought the album because the review compared Gram to Ray Davies of The Kinks, my favorite lyricist at the time. What I got when I played the album the first time was way more than I bargained for.

Although I loved Poco, Pure Prairie League, and the other alleged Country Rock purveyors of the period, even The Eagles, I was in no way prepared for what I experienced for what I heard and how I felt when I dropped the needle on *Still Feeling Blue*, the first track on the album. The rousing sound of fast paced steel guitar and fiddle coming through the speakers harkened back to an earlier time as I hosted visions of childhood trips to Hendersonville, NC, where my mother's family was from, a town situated in the foothills of the Great Smoky Mountains and only 22 miles from Asheville. Jukeboxes at diners blasted George Jones, Merle Haggard, and Buck Owens. Working class music about divorces, alcoholics, and, of course, a heady dose of Southern Baptist guilt about the same.

My father, who to this day thinks the only music is country music, conducted a constant power struggle with his children as they sat in the "far back" seat of our Mercury Colony Park paneled station wagon (you remember, the seat that faced backwards), leaving our poor little soda changed brains adrift in a convoluted mess of a mix between *Yellow Submarine* and *Okie From Muskogee*.

Listening to *GP* transported me back to the station wagon, the diners, and the jukeboxes. It was like rediscovering roots you had forgotten you ever had! Not only was it OK to like George Jones, but it suddenly felt like it required listening. Maybe it didn't hit that same chord with everyone, I don't know, but to this day, over 40 years later, his cult not only thrives, but continues to grow, even supporting several small industries. Gram made it OK to show your Southern roots to the hippies.

The problem was that the way he died and the strange events surrounding his departure far overtook his musical legacy, at least for a while. GP was unusual in the musical world in that not only did he come from the South, but he came from wealth. His family, the Snivelys, owned a vast empire of Florida orange groves. Old Gram had grown up being waited on in mansions with man servants and maids galore.

His mother only lifted a finger to take a drink with it and Gram followed suit. He never met a substance he wasn't willing to abuse and any substance worth doing was apparently worth overdoing. Gram finally settled in on booze, pot, and heroin as his choices in his last few years on the planet, although it was actually morphine that did him in.

His departure became a story in itself when his road manager and best friend came through on a promise that should Gram die, he would take his body out to Joshua Tree and burn it. The problem was that Gram's stepfather wanted to get the body to Louisiana to establish his right to the Snively family money, so Phil and an accomplice were forced to steal Gram, casket and all, from LAX. The drunken misadventures and journey that culminated with the partial burning of GP's remains in Joshua Tree was bizarre and actually quite humorous, so much so that the entire event was eventually chronicled in the film *Grand Theft Parsons*.

Gram was, by all accounts, basically a sweet although extremely unreliable guy, a person who could afford all the condiments of the rock n' roll lifestyle without doing much of the work. He wasn't one to let work get in the way of the party, that was for sure.

As a musician, however, GP took his melting pot approach to American music quite seriously and, when he was at his best, insisted on the authenticity of the spirit of the music which inspired him. Although perhaps there was a twinge of jealousy due to their hits, Gram famously referred to the Eagle's pop music as being like a "plastic dry fuck." He (or more appropriately, what was left of him after Phil Kaufman's failure to crisp him completely) was probably rolling and laughing simultaneously in his grave when the Eagles recorded *My Man,* a posthumous tribute song to him.

Winter and Spring 1974

By the time Lila returned to Charlottesville in early January, sporting a brand new Camaro (what was it with Camaro's?), she would drop on me the first of Lila's greatest hits of the 16-year-old breakup lines. "I think we should see other people." The bloom was clearly off the rose.

Remember Lila's first boyfriend, Daniel, and how she didn't actually break up with him? How was it more like the breakup 'evolved'? I told you I should have paid more attention to that. The lines were never clear with Lila. She was the originator of blurred lines. Now you see them, now you don't. "Lines? What lines? I don't see any lines."

Thus the spring of 1974 morphed into the Spring of our discontent. More appropriately, the Spring of MY discontent. I wasn't always sure what Lila was doing. I spotted her out on a date with her old boyfriend Daniel as they walked by me hand in hand at a party in mid-April. We still saw each other, but it was uncomfortable at best. After the devastation Grace's unfaithfulness had wrought upon my being three years earlier, it felt like déjà vu all over again, to quote the immortal linguist Yogi Berra. Whatever cool I had equipped myself back in that Autumn of 1973 to weave my spell over Lila, I was totally devoid of any mechanism that could provide the capability of dealing with a multiple dating situation that Spring. While it was certainly possible, even probable, that Lila still cared for me, at least based on our interactions, the demonic jealousy that had housed itself deep inside my being since Grace's infidelity left me unable to deal with things in any normal fashion.

My response was simple. Take as many drugs, and drink as much alcohol as humanly possible in a vain attempt to bury my disillusion with love and with Lila. Any woman within range was a target, thus my one night dalliance with Grace in late April 1974. After that, I made a deal with myself to try and work with Lila, hormonal male pride be damned.

The low point was a Saturday night in March when I sat parked outside Lila's dorm all night drinking Vodka mixed with water, finishing an entire fifth while waiting to see if one of Lila's male friends from Marion was going to leave the dorm. Lila had told me he was staying with Daniel, although years later she would relate that he slept on the couch in the common area of her suite. He never emerged that night and neither did I, waking up laying across the front seat at around 6 am, smelling like a Skid Row bum.

There was nothing epic or noble about it. It was purely pitiful, a record low in terms of self-indulgence, self-pity, and pure stupid neediness.

Unfortunately, the drunken self-indulgence continued even on the rare occasions when I was able to capture Lila's time and get her out with me. I suppose I was thinking that since alcohol had seemed to help fuel her love for me back in the fall, I could somehow drink my way back into her heart.

By the time we all took a school year ending trip to Virginia Beach in late May, me with my friends and Lila with hers, it was all over but the alligator tears. On that trip, Lila would come over to see me and my pals during the day a few times, hanging out on the beach with us, maybe having a few drinks, in fact there was some interfacing between the two groups. Lila, for her part, was very uninterested in any conversation with me. It seemed to me that every time she and I were in proximity to each other she drew up like a clam being poked with a small stick. Almost 40 years later, she would attribute that to wanting to be respectful of my "space." What lover doesn't cringe at the sound of that word? Elusive, mysterious, at once all-inclusive while saying absolutely nothing. Space! A word that offers both hope and despair at once to a lovelorn heart. That was Lila. That was, and perhaps is, our relationship. Like "space." It never really begins, but it also never ends.

As the week ended and we all headed back to our various homes, meaning Lila to Marion, me to Charlottesville and another exciting summer as a construction laborer, I was painfully aware that we had "evolved" into a breakup.

<u>Summer 1974: Hot Fun In The Summertime</u>

My pitiful descent into full alcohol abuse continued as the summer ensued, days spent laboring on a rooftop in the hot sun, nights spent drowning my ever present sorrows in whatever libations I could get my hands on.

Still, I somehow managed to rally my incurably romantic heart enough to come up with a well constructed, if needy, appeal to Lila to consider a fresh start and perhaps begin by allowing me to come to visit her in July in Marion. I mailed the letter sometime in June and waited with bated breath for what seemed like an eternity for that phone call that I just knew was going to come, the call that would turn everything around, the open armed invitation. Yes, Rick! Yes! Let's start again. I do love you! I do! When can you get here?

The call never came. As I worked and imbibed my way through the hot June weather in my orange hard hat, that expectation was constantly in the back of my mind. Finally, one day in mid-July, a week before I had proposed the weekend visit. I rushed to my parent's mailbox to find a letter with that familiar handwriting and immediately glanced at the return address long enough to see the name. L. Wylde.

I rushed into our Earlysville home, heading back to my room in the very back of the house, and sat down on the single twin bed where Lila and I had consummated our lust so many times the previous autumn after waiting for my mother to go to work.

Finally!! It's about time. False hope (remember false hope?) was dancing around the room high 5-ing me. I briefly glanced at the closet to see what was clean. Who knows? We might go out to a nice dinner. Briefly, I tried to remember if I had even seen a nice enough restaurant in little old Marion to have a romantic dinner at. What the heck? It doesn't matter. I'm going to Marion, I'm going to visit Lila.

I opened the envelope carefully, taking pains not to rip the flap. We might need this for posterity down the road. I was picturing that shoebox full of stuff that we would hang onto and show our kids. The letter was thin, written on stationary size paper, a single page folded in the middle with the handwriting side turned in. I opened it with both hands.

Hi

I hope you're having a good summer. I think about you. Not much is going on here, but I've been having a nice summer working at Hungry Mother Park. I'm sorry it took so long to reply. I needed a little time to think.

I think we should take a break. The spring was so painful and hard on us. Let's take the summer to sort things out and think about us.

I'm sorry, I hope you're not mad. I don't want to hurt you. I care about you, I just think it would be best if we wait to see each other.

Thanks for writing, please don't be too upset with me. Take care of yourself and enjoy your summer.

Love, Lila

I remember just sitting there on that bed for a good 15 minutes, staring mostly into space, every now and then lifting Lila's letter, rereading it to be sure I hadn't missed anything. Thoughts sped through my hapless brain like a runaway train.

What does this mean? Is it over? Is there still hope? Is she saying she wants to get back together in the fall? Pitiful, sad, almost ridiculous for a grown man of 22. False hope is staggering around my bedroom with a gashing head wound, gasping for air but still breathing, struggling, struggling to survive.

Finally, I regained enough equilibrium to go out and have dinner with my folks, but I spent most of the evening in stunned silence. I didn't even leave the house that night, I just sat in my bedroom with the TV on, staring right through it into what felt like a pit in the bottom of my soul. By the next morning, life intruded again on my misery in the form of a rooftop concrete pour, a lovely task which involved pushing wheelbarrows full of wet concrete along 6' x 2' boards for 30 feet or so before dumping it so you could roll back and get another one. Nothing like a little extremely strenuous manual labor in the 89 degree heat while 150 feet in the air to take your mind off your problems.

September 1974: My Old School

I survived the rest of the summer despite myself. When September rolled around this time, there was no more Stribling Avenue, no more long-time buddies, and there was just me, the Lone Ranger trying to negotiate his way through one more semester to bring home the gold, to graduate. Lila and a few of her dorm mates from her first year took up residence at a tiny house on a side street off of Preston Avenue in Charlottesville.

As for me, I didn't know what the heck to do. Should I call her? Drop by? Leave a note on the door? Were we going to start seeing each other again, as her letter, which was safely tucked away in one of my desk drawers, implied? Or at least, I thought it implied. There were no cell phones, no texting. Contact was made the old fashioned way. Just go up and bang on the door.

Fortunately, I didn't have to do anything as the issue resolved itself when I ran into Robert Grant, one of the Stribling guys who asked me if I had seen Lila since she got back.

"No, I haven't heard from her. Have you seen her?"

"Yeah, she and I went to the Rock last week one day." The Rock was a local swimming hole popular in the 60s and 70s. It was out in the woods and considered a primo day date spot. Some skinny-dipped, some brought suits. It was the 70's folks!

My curiosity got the best of me. "So what's going on with her?"

Robert didn't miss a beat as he answered. "Aw, she's got some drug dealer boyfriend."

Well, there it was, the truth was out there. Very few people tell the truth about themselves. 40 years later, Lila would tell me that Robert chased her around those woods the entire day, finally causing her to knee him in a very inappropriate, but extremely painful spot.

40 years later, Lila, with her memory for details a casualty of her lifestyle, would tell me about working that summer at Hungry Mother State Park in Smyth County and being picked daily by a local drug dealer named Denny, who immediately shoved whatever the drug flavor of the day was down her throat or up her nose, apparently the beginning of what ended up being an odyssey like exploration of her sexuality and ability to ingest copious amounts of illegal substances.

In the old rearview, I see things a little differently now. I should have just walked up to that door and banged on it like I expected Lila to resume our relationship on the spot. I allowed her to 'evolve' things by drawing back. It took me over 40 years to finally figure it out. When someone you care about is acting totally inconsistent and crazy, just act normal. What better way to get to the reason they are acting that way?

Lila was a bird that couldn't be contained long in a cage and it would be many, many years later before I would realize that while free birds are the best kind, you shouldn't get too attached to them. As for her, it was pure subtle irony, perhaps even karma, that she was destined to spend her adult life being kept in a cage by a man who almost perfectly fit the expectations of her father.

It really was all my choice, though. Lila tried to warn me. It's not like she hid who she was or what she was about. But love, love is blind, if nothing else. I thought I could change her. Twice! Maybe three or four times if you're really counting! It's taken just a shade over 60 years to realize that there is only one person that any of us are capable of changing and that person is the man in the mirror.

Chapter 5
Big Yellow Taxi

August 1976: Be Young, Be Foolish, Be Happy

Late August 1976. The area known as the Corner near the UVA campus was a rustling hotbed of activities related to the school, students, and young adults in general. It was and is the place to be if one is traveling through those ever so formative and easy to waste years between the age of say, 19 and 26. A veritable cornucopia of shops, restaurants, and, more importantly, bars, in 1976, the Corner was a center of not only collegiate, but local interest. As both a UVA graduate AND a local or townie as we were called back then, I easily fit into both worlds.

The Corner was truly thriving back in the 1970's. There was Poe's, a bar with RED velour wallpaper that had been a mainstay since the late 1960's. Poe's featured a Tuesday night Ladies' night with Memory Bank, the first guys I had ever seen actually playing "recorded" music. Two guys sat behind a long table in the dark and dingy downstairs bar on those Tuesday nights. On top of the table sat two giant REEL TO REEL tape recorders with the sounds of music that permeated the frat parties blaring from the huge 4 foot speakers sitting on either side of the table...beach music, Motown, a touch of disco, and, of course, Bruce Springsteen's "Rosalita", the optimum party Maximus song of the day. OK, maybe that was just for me. I would stupidly, semi-drunkenly, request the song every Tuesday night, never bright enough to figure out that no matter when I requested it, the tune was played at the same time every night. Reel-to-reel. Think about it, I didn't.

The Virginian was one block up from Poe's and along with Mincer's Pipe Shop, formed the historical foundation of the Corner. The restaurant had been there since 1923. Known for great burgers, steaks, and basic American bar food, it was atmospheric to the max with dark wooden booths that sat on one wall and a long bar with those round spinning bar stools with vinyl seats on the other. More importantly, below it was a dingy cellar with a makeshift bar in the middle that was the West Virginian, a brief lived music bar from the mid to late 1970's. In the other direction, at the corner of 14th and Main, was the Mousetrap. It was a worthy stopping place, especially on the way even further down Main to the Mineshaft, literally a downstairs basement that had been converted into a teen night club in the late 1960's.

By the mid-1970's, The Mineshaft was actually a live music club that hosted nationally known artists as well as local bands. From the fall of 1976 until early 1978, I would be in the employ of the Mineshaft as a doorman/bartender, the flat out coolest job that I ever had, one that allowed me to meet the likes of Muddy Waters, Robert Palmer, and one Domingo Samudio, commonly known as Sam the Sham. Sam spent a week at the Mineshaft in the winter of 1977, playing two shows a night while being backed by a local band called Hammond Eggs.

More importantly, I was the one responsible for driving Sam back to the Holiday Inn on Rt. 29 North every night, but not before he would nightly regale the after hours collection of bar staff, waitresses, and other hangers on looking to partake in free drugs and alcohol with his philosophically grounded stories of his pre and post fame life. It's a little hard to believe that the man who penned "Wooly Bully" and "Lil' Red Riding Hood" was a deeply spiritual and philosophical dude, but that indeed was what Sam was. A gentle soul, I was not the least bit surprised years later when I heard that Sam had devoted himself to a musical prison ministry. I remember feeling very privileged for the honor of giving him that 15 minute ride every night, during which time he advised me about all things of my life as an extension of the Ted Talk he entertained with every late night between 2 am and 4 am.

For all I know, Sam may have offered some advice about Lila, sometime during that week. Oh yeah. Lila. Back to that day in late August of 1976. Well, before that...

Paradise and a Parking Lot

Once I FINALLY graduated UVA in the spring of 1975, I felt the pull of the real world and, thinking I needed to put my degree to work, I took a job as a "management trainee" at a local electric supply house called Piedmont Electric, which actually made about as much sense as trying to pour BBs through a garden hose since my degree was in psychology and my temperament was artistic despite my tendency to lay all things aside in pursuit of the party. You know, life in our 20s. It's a damn shame we can't relive it in our 60s. Damn, wait a minute, I guess I've been trying for the last 15 years. Well, never mind then.

It took me less than a year to get my butt fired from Piedmont, a fairly inauspicious debut into the post-college corporate world. Two years later, after the Mineshaft experience, I would take ANOTHER job with ANOTHER electric supply house and, less than a year later, get fired AGAIN. Starting to see a pattern emerge here, my friends? Definitely not the smartest cowboy in the rodeo when every bull has to kick you in the head at least twice before you finally begin to think, "Maybe I should switch bulls..."

I lived in my grandmother's partially finished basement during the mid-1970s and when I got fired from Piedmont, she somehow managed to talk my grandfather into giving me his job as a parking lot attendant at where? The UVA Corner, the Elliewood Avenue parking lot behind Arnette's, a gift shop situated at the corner of Elliewood and Main. The owner, Jim Arnette, was such a nice, laid back guy that he easily accepted the fact that his 70-year-old employee had turned his job over to his 24-year-old unemployed grandson. My relationship with my grandparents? Well, that's a whole other book.

The job was perfect for me. I spent most of the time stoned to the core by using an old trick that I had learned during my college years of rolling the tobacco out of the end of a Merit Light and tightly packing the empty space with marijuana. Every day I put two or three of these mutant cigarettes into the pack I took to work with me. There was a tiny wooden booth, but I carried a lawn chair every day and took up residence a foot or so outside the booth. From that vantage point, I could pass out the handwritten parking tickets to cars as they pulled in and direct them to the space, not to mention dissipate the pot into the fresh air. I enlightened myself by diving into the esoteric literature of the day, reading everything from Robert Pirsig's *Zen and the Art of Motorcycle Maintenance* to anything written by the man who became my favorite fiction author, Tom Robbins. I was particularly enamored by his debut, *Another Roadside Attraction*, and its follow-up, Robbins masterpiece, *Even Cowgirls Get The Blues*. Wildly drawn characters, lesbians, violence, Buddhist monks, mountain goats, and peyote buttons. Robbins was my kind of guy.

From what I remember, I was walking out of that little booth that late August morning to collect the fee from an older woman with short frosted hair when I noticed the familiar face following behind her.

"Lila?"

Lila's head did that little sideways turn that people do when they look at you quizzically, then straightened back up when her brain had fully processed the sight in front of her. "Rick!!"

Autumn 1976 and Winter 1977: Killer Queen

I can't remember exactly how I managed to contact Lila again after we met in the parking lot that August day in 1976. She had an apartment near the football stadium. It wasn't long after we met again, perhaps in September of 1976, when I took up employment at Mineshaft. My grandfather had no desire to return to the parking lot at this point, so I doubled as a bouncer/doorman at the Mineshaft by night and a stoned parking lot attendant by day. Once I got down to one job, I began to visit Lila's place on days and nights off. We became pot smoking, drinking buddies. Lila had a boyfriend, Elwood, back in Marion. Oh yeah, Elwood. I'm not sure if my knowledge of him was to her chagrin any more than I know if she would have told me about him if I didn't already know, but know I did.

The previous August, I had driven to Southwest Virginia to join Sam David and a dubious collection of Marion based derelicts for the Old Fiddlers Convention in Galax, Virginia, a town that slept like Rip Van Winkle for 362 days of the year. The second weekend every August, little Galax not only woke up, but becomes the dead center of the old time and bluegrass music universe for the Old Time Fiddler's Convention. The subtle irony was that many of the fiddlers and pickers were anything but old. In fact, pint-sized and freckle faced fiddlers were not the exception but practically the rule of the three days. Most of the fiddling and picking action was stretched out through the campground in congregations gathered around pickup ticks and tents, but there was a main stage and that's where the climax of the weekend took place on Saturday night in a fiddling, picking, clogging epiphany. That was where I was headed on that Saturday night in August of 1975 when I spied a familiar face in the crowd out of the corner of my eye. Yep, it was Lila. She and Elwood, who already had gray hair at the ripe old age of 28 (eight years Lila's senior), were wrapping each other like a couple of mating snakes.

I turned around and scurried away like a tardy student who had just seen the principal, never looking back, never turning back, never to return to Galax again. Oddly enough, something happened inside me then that changed things. Through the auspices of snooping through my buddy Sam I already knew all about Elwood, but seeing Lila in the arms of another man was a defining moment. We can't completely chase away the demons that haunt our hearts, that's not always in the cards, but we can lock them away in a dark cell and refuse to feed them, hoping eventually they cowl off into a corner and starve to death. Thus it was with my Lila demon over the next year, so when she walked up to me in that parking lot, false hope was nowhere to be found. Over the last year, I told false hope to take a long vacation, find the slow boat to China, you won't be needed around here anymore. The job at Piedmont sucked from day one, but getting canned helped stamp false hope's ticket as I settled into who I really was and, in so many ways, still am. Lila was in the proper place by the time we reconnected.

It was an easy friendship. We focused on all the things we had in common. Drugs, alcohol, music, and humor. We lost sight of the thing that drove us apart. Basically, that was the fact that I was in love with Lila while she saw me as 1970s version of a "friend with benefits." Back in the Mineshaft days, I was in my own "friends with benefits" stage and I had lots of friends. Waitresses, bar chicks, college girls, and bridesmaids at weddings. I had no shortage of friends and they were easy to come by when you were 25, worked at a cool rock n' roll club, and offered a comprehensive menu of everything from free drinks to an unending supply of pot and other exotic substances. It all passed through the Mineshaft and I passed it all through my female "friends".

I'd visit Lila, drag along some albums, some pot, and whatever the liquor of the day was. She reminded me years later of one night when we knocked out a whole bottle of Schnapps, yet even then, I somehow kept that demon locked away. I turned her on to The Kinks and she shot back with Queen. We went out together, occasionally dragging one of my drug dealing buddies along as the provider of the high. We went to perhaps the coolest restaurant ever in Charlottesville. Tucked away on a hilltop within incredibly close vicinity to Lila's apartment, Richard's Hilltop Hideaway was only around for a few years, known about by a few local residents, but once you parked and walked inside of this converted hilltop home, you found yourself transported to the atmosphere of a 1930's speakeasy, barely lit, deliciously mysterious, and with a behind closed doors back room that said "only the cool and dangerous allowed."

Once you got behind the doors, your transportation to the Prohibition era was completed. Absolutely zero lighting except for the spotlight highlighting the small stage from which you were entertained by a jazz trio featuring a piano, a standup bass, and an incredibly dark skinned, usually red velvet clad black female singer who was the apparent reincarnation of Billie Holiday. Owned by an African American businessman who I only knew as Richard, offering the cheapest and most delicious Surf n' Turf in town (how in the hell he got fresh Lobsters into Charlottesville was beyond me), it was a place to which the term legendary applied as an understatement.

Along with my buddy Driver, Lila and I also went to a legendary Kinks concert at Constitution Hall in DC in May of 1977. The Kinks, led by brothers Ray and Dave Davies, had a reputation for not getting along with each other and we witnessed it first hand when a shouting match between brother Dave and drummer Mick Avory escalated to a spitting match, then reached a crescendo when Mick threw his drumsticks at Dave and stormed off stage. Dave retaliated by stepping up on the drum stand and kicking the entire set off the front of the stand, sending it crashing to the stage. Brother Ray, with the occasional glance behind him, led the audience into what eventually turned into an acapella version of the song "Jukebox Music", eventually getting us all to clap and sing the chorus as he announced, "Well, thank you so much...goodnight!" It was the last time I saw the Kinks. How were you gonna top that? It was so well known that in April of 2014, I struck up a conversation about it with a fellow musicologist wearing a Kinks t-shirt who not only knew about the fight, but held me in heroic regard for my attendance.

Occasionally on weekends, Lila would show up at the Mineshaft with Elwood. In addition to making sure they got a pass on the cover charge, I would spot them free beer as well. They normally arrived in a stupor and left in even more of one. It would be almost 40 years later before Lila would let me know that Elwood had no idea she and I had ever been more than friends until I "had to go and tell him." Even then, those little red flags were waving. Here's the kind of friend I am, here's the kind of person I am, you would be bone dead stupid to trust me. Love me, yes, trust me, no. Rearview mirror. 20/20.

Spring 1977: Me and Mrs. Jones

In the spring of 1977, false hope was halfway round the world on that slow boat to China and I was riding high with confidence of a man who could resist all temptations of Lila. Yet, unbeknownst to me, that little demon of my heart, locked away in that corner cell, starving, somehow managed to smuggle a note out which found its way to that boat carrying false hope to China. "Make your way back here if you can, I see a little light coming from under the door. Get me out of here...pleeeease!"

I don't even recall us being drunk or wasted in any way the night it happened. We were just sitting around. There was no warning, perhaps the conversation took a turn in a certain direction, but somehow Lila ended up on the couch beside me and we turned our faces to each other. Perhaps she grabbed my face just like she would when we met again in August of 2013. I really don't know. I was sniffing the crack, looking for the pipe. All I know is that somehow our mouths, tongues, arms, and bodies ended up tangled together on that couch. Boyfriend? Elwood? Elwood who? Who's that? It was maybe five minutes before she suggested we retire to the bedroom, maybe 10 minutes before we were naked in that bed. The demon was at the door of his cell, whispering through the tiny window like Gandalf tempting Bodo, "Tell her...tell her you love her, tell her you've always loved her, you've got her back..tell her." False hope has been dropped off with its bags on an island and is just waiting for the next flight back to my heart, smiling, checking its watch.

Suddenly, in the middle of the act from somewhere deep, very deep inside me, a voice said, "It doesn't work". I still don't know where that voice came from. Was my friend Jesus still sitting somewhere in the back room of my soul, waiting for the time He could save it? Was it old Gram's ghost making his first appearance? Again, I don't know, but somehow I kept it inside that night and when Lila denied my advances the following night, I would amazingly declare that she was right, we were better off as just friends, a statement she would reiterate to me quite a few times almost 40 years later.

Later, Elwood would actually move to Charlottesville only to be ejected from Lila's apartment within two weeks of his arrival. Since I was the only person he knew in town, he and my sleeping bag ended up taking residence on the living room floor of the apartment a friend and I were subletting from my sister during the summer of 1977. In the old rearview, 40 years later, I would realize that such was the depth of my affection for Lila. I was willing to let her boyfriend live with me just to keep her close.

I actually liked Elwood. You couldn't help it. He was sort of like the guy who tries to sell you that lemon of a used car but you just can't help but admire his charm, even as his hand is in your back pocket. My final memory of poor Elwood was Lila standing toe to toe with him in that same living room, smacking him as she declared what a total deviant he was for taking advantage of her friends when a drug "opportunity" went bad and nearly got my poor roommate, Dave, offed by some Connecticut mafioso. I do remember from my month or so of hanging with Elwood that he was no more faithful to Lila than she was to him. The national anthem was playing, but the Stars and Stripes were nowhere to be found, just a long line of red flags. I had dodged the last bullet that Lila would fire my way for almost 40 years.

Interlude: Bubba and the Cocaine

The 1977 version of Lila would intersect my life one more time before a 30 year disappearance. Sometime during the summer of that year, I would receive a letter, or was it a call? I mean, come on, it was the 1970's and you know what they say about the 1970's. Like the 1960's, if you remember it then...well, you know the rest.

By the time I heard from Lila, Sophia, hereafter known as my best wife, was already in my life. Sophia and I had met at the Mineshaft in the late spring of that year, long after the wind had blown Elwood, Lila, bad drug deals, and all the idiocies attendant to them back to Southwest Virginia or some other point South. Sophia sailed in on a ship of normalcy on a sea of calm, one whose still waters I wasn't blessed with brains enough to appreciate correctly until almost 35 years later when the cuckoo bird named Grace flew out of the coop. To this day, those calm waters keep our children on the straight path, far away from the crazy tapestry their semi-irrational father has woven of his life.

Back to Lila and Bubba...oh yeah, Bubba. That's right, I said Bubba. Once again, I can't make this stuff up. Bubba was the reason I heard from Lila that summer, which was probably one of the few times Bubba and reason were in the same room together. To this day, I don't know Bubba's real name, although he did come up frequently during the second coming of Lila. Bubba was Lila's fiancé. What? Yep, Lila's fiancé. Apparently, after the falling out with Elwood that occurred in my apartment that day and her graduation from UVA, Lila had followed the call of her old high school friend, Pamela, to join her in the Sunshine state, where on the way to the Cocaine Cowboys, The Eagles, and the Miami Dolphins, she hooked up with Bubba. Sophia and I were personally invited to the wedding in September in little old Marion when we visited the happy couple on their way through Charlottesville that summer. As a testimony to his appeal to the late 1970's-early 1980's version of Lila, Bubba kept our heads filled with primo Floridian nose candy of the finest kind during our brief evening with them, leading to a later discussion in which Sophia, the one normal woman in my life, would declare them both "over the edge." More like being lost in the ocean, riding the storm out, two ships crashing into the waves together. The obvious thing about Bubba was that he had plenty of money, drugs, and time to indulge himself and Lila in both. Though I didn't have the clarity to see it through the front windshield of 1977, it's clear as a Hermosa Beach morning through the rear view mirror of 2014 that the die of the Miami era Lila was already cast.

I would actually hear from the Miami version of Lila in 1978 upon the occasion of her being issued an invitation to me and Sophia's wedding. Lila would write back in a letter about how she was already a divorced woman. Of course, in retrospect, I realize that as that letter was being written, the space around Lila was already filled with Eagles, Dolphins, and Cocaine Cowboys.

With that letter rejecting our wedding invitation, I heard the absolute last from Lila as she passed into hints, allegations, and rumors for the next 30 years.

Chapter 6

Family Affair

"May your fountain be blessed, and may you rejoice in the wife of your youth." **Proverbs 5:18**

Some people just do things right. Everything. Good things, bad things, all things. They never do the wrong thing, even if you don't like what they are doing. My first wife, Sophia, is one of those people. God bless her. She kept me on track as long as she could, which was about five minutes. To this day, my aging parents, and, of course, her children, love her like no other, especially me.

In fact, Sophia was probably the first person to truly save me from myself, even though she was never aware of it. If it hadn't been for her grounded presence in my life, I might have scooted to Florida back in 1978 when Lila wrote that letter saying she was divorced. I would have dived headfirst into the cocaine, the sex, the celebrities, the madness. What a disaster that would have been!

Early Summer 1977

When Sophia and I first started seeing each other, we both saw other people for a while. I was still at the Mineshaft and became embroiled with a slightly insane earth mother waitress named Ally who treated sex as a religious pursuit. Tall, lanky, and natural, she was as needy as life would eventually reveal me to be. Determined to win, she filibustered me daily to upend the presence of Sophia using an impressive array of creative sexual weapons, asking to move in with me, and finally breaking me down after about a month. See? Lest you think my weakness was merely a function of middle age, it was a lifetime pursuit.

So, one Friday afternoon in the summer of 1977, about 30 seconds after I told her it was OK, Ally was at her parents home loading her things while I dutifully went to Sophia's apartment to give her the news. When I told her that Ally was moving in, Sophia taught me the first of many life lessons that I would forget over the years by her reaction.

Perhaps it would be better classified as a non-reaction. There was no crying, no gnashing of teeth, merely a purposeful sad look as she declared, "but I thought we had a really good time together."

What? Where are the tears? Where is the begging? Dammit, this is cruel. How dare she assaults me with common sense!! Not fair!! What was I supposed to say to that? I looked up and right into her eyes.

"Yes, we do. You're right. We do have a good time together." I looked down at my sorry feet pensively. "A really good time. The best time I've had in a long time." I looked back up at Sophia and she had no more words. She knew she didn't need any. She was a woman who knew the value of economy in all things. It was brilliant.

Apparently, the good sense that had paid me a visit earlier in that spring of 1977 when I had somehow summoned up the courage to declare to Lila that we were better off as just friends had lingered just long enough. I immediately walked into Sophia's bedroom, sat down on the side of the bed and picked up the phone, dialing Ally's parent's home. Her mother answered and I asked for her.

"Hey, I'm almost all packed. I should be leaving in about an hour," Ally declared upon realizing that it was me.

"Well, I'm sorry but you'll have to unpack. I changed my mind."

"Changed your mind? I'm all packed up. I'm ready." Already learning from Sophia, I went to a cold place where I instinctively knew such business must be conducted.

"Well, I don't want you to come. I don't want you to move in." The line went silent save for a slight whimper from Ally, a whimper which grew by the second. "As a matter of fact, I don't want to see you anymore. From now on, I'm only gonna see Sophia." For the third time in my life, I wondered if the voice emerging from my vocal cords was indeed mine. Ally's whimper evolved into a full on cry. I stoically told her that I was sorry and hung up.

Sophia came back into the bedroom with me as she heard me hang up. I looked up at her. "I'm sorry, sometimes I don't have enough vision to see the sunshine in front of me for the storms that are behind me." She just smiled and we fell into each other's arms and finally back into her bed to appropriately celebrate what felt like a reunion, although we had never really been apart.

Summer 1978

After that day, Sophia left her other dates behind and we became inseparable, finally tying the knot on a warm July day in 1978 at the University of Virginia Chapel. As perhaps a pre-warning that my peculiar brand of insanity wasn't completely gone, I dressed my groomsmen in God awful gray tuxedos that looked like rejects from *Saturday Night Fever*, causing Sophia's father Ray, the apparent originator of her good sense, to exclaim upon relieving himself of it, "thank God I'll never have to wear that again."

1978-1995: The Good Marriage, The Bad Husband

Sophia and her family took me in like a lost child, an apt description of me up until the age of, I don't know, say 60. They took me to Europe, and they gave us primo seating at UVA football and basketball games for years while their daughter followed my wonderings related to my work in the dying field of newspaper circulation for 12 years.

Every time we moved, from Lynchburg to Culpeper, from there to Woodbridge, then finally back to Charlottesville, Sophia would not only land on her feet, she walked ahead tall and resolute, in stark contrast to her mere 5'1" stature. Meanwhile, I followed an egotistical muse which was constantly glad handing me because of my swift rise in the highly political world of newspaper publishing, a rise that was considerably more attributable to my ability to string together bullshit like a beaded choker than to any business acumen. It was the age of mixing business meetings with alcohol and cocaine, which was perfect for me.

The age of Wall Street, although I was more likely to be found delivering newspapers on a Rural Route than pounding on a boardroom table, testified by a near permanent imprint of newsprint on my battered hands that lasted until the mid-90s. I mixed business with alcohol, pot, and whatever other substances found their way into my ever spanning orbit. And there were the women. As we traveled from place to place, it seemed I never met an office that didn't have a woman I could lust after, usually several. These forays met with varying degrees of success and eventually fostered a heartfelt and honest confession to Sophia almost 20 years later when my conscience was finally allowed to return home like the Prodigal son.

That wandering and hugely deficit conscience finally did my good marriage back in 1995 when, having switched from the responsible lifestyle of a newspaper executive to the hugely irresponsible lifestyle of a night club and radio DJ, my erstwhile ego led me to a woman I took up with seriously. Well, at least I was serious. I wish I could tell you, friends, that this particular woman was worth the desolation I wrought on my own life, which began at the time I met her, but frankly she wasn't worth the paper that I am writing this on right now. In fact, after pushing me for a few months to leave Sophia, when I finally did, she actually broke it off with me that same night.

It wouldn't have mattered anyway. If it wasn't her, it would have been something or someone else. I was bent, bent on the pursuit of damaged goods, bent on becoming damaged, bent on a self-destructive path that would take me through rough rocky roads, nightmarish storms, and impossibly dark waters for the next 20 years. Nothing or no one could have stopped me.

1995-1999: Papa Was A Rolling Stone

My divorce from Sophia was final in 1995. After 16 years of perhaps not blissful, but at least peaceful co-existence with her, I had taken a walk, more appropriately, my overblown ego had taken me for a ride, right off a cliff and into the abyss.

The term long suffering wife would have been fairly accurate in application to Sophia. Meanwhile, I was deserving only of perhaps a t-shirt reading "World's Worst Husband". I drank, smoked pot, and eventually ran around, all while she did a stellar job raising our three children. Ultimately, when I left her, I was pretending to be noble when I took up with the other woman, doing the "right thing". Sure. Like you can correct doing the absolute wrong thing by doing something noble in contrast to the absolutely shitty way you've treated another human being!

Sophia deserved better, much better, and she got it when she married Adam Harris, an old high school flame of hers. He was a great guy, he made her happy and turned out to be a truly stellar stepfather to my kids.

God, at the same time, is tallying His score card on me and it's not looking good. I am allowed to follow my egotistical muse for a while, but my sins are piling up faster than a blizzard at the South Pole. After chasing random sex, drugs, and the party life for about six months, even a rampant ego can begin to feel lost and empty. That what exactly what happened to me when I found myself on the phone with one of my conquests, Deana Russo, telling her that just having sex wasn't enough. What? Not enough? Really? Who is this walking around inside my body? After I hung up, I remember getting a distinct feeling that the man that just spoke those words on the phone was not me. Who is that guy?

Over the next few years, I would get to know that guy, even though I was too dense to realize it. My search for sexual satisfaction had morphed into a search for love. God planted love right in front of me in the form of my three beautiful kids. I lived in a tiny bachelor pad with only two bedrooms, leaving me and my two sons sharing a bed on the 3-4 nights a week that the kids stayed with me. I became a very proud single dad, talking the kids to concerts, on trips to the beach, everywhere. It was common to see me and the three kids almost anywhere around town as we established traditions of our own. The kids were educated in the fine art of Elvis movies, Beach Party movies, and music of all types.

Do you know that Carly Simon song *Anticipation*? The chorus chides you to "stay right here 'cause these are the good old days". If only we could really live like that. That's how God works. There is always something good, usually great, right here, right in front of us! But we don't see it, do we? We're too busy trying to get what we WANT to see that we already have what we NEED.

I was too busy looking at the empty part of my glass to see the full part. I was even sent the occasional messenger to drive home the message, such as my work buddy, Matt Moyer, who sat on my couch one night listening to me whine about the missing woman in my life without appreciating the bundles of joy that God had put in front of me in the form of my kids. I'll never forget Matt's words, "Rick, I promise you that you will never grow up and say, 'I wish I'd spent less time with my kids." It couldn't have been drawn out any more clearly. Still, I refused to learn. Instead of letting my actions be dictated by the wonderful things I already HAD in my life, I was driven by strong desires for those things that were MISSING. At least, I thought they were. Who knows? They might have been right in front of me, but I didn't see them because I was too busy looking.

Daddy, Don't You Walk So Fast

If anyone were to draw a graph of my abilities and effectiveness as a father, the last 15 years would resemble that of a patient in dire need of CPR. One step up in improvement equals five steps back down in the cellar. I'm trying, sometimes just too hard. Actually, the first few years of that parenthood graph would be a pretty nice line fairly above the curve, then perhaps level out sometime during the late 80s, seriously dip in the early 90s, and then make a huge jump in the late 90s during the time between my marriages before taking the ultimate nose dive around the time I met Grace again. It still remains in that cellar, despite my many frustrating attempts to pull my grade up. I am nothing, if not inconsistent as a human being.

Amelia, still a Daddy's girl (is there any other kind?), joined us in 1983, showing up five weeks early, yellow, jaundiced, and mostly crying. I remember the first time I saw her when she arrived and the doctor put her on Sophia's stomach so we could bond. Tiny little thing that seemed all eyes, and dark eyes at that, my first impression was that Sophia had just birthed E.T. Still, I was, of course, in love. Still am. Jaundiced as she was, Amelia spent two hours twice a week under the heat lamp for the first three months of her life. My fondest memory of her is from when we lived in Culpeper, Virginia and she was still a solo act. Christmas night, she is lying in her crib and rambling in her sleep..." more Christmas, more Santa Claus." Aw geez, it brings tears to my eyes just writing it.

The second born was Darin. His entry into the planet was not exactly smooth either. Born just before we left Culpeper, he was rushed down the birth canal like a passenger late for a subway when he stopped breathing temporarily, getting out by the skin of his teeth, a habit he continues to this day at age 28. Little Darin had light brown curly hair and a mischievous bent that had given way to the occasional mean streak as he grew into adulthood. Darin would get mad at me constantly when I was in my golden years of single parenthood, prompting me to make multiple trips into the bedroom after he laid down for the night, determined to drag a smile and a hug from his little tortured soul before he drifted off to dreamland, mainly due to my lifelong belief in the principal extolled in Ephesians 4:26 "In your anger do not sin: Do not let the sun go down while you are still angry."

This principle always worked until I met up again with Grace and subsequently, Lila, neither of whom had any problem letting the sun set on their anger. I was brought up southern mannered and never even had the experience of anyone hanging up the phone in anger on me before first Grace, then Lila.

My strongest memory of the young Darin was his insistence on spending the night with me every Christmas Eve after his mother and I divorced, not wanting his Dad to be lonely at Christmas. I'll never forget the Christmas he so gently broke it to his single dad that he wanted to spend this next Christmas Eve at home with his mom. It seemed it was anticipated that Santa would be dropping a new bike under the tree and Darin didn't want to let any grass grow under it. Thus I spent my first Christmas Eve ever alone.

The third child was Joe. He was a surprise all the way around. He was only three years old when I left his mother, yet, somehow, miraculously, I ended up being the total apple of his eye, at least until I blew it. Little Joe loved his daddy more than life itself for those golden years between 1994 and 1999, before I fell into the abyss. He drug himself around behind me everywhere he could go with me. I'll never forget the sight of little Joe when I picked him up at his Mother's house for his first concert, a Third Eye Blind show in Richmond. His tiny little form sat at the end of the sidewalk dressed in shorts, a t-shirt, and red Chuck Taylor high tops just like his daddy wore, adorned by a gold neck chain, a pair a wrap around shades, grinning from ear to ear with a smile that said "cool like you, Dad."

I can only imagine his pain upon discovering in 1999 that the man he loved was leaving him and moving to Florida. He must have thought she must be some special woman to get his beloved daddy to leave him. My God, what a disappointment!

My Family: Remember When

It's a yucky feeling to realize you've pretty much not only turned your whole world to crap, but you have no one to point the finger at except that guy in the mirror. My parents sure couldn't take any of the blame. Not only did people occasionally refer to me as Ricky Nelson, but Mom and Dad were such good parents that our house could easily have passed as the set for "Ozzie and Harriet".

Sports were life for Dad. He lived and breathed them. At the tender age of four, I became a force fed fast pitch softball fan, spending three nights a week at McIntire Park with my mom watching him play for the Charlottesville Lumberjacks with all his cop buddies and a bunch of other cronies. The town seemed so much smaller than, neighborly. The guys he played with, populated with names like Foots, Cracker, and Doodles, became legends in my little mind, as did my Dad. As I grew, Dad moved from playing into coaching and I found myself playing under his tutelage in baseball, basketball, and eventually football. From the age of around 9, until I was 15, Dad was either the coach or one of the assistants on every team I played for.

It wasn't easy ALWAYS being the coach's son. Dad and I have had this discussion perhaps somewhere between 100 and 100,000 times over the years when I would try to explain some incident where I was ostracized, criticized, or pulverized by virtue of my last name. It was a damned if you do, damned if you don't thing. You did something great. Yeah, well you're the coach's son, no wonder. You did something crappy. Yeah, well, the only reason you're still playing is that you're the coach's son.

Then there was the issue of being a cop's son, a whole different kind of challenge, especially when one came of age during the cultural upheaval that was the late 60s and early 70s in America. It's taken another 40 years to tear down the wall that existed between my father and I with the key factor being my own realization that the architect of those walls was the man who stared back at me from that mirror. It took that guy finally seeing his own father for the special guy he was to hammer down those walls.

Dad not only coached sports, but he and several other men also STARTED the boy's football league in little old Charlottesville back in 1960. He not only was a cop, but he also STARTED the traffic division in that same little burg, an accomplishment that never really occurred to me as significant until I was driving around one autumn afternoon in the 90s and it hit that without my father, those school crossing guards might not be there, that he had, several times in life, created something where nothing existed before, something that made the lives of others better. That, my friends, that dawning, was a truly humbling experience, especially in light of my own experiences, which bowed to the less than humble throne of self service.

At the same time, his dedication to my mother, my sister, and myself created an entity of a whole different kind. A traditional family, one which was functional in a dysfunctional world. It wasn't his fault that his functional family suffered from the participation of a dysfunctional member, that being his oldest son. He stayed by my mother even when her manic depression created storms in our lives, standing by her as she went through depression, shock therapy, and years of taking various balancing drugs administered to those in the bipolar realm.

As for my mother, when she was healthy, she gave up everything for her only son, using her inheritance to put me through my first year at UVA, paying for some psychological assessment group to give me a battery of tests in the hope that I might find myself. I suppose I eventually did, but like the Israelites, it took 40 years of wandering in the wilderness to do it.

Whatever mess I am, and I am, I can't blame anyone in my family for it. They were always there. In fact, the only shortcoming I can really see in my family is that they were just too easy on me, supporting me as best they could through every awful, selfish decision I made.

"We all suffer from dreams."

— Bernard Cornwell, Death of Kings

Nothing happens in a void, nor did the massive avalanche of poor, selfish decisions that drove the train of my life into the tunnel of hell for the next 15 years begin in a void. It began with a purposeful foot kicking the first rocks that tumbled an unstoppable mountain of rocks down on me and those I truly cared about in life. That foot belonged to an old nemesis of mine, one I hadn't seen in almost 25 years.

The thing about my old enemy's false hope was that he was like a chameleon. It would be damn easy to spot him if he dressed in shiny cheap polyester suits and pointy shoes like the snake oil salesman he really is, but that's not the case. He's like your daughter's prom date from hell. He dresses to impress and you completely overlook the fact that he's going to ply her with liquor and ravage her.

When he came dancing back into my life in 1999, he wasn't even dressed as a man, but rather as an ageless, impossibly beautiful, blue eyed, blonde, and sweet soul of an angel sent from heaven above.

Chapter 7

I'm A Believer

October 1999: A Reunion

My 30th high school reunion looked to be an easy gig and I was looking forward to putting the oldies set that I had pre-recorded the day before on my system and then catching up with some old friends from the Lane High class of 1969. It was October 15, 1999, and to semi-quote FDR, it was a day that would live in my personal infamy forever. For my nemesis, false hope, it was a red letter day, sort of like his Christmas, Thanksgiving, and Easter all rolled into one. By the end of the day, he would be breaking out the cigars and champagne, toasting his comeback.

Actually, myself and my classmates from the year of 1970 were celebrating a year early so we could combine with the classes of 1968 and 1969 so we could have a better, bigger party.

My personal mission had been to provide appropriate tunes for a Friday night gathering of the 1970 grads in preface to the three class get together planned for Saturday night. My compensation was free admission. I had painstakingly assembled the soundtrack for 1970 using the latest in digital technology, the mini disc, in the process dredging up memories of embarrassing moments, awful bad dates, and a scary trip to Virginia Beach taken upon conclusion of said year where my we etched our spot in infamy forever by becoming the only group ever evicted from a house we had paid for in full three days before the lease was up. Unjustified, of course, some malarkey about holes in walls, eight foot tall beer can pyramids, rampant underage drinking and sexual activity. Like it was our fault, the legislature couldn't get the drinking age correct. We were high school graduates now, for Pete's sake. What? Are we supposed to celebrate with soft drinks? OK, there were plenty of soft drinks, they were just mostly mixed with bourbon.

Enough about bourbon and beer stained memories, back to October 15, 1999. The century was getting ready to turn that year and, although I didn't know it at the time, it was to be the beginning of a long spiral of unlikely events that would take myth and journey to where we are right now, with you reading this page and me writing it.

I had a solid plan for Friday night. Start the disc I had created for the 1970 grads in the back room of the Charlottesville Ice Skating Park, where our reunion was, then head a block over to the Omni Hotel where the class of 1969 was assembled, the class of all my drinking buddies and, more importantly, most the cheerleaders that I dated. Yes, as shallow as I seem now, I'm pretty sure that I was actually worse in high school. Every autumn, I would pick a cheerleader, ask them out, date them long enough to have beautiful accompaniment to the fall Homecoming dance, and then proceed to the position of either dumper or the dreaded dumpee once the football season ended. There was Samantha Snead, though, from the class of 1969. Sam was special to me. She wasn't easy and you, my friends, have certainly read enough so far to know that when it comes to women, easy and I are not often found at the same party together. Before the Graces and the Lila's entered my orbit, Sam had the dubious honor of being the first woman I went above and beyond to pursue, taking a Trailways bus to Greensboro, North Carolina in October of 1969 to accompany Sam, at her invitation, to her homecoming at The UNC-Greensboro woman's college. I don't remember too much about that weekend outside of sharing a hotel room with a guy I didn't know whose girlfriend was Sam's roommate. He had a Dodge Daytona that wouldn't have looked out of place at the Charlotte Motor Speedway and we, Sam and I, rode around all weekend in the back seat. The last thing we did that Sunday before I got on the bus back to Charlottesville was go to the campus auditorium where we saw The Fifth Dimension. Yep, the *Stoned Soul Picnic, Sweet Blindness, Wedding Bell Blues* Fifth Dimension. Laura Nyro became one of my early musical heroines and there was no one who could work Laura's catalogue of amazing hook laden songs like The Fifth Dimension, not even Laura.

Needless to say, I had to see Sam at the reunion and even met her husband. OK, the name eludes me. Can we just call him Sam's hubby?

My old friend Mick Hubley was staying with me for the weekend, having come up to Roanoke. Mick and I had the distinction of being suspended from Buford Junior High School together at the ripe old age of 15 when we decided to liven up the school sponsored sock hop by downing a fifth of Kentucky Gentleman completely straight up in about 30 minutes. I don't remember much of the evening other than every vehicle that approached having multiple sets of headlights and the fact that *"Penny Lane"* and *"Strawberry Fields Forever"* seemed to be in endless rotation from wherever the music was playing from. Honestly, to this day I'm still not sure whether we actually threw up in all the places they gave us credit for. All I know is that by the time we got to Lane High School together the next year, we were walking legends, albeit infamous ones. It was sort of weird being 16 and having 18-year-old girls intimidated by your mere presence. "Are you Ricky Trax?"

"Yes, why?"

"I know all about you, I just wanted to see what you look like." Coming from a girl who was two grades ahead of you, it was just strange. We were like lepers, but instead of being castigated, we were revered.

As Mick and I prepared for an evening of nostalgic reconnection with old friends, girlfriends, and fellow derelicts, the furthest thing from my mind, in fact, not even in the universe of my thought patterns was an old love that I hadn't talked about to or laid eyes on in 25 years.

The Second Coming Of Grace: Sweet Blindness

I was standing right in front of my gear when she walked in, just like the sitting duck that I would eventually end up being. I hadn't seen that face in over a quarter of a century, so how was it possible that it not only had not changed, but it even looked more impossibly beautiful than it had that late September night back in 1970?

Just like that night, when Grace entered the reunion that Friday night, a night that was destined to change and perhaps corrupt the lives of so many, she was proceeded by that same light up the heavens smile as she had over 29 years earlier. It had been advertised that I was providing the music, so she turned immediately to the sound of it and made a beeline my way. She floated across the room as if she were riding on a breeze and landed right in front of me with outstretched arms, which immediately found their way around my neck. I have to say that for the second time in my life, she was the most beautiful creature that I had ever seen. How is it possible she looked younger, more beautiful than she had back in 1970? She looked so good she didn't even look real. I may have even rubbed my eyes a bit just to be sure I hadn't dozed off and started dreaming. Nope, she was there. I could touch her, and feel her arms squeeze my neck.

Eventually, she spoke. Oh hell, let's be honest, I can't remember who spoke first or even what was said. Like Commander Cody, I was lost in the ozone again. Years later, people who knew Grace, who met Grace through me, would ask me many times what it was about her that drew me to her. Twice. No, make that three times counting that one night stand in 1974. I have examined and examined myself, like Perry Mason scrounging through the evidence over and over, looking for clues that will let him once again emerge victorious over Hamilton Burger. Unfortunately, as much as I have dug, exposed, and scrounged, it all leads back to a single one word verdict for the defendant in this case, one Rick Trax. Guilty!

The bitter truth I have had to admit to myself is there is nothing, not a single thing, outside my own shallow, irreconcilable desire for her beauty. I have no reason, no excuse. I was drawn strictly to her beauty. In pursuit of that, I tossed away nearly 15 years of my life. In pursuit of that, many around me and her, my parents, my children, her children, her ex-husband, people who were not complicit and likely would not have even gone along with my crimes voluntarily, ended up serving virtual life sentences handed down from the throne of mine and Grace's mutual selfishness. It is a sobering realization, a cold and harsh truth, but one which can't be put aside. A verdict that doesn't deserve to be overturned or amended.

But on that October evening in 1999, the jury hadn't even been assembled yet. On that night, I was kicking my loneliness demon to the side. Get out of here, and I won't be needing you anymore. Nope, take a long vacation, Buddy.

From that point on through the rest of that weekend, Grace stuck to me like glue. After the party that night, Grace, myself, Mick, and Grace's friend Sheryl headed out to my tiny two bedroom duplex on the north side of Charlottesville. While Mick and Sheryl fixed cocktails, Grace sat down beside me on my couch, putting her arm around my shoulder, using her beauty and touch to draw me towards her.

"I'm sorry, Rick, I'm so sorry." What? Had she done something I hadn't seen? What the hell is she talking about?

"Sorry for what?"

"Everything. Life. Sleeping with another man. Marrying another man." Now you would think logic would jumpstart my pot and alcohol addled brain at some point here and declare, don't you mean marrying TWO other men, including the one you cheated on me with almost 30 years ago? Including the one who is the father of the two sons, you told me about? Aren't there a couple of details you're leaving out here, Grace?

But no, there is absolutely no way a single word that might drive Grace away, back to her home in Boca Raton, Florida, back to her two sons, back to her husband, there is no way any of those words to that effect were going to slip past my beauty clouded brain and escape from my mouth.

Later that evening, Grace would invite me back to my own bedroom and open her arms as if to display her wares. "Remember how flat chested I used to be, Rick?" Um, maybe...no. Honestly, once I saw that face your breasts were not even close to my consciousness.

"I had these done in Venezuela!" No, Grace, please don't show them to me. I don't need to see those. You're married. I'm trying to be good here. Of course, eventually, before the weekend was up, she would indeed show them to me, as well as press them against me and put my hands on them. Eventually, before the weekend was up, I would ascertain that the timelessness in Grace's face that also left me bewildered was, in fact, also surgically induced via a facelift that occurred apparently with a sense of strategic timing in consideration of her possible reuniting with me.

She told me about her family. Her husband was "sick" and only had maybe 8-10 years to live. Of course, 15 years later he is still walking around, pretty damn healthy to boot. Her name was now Grace Jones Rio, a name that perfectly suited her chosen path as a top fashion model, thus the tax deductible surgical improvements to her physical manifestation.

Her sideline as a hair dresser took up far more time and brought in far more income, but the model status, even with minimal income, allowed Grace to dress in the highest fashion available without it being on her own dime. Not that I cared. As a mobile DJ, I learned to take advantage of creative financing, at least as much as the law allows, as well.

She told me all about her two sons, Chet and Chaz, tossing in that both of them had also been and were models. Grace didn't carry around family pictures to show her kids off. She had comp cards. Comp cards, I'm not kidding!

So Grace and I spent the weekend together, even sleeping together Saturday night, I'm ashamed to say. She characterized her husband as controlling and mean spirited, I'm sorry to say that was good enough for me. When I say sleeping, that's actually not an apt description. We slept some, but I spent the vast majority of that evening fighting off Grace's advances, a far cry from the Grace I met at age 19. I had been an adulterer and I was determined that I would not allow my sweet Grace to follow that path, to deal with all that meant you had to deal with. Still, we acted like lovers. It was like 25 years had never passed. The truth is that the sin is in the intention and despite my outward appearance of propriety, the inside was consumed with lust over the beautiful creature in front of me. I'm pretty sure Jesus knew that.

It was an incredible weekend and suddenly, my loneliness demon was floundering in the background, running short of breath. But there was another demon lurking.

In the back of my mind, God was playing a movie. It showed Grace, her 21 years of marriage, her sons, my kids, my life...all designed to make a point I completely ignored. I was too busy listening to the flesh demon whispering in my ear, "You'll never have another chance like this...look at her...she's beautiful and she's yours for the taking. Take her!" While saying this, the flesh demon was simultaneously whacking the loneliness demon into total submission and it went whimpering off. I DESERVED this!

Deserved! What a dangerous word. Every time in my life I have entertained thoughts summoned up by that word, it has ALWAYS led to a precipitous place. That's a word to be wary of. When we give in to that word we may as well admit it. I want what I want. I don't care if it's what I need, I don't care what anyone else thinks, I don't care what happens to anyone else, I DESERVE this!

I took Grace to the airport that Monday afternoon after the reunion when she flew home. We sat in the terminal holding hands. I knew the RIGHT thing to do, but lacked the courage to do it. This is where we have to understand God's will. You can get what you want. Anything, just like the motivational books and speakers say. If you can think of it, you can have it. But what you need, that's different! God puts it right there in front of you, holding two hands out like the scales of justice. Here's what you want, but here is what you need. Now, YOU choose. Over and over, I made the wrong choices. Free will. It can be a bitch!!

The best that I could muster when Grace was getting ready to go through the gate was, "We'll have to see what happens."

Really, Rick? That lame? Yes, even though it was very clear in my mind even then what I SHOULD do, I was listening to that flesh demon. Made sense to me. So I saw Grace off, thinking in the back of my feeble mind that I had done the right thing when in fact, I had just done the wrong thing lite.

I returned peacefully to my desk job selling audio parts for cars and home via email/phone, proud of myself that I had resisted the urge to commit adultery and courageously put Grace on the plane without making further plans.

It was about two hours after I saw Grace go through that gate when the phone on my desk rang. Despite not hearing it on the phone in 40 years, I recognized Grace's voice immediately. Honestly, I'm not even sure what she said on that phone call, but that's because I was hearing other voices in my ear. This time it was not the flesh demon or the loneliness demon, at least I don't think so. What do you expect from a man who hears voices? It could be worse. I could be seeing ghosts, imaginary leprechauns, non-existent apparitions of all manner. This voice was very cooly and very clearly saying the words I did not want to hear in my ear. "Let her go. Tell her to go back to her family. Let her go."

I don't have to tell you that I didn't listen. It was just inconceivable that God would drop such an amazing incredible gift in my lap and then ask me to return it. Right? What would the point be? Just to tempt me? Yep, that would be it. And it was another fail, no, another epic fail!

Finally, my sin has to be logged. My days as a great dad were over. My march towards normalcy is finished. The train to sanity ran off the tracks. It's done. Now I was on board the train of inevitability that would become my 13 year marriage to Grace. There was no stopping me now. I had left God no choice. He had given me every possible escape route and I had ignored them all like homeless people at a banking convention. I had finally, again, committed a sin that would HAVE to be paid for.

January-July 2000: Life In The Fast Lane

So in November 1999, Grace moved out of the home she shared with her husband and two sons, taking Chaz with her while Chet stayed behind with his father, Paco. OK, his real name was Peter, but Paco was what he was called. Grace found a Christian therapist who within two weeks, labeled Paco a narcissist and justified her desire to leave him. The woman knew how to wrap a weak man around her little finger in a skinny second. Honestly, over the next few years I would come to know Paco, and while he was a pretty typical alpha Latin male, I never found him to be a narcissist. In fact, he seemed to put his children first, a trait I admired greatly despite my apparent inability to emulate it.

Grace, for her part, announced the impending separation from her husband of 21 years by telling her oldest son, Chet, first. Chet, in turn, broke the news to his completely unsuspecting father when Dad jumped on him about something by exclaiming. "You're an asshole, that's why Mom is leaving you."

Grace described a sad scene with poor Paco down on his knees begging her not to leave him. I felt as complicit as Blanch Barrow was to Bonnie and Clyde at this point, but still I just continued to lazily float down the river of moral turpitude towards the rapids of self destruction, oblivious to my own responsibility and complicity in Grace's behavior.

Grace, for her part, pulled me back in the water every time I threatened to wade out. When I questioned whether she should give the marriage a chance, she quickly dismissed it. "You just really don't love me, do you, Rick?"

 I couldn't capitulate quickly enough, "Yes, Grace, of course, I do. I always have, " I lied. Grace always knew how to beat me into submission.

She wrote flowing letters. OK, maybe not so flowing. Let's be honest. Literary and Grace didn't hang out together too much.

So in January of the year 2000, after almost two months of honing my telephone sex skills (which actually turned out to be quite substantial), Grace and I began a long distance relationship between Charlottesville and Boca Raton, Florida. It was a jet-set relationship, with the problem being I had a VW budget. That would haunt me later.

Marriage never even had the chance to appear on the radar. That plane had landed and the passengers were in the terminal, before the relationship plane had ever so much as reached the runway to take off. Grace had a way of gently bludgeoning my wishes, if I had any, into submission.

There was a seminal moment that happened by telephone in mid-December. Grace was talking about the assumed result of first loves being finally reunited in matrimonial bliss and said, "I suppose I'll have to start to look for work in Virginia, begin to look around up there."

Somehow, incredulously, stupidly, without a hint of foresight, I found myself saying, "No, I can move down there." Why I said this I, to this day, haven't a clue. I had three kids, and she had one with her, I had a good job and a business, and she had skills that were fairly easy to move around. Grace is an outstanding hair stylist, and she would never have an issue finding work. I can only assume that I was as much running away from my life as I was running towards Grace. It remains a mystery to me over 15 years later as to why I so freely made that colossally bad decision with absolutely no hesitation.

We actually held off on consummating the sex act until April, but once we did consummate, it was intense and frequent.

Grace's divorce was scheduled to be final in mid-July. On the Fourth of July, Grace was visiting and we were at McIntire Park for the traditional fireworks with Grace's old friend Sheryl. Somehow it came out that in our selfish pursuit of each other, Grace and I had never really discussed the issue of children, of blending these two families. Sheryl suggested out loud that perhaps we should wait a year to marry and work out those details for the sake of the children. Later when Grace and I were alone, I mentioned the conversation.

"Grace, maybe we should wait a year. What could it hurt?" If Grace had been a cat at that moment the fur on her back would have stood straight up. She got that same look on her face that she had when I ran her Camaro off the road in 1971.

"Oh, I see, Rick! You let Sheryl get to you! You'd rather listen to her than me. Why don't you run off with HER?" Wow!!! Talk about a cat on a hot tin roof. Needless to say, I capitulated again right away and we marched towards an early August wedding less than four weeks after Grace's divorce would be final. This one continues to trouble me with 'what ifs' in that rearview mirror. My kids could have used my vote at that time, but I was too weak to cast it.

Eagles Interlude: A Not So Peaceful Uneasy Feeling

Oh yeah, you wanted to know about the Eagles, right? I promised you two women from my past who had been with the Eagles. Well, I heard Grace's Eagles story shortly after we got back together again. We did a lot of talking to catch up for 25 years. We were talking about Grace's years in Europe when she started referring to her night with the Eagles. It turns out her night was a lot less, well, active, than Lila's nights with the group. She and a group of models had been lined up to have dinner with the Eagles after the show, at least that was Grace's story. "You know, Rick, models and rock stars, they kind of go together?"

Sure, sorta like bartenders or waitresses or just girls who have cocaine and rock stars, they kind of go together too. Knowing what I do now, I think it's possible that Grace may have just been part of the band's infamous third encore, when audience members, specifically hand chosen female audience members, were issued third encore buttons and told to join the band backstage, where the party ensued. Who knew what happened, but I doubt that even the Eagles could look past Grace's density. When she explained that they were just a bunch of country boys who made good, I knew Grace hadn't gotten too close to the Eagles! One might say that while Grace's Eagle experience ended up being somewhat of a whimper, Lila's was definitely a bang.

Chapter 8

Life In The Fast Lane

August 2000: A Knot That Can't Be Broken

I took my promises to God seriously, probably one of my few redeeming qualities, so when Grace wanted my friend and pastor, Jimmy Rose, to perform a straight up Christian ceremony for us, I took it to heart. Honestly, Sophia was so dead set against organized religion that my first wedding was a completely secular affair. Taking vows before God, though? I took that to heart.

Of course, I didn't take it to heart enough to speak up when Grace convinced Jimmy that her divorce was justified because Paco had cheated, despite there not being anything resembling a shred of evidence that he did, that in fact all he had done was take care of his sons while Grace travelled the world in pursuit of modeling dollars. I didn't take it to heart enough to question Grace when she said she didn't have time to watch the marriage preparation films that Jimmy said we needed to complete in order for him to perform the ceremony, nor enough to refuse when she and I were asked by Jimmy to sign off on watching the films.

In the old rearview mirror and armed with a much deeper knowledge of what God actually had to say about marriage and divorce in the Bible, I know the cheating, adultery, was a trump card. Grace, whether calculatedly or not, knew that once she played the adultery card against Paco, Jimmy would agree to perform the ceremony.

Not that anything lets me off the hook. I was complicit in every single step of this nasty game. I signed off on the films, and I didn't say a word when Grace took poor Paco out to the woodshed for cheating, I let my friend and pastor Jimmy believe every single word without a breath of protest.

So it was that on a warm August day in the year 2000, Grace, myself, and all five of our mutual children stood before Jimmy and God. As Jimmy said those words, "for better or worse, for richer or for poorer, in sickness and in health," another thought was rolling around in my muddled mind.

You can't get out of this, you're in it for life. Where are you taking your children on this journey and why? I steadfastly told myself that I would find a way. On the surface, I was a happy man, and friends told me they had never seen me happier. Even then, I must have been a decent actor.

Looking back on that day, the thing I remember most was the shock to on the faces of the children, the collective deer in the headlights look that was the only thing they seemed to all have in common. Grace's son Chet, who gave her away, got sick to his stomach first thing that morning, never really recovering although he was able to make it through the ceremony. Her youngest Chaz, grabbed her calf and fell down almost crying, making her drag him behind until he was extricated. After a brief reception, the kids were turned over to the charge of my poor father while Grace and I retreated to a Bed and Breakfast on the south side of Charlottesville called the Inn at The Crossroads.

When we got there, Grace wandered around the gazebos and swings set up to watch the beautiful sunsets over the Blue Ridge in her much too traditional for a 50-year-old bride's wedding gown, smiling and talking to the camera like it was a model shoot. I tried to look past the awful and selfish shallowness of it all, but it was like I was driving a train I had no control over right into the precipitousness of unhappiness and self-conceit. What had I done?

The Honeymoon: Destination Boca

The trouble started right away with Grace. Well, not right away, but right after we were married. Up until the preacher said those magic words, Grace treated my three kids like they were made of gold. Then as soon as we were officially hitched, she dropped the boom like a sledgehammer on a railroad tie. I have thought since then, and it's probably like that if you go to hell, you know. Old Satan, dressed like a $5,000 prostitute, leads you to a door that looks like the entrance to the Venetian in Vegas, then once you're inside, it's Mick Jagger with horns and dressed in red..." Please allow me to introduce myself!"

My personal hell with regard to Grace and my children started the second morning after we got married. In a life filled with brilliant therapists, an oxymoron similar to generous lawyers, Grace's Christian therapist, the same one that told her she was right to get her divorce because her husband was a classic narcissist, told her it would be a good idea to spend the first two weeks of our married life with ALL of our children.

We took off to Florida in two vehicles, one a rental truck carrying all my stuff as well as Darin and myself, the other my work mini-van with Grace driving plus Chaz, Amelia, and Joe. After spending the night in a co-joined room that cost maybe $35 for the night, the next morning, we hit the road very early to make it to Summerton, South Carolina and the Summerton Diner. I mean the hotel room was blue, perhaps a foretelling of what my kids were worth to Grace.

The Summerton Diner, which Grace, who would 12 years tell me that it was no treat for her to eat breakfast in a diner, insisted would serve us a southern breakfast beyond our wildest dreams. It was a diner, you know, they served a diner breakfast. Sure, they had great grits, but that's a staple in South Carolina. The main thing about Summerton Diner is that stopping there had been a Rio family tradition, so there are two big lessons here if you're keeping score. And you know you are.

First of all, should you ever marry anyone, anyone at all, spend the first week or so with just the two of you before introducing the adopted family into the atmosphere. Second of all, should you actually make the above mistake and end up with a van, or perhaps a truck, or both, full of your newly blended family members, work to establish new traditions for THAT family without co-opting the singular traditions of either family. There's a part three, but wait a minute. Back to the Summerton Diner and that early August morning in 2000.

As our newly blended group sat together at a large table, Joe asked me if he could possibly have a Coke to drink instead of Orange Juice. When I suggested that perhaps he have something healthy and THEN move to the Coke, he began to whine just a little as eight year olds are wont to do when they don't get their way initially.

I was fully prepared to wait him out when Grace jumped in with both feet, mostly in her mouth, "Joe, we're not going to whine, no whining, stop it...just drink Orange Juice and be happy with it."

I'll never forget the look poor Joey gave me, a cry for help. Are you gonna let her treat like this, Dad look? The war had begun. Meanwhile, Grace's son Chaz picked up on the obvious fact that he was in the catbird's seat here, a fact he would use to his advantage over and over in the next eight years. Imagine an eight-year-old, already spoiled rotten, who has just been given a free pass due to the fact that there is another eight-year-old he could shift the blame for EVERYTHING to. That, of course, brings us to the third point. Stand up for your kids, early, often, and vociferously, even against your new significant other if the situation calls for it. No one to blame but myself, but once Grace and Chaz smelled the blood in the pool, they were like sharks circling their dinner with regard to poor Joe.

September 2000- June 2002

Once my kids returned to Virginia, Grace and I spent the better part of the next year or so living like single people without responsibilities. Paco did his fatherly duties and kept Chaz whenever he could while Grace and I fell into the socialite party scene of Boca and Miami, living like two people with no responsibility.

"Fathers, do not exasperate your children; instead, bring them up in the training and instruction of the Lord." **Ephesians 6:4**

Many would likely call me a liberal father, but I never really punished my kids. Talk to them, yes, take away privileges, yes, but punish? Never. Consequences serve as their own punishment, yes? Now Grace and her husband, Paco, who was from Venezuela, were all about "spare the rod, spoil the child," and they were constantly whacking Chaz, who often laughed while and after the punishment was happening, mostly using belts. Chaz would often proudly show off his reddened butt cheeks after he received a whacking. Did it work? Well, one of the few times I did effectively discipline Chaz, I sent him to time out, causing him to inquire why I couldn't just spank him like his mom. I rest my case on the effectiveness of corporal punishment on that statement.

This would come up again and again for the first five or six of our 13 years together, causing Grace to castigate me many times, "No wonder Joe is so spoiled, Rick, you're afraid of him."

My kids as a family made two visits to Boca Raton before the oldest two, Amelia and Darin, declared enough. One was the first Christmas of 2000. That one actually went well, except for a brief moment when Grace beat me into going to look at Christmas lights on palm trees when Darin begged me to bond with him by staying home to watch UVA play a Christmas Eve Hula Bowl game. Guilty!! Remember point number three. Stand up for your kids. I didn't. True that Grace was constantly maneuvering me to choose between the kids and her, but that goes back to point three.

The second more damaging trip was in the summer of 2001 when all the kids came down and we took them to Key West. To call this trip disastrous was putting it mildly. Grace was her usual dominating self, insisting we go on a stupid tram ride around Key West that the kids, even Chaz, universally protested.

"But it's history," she exclaimed, apparently blind to the fact that the tram was empty except for us and outside of Grace and myself, the remaining four passengers were ages 9, 10, 15, and 17. To say their interest in the history of Key West was questionable is perhaps a wee bit north of obvious.

The audacity continued when Chaz decided it was time to call Mommy every single time he didn't get exactly what he wanted. Two incidents stood out and pretty much encapsulated the decision my two oldest children made to never visit their father again in Florida.

One evening Grace and I turned in early, leaving the children on their own in front of the TV. When Chaz and Joe got into it over what to watch, struggling for control over the remote, Darin took it on himself to relieve them both of it, negotiating a peaceful end to the dispute. I went out to check on the fray, seeing Darin successfully bringing the conflict to an end, I just stood back and watched. At that moment, the predator version of Grace came storming out of the bedroom, screaming at the top of her lungs.

"WHAT is going on?" Darin barely moved his lips to explain, when Grace turned her rage towards him, upping the volume.

"YOU SHUT UP, DARIN! Stay out of it!! You're not the parent here!!!" Darin has never known fear and he certainly wasn't afraid of the monstrous apparition in front of him, albeit disguised as a beautiful woman. He threw the remote down and stormed out the door, never to reappear until the following morning after spending the night with a buddy he had made who was in another part of the complex.

The second, more damaging incident again revolved around Joe and Chaz. After walking around the part of Key West adjacent to the dock that hosted the daily sunset show, we retreated to a nearby Burger King to feed the hungry teenagers. There Chaz began downing French Fries with the speed of the Road Runner, escaping a failed Wily Coyote trap. When Grace told him to slow down, Chaz blurted out,

"Yeah, if I don't slow down, I'll get fat like Joe." No, Joe wasn't overweight, but at age nine, he still retained a little of the baby fat he had been born with, later he would slim down to a skin and bones version of himself.

What Grace blurted out next was the stuff of which psychiatric legends are born and sustained.

"No, you don't want to get fat like Joe."

It was as if someone had shot a gun through the table. Everyone and everything stopped, everyone aside from Grace, apparently completely oblivious to the incredible ugliness that had just escaped from her lips.

I spent two hours that night driving a crying Joe around, "Why did she have to call me fat, Dad? Why did she say that?" Years later, Sophia would tell me how a month or so after he returned and had gone to therapy, he had turned to her in the car and said.

"It doesn't matter what she said or thinks, Mom. It's what's inside that matters." Profound, just too bad Grace couldn't look inside herself, see herself.

My Folks: Two Lonely Old People

My parents were in their early 70s by the time I married Grace. They supported me 100%, although I know deep inside they suspected that Grace was the same person who had absolutely crushed their only son like an empty juicy box when he was a mere 20 years old. They even contributed by taking both Chaz and Joe with them on a family trip through Tennessee and North Carolina, a contribution that nearly drove them off the edge of the cliff as two eight-year-olds jockeyed for position. My mom looked like she was in a state of shock the entire wedding weekend. In the rearview mirror, someone should have pulled me aside, smacked me really hard in the face and screamed, "What the heck do you think you're doing?"

Dad stood in for me in Virginia for two years while I dallied in Florida with my selfish side, taking the boys to football games, and letting Darin learn to drive in his car. It actually became somewhat of a golden era between Dad and his grandsons, who still tell stories about their exploits at football games with their Grandad, proof that God can bring forth some harvest out of even bitter fruit. Where Dad wasn't, Sophia's husband Adam was, building a soap box racer, enrolling, and getting Joe prepped for the Soap Box Derby for the two years he was eligible. Let's face it, friends, God just gave me many blessings that I, frankly, never, ever deserved.

Summer 2002: In The Name Of Love

At the age of 10, Joe did the bravest thing any man or person could ever ask anyone to do in the name of love. Despite Grace's constant admonition of him, despite my stepson Chaz's ongoing torture of him, against the advice of both his mother, his therapist, and any other human being around him with any semblance of sanity, he came to spend the summer of 2002 in Florida with his beloved daddy. For my part, I spent every minute with Joe, taking him to work with me daily in the restaurant where I served as a barista and occasional waiter in.

The mostly Haitian kitchen staff fell in love with Joe, as did the waitresses, only serving for me to delineate the wide gap attitudinally between those I loved the most, my children, and my bitchy wife with her bratty son, both of whom tortured poor little Joe unmercifully during those summer months.

Perhaps the single most heart wrenching, guilt inducing moment of my life occurred one night that summer when Joe, wrongfully accused by Grace of doing something minor that she blew into a crisis, something that Chaz had actually been responsible for, went running down the street crying. I pursued him and sat down with him on a park bench where my heart was ripped out of its cradle by his teary voice exclaiming, "You shouldn't have left me, Dad. I needed you!"

August 2002 to January 2003

One thing I knew for sure was that when I drove Joe back to Virginia in early August, none of my children would be returning to Florida to visit me as long as I was living with Grace. I had built my own pen, there was no one to blame but myself for there being no escape hatch. I would have to break myself out of the personal Alcatraz I had locked myself into. Unfortunately, prison breaks, like decisions, have consequences, ones that, like everything else are so much clearer in the rearview mirror than they ever were through that front windshield.

If the kids were the only problem, I might have hung in and still be living in sunny Southeast Florida. The kids, however, were just the tip of the iceberg. Employment wise, I went down the quick trip to Never Never Land. Southeast Florida, like LA, was a place where you either brought it with you, meaning prosperity, or you just didn't have it. Not only that, you weren't going to get it either. That would be me. I came to Florida pretty broke, left even more broke and carrying a personal bankruptcy with me. In addition to being an apparently awful judge of female characters, I was also a horrible money manager.

While we discussed my bankruptcy, which Grace was encouraging, our backyard was filled with well diggers putting in Grace's swimming pool. Nothing like contemplating going belly up financially while looking out the window at the construction of a $13,000 backyard pool that your wife is paying CASH for. Indicative of my flawed character is the fact that I never really, truly saw what was wrong with that picture. Clear as a perfect spring day to the normal human eye, but through my front windshield, there might as well have been a sandstorm I was driving through.

Another thing that hadn't changed about Grace was her temper. When she would, at times, come storming at me like one of those cartoon

Bulls, snorting out of both nostrils, it would dredge up unpleasant memories of that long drive to Alabama to see her family when we were 19 during which Grace's temper displays had me seriously considering a stop in Chattanooga to get a Greyhound back to Charlottesville. Her temper was legendary with her co-workers, one of whom, a nice older woman named Marie, once imparted to me that she felt sorry for me cause I had to live with that for the rest of my life. Nice thoughts, huh?

As the tensions and unhappiness grew between Grace and I, she suggested counseling, which I agreed to. So here I was, friends, living in an extremely strange place for a simple minded Southern Baptist boy, underemployed, estranged from my family, in the midst of legal pursuit of bankruptcy while a nice underground swimming pool was being built in my backyard, and, oh yeah, I'm in marriage counseling too.

Our first counselor, a very nice lady with the improbable name of Glory, was only a wee bit of a quack. I can clearly remember her vain attempts to hypnotize me, to which I finally responded by telling her to give it up. I didn't need hypnosis to know what my deepest seeded desire was, I already knew. I wanted to go home, back to Virginia, back to my kids, back to the life I had left behind, too stupid already to realize that you can't go back and, even if you do, nothing is ever the same. But I didn't need Glory to tell me that. I just needed her to be my fall guy. It wasn't me who said I wanted to go back to Virginia, Grace, it was Glory, she dug it out of me, but since she dug it out, it must be what I really want.

Grace, for her part, was like that old joke. My doctor told me to stop drinking, so I got a new doctor. Like in the Springsteen song, the Glory days were over. Grace dropped Glory's therapy like a lead weight. No half-assed pseudo new age hypnotist/therapist was gonna disrupt Grace's plan for the perfect trio family of her, Chaz, and me. Eject button! Bye bye, Glory!

Grace lined us up with a Christian therapist recommended by a friend. We had one visit with this guy, whose limited therapeutic abilities were far surpassed by his huge ego. When about 30 minutes into our session, he looked me straight in the eye and said, "Rick, isn't it true that deep down inside, you might feel like you are just not good enough for a woman like Grace?", I immediately said no, but took note of the fact that his eyes wandered to Grace and, that, in putting me down, he was also pretty much hitting on my wife. Once I wrote my check that day, I effectively swore off therapy for life.

So, in early February of 2002, back to Virginia, I went in a snowstorm. Pretty stupid time to leave Florida. Note to self; next time you're living in Florida and it's winter, wait until at least April to move out. That should have been the end of the story, at least as far as Grace and I. It should have been, but as the rest of this little story demonstrates, my ability to say no to either Grace or Lila falls somewhere between 0 and -10

The Long Road Home: February 2003 until September 2012

One thing I forgot when I moved back to be with my kids was that even though two years is a short time in the life of over 50 of them, it was a long time in the life of kids who were under the age of 16. Time for them to adapt to a father who lives 1,000 miles away with a woman they aren't so sure about, time for them to establish different patterns, ones that didn't include said father, who was in absence. In my short sightedness, in the same blindness which had carried me to and from the sunshine state, I stumbled around the family dynamic like a bull in a china shop, building expectations in myself for a renewal of relations with my children, who frankly, and correctly, looked at me with the jaded eyes of a judge who is seeing the same criminal before his bench for the 100th time. So you promise it will be different THIS time. Right!!!!

Then there was the wild card of Grace, still determined to make things work. After two years of delaying tactics on my part, I finally allowed her to move back to her hometown and we bought a house. It was a house built on sand, a family built on sand. Eight years later, my kids still didn't feel like part of this highly dysfunctional unit, which is probably a good thing. In fact, the main beneficiary of our renewed relationship was Chaz, who dodged the bullet of going to the awful Southeast Florida Public schools.

As for Grace and I, rear view mirror time, I think each of us in our own way, realized the move was a mistake almost immediately, me by losing myself in the fog of constant alcohol and "secret" marijuana consumption, her by expressing her unhappiness with almost all things from the house to me, stopping along the way to berate my kids and parents for their lack of support for her. Grace kept her Florida home the same way she kept her husband's last name, all to the chagrin of my father, who saw it as a way of hedging every bet. Things rolled this way for eight years. Every now and then, Grace would confront me about the beer drinking, telling me to choose between the alcohol and her. With her traveling almost a quarter of the year, to me it felt at the time like a choice between awful and terrible. Incremental at best. I know, I know, flawed thinking.

At some point, a few women, apparently sniffing the unhappiness that even I didn't know I suffered from, made a few overtures, overtures I not only resisted but walked away from resolute in my dedication to the marriage, yet still unable to leave the pot and the alcohol on the table. Then there were the kids, now closing in on adulthood. When Grace was gone, they freely populated our house whenever the urge struck them. When she was there, they avoided it like a house trailer in a hurricane, the hurricane being Grace's temper. I'm not sure what would have happened if I had given in to Grace's requests, some would say demands.

I mean, her last husband Paco had given in when she demanded he give up drugs, yet still ended up on the trash heap of marital discordance when I strolled into her life. All I know is what once were kisses turned into pecks over those last few years. My sense was that Grace would find something to be unhappy about no matter what.

Over those last few years, the one thing that seemed to juice her had nothing to do with her son, my kids, me, or anything else remotely connected to our life together. It was her wealthy clients/friends, the ones with husbands who "adored" them. It was them and her travels around the world, allegedly solo, which seemed to bring her boat closer to the island of happiness than anything that was part of our common reality.

Even then, when those wealthy clients/friends didn't tip her enough, buy the overpriced facial products she pushed or, God forbid, fail to give her a gift at Christmas or a tip she deemed worthy, even then she was unhappy. I served as the listener and sympathizer to those complaints. It would be a few years later before the dawn would come and light would shine on what she told these "friends" about her loving husband, portrayed as a rogue who didn't pay his share and was about to let the mortgage on our home be foreclosed on, a total load of poppycock.

Thus, the scene was set for the next act God had in mind for this little play He had going. That scene would begin on September 22nd of the year 2012.

Chapter 9

Lyin" Eyes

September 22, 2012

When John Lennon was murdered, there was some speculation about he and Yoko's connection to numerology that was accompanied by a theory that someone close to the couple should have noted the significance of the date 12-8-80. Certainly, in the PC "spiritual but not religious" world of the early 21st century, the date of 9-22-12 would be my personal numerological Armageddon. That was the exact date my life began to unravel and spiral out of control, although I had no way of knowing it at the time.

It was a Saturday and I had a wedding to work at one of the nicest vineyards of the dozens that had sprung up in the area surrounding Charlottesville, hereafter known as Napa East. This one featured the most spectacular sunset around, hands down. It was my first time working with Brian Patrick, a rare bird in the officiant end of things in that Brian both counseled and performed ceremonies that were purely Christian in nature. This was in contrast to the vast majority of officiants, who ran like the wind at the mere mention of the name Jesus. After all, Charlottesville was squarely centered in the spiritual but not religious universe.

On the way, I made my daily obligatory phone call to my parents. Dad sounded down.

"What's wrong, pop?" I asked him.

"I'm just not feeling well. I feel weak, maybe I have a cold or something." What he had was what I would recognize from this point on as low blood sugar, but on that September day, I was as clueless as a kitten in a clothes dryer.

"Well, just stay in your chair and take it easy. Don't get up unless you have to."

"Oh, I won't." Satisfied my duty was done, I moved along to my job.

It was a stunningly beautiful day. The ceremony was scenic and meaningful, thanks to Brian Patrick's fine words. While the iPod cocktail mix played over the house system, I took the chance to pack up my ceremony sound system and get it back in my work van. That was when I noticed the missed call and voicemail. The call was from my parents. They would NEVER call knowing that I was working. On the voicemail, my poor mother was in a panic mode.

"Rick, it's Mom, your dad fell down in the bathroom and he can't get up". I thought about that old ad for a Life Alert pendant that permeated our culture for a few years. I believe the woman was called Mrs. Fletcher..." Help, I've fallen and I can't get up." The ad had played so much the phrase sort of became a joke. This was to be my destiny for the next almost two years, however, as I would have to go and help one of my parents up no less than six times.

No time to spare. Maybe thirty minutes left in a cocktail hour to manage the situation and then back to work. I took a chance and called my eldest son Darin. By the grace of God, I got him. He would head straight over.

Then I called Mom again, only to find out a couple of neighbors had come to help and that the Rescue Squad had just loaded Dad up and taken him to the hospital. This generated another quick call to Darin to redirect him. He would go to the hospital, assess the situation and sit with Dad until I could get there later. Just in the nick of time as I headed straight back to introduce the bridal party after hanging up.

Sweet Blindness

Grace? We were still married, yes. Grace had travelled back to Florida for one week a month to service her Florida beauty clients for pretty much the entire eight years she had been in Virginia. While Grace made a lot more money than myself, my job had been to hold down the fort and attend to Chaz. In addition to her Florida trips, a couple of times per year, Grace would score one of those Cruise Ship modeling jobs that would result in a free international trip. Grace would commonly explain that these weren't pleasure trips, this was hard work, but to the layman's eyes, a trip where you cruised international waters on a huge boat that had swimming pools, bars, restaurants, and night clubs didn't resemble any recognizable form of real work.

As time went on, Grace got the fever to travel internationally again. She had lived in Milan for a few years, so I thought nothing of it when she began to take a summer "girlfriend" trip to Italy every year. Since these trips were always during my busy season as well as beyond my financial means, I placidly stayed home. I didn't even become suspicious when she declared all girlfriends unworthy and began making these yearly pilgrimages alone. After all, Grace knew Milan, people there probably knew her. I didn't blink when Grace told me she had talked with her old Italian fiancé, Guido. I even suggested that she try to get together with him while she was there.

I mean, we were married, Grace had begun this round of our relationship by apologizing profusely for the infidelity of our youth, which had actually resulted in her first marriage, another thing she apologized for. Marriage is built on trust, a home built on rock, not sand, that sort of thing. You have to believe, right? I guess you're thinking, how could a grown man be so stupidly naive yet still have written the words you are now reading? Dysfunctional brain syndrome? Alcohol poisoning? Delayed retardation?

Heck, I wish I knew. Again! Trust me when I tell you I am not totally stupid. I HAVE a college degree. I am what I would call "specific stupid". While I can look at virtually anything else in this old world with a wise eye, apparently just the thoughts of Grace, or Lila, drove me into a state of babbling idiocy. God forbid I should actually be in their presence as any semblance of common sense that I have seems to get up and take the bus home immediately.

A Bible Verse: For What It's Worth

This all brings us back to that fateful day, September 22nd, 2012. There are days in all of our lives that serve as a catharsis for what follows. Rarely are we aware of what is happening until the events of those days are in the rearview mirror. Somehow I felt the significance of what was happening on that day, although I most certainly had no inkling of the unstoppable landslide of circumstances and events that would follow in my life, I could see, in the words of Stephen Stills, that there was definitely *"something happening here,"* and what it was was in no way clear. Not yet.

I even texted Grace what was happening, typing that God was talking to me. She text me back, "Yes, He is". What even poor Grace couldn't realize was that she was one of the pawns being moved as God directed my life to checkmate.

I remember, although barely, introducing the bridal party and then punching the button on my preset dinner mix, happy to have the pressure off for a bit. I must have looked distressed. Brian Patrick blessed the food and then asked me what was wrong. I explained to him that I was experiencing something I had bad dreams about. Worst case scenario. Locked into someone's wedding until 11:30 pm, Dad at the hospital and Mom at home...alone. Me unable to lift a finger to help. A nightmare come true.

I retreated out to the foyer to allegedly continue to pack up my ceremony system, but really just to sit and figure out where I was and where I would be once the dust settled. On his way to leave, my new friend Brian came by to check on me one more time. He pulled out a laminated index card saying, "I carry these around with me and just pass them out as the spirit moves me.... somehow this one feels right for you." He handed me the card as I told him goodbye. I glanced down at the verse on the card.

> *"My son, give me your heart, and let your eyes observe my ways"*
> **Proverbs 23:26**

What? I stuck the card in my pocket, wondering why that particular card. It would become clear in the months ahead. One thing I would come to realize is that when God talks to you, it doesn't always make sense. He knows the future, you don't. It's pretty much as simple as that.

So after the wedding, around 1:00 am, I went to the hospital and began what ended being a six week vigil of caretaking for my parents. It was tough to see my father, the man who had coached me in every sport, incapacitated by a combination of low blood sugar and general weakness attendant to his advanced age. Between September 22nd and November 8th, I would spend a grand total of two nights in my own bed, the bed I shared with Grace. Well, at least I shared it with her about 35 weeks of a typical year. In fact, Grace, who returned from Florida on the following Monday, September 24th, would encourage me to stay with my mom in my parent's home. It would be March of the following year before I realized why a woman who instinctively put her own needs above all others suddenly turned altruistic to a fault.

I picked Grace up at the airport sometime around mid-morning that Monday. As usual, she emerged from the baggage pickup area at Charlottesville Airport, pulling her bag behind her. She may have even waved goodbye to a fellow passenger, a not uncommon occurrence during the 15-20 times per year that I was picking her up at that airport. I never paid attention. I trusted. Idiot. Remember?

If I had looked up on that particular morning, I may have noticed a slightly stocky semi-handsome dark haired 40 some Englishman. I would later find out his name was Clifton Jenkins during the tree shaking that took place between February and March of 2013. Grace met him on the plane that morning. 2 weeks later she would be back in Florida and Clifton Jenkins would fly into Fort Lauderdale for the purpose of taking my sweet, once virginal wife, Grace, out to dinner. She would have too many martinis and spend the night in his luxury hotel room. Her rental car would be ticketed and she would pay that ticket before she returned to VA. A glitch in the rental system would still generate a charge of almost $90 to Grace via mail.

Of course, I would help her get this mess all straightened out since I took care of 100% of the computer and fax stuff around the house. It wouldn't be too much of a stretch to say that despite being her husband, there were times when I would feel more like "staff" to Grace. I helped fix the mess in late October. It would be March of the following year before I really took a close look at that parking ticket. Otherwise, I might have asked my sweet and innocent wife what she was doing in Fort Lauderdale at 2:00 am on a Tuesday night. I trusted. I believed. Idiot.

It just never occurred to me that Grace's encouragement to not let my mother stay alone was driven by anything other than warm family feelings, at least not until I later discovered the steady stream of emails between her and Clifton. It never occurred to me that when she suggested that the upcoming Rolling Stones in Hyde Park London was THE way to see the Stones, said the suggestion was made with a wing and a prayer that her new pal Clifton would spot her the ticket and perhaps his London flat as a place to light down. Trusted. Believed. Idiot!

See, Grace WAS actually telling me who she was. She just didn't tell me she was telling me who she was, so, at least in this case, how could I believe it? In fact, when all the monkeys were ejected from the tree during the shaking, I was dumbfounded when I realized that Grace had subtly announced every last one of them to me. All five. Yep, there were five monkeys in that tree.

So how did that shakeout happen? What brought the monkeys down? Well, it all started in late October of 2012 when a South African real estate developer named Caleb Cobb and his wife made an offer on the home Grace and I had lived in for almost 10 years. The house had been on sale for at least six of those years. Grace had complained about that house from day one. Too small, too dark, no storage, pick your reason. It all fits Grace's basic MO. Whatever it was, it wasn't enough. The house, me, and the kids were never happy. Being the puppy dog I was, I went along, every time. I worked my ass off to sell that house, at a loss, all in the desperate hope that it would keep Grace in the marriage. For the first time in my life, when Grace and I married, I had said Christian vows, complete with a reading of the Love Passage, Corinthians 13, the chapter where God reveals through Paul the true nature of unconditional love, agape love, and love as a decision.

> "4 Love is patient, love is kind. It does not envy, and it does not boast, it is not proud. 5 It does not dishonour others, it is not self-seeking, it is not easily angered, it keeps no record of wrongs. 6 Love does not delight in evil but rejoices with the truth. 7 It always protects, always trusts, always hopes, always perseveres. 8 Love never fails. But where there are prophecies, they will cease; where there are tongues, they will be stilled; where there is knowledge, it will pass away." **1 Corinthians 13:4-8**

It was early November 2012 when Chaz and I had the conversation in which he revealed his mother would be leaving me after the house was sold. What could I do? Not a thing. It turned out that Chaz had actually spoken up for me, and gotten angry with his mother, but even he knew there was no stopping the runaway train that was about to run me over. I dutifully gave up my beer and the little bit of pot I allowed myself to indulge in immediately and announced as such to Grace on a brief Thanksgiving trip to Williamsburg that we took.

On the way back, I took up the subject of Grace leaving. Let's be honest. At this point, Grace leaving me, actually divorcing me after all we had been through, seemed inconceivable. But that was her plan. Would I get another chance? We looked for rentals and in the process, I thought I had Grace talked into giving it a chance. But I didn't know about the monkeys in the tree. Heck, I didn't even know about the tree yet.

It was early December when I finally found the right rental, meaning the one that would be acceptable to Grace. How desperate was I? Here was a woman who had already stated her intention to leave me, left me with less than a 50/50 chance of keeping her in the relationship, yet I still virtually allowed her to choose our abode, the home that I would be paying the complete rent on.

Then there were the cats, the cats I would eventually inherit. Not one cat, not two, but three furry little creatures. When Grace and I married 13 years before, I not only had no animals, I did not WANT any. The new place was in a tightly packed neighborhood and if the kitties were going outside, they would need tags. That's why I was in the pet store on December 7, 2012. And the pet store was where I would look up and see a giant of a man who looked like he should be coaching an NBA team but instead was doing the work of The Lord.

Pastor Wilt Levine and I had actually worked together on a few occasions, but it was as the resident pastor at tiny Laurel Hill Baptist Church near the Charlottesville Airport that I really knew him, a church that I had attended with my dad several times. I approached him in the store with the announcement that I was Olly Trax's son. We made a bit of conversation for a few minutes as I told him about Dad's fall, his time in rehab, and my caring for Mom.

It was only a few minutes before I was pouring my heart out to this man of God about the marriage and its impending end. Wilt re-introduced me to my best friend, Jesus right then and there. Before we left, we shared a prayer and made a plan for me to go see Wilt as soon as possible, a plan that would eventually lead to Wilt becoming my pastor, counselor, and most trusted brother in the walk I was about to begin with Jesus. I still didn't know about the tree, the monkeys, and all the other rain that was about to fall on my life. The really funny thing, friends, is that Wilt had no pets and could offer up not a single reason why he was even in that pet store on that day. Cue the Twilight Zone theme....

January 2013: A Trip To Boca

January 27, 2013. I am sitting in the Richmond Airport waiting to board my JetBlue flight for Fort Lauderdale when Grace's call comes in. I check my watch and it's already 12:30 pm. I had been expecting to hear from her all morning.

"Hi, my flight is running a little late. I'm not on board yet. Did you go to church?"

"No, I actually just got up." It was a groggy voiced Grace on the other end of the line, explaining how she had gone to a nightclub with her friends the night before. Didn't get home until after 2:30. Woke up once, then had to lay back down. What time would my flight get in? Around 4:30 or so. We hung up and I boarded. I didn't sleep at all during the three hour flight, excited that I was going to be in Florida, excited that I would have a week with Grace away from the somewhat depressing townhouse we now lived in. It just wasn't the same as our house, which I had loved despite Grace's bitter complaints about nearly everything about it.

On the flight, I shared the row with a couple of young guys, both of whom were Florida residents. As we flew over the waters of Southeast Florida and turned landward across the Port of Fort Lauderdale, the cloudy skies began to drop a little rain. I mentioned the on-the-beach nightclub I anticipated going to with Grace that night, bemoaning the falling rain. One of the young guys noted that this was Florida. If you don't like the weather, wait five minutes, it will change.

After we landed, I grabbed my bag from the overhead and made haste to the baggage claim area, outside of which Grace was waiting in her Jeep. As we headed out and up the road to Boca, I noted two things. First, Grace, who had insisted on listening to the oldies station exclusively for years, had a Top 40 radio station on. Second, it was LOUD. In fact, it was almost as if I were riding with a teenager. One that was also driving like a maniac, I might note.

After we safely arrived at the Boca home that Grace had kept through all those years, the home she had rented with my assistance doing virtually all the contracts, emails, and other computer stuff while she collected the rent, we were joined within an hour by Grace's close friend Darla, another model. Darla's husband, David, a man I truly loved, had passed away the previous July from hepatitis complications. David was a former addict who successfully conducted a prison ministry in Miami before his health waned completely. The ladies drank wine and we ate a light dinner while listening to the Laura Nyro cd that I had made for Grace.

The Club: Three Little Birds and A Monkey

The women were about three glasses in by the time I poured them into the Jeep and we headed south to Deerfield Beach and a nice little spot called JB's On The Beach, where a top-notch reggae band would be playing that night. I made a very small mental note about Grace's wine consumption, which had heretofore been limited to around two glasses for the evening. The music was great, the vibe was awful. The joint was filled with 50-60 some year old dudes with shirts open to the chest hair and gold chains around their necks.

Most of their heads sported a neon sign that said "Horny, Rich, and Ready to Roll." OK, I'm making that last part up, but you get the picture. One particular fellow, a brutish bear of a man named Dan, was introduced to me by both Grace and Darla, who obviously knew him. He proceeded to hang with us the rest of the night, much to my chagrin. I made another mental note of the fact that Grace introduced me not as her husband Rick, but simply as Rick. Once, when I returned from an excursion to the head, to find Dan and Grace engrossed in conversation. Grace looked up as I approached.

"I told Dan we've known each other since we were 19." Oh yeah, Grace? Great! Did you manage to slip in the fact that we've been married for 12 years? To say Dan had few redeeming qualities would be to say he had zero redeeming qualities, which was true, at least to my eyes. Of course, at maybe six feet, five inches, and 260 really solid pounds, I sure as hell wasn't going to tell him.

"You want me to tell him? I'm not scared of that son of a bitch." I turned to the empty chair beside me to see a familiar young handsome face poking out from underneath long hair with slight bangs which framed it. Slipping back in my seat, I note the way my new table mate is dressed, sort of like an urban cowboy with a kerchief around his neck and an obviously custom designed leather jacket. Then I note that he has what looks like a fat joint in his right hand while his left hand is wrapped around the neck of a bottle of Jim Beam. Who the hell is this guy and how did he get that stuff in here?

Grace and Dan continue the dumb down contest that is masquerading as a conversation as I look closer at the seat beside me and begin to recognize the apparition seated there. Straining, I lean forward. "Hey! You're....."

"Yep, it's me. GP." The ghost of Gram Parsons smiles at me and takes a deep hit off of the joint. No wonder Dumb Dan and Grace have continued to warble, this hallucination is earmarked for me personally. I lean further forward and touch the leather of the coat. It's real. "You can see me, you can touch me, them...no!" Gram exhales and takes a big swig of the bourbon. What do you say to the ghost of a dead rockstar you meet in a bar on the beach in Florida?

"So why are you here?"

"To help."

"With what?"

Gram smiles and takes another swig, then a hit on the joint. Holding the hit in, he speaks, "Oh, you'll see."

Just then, I am distracted by Dan asking me a dumb question, the inanity of which causes me to look at him and Grace while answering. When I turn back towards the seat, it's empty again. No GP. Maybe I had entered the Twilight Zone.

That Dan had an affinity for Darla was another obvious fact, as well as that Grace and Darla knew Dan from nights out and had danced with him before. Grace gave me a brief glimpse of where she was headed when she and I went to the restroom. She said she couldn't understand why Darla didn't like Dan, implying that even if she didn't, she should take advantage of the fact that he wanted to pay for her drinks. "Besides, Dan is rich." Grace made that statement with an almost perverse delight that was an early clue into the nature of Grace's growing materialism.

When Dan began to lift Darla like a barbell during a few of the more energetic songs of the excellent reggae band, all I wanted to do really was smash his big dumb skull with the nearest wine bottle. It was a lovely fantasy, but one I had to let go. Grace and Darla were both downing wine as fast as Dan could buy it for them, but I was tolerant as the situation found Grace in more physical proximity to me than she had allowed in quite a while, wrapping my arms around her, bumping her butt against me as she danced. Still, another mental note that I was clearly being treated more like a date than a husband.

The coup d'état was when the band quit at about 11:30 and my sweet non-party girl Grace exclaimed, "What? They're quitting, I'm just getting started," a statement that was about as out of character for Grace as wearing combat boots.

The ride home, well, ride for Grace and Darla, they sure weren't driving after 20 or so glasses of wine between them. The ride home was, umm, interesting. Grace asked how much wine she had and when I replied that I had counted eight glasses, Darla, who had the other 12 glasses, jumped to her defense.

"No way, Grace."

When Grace exclaimed to me, "Yes, honey, I've been driving drunk," in the middle of a brief conversation about how they met Dan the dick, it was Darla, one of the western world's premier drunk drivers, who proclaimed, "No you haven't!" Seriously, folks, I've seen this woman drive like a champ after drinking enough alcohol to sink a sizable yacht. What did they care? They were models, they were beautiful. If they got pulled over, they'd just flash a smile, a little leg. What cop in the world could resist?

When we arrived back at Grace's house, it wasn't what happened that surprised me, it was what didn't, which was sex. After 13 years of marriage, I had a fairly good concept of the situations my darling Grace would get frisky in and 8 glasses of wine most definitely qualified as one, yet we said goodnight with a tongueless kiss and a brief hug. The mental notebook in my head was now filled to capacity. I was beginning to see the tree, still clueless about the monkeys.

Whoever it was, I went to bed with that Sunday night, by Monday morning, I was waking with the Grace that I knew and loved. Monday Morning Grace swore off alcohol and the party life that last night's Grace was embracing like a teddy bear in a bassinet. It would be much later when the dawning would occur in my consciousness that what I had witnessed that Sunday night was the Grace that had been traveling to South Florida for a while. Even when Darla's husband David was alive, she rarely missed a party. Even when David was alive, Darla played with men like they were lab rats, pulling them into her orbit. Then as said men would begin to gnaw at the bait she had knowingly tossed in their ocean, she would draw back into the aghast posture of a nice girl shocked at the attention. "But I'm married." Once David passed, once her mourning was done, the gloves were off. Don't get me wrong, she was totally dedicated to his care, but at the same time it was as if she was discovering dormant superpowers.

Sunday Night Grace had merely let her guard down. She had given me a glimpse behind the curtain and dropped the facade. Feeling good, she had a weak moment and forgot that I was there. It would be months before I would dig up the Facebook pictures of Grace, Darla, and a bevy of South Florida models partying at various spots around Southeast Florida. It would be even longer before I would single out an accessory she had been wearing for over 10 years as missing in action. Her wedding ring!

The tree was now obvious and I was beginning to hear the distant, dim sound of monkeys. By the end of the week, they would be screaming at me.

Chapter 10

At the Dark End of the Street

<u>Late January 2013: Boca Raton</u>

I could write an instructional book on cheating. How to do it, when to do it, when not to do it, and, of course, how to keep from getting caught. That's important. I cheated in church, cheated in school, cheated at board games, cheated on pretty much every girlfriend I ever had. Oddly enough, I never cheated in sports. Go figure. Warped sense of honor.

Grace was an awful cheater. She left such a broad trail even a hound with no olfactory sense could follow it. Or she simply was not the sharpest tool in the shed? Your decision, my friends. I'm just telling the story.

When the first monkey came down, it happened quickly! Bam, boom, crash!!! It was late Wednesday afternoon when Grace and I were sitting at the table, her eyes on her iPad, my eyes on her. I was not a hound with damaged olfactory senses. I could smell a rotten fish from the next block, so I took note when a wry smile crossed Grace's face as she checked her email, as I did when she dropped that smile like a cat caught with a canary. I made sure to walk around the table and glance at that iPad as I went out to work in the yard. What was so interesting, Grace? While she closed down the email it wasn't before I caught a glimpse of a broadly smiling man in a picture.

My inborn Scorpio detective drive kicked in like a diesel in high gear. Grace, oblivious to anything outside her world, the one that revolved around her, left the iPad laying on the table that night. No password, no pin. See? Awful cheater.

What I saw was a series of emails between her and an overweight goateed man that would turn out to be Mark. The best word I can use to describe the exchange is "goofy". Here is an obviously very successful man reduced to a pile of mush by Grace's beauty, a beauty that was clearly beyond his reach to this point. The picture was captioned; "me with the governor. Trying to impress you." The exchange had started with Grace writing that they should "stay in touch. Here's a few pictures." Those modeling pictures were all Grace had, she had to lead with them. There was nothing else. What was she going to do, share her treatise on the decline of the American family, a treatise which, by the way, did not exist? Grace had her beauty, her status as a professional model (barely, she only worked once or twice a year) and, oh yeah, her worldliness due to her stint in Milan during the days of her youth.

My mind tried to zero in on these emails. What is this? An online dating site connection? Mark's response to her picture drew me towards that conclusion. "I love your eyes. Can't wait to see the real thing."

Sleep and I didn't get along so well the rest of the week. Didn't matter. I was a hound dog on the trail of a rabbit, one that turned out to be a monkey. Despite the lack of rest, my personal energy level, metabolized by the Scorpio detective drive, was high. Grace's Florida house...I mean, she KEPT her Florida house, that should have told me something...was on a rental for the upcoming month, so I voluntarily helped her get it ready. Thus it was when I was in the back bedroom, the one we shared for two years, cleaning up on Thursday morning. Grace's iPhone was setting on the dresser and I heard the text notification. The texts appeared on the front screen for a moment before disappearing. I usually checked them to let Grace know if it was something that required her immediate attention. I walked over to the dresser and checked the text.

"Just wondering what was up for the weekend. Wasn't sure how long your friend is going to be around. Mark". Just like that....MONKEY DOWN!!

A Well Respected Man

Rick, the Scorpio detective, won't stop there, though. Hound dog on patrol! The next time I see my sweet Grace putting entering her PIN code, I casually slide behind her and easily pick up the four numbers that will eventually open Pandora's box and knock all five monkeys out of the tree.

Grace met Mark the very night before I flew out for Florida. The text revealed they had met and been together in a bar until 5 a.m. More appropriately, a "bottle" room. The bar, the Blue Martini, had a private room adjacent to it. In order to gain entry to the room and get a table, one had to buy a bottle of liquor. The mixers were free. Liquor bottles were $200...really. I can't make this crap up. Once the customers, who were ironically all male, gained entrance to the private room and secured a table, they could saunter back out to the main room and troll for female companionship to join them at the table or just to invite them to the bottle room. I already knew about the bottle room as Grace had explained how she, Darla, and the other models had been invited in by some 30 year old guy who apparently revealed Grace as the reason for the invite. Red flags came up when I asked Grace if she had told the upstanding young man that she was married and she replied, "I had the ring." This was technically a truthful answer as she did indeed still have possession of the wedding ring, which was safely tucked away on her dresser at home.

The initial texts between Grace and Mark indicated that he had swooped her away from the 30 year old, although my gut told me finances likely played a part in the swooping. The remainder of the texts from that first night were as goofy as the email exchange I discovered earlier. The most outstandingly regurgitative text had Mark saying, "I can still see you looking into my eyes and feel your hand on my chest." Talk about gagging yourself with a spoon!

The Thursday texts were a little less goofy. Mark asked if Grace had an opening to get a meal together and Grace cited work and the presence of her "friend" (Yep, that's me!) as the reasons for her denial of the invitation albeit with the caveat that she may be able to work something last minute out. Mark played a good puppy dog.

Somehow, I made the decision to keep digging, not play my hand until it was called, which would be soon enough. Friday was our last day in Florida before making the two day car trip up the East Coast on I-95. I dropped Grace off that morning at the beauty parlor she worked at in Boca. Then I dropped her car off to have it road checked for the long trip and walked back to her house to continue the cleanup for her renters. That's right. I was still doing my duty, folks. You can smack me with the stupid stick later.

I picked up the car in an hour. That's when Grace called. "Hi honey, I wore the wrong shoes again. Would you mind bringing me the tan pair that is by the dresser?" She waited while I found the correct pair and confirmed them. "Oh yeah, can you also bring my Ray-bans from the car and the bottle of makeup foundation that's setting on the dresser?" Sure I could. "Thanks, honey!" After hanging up, I look up. There is a virtual army of monkeys in the tree, all frantically waving red flags!

Having received my directives, I walk back down Boca Raton Boulevard the three or four blocks to the garage where Grace's Jeep is being serviced and after a few parting words with Chuck, the owner of the shop, get in the Jeep and drive back to the house, grabbing the shoes and makeup foundation requested by my wife. I hop back in the Jeep, quickly opening the console to confirm the presence of the missing Ray Bans. Upon that confirmation, I take off to the shop. As I drive down Boca Raton Boulevard, I feel a presence and look at the passenger seat beside me.

"Want a hit?" Gram Parsons holds out his ever present joint to me. "Drink?" He turns up the bottle and takes a swig, finally turning his face towards the windshield. "You starting to figure a few things out?"

Huh? Excuse me? You've been dead for nearly 40 years, and now you're sitting beside me, still dead as far as I know, in a Jeep in Boca Raton, Florida, offering me a toke and a shot and asking me if I'm starting to figure things out? Hell no, I'm not figuring things out. When I turn to speak those thoughts out loud to the apparition, he has vanished. I just shake my head as I pull into the lot of Grace's shop and park the Jeep.

Always at Grace's service, I had arrived at the shop within an hour of the original call. The first thing I notice is that she is already wearing flats while the shoes that I am bringing her have a small heel on them. Now, Grace and I had been married for over 12 years at this point, so I had actually witnessed her transition from the ridiculous heels that she wore to work in the first few years that had ruined her back to the athletic shoes she now wore at her shop in Virginia. I might have fallen off the turnip truck a few times, but the brain damage wasn't permanent. I still knew when I was being sold lemons. I made the lemonade by asking Grace if she wanted me to take the shoes she was wearing with me. Even the monkeys were laughing as she gave her answer.

"No, there are some clients that I like to dress up a little more for." Really, Grace? So you're inside a beauty parlor on your feet styling hair in high heels with your Ray-bans on, but you still can take the time to freshen up your makeup? I didn't even need the Scorpio detective drive to figure this one out. It was a virtual layup of a conclusion, one that drew itself like a baby scribbling with crayons. The a-ha meter was clipping into the red.

Darla had been getting color and Grace asked me if I would mind driving her home. On the way, I began to "question" Darla as my Scorpio detective kicked into mega gear and overrode my common sense. Darla had been with Grace the previous weekend when she had met Mark, and I suspected Mark was the reason I was carrying heels, makeup foundation, and Ray Bans to my lovely wife of 12 years. Darla eventually protested.

"I have my own shit, Rick," she blurted, obviously frustrated by my semi-confrontational questions, "you two are going in different directions." Huh? Different directions? That seemed a vast understatement. As Darla disembarked from the Jeep at her home, just a few blocks away from Grace's house, I just blurted it out.

"I know about Mark, Darla!!"

"Mark? Who's Mark?"

"The guy from the other night."

"Which one?" Which one? Which night? Geez, how many are there? I let it and Darla go, watching her go into the house, then driving back towards downtown Boca.

I drove back to Grace's shop, drove around the block and took up residence on an adjacent street in Grace's Jeep, a spot where I could see the door. It wasn't longer than 30 minutes before she emerged wearing the shades and the heels, primping herself as she walked down the sidewalk towards the downtown Boca area known as Mizner Park, so totally into herself that she failed to notice her own car parked in plain view, not to mention the husband sitting behind the wheel. I followed at a close distance and watched her turn the corner. It was easy to deduce that her destination was the Starbucks that was on the corner. I rounded the block and parked across the street, again in plain view.

It was about 30 minutes later when she walked out arm in arm with the overweight goateed man that I recognized from the email. As they turned the corner onto the side street, I pulled out and headed that way, reaching them just as they stood under the overhead walkway between two parking garages. They were just preparing for the inevitable goodbye kiss when I drove by them in Grace's Jeep. If eyes could really jump, Grace's would have traversed the Grand Canyon in a single leap at that moment. I drove on, turning the corner and beginning the first of several trips around various blocks as I tried to figure out my next move. Grace called my cellphone several times until I finally pulled up to a stop sign and she walked through the crosswalk right in front of me, still not noticing her own car. I blew the horn and a visibly nervous Grace got in the passenger's seat.

"What are you doing down here, honey?" Grace's demeanor was that of a kid caught with the cookie jar. Why dropping off your dry cleaning, of course? Thinking quickly, I remembered that from the task list of the day. I wasn't ready to show my hand yet. Where the hell is GP? I have a few questions for you, Mr. Ghost.

Grace made what may rank as the worst attempt at damage control in the history of philandering when she said, "I went out for a cup of coffee...I just needed a cup of coffee." I nodded like a zombie and let her out in front of her shop. An absolutely AWFUL cheater.

Chapter 11

Got My Mind Set On You

To call the next few days uncomfortable would be tantamount to calling the Grand Canyon a gully. First of all, it was laughable when Grace said, "you're checking on me!"

We finally did have the conversation, though. Did Grace apologize or admit anything? Well she said, "Rick, I should have left you two years ago." What do you think? Is that an apology or admission? She seemed particularly disturbed when I described the feeling that I got from catching her with Mark as a sense of Deja Vu from her infidelity when we were young.

As we discussed the incident while driving north on I-95 the next day, Grace at first declared, "I didn't even know that guy!"

I watched her wiggle a little as she recalled the small detail of them leaving Starbucks arm in arm, finally dropping back and punted to "Well, we danced together one night."

"Does he know you're married?"

If Grace was a cat when I asked that, the fur on her back would have been standing straight up at attention. "I told him I was divorced, Rick!!!" She snapped.

That fact that would be confirmed when I later saw a text to him apologizing for being distant when they said goodbye that day. It seems her "ex" was stalking her. Holy cripes!

When that statement came out, I could almost see my friend Jesus standing over in the corner shaking his head like a teacher who has caught you skipping class.

21 "With much seductive speech she persuades him; with her smooth talk she compels him." 23 ……" he does not know that it will cost him his life." **Proverbs 7: 21 & 23**

I was a sinner and destined to pay for my sins. I was an adulterer. Did the women who participated in the adultery with me know what they were doing? To a woman, yes. They were willing participants in the sin. They knew. In fact, all the women I committed adultery with initiated the act themselves, but not a single one twisted my arm to join in. Willing participants. Me. Them. I plead guilty, Judge Judy!

While Jesus is shaking his head over Grace, He is making motions with His eye to me. I know, I know, first remove my own plank then we'll talk about Grace's.

"You hypocrite, first take the plank out of your own eye, and then you will see clearly to remove the speck from your brother's eye." **Matthew 7:5**

Even though my own adultery was now 20 years past, even though I had confessed it before God, I was in no position to judge. I had learned. A few women had tried to tempt me during the 13 years with Grace, but I wanted no part of it. I knew exactly what guilt felt like, how having the knowledge that you had put your very soul in jeopardy ripped at you, your being, your fabric, your happiness and your well-being. It was like rats gnawing on a carcass. Slowly, but very surely you disappeared. That, my friends, is how God teaches us real repentance.

And that is why I was willing to forgive Grace. That and remembering the promise for better or worse we made during that wedding ceremony 11 years before. Through all I was about to find out, as monkey after monkey fell out of that tree, I was willing to forgive. A fool or a believer, you make the choice, but I was always willing.

There was only one woman in the world who could knock me off my path and by the time Lila showed up, it was a technicality.

Unfortunately, as I was to learn when I went to LA, with God, as in sports, you can lose on a technicality. Fortunately, as much as I was willing to forgive Grace, our Father is even more willing to forgive us. Just ask. Ask.

"Always forgive your enemies; nothing annoys them so much."

— Oscar Wilde

As we headed up the coast that first day, I thought perchance that I could reason with Grace, and talk her into staying in the marriage. I remember saying, "Don't break our covenant, Grace. Trust God. He can fix this." She gave me the answers I suppose she had to give a man she would be stuck in the car for two days with. It wasn't yes, it wasn't no, it wasn't even maybe...more like a nebulous cloud floating in the sky...maybe it would rain or maybe it wouldn't.

We stopped for that first night at a hotel near Savannah that was our customary stopping off point. Grace loved the beds and the fact that there were two of them. I'm just gonna say it here. If your significant other starts wanting their own sleeping space, away from you, then you just as well stick a fork in that relationship. It was a hard lesson, but now I know. On this particular night, it turned out to be fortuitous, although perhaps not so much for Grace. As I sat in the front room watching late night talk shows, the text alert went off on Grace's phone again. Yep, she still hadn't secured that phone. As she slept like a log, I grabbed the phone to let my detective tendencies satisfy themselves and looked at the incoming message.

"Just saying hello, beautiful. How are you?" Who's this from? Has to be the Mark dude. To my surprise, the name of the incoming text was not Mark, but Adam...Adam Gotman to be exact....and that my friends, is how the monkey tumble began.

One by one over the next month, the monkeys fell from the tree, each with his own outstanding characteristic. They weren't boring monkeys, to be sure, perhaps boorish. Some were handsome, some would turn your stomach, but they all had one thing in common...MONEY!

"While money can't buy happiness, it certainly lets you choose your own form of misery."

— Groucho Marx

Enough pre-game, you want to know about the monkeys, right? Grace, even after she knew I knew she was being unfaithful, still didn't cover her tracks. She left every door open, all I had to do was walk in like an addict in an electronics store in the middle of a riot and take whatever I wanted. It began with grabbing the phone nightly, following the trail of texts and emails. Then she upgraded her phone and left the old one on the couch in one of her bags. It was really like taking candy from a baby, as it would be months before she even realized the phone was missing. By then I had pictures, videos, texts, emails, and everything I needed for any impending legal battles, just in case. That's right, I said pictures and videos right there, on her phone. She didn't delete a damn thing. Absolute worst cheater in the world. Too bad she didn't tell me what she was up to, I could have given her a few pointers.

So, the monkeys came tumbling down, hitting branch after branch along the way, each branch a new revelation, each revelation tearing a new rip in my soon to be crushed heart. Funny, in looking back I can see how the Scorpio detective drive actually saved me in a way, allowing the cracks that were splitting my heart to settle in like a slow moving and gently rolling earthquake rather than the violent, immediate, damage inflicting 7.9 shocker it could have been. Oddly enough, my need to know saved me from a reaction of NOOOOO!!! Maybe this is how warriors maintain a cool, calm demeanor when staring at the jaws of death...focus on the process.

Mark, of course, was the first monkey. He is the one still standing. I'm sure to this day he is Grace's puppy dog as much as I am sure his success and his puppy tendencies made him the most appealing candidate in Grace's pre-emptive and clandestine search for my replacement. He would maintain contact with Grace, always a gentleman, never forcing the situation. In fact, I'm sure Grace was the driving force behind the wheel of their eventual relationship. At the bottom of it all, I have no reason to think he even knew what he was getting himself into and by all accounts, he comes across as a very nice guy, one that can't be held responsible for pursuing a beautiful woman, especially one who told him she was already divorced. In many ways, I actually feel sorry for him. He simply had the best resume of the available candidates. When he traveled to Europe with a beautiful model in the summer of 2013, paying all the way I might add, he had no way of knowing she was, in fact, still married.

When Grace and I had the conversation after I discovered the email less than two weeks after she moved out of my townhouse confirming that she and Mark were going overseas together, she justified the trip to me by saying, "I'm not paying for any of that"...you read that right...oh, yes she did! Poor Mark. Again, seems like a nice fellow...I just hope in the long run, he has enough vision to see the tree before HIS monkeys start tumbling down. That beauty of Grace's can be so blinding.

He who loses money, loses much; He who loses a friend, loses much more; He who loses faith, loses all.

—Eleanor Roosevelt

Monkey number two was Adam Gotman, the man who texted Grace that night in Savannah. It turned out that Adam had been around since early March of 2012, a fact that was proven by the pictures of Grace and Adam wrapped around each other the night they met. Since the pictures were texted by Darla and also in the picture was Suki, another close friend of Grace's, it begged a question, girlfriend. If you're a girlfriend and your married girlfriend starts dating around, at what point do you make the suggestion that perhaps she should get divorced

BEFORE she starts the shopping? Adam didn't appear to have the cash the other monkeys tumbling had, so I'm not sure what the attraction was, but, based on the texts, I would put my bet on the horse called Pure Lust to win. You know how things that seem absolutely horrible at the time can be funny in retrospect? That's the definition of my outlook on Grace and Adam's relationship, which actually had about a 10 month run. Of course, the one thing old Adam didn't know, the one thing he had in common with me, which he never knew, was that he wasn't the only one. There never was an only one with Grace. Remember? Never happy, always looking for greener grass. That's Grace!

One of the funniest exchanges involving Adam is actually a text between Grace and Darla as Grace anticipates Adam coming down to Miami to take her to dinner. Grace texts that she hasn't "been out on a date in years." I can't make this stuff up, folks. Why would I? The absolutely funniest thing occurred after that date when Adam dropped Grace off at her nephew's apartment. Oh yeah, her nephew, Judd. Let's just call him a monkey assistant and let it go at that, but you're starting to get a feel for how many people in Florida were in on this little soirée before it was even a distant blip on my personal radar screen. Now picture the fact that I made at least three trips to Florida with Grace while this drama was unfolding and each time each of these fine people treated me as if I were their best friend. Geez! Talk about thieves in the temple, wolves in sheep's clothing, or whatever other analogies you want to throw out there.

So Adam dropped Grace off and apparently headed back to Boca and the following text exchange occurred. Do yourself a favor and set your coffee down way away from your keyboard before you read it.

March 11, 2012 1:44 AM

Grace: Hi, let me know u made it home ok. I really had fun. U r so hot. I like u alot.

March 11, 2012 3:12 AM

Adam: Hi..just arrived home... Soooo tired ... And you are even hotttter ... and like you mooooore ... Xoxo

Wait! Don't pick that coffee up just yet, there's more. Here is the text that I got from my darling wife Grace at 1:46 am, two minutes after her text to her date for the night, Adam.

March 11, 2012 1:46 AM

Grace: Honey, Can u please water the orchid?

March 11, 2012 1:48 AM

Rick: Ok

Glad you didn't pick up that coffee now, aren't you? I know the question begging you for an answer. What the hell is wrong with me? Well, you'll just have to add this little guffaw to the stupid stick smacking score you've been keeping on me. Tell me this. Why would a man who is too stupid, or trusting, to ask why his wife is in Fort Lauderdale getting a parking ticket at 2 a.m. subsequently be bright enough to wonder why the same woman, the one who insists on hitting the sack by 11 p.m. every night at home, would be texting him at 1:46 am from Miami to water the orchid? Love is blind. In my case, it also seems to be deaf, dumb, and retarded.

The Poor Side Of Boca

Old Adam hung in there through months and months with apparently no payoff. In fact, when Grace and I had the talk later. OK, maybe talk is putting it too lightly. When Grace and I had the confrontation later, her statement about Adam was, " I haven't EVEN kissed him yet." Oops...sorry about that coffee. Should have warned you again.

Grace must have eventually figured out that Adam just didn't have the cash reserves to be a serious candidate. My Scorpio detective drive was easily able to locate his arrest record with a simple Google search. It was quite impressive. Over the course of 15 years or so, he had attracted lawsuits like sewers attract flies, not to mention an awesome collection of traffic charges ranging from several DUIs to coke possession. His crowning achievement, however, was a more recent charge for felony stolen property, meaning in excess of 100 grand. Oh yeah, let's not forget the domestics, a series of charges brought by an ex-girlfriend named Diana, truly a beautiful lady. You couldn't fault his taste in women.

Grace knew of at least some of the issues since there were a few text exchanges about his day in court and he was obviously under some sort of house arrest in the waning stages of their "relationship". Then there was this interesting text exchange.

Grace: I am sorry, I am not into casual sex. I guess I gave u the wrong impression before.

Adam: Well I'm sorry I gave you the wrong impression I'm not either.

Grace: Suki and I wanted to thank you for a beautiful dinner!!! You're hired!!!

Adam: Deal.... And plus I respect you much much more than just to look at you for casual sex..but u cant blame me im only human and i am so dammmmmmmm attracted to you ...anyways you're a sweetheart.. bigggggg kiss,

Grace: Thanks for your honesty. It makes me feel better. When the times right, it will be great!

Adam: Cant wait ......xoxoxoxoxo...have a good day ....and I love cooking for you.

The dime drops in the jukebox in my mind. George Jones is singing his classic *The Race Is On*, wherein he describes his breaking heart as a losing horse on the track. In my vision, I see a few more horses, namely Greed and Pure Lust!

February 2013: Money Honey

Excuse me, sir! May I have my winnings? I believe I bet on Pure Lust to win. Around the time Adam goes under house arrest, which was likely con-current with the time sweet Grace figured out that he didn't have a cent, poor Adam sinks from view quicker than the Titanic after it hit that iceberg.

It's a process, you know, this monkey tumble. A vetting process.

Then there was Clifton Jenkins. We've already met him, a 40 year old London based insurance executive who traveled to the States regularly and appeared to travel to many of the states. He and Grace only had two or three recorded meetings over an almost seven month period, the one in Fort Lauderdale in which she ended up in his hotel room, one in Boca in which he ended up sleeping in the marital bed Grace and I shared, and perhaps one more in Miami, unconfirmed. I mean, even for a Scorpio detective drive, there does come a point where the evidence is overwhelming and further pursuit of it can only be classified as mere obsession. I was well beyond that point by the time Clifton and Grace may have had their final date in late February 2013, not to mention beyond the point of caring. It was pretty funny reading texts from Grace to Darla, nephew Judd, and a variety of the other unintentional thieves in the temple of Boca..." Do you think Clifton is too young for me?" Like I said, it's a vetting process. So complicated for a 62 year old philanderer. So much to be considered. Age, looks, and, of course, financial considerations. Poor Grace, so many decisions, so many thoughts crowding her pretty little head.

When Grace and I actually talked about Clifton in mid-February, she came closer to an admission of guilt than at any other time during the monkey reveal. It started with Grace denying that she ever said she shared a bed with Clifton.

"I did NOT say that Clifton and I slept together!"

"Well, you did say you spent the night in his room in Fort Lauderdale the night you got that parking ticket."

"I had too much to drink, that's different!" Grace's head snapped to a little when the absurdity of what she had just said hit her.

"So you had too much to drink...and did he have a second bed? Did you take along pajamas? What did you sleep in?" I just stood in the living room floor when I asked that question. Grace, sitting on the couch, just hung her head straight down. She never answered the question. I surmised the hanging head was her answer.

I also reasoned that her head-hanging shame was at least partially due to the fact that Clifton was only 40 to Grace's 62, but it also could have been that Grace had finally deduced that when a 40-year-old man travels coast to coast, then disappears back to his London flat while she only hears from him intermittently and he only spends the night with her twice in those six months, perhaps she is not the only monkey in HIS tree. One more quick note about Clifton before we bid him adieu. Actually, it's more of an admonition to those of you who are starting to use this book as a how NOT to cheat manual. Nix the selfies. It was hilarious finding the selfie that Grace took of her and Clifton at her house after their night on the town. Grace looked drunk and Clifton, well, let's just say it. He was only 40, so he obviously had not missed too many cocktail hours in the 20 or so years he had been eligible for them.

If you're counting, that's three monkeys down, and two to go. Saved for last by virtue of their opposing poles in terms of involvement with my lovely soon to be ex-wife. Like heads and tails.

The first of the remaining two is what I call the "incidental" monkey. His name was Anthony Gunn and he was sort of a "one night stand. I was drunk and didn't know what I was doing monkey." Grace met Tony, as she called him, through the auspices of her friend Lori Chavez. Lori was a former real estate salesperson who hit the jackpot when she met Larry Feldman, an extremely wealthy international gold and silver trader. I had attended one of Larry and Lori's yacht parties the previous year with Grace and Darla. The stench of greed and bullshit permeated that yacht in a Palm Beach harbor. It was on that yacht that I first observed Darla's manipulative mastery as I watched her twist man after man around her little finger before dropping the "but I'm married" bomb on them. Practice. Spring training. What I didn't realize at the time was that Grace was taking it in, learning, making mental notes of her own. On the way home that day, Darla treated me to a demonstration of her drunken driving abilities, which were incredible, especially in concordance with her strategic conversation about how easily a beautiful woman can talk that officer out of that traffic stop.

As for Lori Chavez, like Adam, she had a Google-able legal record. That's what happens when you have an online article about your vehicular manslaughter of an elderly gentleman whose mistake had been crossing the street in front of her as she was heading home from cocktail hour. It's especially interesting if that article is accompanied by a picture of you in your disheveled drunken glory wearing prison blues. I'm sure her rich catch Larry didn't have sense enough to Google Lori, otherwise he would have found some comments by a number of men about Lori's picture from a cocktail party in 2010 in which she is referred to as an evil snake which snares its prey with its poisonous ways.

Back to Tony. It seems Tony was in attendance at dinner and cocktails, LOTS of cocktails, on Larry and Lori's yacht on March 8, 2012. If you're taking notes, that's 2 days before Grace's "first date" with Adam. My sweet Grace was on a tear in early 2012. The search was on in earnest. Grace had let me know she was going to the yacht that night and I had given my "have a great time, Honey" blessing as well as an admonition to tell Larry and Lori hello for me. Unlike my friend Jesus, I didn't know Judas even when he was staring in my face.

Like Mark, Tony was another guy who likely hadn't spent much time with women of Grace's beauty. He was a heavy set guy from a New Jersey factory town with a face to match. He was also married, a fact that I am sure Grace to this day is not familiar with. Easy to find out. Google again. Grace. Bad cheater. Rick. Excellent detective. Not a good combination for Grace.

It was a strict text trail that exposed this dalliance, such as it was. I deduced that Grace arrived at the yacht that night and, purposely or not, Lori had arranged for a fair number of Larry's male clients to attend. Tony was just one of the horses in the race. Since once again there were pictures (AWFUL cheater), I could easily ascertain that Tony was by far the least attractive of this particular stable of potentials. I guessed that Lori had also provided a pre-program of financial background so that Grace wasn't going in blind. She may have come out blind cause those pictures showed LOTS of drinking. Whatever happened, there was the text trail between Grace and Tony that started at 2:46 am on March 9th, including one in which Tony laments Grace not spending the night because "then even better in AM". Huh? What's even better?

The next day, Grace gives Tony a ride to the airport and there is a text exchange in which he says how nice it was to meet her, and how much fun they had, with Grace coming back with the same sort of stuff and eventually leading to this:

Tony; I will send a gift only catch is you need to tell me how it went?

Grace: It went well, I thought. How did u think it went? I like u a lot. It was only one night.

Tony: Yes very well! Think we can have some fun! Let loose and enjoy life!

Grace: Me too! Sleep well on the plane and dream of me. I will think about u too.

Tony: Oh baby! Dream and fantasize!

Grace: R u on the plane yet?

Tony: Yes I am a little delayed! Can't wait to send you a present! You will have to give me complete details!

Grace: We will see what the outcome is. Thank u, u r so much fun!

Tony: So do you have multiple orgasms, just one or maybe rare?

Tony: This will help determine the right toy for you

Grace: Can u be more specific?

Tony: Answer the earlier question! Are you a multiple orgasm girl, only one or rarely happens each time you have sex? I know it depends on the situation, but on average.

Grace: It happens every time

First of all, I wasn't aware Grace had an orgasm every time...hmm. When Grace and I finally discussed the above exchange, she exploded.

"That guy was a CREEP! He was awful!"

"So why would you be discussing how many times you orgasm with a creep like that?"

"It was a game we were playing." Once these words escaped, Grace clammed up tighter than a machine wound tire nut. Whoops!!

Once again, I didn't need to say another word. I looked over in the corner and there was Gram, a joint and a tequila bottle in hands as usual. He turns up the tequila and swallows what looks like a quarter of the bottle with a single gulp. Then he hits the joint and smiles at me with that killer smile, words escaping from the back of his throat as he holds in the joint, "Incriminating silence, brother!"

A question briefly floats through my brain as to why one would even want to catch a buzz in the afterlife, but is immediately replaced by the sublimely absurd thought that I am now taking Dear Abby style romantic advice from a dead junkie rock star who never had a hit record or a successful relationship in his life, unless you count his devotion to heroin and self destruction. And this is four months after I quit drinking.

The Big Gorilla: Monkey Man

That leads back down this mountain to where the trail actually begins, the first monkey to climb the tree. The fact that I discovered him last is evidence of his ability to hide in plain sight, because he was the most obvious monkey of all. If Tony was the "incidental" monkey, Guido was the big BAD gorilla. Guido and Grace had been engaged when Grace lived in Milan in the late 70s. Grace had flown like the wind when she caught dear Guido ("he treated me better than any man ever had") cheating on her with one of her model friends. Guido was an Italian Count with official royalty status. Funny story. The first time I became even slightly suspicious about Guido and Grace was when she asked me in late 2012 what a Count's wife was called as far as a title. When I told her a Countess, she said that's what her Italian boyfriend was. How was I to know she was talking about the present day?

Back in the 70s when Grace left Guido, he chased her to the States so she ended up down in South Florida to escape his reach. This would be, you guessed it, the "cocaine cowboy" era.

Thank you for joining us today, Ladies and Gentleman! Welcome to "Flashbacks"! Before we begin today's game, let's take a glance at our "strange coincidence" board and check our champion, Rick Trax's, scores so far:

1. Two women from the 70s
2. Two replayed relationships
3. Two replayed endings to said relationships
4. Two women who had "personal time" with the Eagles
5. Two women who were in Miami during the Cocaine Cowboy Era
6. OK, this might be stretching it a bit, but TWO sets of silicone boobs...really!

You're hearing that Twilight Zone theme now, right? Geez! How in the hell did all this happen?

When Grace went to South Florida, she immediately met Paco Rio. Paco, whose real American name was James, was from a wealthy Venezuelan family and lived on the fringes of the Cocaine Cowboy range with a fairly inexhaustible supply of the potent nose candy. In fact, Grace's stories always had me picturing Al Pacino sitting behind that giant mound of snow at the end of *Scarface*.

The Guido Shuffle: I'll Tumble For Ya

It was the summer of 2011 when Grace took her first solo trip to Milan. Sometime a couple of months before that, she told me she had heard from Guido. I encouraged her to have lunch or coffee with him, and such was my trust. Misplaced trust. The only slick move that Grace ever pulled was telling me that she had no desire to see him. Believed her, bought in hook, line, and sinker. Take me home and pan-fry me. It would be almost two years later before I would discover Grace's emails from August 2011 to Guido saying that she knew from the first time she saw his "handsome face again that her life would never be the same." Based on the pictures and videos that I have seen, one of us was blind and if Guido was still handsome, it was most assuredly me.

The thing about European men that is just a little scary is that they insist on wearing those tiny Speedos no matter what the condition of their body is. I'm not saying anyone should ever be ashamed of anything but there are some cases where a little well placed shame could carry you a long way. Try to picture a whale in bikini panties. Those pictures were scary. If that's what your significant other wants in life, how are you gonna compete with that? What should you do? Buy a box of donuts and shop one size down at Victoria's Secret. The realization sank in that when it came to Grace at this point in life, the attractiveness of a male of the species most assuredly had to be run through the financial vetting process, the scoring which obviously was weighted heavier than the other potential considerations in this once clandestine search.

It turned out that Grace and Guido had been traveling together for over two years, occasionally taking his daughter with them and often spending time with his family. It seems even the Italians were in on this little joke that I was the apparent butt of. Guido actually had an attack of common sense at some point however, breaking it off with Grace by telling her that she was a dream and dreams must be given up at times, that fact that he also said he had to take care of those close to him tells me that he sniffed out the gold digger that was hard on his trail, the blond beautiful one. Two things stand out here, my friends. One was that Guido absolutely knew that Grace was married. Being Italian, her being married not only didn't discourage him, but it likely made Grace more appealing, thus my connotation of him as the "bad" monkey. That leads to the second thing, the fact that Grace told me that "Guido" was the future she thought she had...I cannot make this up, why would anyone make themselves look so dumb on purpose? I'm guessing when Guido figured out that second thing, HIS greed kicked in. No wonder he and Grace got along. They had that in common. Soon after that, Guido made himself history again.

OK, there could be a third thing, but in order to state that, I would have to describe the visual of a vastly overweight balding man in his 60s squeezing into a pair of tight panties while promenading about like an effeminate weight lifter. You'll have to wait for the movie for that.

And with that scary apparition of a vision, we leave the monkey tumble behind. As for Grace herself, well, I guess she just did not want to wait until the cupboard was bare until she went to the grocery store. The preponderance of evidence she left in her trail was truly amazing. I may as well have been there. I was going to pay for my sins, but all that evidence made it easier for me to make Grace pay for hers.

Chapter 12

Heartbreak Time

The Testimony: Power

Jefferson Park Avenue cuts through the soul of the University of Virginia like a butcher knife through cheesecake. It starts way out on the west side at Fry Springs, the site of the beach club where I spent every summer day of my pubescent years and made my first attempts at discovering the intimacies of the female anatomy in the Olympic sized pool. From there, it meanders in an easterly fashion through the neighborhoods where so many of my friends grew up in the 60s, streets and offshoots now dominated by overly priced student rentals, including the aforementioned Stribling Ave., site of my first encounter with one Lila Wylde. As the road itself heads into the heart of the campus, the dorms, the football stadium, the route that I took following Lila after that first meeting, eventually becoming Alderman Road, JPA (as it is commonly known) takes a right turn down lines of apartment complexes and buildings constructed with the student population in mind. It snakes another right turn, taking it down the backside of the academic village, behind the area known as the Central Grounds and Cabell Hall, flanked on the right side by more off campus student housing, eventually working its way right through the massive complex of the University of Virginia Hospital and intersecting Main Street at the eastern edge of the UVA corner.

Dead at the intersection of JPA and Main sits The University Baptist Church, a deceptively large brick structure with wide inviting steps and tall columns that extends back behind its tiny parking lot, taking up an entire block for the most part.

Between my grandmother's old TV that was constantly on either Billy Graham or Oral Roberts and my parents taking me to Sunday School, services, and other activities during the week at the church, one might say the first 10 years or so of my life was dominated by the church. I loved Jesus...and football! Like Vince Lombardi, I loved God, my family, and football, in that order. At the ripe old age of five, I had my life already laid out before. I would be a professional football player, and then during the off-season, I would be a preacher. I practiced football by beating the crap out of my imaginary opposition in the front driveway of our apartment building on Monte Vista Avenue and practiced preaching every Sunday afternoon from a makeshift pulpit I constructed in my grandmother's living room, occasionally chastising my poor sleep deprived father (who was working the midnight shift on the Police force) with the admonition that "someone in the congregation is sleeping."

"After me comes the one more powerful than I, the straps of whose sandals I am not worthy to stoop down and untie. I baptize you with water, but he will baptize you with the Holy Spirit." **Mark 1:7-8**

Through the Sunday School classes, I learned to love Jesus. He became real, a gentle yet strong figure, a pied piper of sorts for kids. I felt the presence of my friend Jesus strongly back then, but I was still as surprised as everyone else one late summer morning in 1958 when I found myself getting up from the pew and walking in upfront of the huge church to announce to the pastor that I was ready to accept my friend Jesus as my Lord and Savior, ready to take my dunk in the holy water of the baptism pit. When this actually happened has been a source of family controversy between my mother and myself for years. Mom insists that I was 9, but the Bible given to me by my Sunday School teacher, Mrs. Waylon, to commemorate the occasion was clearly inscribed November 21, 1958, making me 7 at the time.

The University Baptist Church was, and is, as beautiful on the inside as the outside, with rich wooden pews, and a balcony that traversed the entire semi-circle of the sanctuary. Behind the huge wooden pulpit straight out of Protestant England was a choral pit that was huge, the mandatory pipe organ off to the right side, and way up behind that was the baptism pit, painted white and with a curved ceiling. Aside from my memory of expressing my concern to the pastor that I couldn't swim and had fear of going under the three feet of water, I clearly remember walking down into the pit and gazing out at the sanctuary thinking there was no backing down now with all those faces staring at me. I also remember the pastor's gentle demeanor as he assured me that I would be safe under the water as he squeezed the sides of my nose together and laid me back into and under the water. I can still see the curved white ceiling as I came back out of that water and opened my eyes, wondering what the change would be like now that I was saved. Of course, at the ripe old age of seven, while I understood the gentility and unconditional love offered by my friend Jesus, what I didn't understand was this thing called will that is implanted in us by our Creator or that there is another force in the world that also takes a very personal interest in each of us, a force capable of attaching itself to either unsuspecting people or things for the express purpose of tempting us to listen to the most base callings of our flesh while turning our back or, more conveniently, misinterpreting the higher calling of our Lord.

I stayed pretty close to these roots until I was about 15. My first almost girlfriend, Lindsay Hall, was a friend from the church youth group. Of course, at the same time, I was spending my summers at the Fry's Springs pool, luring girls into the shallow end so I could explore the intimacies of the female anatomy, so the struggle between flesh and spirit was already amping up inside my little, soon to be tortured, soul. Then, when I was 15, I went back to church after about maybe six Sundays of sleeping in and one of the deacons made this comment "Well, we haven't seen you in a while."

How dare he say that? That bastard!! Hypocrite!! Once I declared the hypocrisy, I banished myself from the house of God. I am not going hang around some joint filled with hypocrites, especially if I have to get up at 8:30 on Sunday to get there.

Except for Christmas, Easter, and my marriages, I was to be found nowhere in the vicinity of the pews or the pulpit for 35 years.

During those years, God would only make His presence known when it was time to save me as I woke up in parked cars, under trees, ran my car off the road while dead drunk, cheated on wives, drank, and ingested every substance which promised to lift me to a higher level of 'consciousness'. What He was saving me for, I still don't know, but the fact that I am still walking around on this planet after everything that happened is a testimony to the reality that miracles exist. Except for a little injection of new age and earthy spiritualism between my marriages, this is pretty much where my friend Jesus found this prodigal son in late 2012 when Grace's intentions to leave our marriage became apparent.

"He was oppressed and He was afflicted, Yet He did not open His mouth;

Like a lamb that is led to slaughter, And like a sheep that is silent before its shearers,

So He did not open His mouth." **Isaiah 53:7**

Grace didn't actually officially announce that she was leaving the marriage. More like it sort of evolved from her agreeing to give it a shot to her looking for a place to live as the five monkeys tumbled from the tree. In one of the few recorded instances of me standing up for myself regarding either Grace or Lila, I announced to Grace at some point that in order to continue residence in my townhouse during our reconciliation, she would have to give up dating. I mean, it seemed only fair since we were still very married.

The conversation went something like this.

"Grace, you can't live here while we're married and date other guys."

"Come on, Rick, they're really just friends." Seriously, that was the answer. For the first time maybe ever, I actually set a boundary. I gave Grace one month to cut all the monkeys down and release them. It was

Valentine's Day 2013. Later, I would hear that Grace complained that I "only" gave her a card, some roses, and a bottle of wine.

December 2012- March 2-13: The Love Dare

Before the monkey tumble began, I headed down a completely different path, giving up alcohol, and pot and again returning to the waiting arms of my friend Jesus via *The Love Dare,* a book featured in a generally panned Christian based marriage film by Kirk Cameron called *Fireproof,* a movie which church members came in droves to while the general public shrugged its shoulders and rolled its eyes. And why not as the film depicted a marriage resurrected from the dead when the husband demonstrates his unconditional love for his wife via 40 days of Love Dares.

While the film absorbed some well deserved critical arrows like a dartboard in an Irish Pub, the book was a slightly different story, emphasizing that what seems on the surface to be an attempt to keep your marriage together was instead a well disguised instructional in the way to walk with Jesus. For myself, that meant being woken up sometime between 3 a.m. and 5 a.m. so many mornings that I began to refer to that time as "God time." Normally, I would take the time and expend the energy into working on my online Love Dare journal of my experiences (Yep, it's all out there in cyberspace somewhere), but the morning of December 28, 2012 was different.

Grace was in Florida and it was approximately 4 a.m. when I shot up out of bed. Not wanting to dwell on Grace and the marriage, I always grabbed the Love Dare book to survey the day's assignment. The dare had absolutely nothing to do with Grace. It was day 20.

If you declare with your mouth, "Jesus is Lord," and believe in your heart that God raised him from the dead, you will be saved. For it is with your heart that you believe and are justified, and it is with your mouth that you profess your faith and are saved. **Romans 10:9-10**

The title of the chapter was simply "Jesus is Love." The chapters were filled with verses and my standard procedure was to read the chapter, study the verses, and pray. It was during the prayer that it happened. A wave of I am not sure what washed over me and I found myself on my knees, then my face, eyes filled with tears as, for perhaps the first time, I came to the complete realization of what the Trinity was, who my friend Jesus really was, and what that knowledge did to me. It wasn't knowledge gained from some detached spirit that was in the room, it was from inside me, informed by the presence of the Holy Spirit in me as, for the first time, I understood that God, Jesus, and the Holy Spirit that completed the Trinity and resided inside my heart were all one and the same. There was no separation and I understood the Crucifixion, the Resurrection, and why it all HAD to happen the way that it did. It was a pivotal and painful moment filled with grace as understanding swept over me like a tsunami in the Indian Ocean. Grace wasn't really my first love, He was, and Jesus was.

He never really left my side for long during this Heartbreak Time, comforting me, and acknowledging the pain while occasionally showing me a glimpse of where I was heading.

11 For I know the plans I have for you," declares the Lord, "plans to prosper you and not to harm you, plans to give you hope and a future. 12 Then you will call on me and come and pray to me, and I will listen to you. 13 You will seek me and find me when you seek me with all your heart. **Jeremiah 29:11-13**

Trust, that was all He wanted. Take your licks, suffer your indignation, love unconditionally, and trust Him to get you through it all. As monkey after monkey tumbled from the tree during January and February of 2013, He cautioned me to hang in but set boundaries, a concept that I didn't really understand but did put in place when I informed Grace that continuing to go out with her male "friends" in Florida would not be contiguous to living with me in that townhouse. By early March, she had made her decision and I aggravated my many personal advisors by assisting her with the move in the first of many acts of what I came to call "undeserved grace". Or maybe undeserving Grace. As the spring of 2013 rolled around, Grace and I were officially separated, despite my resolute refusal to sign separation papers.

As for Grace herself, she would occasionally show back up, usually for the purpose of manipulating me into signing something I refused to or making a concession that I had no intention of giving in to. Bad as Grace was as a cheater, darned if she wasn't even worse as a manipulator. She was as easy to read as a children's book with a magnifying glass. The best attempt was when she showed up at my place with the intention of talking me down from the ledge of the small settlement that she knew I would be asking for, primarily because of the monkeys. I watched her twist and turn like a fly avoiding a swatter, finally giving up that I knew about the trip to Europe that she and the chosen monkey, Mark, were taking together in late June and early July. I had just intercepted the email that Mark had sent Grace with confirmation of his flight to Milan in late June.

Grace spent the better part of an hour trying to manipulate and maneuver around me that day. As we went out to her Jeep, for which she had paid $17,000 in cash five years earlier, she continued to whine about her financial situation. Suddenly, I lost it.

"Well, you can afford going to Milan and Paris with your boyfriend!" I exclaimed.

"I'm not paying for any of that." Oops! There it was. It was out there. Those words hung out there in space like a black hole, just waiting to see what matter could be swallowed up. Suddenly this woman who had tucked away cash while I went bankrupt used timeshare points for our trips together while saving her cash for her personal treks to Europe, suddenly this woman peeled away every layer of her personal onion at once to reveal that "yes, it IS all about the money!"

Grace is nothing if not oblivious, yet when she uttered that she wasn't paying anything for that trip, even she paused as she realized the implications of what she had just said. I didn't say another word. How was I going to top the ones that had just come tumbling out of her mouth?

How's that gonna be, my dear Grace? How's it gonna be that you, despite the small detail of still being married, are going overseas to stay in hotels with a wealthy boyfriend who is likely not aware he is spending time with a married woman, but is paying 100% of everything? Hello Jezebel!!

Spring turned into summer, Grace took her trip with Mark after swearing to me that he knew she was still married, then returned to her previous pursuit of frantically trying to get me to sign papers. I knew Grace could get her divorce without me but I was determined not to help. I considered it part of the deal that I had made with God. My heart, meanwhile, was aching like a toothache after chocolate.

"The heart is more deceitful than all else and is desperately sick; who can understand it?" **Jeremiah 17:9**

Lest you think your already extremely doubtable hero is a religious fanatic as well, I did manage to summon up the common sense to hire a legal advisor, an old friend named Dan Tartino, who had once been the mayor of Charlottesville during my radio days. Dan was kind enough that, for a nominal fee, he assessed the evidence I had via email, text, pictures, etc. of the monkeys and declared it a worthy case, that in fact, I may have a good shot at obtaining a settlement in the legal arena.

In one of the few moments of comic relief in the tragedy that was on the stage, Grace, declaring she would never, ever trust my attorney to draw up settlement papers, instead went to an attorney recommended by one of her wealthy friend's clients. I laughed despite myself when she texted me from the office 'This woman wants $2,500 to draw up these papers.'

Grace had somehow managed to find one of the divorce attorneys who actually WANT you to go to court, a clear profiteer. Eventually, she would trust a Florida attorney to draw them up. Eventually, in early September, I would sign them.

I didn't want a settlement, though, I wanted the marriage back. Despite everything, despite the monkeys, despite the trip with Mark, I wanted Grace back. Maybe it was just the idea of Grace that I wanted back. Life went on through late July and early August. I went to work on gigs, went to the gym, stayed busy with musically inclined social events, and especially leaned on the church, constantly bugging my friend Pastor Wilt for his advice.

None of us can get inside the mind of God, so the idea that He may actually punish us for our sins is one most of us prefer to suppress. My own sense of awareness, tempered by my early conversion, was that He is a completely loving God, but somewhere in the back of my consciousness is that memory of admonition via TV from Oral Roberts and Billy Graham. It was that fear that got my attention when Grace had insisted on full Christian wedding vows. It was likely the same thing present one day as I sat in Wilt's office, fully aware that any fight to save the marriage was surely doomed, and made a promise to God that even though I might not be able to save this marriage, I would keep that ring on and honor my commitment to Him until the day those final divorce papers arrived in the mail. Wilt assured me that God would certainly bless me for honoring that promise. I'll let you, my friends, draw your own conclusions based on what happened in the aftermath.

August 2013: A Peace That Passes All Understanding

One Friday, I finally decided to clear my townhouse of the piles, stacks, and remnants of the preceding six months. It was late August and I was preparing for a visitor, listening to the profound sounds of one of my musical heroes, the good Reverend Richie Furay. I had admired Richie from his beginnings with Buffalo Springfield through his days with Poco, a group that was, ironically raided by The Eagles for bass player Timothy B. Schmidt. Remember that irresistible combination...money, drugs, and women. Richie had fallen victim to no such madness but rather to the sacred solicitations of The Lord and Savior Himself. As I progressed along my own personal Christian path, I reacquainted myself with the good Reverend, specifically his latter day gospel music which basically sounded like Poco with with righteous lyrics.

On this particular Friday, I was working with a stack of papers when I discovered the prints of some fairly angry unsent emails that I had written to some of the monkeys. I remember it so very well...it's as clear as the ceiling of that brisk pit when I was 7 years old or the wave of realization that swept over me on that December morning in 2012. I was crumbling up the emails and tossing them in the trash. The song was called "Peace That Passes All Understanding".

"Forget the former things; do not dwell on the past. See, I am doing a new thing! Now it springs up; do you not perceive it? I am making a way in the wilderness and streams in the wasteland."
Isaiah 43:18-19 NIV

As Richie sang, I peered down inside that trash bag and heard that same voice that had spoken to me when Grace had called from the Charlotte Airport after that reunion weekend. "It's over, you're free." I wasn't sure exactly what I was free of, but I started dancing. I danced all day that day, including when I went down to the Fridays After Five.

In fact, I was so out of character that afternoon that an old friend who knew my story from many days of being bored and bombarded to death with it at the gym, stopped me and looked me dead in the face while asking, "Who are you?"

The visitor? It was someone who had rescued me from the clutches of Grace induced heartbreak almost 35 years earlier, a parallel that did not escape me, although I did forget the tiny detail that I had ended up with a heartbreak from that rescue that lasted longer and was worse. That second heartbreak, in fact, had lingered for almost 40 years like a bad relative you can't get to go home. It was there living rent free in the back room of my bankrupt heart for all that time, I just didn't know it.

I had been at a Bible Study the previous Tuesday night when the Facebook message tone went off on my Android. After leaving, I looked at it to see the message. It was from my Facebook friend and old college girlfriend, Lila Wylde.

'Hi. I'm gonna be passing thru Cville either Sunday or Monday. Wanna have lunch, coffee, a walk?'

> Christine's Tune (aka The Devil In Disguise)
>
> *Her number always turns up in your pocket*
>
> *Whenever you are looking for a dime*
>
> *It's all right to call her but I'll bet you*
>
> *The moon is full and you're just wasting time*
>
> (Chris Hillman, Gram Parsons)

"Christine's Tune (aka Devil In Disguise)" as performed by The Flying Burrito Brothers

An old friend once told me she had never seen a miracle in her life except in the rearview mirror. I suppose the same would apply to the train wrecks. I would also add that sometimes it's pretty damn tough to tell the difference when either of those occurrences appears through the front windshield. Such was the third appearance of Lila Wylde into my life.

Lila was in DC for a few days, during which time we messaged back and forth about how good it was going to be to catch-up, I had the dancing downtown experience, volunteered to help her put furniture together, and had a fully satisfying weekend. She messaged me on Sunday morning. She would be leaving DC around 10 am and could we still have lunch?

From the time I received that first message from Lila on Tuesday night until at least Thursday of that week, I had assumed the Lila that would be stopping to have lunch would be a married woman. I remember late in that week seeing her relationship status on Facebook change to divorced. I had no assumptions at that point, only questions, you know? I wasn't thinking, hot damn, here comes Lila and she's divorced, I was still deeply committed to the promise I had made God to keep the ring on my finger and not even consider being with anyone until the bitter end, when I couldn't fight or hope any longer for my marriage to Grace, until the papers announcing that Grace and I were no longer married arrived in the mail. That promise to God was bigger than any relationship, old or new. It wasn't a legalistic promise, it was a proof promise, proof to God that He was number one and that I was deserving of the blessings that He would eventually rain down upon me. Well, at least, I had the rain part right. It was the thunder and lightning that I had missed.

In fact, Lila would reveal later that she likewise expected to be greeted by a married man when she arrived in Charlottesville. Unlike her, I wasn't concerned about the world's perception at this point, so I had no Facebook relationship status. I still don't. Honestly, the only relationship status that ever seemed really accurate for anyone is "it's complicated," and perhaps even that should be amended to "relationships.... they're complicated!"

August 2013: Lila's Back

Since it was a Sunday morning when Lila was arriving, I was, naturally, in church. Not only was I in church, it was one of those days in church. My good friend Pastor Wilt was occasionally inclined to be moved by the spirit. Just as he was about to start the sermon, he would change direction completely, like a halfback spinning out of a tackler's arms to dart all the way across the field until he finds the opening that lets him sprint into the end zone.

"Rather than delivering the message that I have prepared, God has put on my heart that we have many people here this morning in need of prayer". There was to be no sermon this Sunday morning. In lieu of it, those needing prayer were to line up. Wilt, the associate pastor Harry, and a couple of other elders would be upfront to hear your needs and pray with you. Immediately, amazingly, the aisle going up the middle of the tiny chapel was filled with people, all seeking solace. I stood up, and so did my father, who was not only in church that morning, but had driven himself there, as he was still able to do at that point. When I reached the front and was ministered to by Harry, I asked his prayers for the healing of my marriage to Grace.

By this time, even I recognized it was merely an exercise in futility, but I was close enough to the Lord to also know that futility was not a word in the Heavenly vocabulary. There was only hope. Nonetheless, even though God had announced to me Himself that previous Friday morning when I was listening to Reverend Richie and literally throwing the past away that I was free of the marriage, I had enough faith and just good sense to know that he wanted me to finish the race, like a last place runner, knowing the result of the race is already a foregone conclusion. Finish the race, cross that line. Then I could walk away, head held high, dignity intact.

Behind me was Dad, crying as he asked Harry to pray with him for my mother. Dad, always thinking of her, never himself, a picture of love. Later when he was in assisted living and driving me crazy with his obsession on knowing every single thing about Mom's medical situations, I could fall back on this moment to alleviate the aggravation that came upon me.

Once Dad and I sat back down, I felt my phone, which was on silent...hey, it's church..begin to vibrate. I looked at it. Lila was only eight miles from my house. I took off. I mean, Wilt wasn't preaching anyway, just the prayer thing. It's the little things, you know. They seem so insignificant you miss them at the time.

Be alert and of sober mind. Your enemy the devil prowls around like a roaring lion looking for someone to devour."
1 Peter 5:8

I stood out in front of my townhouse on that sunny late August day waiting for her. Soon, a BMW SUV came up the road. Even with the tinted windows, I instinctively knew it was her. Stepping onto the edge of the road, I waved and motioned. Once she parked, the woman that had spent 35 years lingering in the back of my mind fairly jumped out of the vehicle and seemed to be jogging towards me. I immediately noticed the fact that she was no longer the thin little 18 year old I had met almost 40 years ago, but had a little spare tire around her middle.

The long brown hair she had when we were young was now blonde and short. Wrinkles around her eyes. "We're old," she exclaimed as she opened her arms as we hugged. The extra weight, the age, the "natural" blonde hair...it all served to give me a false sense of security. I would be OK. Grace's beauty had spoiled me. No way I was going for anything less than perfection. I was safe. Bring her on. I completely forgot about that sweet southern pecan pie flavored by spices and jalapeños, about sweet southern accents that merely served as a facade for the sexual sauciness that lay behind them. I felt a sense of relief. No lightning striking twice here!

"He who trusts in his own heart is a fool, But he who walks wisely will be delivered." **Proverbs 28:26**

Lila came into my literally humble, but finally clean abode and we began the process of catching up on 35 years, after which we piled into her luxury SUV (little things!) and headed down to the Driftwood Grill, where my son Darin was cooking.

She had expressed a desire to meet him, if possible. The conversation was almost shockingly easy as we shared the details of each other's journey. I told her about Grace and she told me about her husband of 27 years, whom she described as controlling to the max. She even described a scene in an airport where she was asked if she wanted security called. Such was the anger her husband screamed at her with...in public. It was almost like we had never been apart as we sat there for an hour. She loved Darin, who managed to find some time to sit down with us. Darin would later make a note of the fact that Lila had a multitude of piercings in her ears with a declaration that she had "been around". This was long before any knowledge of the Eagles or the "Cocaine Cowboy" era Lila.

From the mouths of babes indeed, even though Darin was no babe at age 27. Lila told me about her own kids, aged 20 and 23 respectively, saying she thought maybe they were spoiled. Signs were already there, but I was ignoring them. I was describing Grace's infidelity, and my attempts to keep the marriage together despite it. She was telling me about blindsiding her husband by moving out when he was away on a business trip after Dr. Alouette, while checking out what was wrong with her tennis game had told her that it wasn't her tennis game, it was her life that was the problem. Therapeutically induced divorce. In the rearview mirror, that truck following me had red flags hanging out everywhere, but I paid zero attention at this point, I just sped up. Maybe I could outrun the flags, although now I can't even see why I would want to.

Instead what I saw was Lila at her most charming, sympathetic, almost loving. That sweet and saucy southern accent was still just as effective despite the physical changes and by the time we were getting back in Lila's car, I was again thinking about the jalapeños in that southern pecan pie.

On the way back to my house, we talked about the fact that Both of us had ALMOST attended William & Mary. I bemoaned the fact that in my decision not to go there, I had actually missed out on the chance to play football for Lou Holtz.

I can still see Lila exclaiming, "But then you wouldn't have met ME!" It had already started, I just didn't know it. We sat around my place and chatted for a good hour afterwards before she had to hit the road to her mother's house in Southwest Virginia.

On the way out, I blurted out, "Hey, why don't you come back Wednesday and go see the Beach Boys downtown?"

There came the second or third appearance of Lila's come hither smile as she answered, "I think my mother might go crazy if I did that, but thanks!" I let it go.

We stood outside my door and hugged. When I went to peck her on the cheek, she grabbed my face and kissed me on the lips. I should have been wary. Remember the rearview mirror? Instead, I was quietly ecstatic. As she pulled away, my heart was rejoicing a little from some injected hope. It didn't take much after the Grace experience. We sent a few pleasant texts back and forth after she left. Meanwhile, it was maybe an hour later the telephone rang and it was my old college friend Tom Strait. Tom never called me and he knew Lila. My internal coincidence meter pegged on over the line to the dangerous message from God level. Tom, upon hearing what just transpired, the connection, the fact that we were both unexpectedly single, declared that it sounded from God. That was really all Rick needed to hear but he followed with the suggestion that I ask her to come back for the football game the following Saturday. I shoot back that she already had flights, plans, etc. and so on. Tom, ever the optimist...I love that about him...just said why not try? I told him to give me a night to think about it.

I didn't need to think about it. I was already hooked. Lila was like a crack to me. All I had to do was indulge myself once. I wrote the message that same night and sent it via Facebook early the next morning. Later that day she texted me.."Sounds like fun. I'll have to let you know." Then the next afternoon. "Guess what? I'm coming. I'll get there Friday afternoon. I'd like to buy you dinner Friday night if you are not busy." My heart jumped out of its seat in my chest and did several cartwheels around the block. I just KNEW this was just the beginning. God was gonna bless me for my faithfulness and Lila's return visit was just the beginning. That was what it looked like through the front windshield anyway.

"For the lips of the adulterous woman drip honey, and her speech is smoother than oil; but in the end she is bitter as gall, sharp as a double-edged sword. Her feet go down to death; her steps lead straight to the grave. She gives no thought to the way of life; her paths wander aimlessly, but she does not know it." **Proverbs 5:3-6**

It was around 5 pm on Friday when I picked up Lila at her hotel near the UVA campus. I texted her as I arrived and went into the lobby, sitting down on a couch adjacent to a very small lobby bar, which seemed to serve the purpose of providing an initial imbibing spot for those entering or exiting. Lila came bounding, literally bounding, down the lobby wearing a loose fitting floral print sundress, sandals, and swinging a fairly sizable purse. Approaching, she proclaimed, "I'm here," and opened her arms for the welcome hug.

"Do you want to have a drink here first," she asked, gesturing to the small bar.

"You can go ahead, I don't need anything," I replied confidently. Her head did that quizzical sideways tilt that people do and I saw the light come on behind her eyes.

"Oh, that's right, you don't drink anymore," she smiled and flashed the come hither look, "I hope you're still fun, Rick." I smiled back, but I'm pretty sure it was a deer in the headlights smile. My muse was already drawing beads on me.

We headed downtown for a free Friday night show, commonly referred to as Friday's After Five. That night, the show featured a supremely nostalgic as well as highly talented band called Soul Transit Authority playing most of the stuff we had danced to in the late 60s and early 70s. That part of the evening was capped off by the appearance of the UVA football team, band, and cheerleaders for a tradition known as Paint The Town Orange. The synchronicity that had occurred between Lila and I on our Sunday lunch date continued and extended as we interacted with people. Lordy, I had forgotten how much pure fun Lila was to hang out with. People were drawn to her and she was as outgoing as me, albeit with the caveat of that sassy Southern accent. Together we sort of made a powerhouse couple that was just fun to be around! I remember thinking, *this is gonna be a fun ride*. Unfortunately, I forgot to check the gas tank.

Dinner was at the most expensive restaurant in downtown Charlottesville, Hamilton's. I had made the reservations and it was here that Lila began to really work her magic on me. Oh hell, let's be honest, it didn't take but so much work. Right out of the gate, she announced that I was to order anything that I wanted, in any quantity. Even if I just wanted a taste, just leave whatever I didn't want, a tall order for someone who grew up in a family where you had been trained to clean your plate. There were always those starving children, we all remember that analogy, designed to make you feel guilty for your over or under indulgences. I took the bait, however, I ordered the appetizer, the steak, and the lush dessert.

The distance from the humility of my friend Jesus, the one who took the lowest place, the one who washed the feet of his disciples, the rebel who shook up Jewish society to the maximum by hanging with the tax collectors, the prostitutes, the sinners, the lowest of the low, was increasing like the San Andreas Fault during the Big One. Unlike the day I passed up that pipe, Jesus wasn't speaking to me. Lila sure was in a virtual assault on my dedication to keeping the wedding ring on, staying the course, honoring the Lord by holding on to the last vestiges of my marriage until it was completely over.

I can still see her leaning across the table, "You know, we're a lot alike, you and me, Rick."

"I guess that's why we're friends." I was trying to hang on, difficult to say the least when the face, albeit slightly wrinkled, that I had passing thoughts about for 35 years was looking longingly at me. "Longingly" for Lila was a strategic term, though. This was just the beginning.

"So why are you still wearing this?" She reached across the table and took my finger, the one the wedding ring was on, in her hand.

"Well, strange as it sounds, I'm keeping it on because I promised God that I would. Once the divorce is final, I'll take it off. I know that might sound crazy, but I truly believe He will bless me for the effort. I know it sounds dumb." Well, there it was. A chink in the wall, that's what that last comment was. A weakening, however minute, of the will. An opening. For someone. Something.

"This is just a symbol of something that's already dead. Set yourself free, you have the key..." Lila gently took the ring between her finger and began to gently tug it off of my finger...." You have the key. Set yourself free. It's just a symbol, just a piece of metal." Our eyes were entwined as her words passed between us. If my faith was a fortress, one might say the outer wall had been breached.

Lila didn't twist my arm. I was a voluntary fool. She slowly but surely worked the ring off of my finger and dropped it into the glass of water in front of me with a seductive smile. Suddenly it was 1973 again.

See, it all escaped me, the irony of it being EXACTLY 40 years later. I don't know how God comes up with the tests He puts His children through, but in retrospect, this one came with a virtual road map that I should have paid attention to. I didn't want to. I wanted to smoke the crack. I wanted to think Lila was my gift. Was she my gift or was she my test? Once again, my friends, I'm just going to tell the story, you make the final decision. I will say, though, that I am the one who smoked the crack. Lila lit the pipe, for sure, but the decision was mine. I have no excuses.

After dinner, the assault continued as we walked down through the circus of street musicians and vendors that is the Charlottesville Downtown Mall. Lila took my hand tightly as we walked down to Miller's, where there was live music. Not only live music, but the live music of an amazing local phenomenon named Eli Cook, a 20 year old with an authentic sensibility and uncanny ability to play the blues. Over the next hour, we watched and listened as he played everything from Delta National Steel guitar sounds to Jimi Hendrix, stopping along the way to revisit Duane Allman and Eric Clapton. It was already 1973 again. Now we're treading on truly dangerous ground. I was having such a great time that I forgot that crack could be addictive. As we sat there listening to sounds that were uncannily like those we heard on many of those first 1973 dates, Lila began to run her fingers through my hair, at least what was left of it, and the assault amped up to a full on attack.

We left and headed up the street to the Sky Bar, an outside rooftop establishment with couches and a huge young crowd, not to mention a bartender who not only knew me, but spotted me for free drinks. The free drinks worked since Lila had steadily been downing wine and beer since we hit downtown at 5:30 or so. We were working very hard on midnight at this point and while she was a little beyond inebriated, Lila was still pretty damn steady on her feet. No cheap date this lady was. It was good I wasn't drinking. At least, I didn't have to suffer the embarrassment of her getting my wedding ring off AND drinking me under the table.

We found a couch in the corner where we settled in. Once we did, Lila became more subtle, and more convincing, while simultaneously announcing that she was basically out to seduce me. She reflected on our 1973 relationship.

"I hate to say it, but honestly, that was all about sex."

"All about sex?"

"I was 18." Lila leaned against me. "You were only the second person, Rick." Her hands found my neck and then my leg. "And the first time I saw you, I knew we were going to have sex." Red flag waving!! Help!!

Lila, who had never been one to share too much family history, began a series of family revelations about her serial cheating father, and her codependent mother, growing up. Truth or seduction, who knows?

"You know, Rick, most fourth and fifth marriages begin when old flames reconnect, when two people meet again." And there came the infamous come hither Lila look as she again sensually ran her fingers through what little hair I had. "It's like, hey, I remember you." Fourth or fifth marriages? Don't ask me, we both only had two at this point. My brain was mud from Lila's fingers at this point. She could have said anything.

It was absolutely brilliant salesmanship. I mean, this woman could literally sell the proverbial ice cubes to Eskimos. Her final piece de resistance was to kiss me deeply. That's when I remembered that darting little tongue of hers. It was gonna be tough to resist.

Lila and I had earlier talked about me taking a trip to LA the following January. She was going to board me in her finished garage, take me to all the LA music places, and trek us out to Joshua Tree, where I would finally get my night in the infamous Room 8 where Gram had died. She looked at me after that kiss and sweetened the pot considerably by declaring just before kissing me again, "I don't think you're going to be staying in any spare room."

The discussion turned philosophical. Well, at least as philosophical as you can get with a half drunk woman in a state of lust. I explained my connection and experience with the A word. Adultery. I had been there, I had done that, asked for forgiveness, put it behind me. It was one thing that looked a lot better in the rearview mirror. It was a technicality, for sure, as both our divorces were a foregone conclusion, but they weren't final. Technically, we were both still married. Then there was the little matter of the promise that I had made to God.

"Look. Lila. I've been an adulterer. Anything that starts between us right now is technically going to be adultery. I know that sounds like a small thing, but anything that starts in adultery is going to end badly. If we are going to get involved, I think we should give it the best chance." I kissed her and looked her directly in the eyes. "The very best chance."

I knew that anything that started in adultery, even if it was a technicality, would be doomed to failure. I had learned patience from my journey through Grace's infidelities, and I could wait for my rewards.

But the alcohol owned Lila at this point and she proclaimed, "I'm from LA. Fuck me or take me home". I decided to take her home. It took a bit, a few passionate kisses and some bumping and grinding beside my van, before we got in. When we got to her hotel, she eventually got out and took off on foot across the parking lot.

"Can I walk you up to your room?" I yelled.

"Nope, you can stay if you want to". I watched as she stumbled slightly across the parking lot and disappeared inside the hotel lobby, then got in my van and drove away.

Here is where it gets a little tricky. I had just turned down sex with a woman I had loved and lusted after for 35 years. I somehow, stupidly, made the assumption that I would feel good about that, like God was some miracle machine who could reward His children on demand for obedience. Instead, what I got was a growing doubt that would gnaw away at me all night long. I expected God would be proud of me for saying no. How could He not be? After what I had sacrificed. Man, did I ever miss the point! I rolled and tumbled all night long, tortured by what thought? The thought that I had blown it! Yep, that little voice kept telling me how stupid I was, how I had blown it. What was I, crazy? I was going to let a stupid technicality keep me away from a chance with a woman I had dreamed about for almost 40 years? How stupid!

Here is where the technicality gets you. Here is where things look a little differently in the rearview mirror. What if I had kept my promise? What if Lila had walked away because I wouldn't indulge with her? What would God think about that? What would I have missed? Maybe 19 days of great sex, getting to be a therapeutic listener to a woman who would turn out to be incapable of returning the favor, a friendship that maybe has turned out to be pretty one sided at best? Almost a year of total heartbreak over a woman I had spent less than three weeks with? See what I mean about that windshield and the rearview mirror? I mean, you be the judge, what if I missed out on Lila? What would God say about that? Maybe so what?

"Submit yourselves to God. Resist the devil, and he will flee from you." **James 4:7**

The next morning, I leapt up despite a torturous sleepless night, thoughts focused on the blown chance that had kept me awake all night. Lila and I had already made a plan to walk around the UVA campus early before we hooked up with Tom and Jane for a ride to the game, tailgating, and all attendant to that. I stopped to pick up some brownies as my contribution to the tailgate, plus some wine for Lila. When I was in the store, a Kinks song came over the sound system. That was it for me. Obviously, it was God who kept me awake all night, not the other guy. I was all clear to go for it. Stone cold sober, my friends, merely under the influence of the crack called Lila Wylde. That is twisted reasoning at best.

August 31, 2013: Another Game

It was a truly beautiful morning on that final day of August 2013 when I walked into the front lobby of Lila's hotel. I couldn't stop watching the elevator door. When she finally came walking out of that door and into the lobby, I took note of the Nike shoes she was wearing. Maybe $200 a pair? I would be finding out much more about both Lila's athleticism and her financial wherewithal in the months ahead.

She was dressed for the walk, light clothing, loose and easy fitting. Nothing I recognized and through Grace, I actually knew a little bit about female fashion. The mental notebook in my head recorded its thoughts...California style, California tan, California girl...uh.... woman? It wouldn't have mattered. I was dying for another hit of crack that morning. I HAD to have it. As we walked the beautiful campus, reminiscing all the way over to the football stadium, it was all I was thinking about. My lips were moving, words were coming out, I could hear them, but the only thought passing through my mind was, "Will she give me another chance?" Had I blown it by denying her last night?

"So, Lila, when I come to LA to visit, we'll be divorced. So then anything goes," I said as we walked. Lila didn't break stride nor look at me.

"Yeah, well, you missed your chance, buddy!"

Ever the temptress, Lila used words like "buddy" on a regular basis, perhaps a leftover remnant of her Southwest Virginia upbringing. Southwest Virginia is basically Tennessee with the discerning difference being the existence of a state line. Marion, Virginia, where Lila, Sam David, his brother Kevin and all the other crazy people I knew from the small town that had somehow taken a large, looming and permanent place in my personal reality, was about an hour north of Bristol. Bristol was a town that couldn't make its own mind up, opting instead to be in both states.

Bristol is also the home of a major NASCAR race, thus further blurring the line between pure Southern gentility and white socked redneck abrasiveness. Lila was like Bristol, and she had a little of both in her. Toss into that mix the wildness of her Miami experience, the sophistication of her working for a New York City advertising agency, finished off with 20 years of Los Angeles country club set, beachside living induced comfort and you had a pretty damn heady mix of woman.

What Grace had lacked in sophistication she made up for in pure feigned sweetness. What Lila lacked in anything, she made up for in sheer cunning that easily hid behind the facade of Southern sweetness she projected at will. I mean, you can see I didn't have a chance. It was like I was Elvis and she was the world. Eventually, she was gonna win and I was going down. With Elvis it took 42 years, for Lila it would take all of 12 hours on this Saturday. The "missed your chance" statement was merely a misdirection. Meanwhile, she was bootlegging it the other way to a clear field all the way. Once I even mentioned regret for not staying with her, she knew she had me.

So we hung out like the old chums I thought we were that morning. Chatting, watching Game Day on ESPN.

"I LOVE Game Day!" Lila knew the real way to a man's heart, or perhaps more accurately, his pants, and she knew that way was more likely to be found on the field than in the kitchen. Wily, customized dissemination of my defenses. End run around Jesus!!

I had lost track of the sports world while married to Grace. What exactly is a man supposed to do when he goes to the grocery store and returns to find college football replaced by the home and Garden channel? When the request to return to the game is met with an icy stare from a woman who is flitting around using the TV as background and semi-angrily sheathed "Go ahead." In the rearview mirror, I see myself as a puppy dog dragging off into the sunset, tail between his legs, dragging one of those old school hobo sacks on a stick labeled "gonads" and "testosterone". Lila gets the credit for dragging me back in the direction of the alpha male train. I'll give her that.

We met Tom and Jane on the outskirts of town and transferred ourselves as well as our limited contributions to their tailgate into Tom's SUV. Once we arrived at the stadium, we were invaded by Tom's son Tommy, a selection of frat brothers, sorority girls and others. Jane took delight in sharing the story of Lila and I being together for the first time in 35 years. I love Jane, one of the few women left in America with a sense of romance that extends beyond the film "The Notebook," we began to attract these kids like a chocolate cake attracts flies at a picnic.

Lila smiled and charmed these kids, especially the males, with a "confusing" sense of purpose, smiling, enticing, and then pulling back the charm at the appropriate moment. I swear I heard her southern accent deepen as she talked to them. The ultimate cougar!

In the front windshield was this power couple, this incredible story of restoration, this DESTINY romance. In the rearview mirror was Lila, my crack, turning on the charm, the smile, the humor, selling, marketing her way into my consciousness and my bed. Like me, love me. Admit it, you REALLY want me, don't you? It was an unfortunate collision of hope and need. The actual destiny was doom. My doom.

Tom had left his drinking behind almost 20 years before and I was verging on a year of sobriety. Jane and Lila bonded over wine, holding up the tradition of over-imbibing at UVA football games. Lila, for her part, held up way more than her end as she continued to try and fill up that same leg she had been working on the night before. The woman was a true pro. Oddly enough, the more she drank, the more charming she became. Also, apparently, the more she drank, the more attractive I became.

Lila and I finally went into the game about halfway through the first quarter, found our seats, and, of course, began to make friends with everyone around us. We had seen about 12 plays when the PA announcer came over the system. Everyone had to leave the stadium as there was a front of dangerous thunderstorms very nearby. What? The sun was shining. I mean, seriously, how many people have ever been to a sporting event where God calls time out? Looking back, rear view mirror time again, maybe it was...no, that would never happen, WOULD it?

Tom and Jane never even made it into the game. We climbed back in their car, along with coolers, tables, tents, and everything needed for a pretty elaborate tailgate party. We sat crammed together for a bit and finally headed out to take Tommy back to his place as the sky opened and the rain rushed down faster than the teams hit the field that day, thunder for a band and lightning for a cheerleader. Lila continued on the wine, providing running and, I might add, quite amusing commentary as we drove along. Southern accent tempered by LA wackiness and the sort of offbeat (and off-target) spiritual meandering found in all those crazy movies you've seen about life in LA. Remember "Bob and Carol and Ted and Alice"? Kids turning a broken water main into a water slide?

"Look at those kids. That's the way you turn lemons into lemonade". Front windshield; charming, wacky, seductive. Rear view mirror; wacky psycho babble therapeutically induced false security.

About an hour later, we finally returned to the stadium, cued by the radio announcer's proclamation that the game would be resuming. Lila and I returned to our seats, and watched ANOTHER 12 plays. Then the sky opened AGAIN and the rain began coming down. It's a blowing rain so even though our seats are under the upper deck, we begin to get soaked. As we walk out to the causeway, Lila takes my hand for the first time so we don't lose each other in the crowd. OK, Lila takes my hand and puts it squarely over her breast and pulls it tight. Uh oh, boob time for Bonzo!! Then 10 seconds later, she turns around and gives me a full out kiss with the magic Lila tongue, right in the middle of hundreds of people. Done! Game over. If Don

Meredith was still breathing and here, his famous fat lady is singing, "Turn out the lights, the party's over". My promise to God is history and my second or third, go round with Lila has begun.

Don't get me wrong, my friend Jesus is still lingering back there, but his demeanor has changed from that of a friend to that of a high school football coach who has tossed the clipboard not to the ground in anger, but to the bench in resignation and acceptance. Back to the drawing board, team, we've got a lot of work to do.

The ghost of Gram has disappeared completely. He's somewhere out in Joshua Tree, sipping bourbon, firing up designer joints, and shooting up high octane heroin while sitting at the bar. Leave it to Gram to find the seedy side of the afterlife, God bless him.

That was the moment. Things are so much clearer in the rearview mirror, so now I can see it, but at that moment I was blind as a bat. It was as if I came to a fork. Down one way is barren land, leafless trees, dirt, gravel, and nary an oasis in sight. The other way is paved, clear, surrounded by lush trees, palm trees at that, and waterfalls in the distance. God's way barren, hope in the distance...maybe. The other way is Lila, LA, material riches, sexual pleasures, and more importantly, hope, hope of love with a woman who had been lingering in my heart for 35 years. There is a word on the road sign that I miss completely though, my friends, it is small, in parentheses and way at the bottom of the sign, perhaps even partially obstructed by weeds. The word is "false".

> *"And the one on whom seed was sown among the thorns, this is the man who hears the word, and the worry of the world and the deceitfulness of wealth choke the word, and it becomes unfruitful."*
> **Matthew 13:22**

There's no way of telling what would have happened if I had taken the other fork. Would Lila and I have ended up together? Would our restored friendship have fizzled out? Who knows? All I do know is this. Once I took the Lila road, she owned me. Like any good owner, she took care of her new things well for a while, but like anyone who is blessed enough to be regularly visited by the material riches of this world, she also tossed aside all new things when the dings and scratches began to appear. The signs were always there. Throw away your food if you can't eat it, toss away your promise to God cause you "deserve" better. It was a matter of respect. Or perhaps no respect.

R-E-S-P-E-C-T...find out what it means to me. Apparently when it came to self and Lila, nothing!

"For the lips of the adulterous woman drip honey, and her speech is smoother than oil 4 but in the end she is bitter as gall, sharp as a double-edged sword." **Proverbs 5: 3-4**

When Tom and Jane headed back to DC due to the awful weather, we took the occasion to grab a ride back to Lila's hotel, not finding the walk back in the pouring rainstorm appealing. Up in her room, we watched football and I pretended that propriety was going to be observed by taking up residence on the couch while she sat in the desk chair. Unable to watch the UVA game due to the delay, TV money, etc. (I mean, her ex was a TV sports executive, she had to know that, right?), we took solace briefly in watching our arch rival Virginia Tech get walloped by Texas A & M.

The act didn't matter, and it was already over for me. As Lila relocated to the couch beside her, not realizing that she had already won not only the battle but the war, her troops continued to advance, burning and pillaging any reason stupid enough to stand their way. The wine she was still drinking served only to amp up the assault. "We deserve this, Rick, both of us." In the rearview mirror, it looks so different, so clear. Here's a man who was cheated on by his soon to be ex-wife, a violation of trust, trying to build a house with a woman whose soon, after hundreds of thousands of dollars in legal fees, to be ex-husband controlled and hounded her, clearly having no trust. Rearview mirror logic. Trump's front windshield "love". Every time.

The coup d'stat was administered when Lila began to explain the acquiring of her new boobs...that's right, I met two women from past relationships from the 70s who had turned away from the flat chested A-cupped ways of the past by buying silicone relief, both of whom INSISTED on showing them to me. The missile destroyed the target when she pulled her top down and placed my hand on her breast.

The only talking after that was when she briefly stopped to say, "Are you sure you're OK with this? Technically, what you're doing right now is cheating on your wife." Technically? I let you decide if that was a fair statement for her to make with her hand down my pants, but the truth is, I was totally on board the train at that point. The war had been over. We were just working out the terms of my surrender. Technicalities!! The devil is truly in the details.

> *"See to it, brothers and sisters, that none of you has a sinful, unbelieving heart that turns away from the living God. But encourage one another daily, as long as it is called "Today," so that none of you may be hardened by sin's deceitfulness."*
> **Hebrews 3:12-13**

Despite what my buddy GP (Gram Parsons) might have thought when he and Chris Hillman composed *Christine's Tune (aka Devil In Disguise)*, the devil truly isn't IN anyone, but the irony is that he can use everyone, at least as long as God lets him. And we don't know it when he's using us. We haven't got a clue. In fact, sometimes we can actually be thinking we are doing the other guy's work when we are in the employ of the man in red with the pitchfork. Lila and I reveled in each other all night long and, to be fair, she visited me with no illusions. The most romantic thing she said all night was, "Well, you fucked your old girlfriend." Just look at that stupid guy in the rearview mirror laying flat on the road. Poor dumb bastard never even saw the truck coming.

On her way to Dulles the next morning, I had her stop by my place and cooked her breakfast. We said our goodbyes and she was off to her flight back to Lala land while I went to work for the first bride and groom of a busy September.

I still remember us standing out in my driveway saying goodbye that September morning. I remember the twinge of sadness that passed through me when our first goodbye kiss ever was a tiny peck on the lips, not a passionate tongue twisting mass of embraces. Lila would later say, "and I didn't even kiss you the way I should have. I was being careful for that little boy next door," referring to the neighbor's child that was in the next yard that morning. There was no sense of desperation as Lila pulled away.

I was content with things, still close enough to the Spirit to have a remnant of trust, still captive to the basic tenant that when we try to control, that's when it all goes wrong. Content to let her go back, live with what happened, plan the January trip that we had spoken about and nothing between. Content to allow time to do its work, her to go back. We would see when January came around if I was in the guest house or the master bedroom. Love is patient, and I believed that.

When she texted me later while I was at the wedding that she was stuck on the runway at Dulles and they were serving wine, that it was too bad that I wasn't there when the alcohol hit her, it gave me a twinge of pleasure, but I was content, content with what happened and patient to see what was next. Front windshield love, rear view mirror logic. You know how it is when you're driving, though. It's easy to get complacent and forget to check that rearview mirror. That's how you miss the train wreck.

Chapter 13

Open Up My Window

"To love at all is to be vulnerable. Love anything and your heart will be wrung and possibly broken. If you want to make sure of keeping it intact, you must give it to no one, not even an animal. Wrap it carefully round with hobbies and little luxuries; avoid all entanglements. Lock it up safe in the casket or coffin of your selfishness. But in that casket, safe, dark, motionless, airless, it will change. It will not be broken; it will become unbreakable, impenetrable, irredeemable. To love is to be vulnerable."

—C.S. Lewis, *The Four Loves*

What happened over the next four weeks after Lila boarded that plane back to LA can best be described as the collision that occurs when an irresistible force meets an immovable object. The irresistible force? Well, that would be all that neediness that disguised itself as love that I had stored up inside myself since Grace had told me she was leaving. I had to face the inevitable conclusion that the woman who had chased me through 25 years of time, broken up two families in the process, changing the lives of virtually every person who spun into our orbit, that woman found me awful enough to leave me despite my being the "love of her life." All that self-pity, determination to make SOMETHING work, guilt over the bad treatment Grace had convinced me I had given her, all that had to be poured out somewhere, somehow, on somebody. Lila found herself in the path of all that repressed emotion and need, perhaps wearing a mask of love. The immovable object would be Lila's heart, safely tucked behind the walls erected in protection of 27 years of the mental abuse of a controlling eternally unhappy man. As time moves us through this round, perhaps the last round, of our fitful stop and go relationship, more factors would contribute to the immovability of that heart. Girlfriends, money, her friend Dr. Alouette's "therapy", and the LA lifestyle to which Lila, ever the princess, had become accustomed. It's all very clear in that rearview mirror, but through the front windshield, all I saw was hope, false hope. Remember false hope? Dresses up just like real hope, parades around saying "Embrace me, love me", then karate kicks you in the nuts when you aren't looking. Well, in the four weeks between Lila's appearance in Charlottesville and our Memphis trip, false hope took up residence in my being like a bad tenant who is never planning on paying a cent of the rent. "My stuff's all in here now, you wanna kick me out? YOU move it!!" I should have recognized it when we signed the lease. It wasn't like I hadn't seen it before. It had just been a while, especially when it came to Lila.

No matter what she may have said over the course of our nearly constant telephone conversation for at least two hours a day for almost five months, the 2013 model of Lila was not the least bit impressed by my stories of Muddy Waters and Sam or any of the other dubious accomplishments that I had previously considered story worthy by virtue of the breadth of my experiences. While I had moved through the world of small town celebrity as a broadcaster and theatrical actor, the grown up Lila had graduated from sex with rock stars and professional football players to the LA world of hobnobbing with the rich and famous. Actors, directors, NBA players. Her divorce attorney moonlighted as the legal consultant for *Good Morning America,* her therapist sidelined as the motivational psychologist for the then current Super Bowl champion Seahawks. As much as I still admire Grace for never falling victim to the traps of sex, alcohol, and drugs that her reality had placed before her, I admit to equally admiring Lila for the pure chutzpah it took to leave the husband whose labors provided not only the livelihood for the lavish lifestyle but also the means of entrance to this world of American fame. Up until that one we would watch together with her good friends two days before she kicked me out of Hotel California, Lila had only missed two of the last 20 Super Bowls and normally viewed them from the vantage point of a corporate suite so exclusive that even Robin Leach couldn't get in to do an expose'. I was drowning before I even realized how far the water was above my head.

Early September 2013: Back To LaLa Land

Once Lila got back to LA, it took me a day to text and make sure she arrived home safely. Again, cool with what happened, patient as I had learned to be, and content to know I could plan a nice LA trip in January. I could wait until then to find out if I was in the outhouse in the back or the master bedroom for accommodations. Lila, on the other hand, had no such patience. After assuring me she was back safely, she texted again, "Any chance you could get away during the week or a long weekend sometime during October or November, maybe New York?" Damn, she was offering another hit of the crack!

Lila had made a big deal of my denial of her lust that first night. I can still hear that sweet pecan voice saying, "I had to BEG you!" In the rearview mirror, I can see that for the masterful piece of salesmanship, it was. Just brilliant!! You barely got that great deal last time, buddy, and it was ONLY thanks to me. Best grab the gusto when it shows up next time, you might not be so lucky. I mean, as a self-employed businessman, I had studied sales through all those high falootin' gurus for years, but compared to Lila, they didn't know shit from shinola!

Of course, I could come up with a long weekend, just watch me. You'll bring that crack pipe right? Then more brilliant salesmanship..."Well just let me know, if you can't, I understand." See what I mean? Pure genius. The woman was like high tide, she comes in, she goes out, she giveth, she taketh away, she twisteth you around like a "candle in the wind". She owned me, which is pretty damn funny because one of her tricks was to tell me that I OWNED her. Brilliant salesmanship!!

In the first week, we exchanged a few pleasant emails, mostly about her home shopping and a couple of shops on the downtown mall in Charlottesville. The Saturday following the one I spent with Lila at the game and in her hotel room, I had a long drive for a wedding for Barbie and Ken. I can't make this crap up, friends, the bride's name was Barbie and the groom's name was Ken. Furthermore, Barbie's mom had hired me for Barbie's intended wedding to ANOTHER groom but they had broken up. No, he was not named Todd. Google "male doll that was Ken's friend" and you'll get that. I was telling Barbie and Ken's Love Story to the guests and the main gist of the story was Ken's unbelievable perseverance as Barbie looked for love in all the wrong places after their initial affair. Under the influence of the crack, I was drawing WAY too many parallels to the story of me and Lila in my own soon to be obsessed mind. That alleged message from God's coincidence meter was pegging in the red again.

Lila, on the way to shopping somewhere in Malibu, had called right when I left on the two hour drive to Potomac Pointe Winery near DC, another beautiful spot, one that would make you swear that you are in Tuscany. We talked the entire two hours, only hanging up when I was forced to negotiate the twisting mountain road that led up to the winery entrance. This was the beginning of our "money" talks. They basically consisted of me admitting that I had none, while Lila would contribute that she wanted to spend ALL of her ex-husband's. Yep, you got it, I was being tempted by Sugar Momma-hood. Would I be able to deal with it? Could I accept that? Would I feel less of a man? All I had to say was pass the pipe and light me up, sister! I WANT CRACK!!

<u>Sex Drive</u>

Lila and I talked on the phone the entire two hour drive back from Potomac Pointe that night after Barbie and Ken's wedding. This was the beginning of our phone sex. I had started the phone sex with Grace when she was in Florida and I was in Virginia. Actually, I had learned the art from an old girlfriend, OK, an old booty call friend, who had visited my life and bed in the 90s between the end of the marriage to Sophia and the second (or third) coming of Grace. I was a natural. It came easy to me, the soft and sexy voice, the imagination, the willingness to go beyond what looked like the boundary into new territory that was essential in driving the phone sex relationship from the atmosphere into the stratosphere. Lila actually started it with the suggestion that she had been thinking about us meeting and my hand going up her skirt on the way from the airport to the hotel. That was all I needed. Once she gave me the ball, I knew EXACTLY where the goal line was and I fancy danced it all the way down the field for a touchdown. By the time I backed my van into the driveway for the night, the pecan sweet southern voice had melted into a puddle of sweet, sticky goo on the floor.

What a saleswoman!! She owned me completely and she hadn't even made a down payment yet. Scary how good she was! OK, excuse me, but forget passing that pipe for a hit. Just fill the whole damn thing to the brim and hand it to me with the lighter. NOW!!!

Masterpiece

By September 2013, false hope was strutting around in its best three piece suit. In retrospect, I have to give some credence to the theory that none of it was actually purposeful on Lila's part, that what in fact happened was a collision between her affection starved being and my need to feed affection to someone, anyone. Bad timing. Or perfect, depending on your point of view. Either way, the email exchange and the phone sex amped up for the three weeks between Barbie and Ken's wedding and the day I left for Memphis, the eventual chosen spot for our long weekend together after Nashville was all booked up. We were looking for someplace, you know, mid-countryish, so either filled the bill perfectly. I knew both towns and Lila neither. She was willing to concede home court advantage at that point. Perhaps lulling me into a false sense of security. The morning emails that I made a tradition were literate masterpieces unto themselves, soul baring compilations questioning the very nature of our existence, laden with random thoughts about my relationship with my friend Jesus, free flowing feelings from my heart to the all new 2013 model Lila, and, of course, sexual undertones, overtones, sexual tones of all kinds. We talked on the phone every night for at least two hours as I ignored my business, friends, and family, giving it all up for a woman who was almost 3,000 miles away. We would talk about everything, occasionally lapsing into phone sex, great phone sex. Later, Lila would explain to me that one of the secrets to true sales success was the ability to listen to her client's problems, citing the case of one New York businessman who seemed to just want someone, maybe a pretty girl, to open up to about his problems with his wife, kids, life. "He just needed somebody to listen." It all sounds so innocent, especially when she told the story with that sweet little southern Pecan accent. Eventually, said businessman would then pull the trigger on thousands of dollars of TV advertising, dollars that would line Lila's already silver lined pockets. Again, friends, I'm just the storyteller. Interpret for yourselves.

We would occasionally share the moon, a connectable dot from West to East coast, one that reminded me of an obscure Christopher Cross song, "Open Up My Window". False hope was fluffing up my pillows, leaving me chocolates at night, prepping me for the kill. When I sent pink roses randomly to the West Coast one September day, it prompted a call from Lila proclaiming, "You are just doing all the right things, I just ADORE you!" Following on the heels of the Grace experience, these words were like a symphony to my beleaguered ears. I wanted to believe them. I did believe them. THAT was a mistake!

"16 Wise friends will rescue you from the Temptress - that smooth-talking Seductress 17 Who's faithless to the husband she married years ago, never gave a second thought to her promises before God. 18 Her whole way of life is doomed; every step she takes brings her closer to hell. 19 No one who joins her company ever comes back, ever sets foot on the path to real living" **Proverbs 2: 16-19**

I have perhaps the stupidest bucket list in the world. While most people want to cross the country, go to China, scale Mt. Everest, and skydive from 10,000 feet, mine contains smaller, more manageable items such as becoming a broadcaster, doing some acting, publishing a novel, and making a film. The fact you're reading this means there's only one item left on that list, so please stop reading right now and write a quick letter to my publisher demanding that a film be made of this story and insisting that I direct it. Thank you.

The small theatrical part I played in a community theater production of The Odd Couple in 2008 was the only part I ever auditioned for. I figured since I was batting 100%, why not quit while I was ahead? So I did.

My brief radio career lasted from 1991-1995. At one point, I actually had two radio shows, an AM (remember AM?) talk show in the morning and an FM top 40 show in the afternoon. The FM show was my showcase as I used a variety of sound drops, music, and song parodies to create an afternoon party with music every day between the hours of 3 and 6 pm. Personally, I thought I was brilliant, which was probably the reason my over-inflated ego was able to take me on a major left turn that left my marriage to Sophia and any sense of normalcy way behind me in the dust. I kept the tapes for years, deducing that certainly the Smithsonian would want possession of this collection of humorous gems posthumously. Then, at some point, I actually listened to the tapes and it seeped into my now more consciousness how absolutely awful I was. A true loose cannon, one that backfired frequently at that.

I mention this because retrospectively, that's about where the daily emails fell when examined. What seemed brilliant at the time appeared ill-advised at best in the old rearview mirror. It was the daily emails where I lost control and my neediness to give some love to someone, somewhere made the quick trip from the sublime to the ridiculous. I mean ridiculous! Like my radio show breaks, these emails seemed so brilliant at the time. Reading them over at the time,

I remember thinking about how even Lila and her traditional fear of commitment. OK, fear of commitment to me. How could she resist my subtlety and smooth blending of humor, sex, love, and faith? She didn't resist...at first. With words that were sometimes eloquent, always heartfelt, I bared my soul, the faith that had kept me walking with my friend Jesus, my insecurities, my pain, and, ultimately, my joy at finding that she was my gift from God, to Lila over the 27 brief days between that Sunday morning in my townhouse and that Saturday afternoon when my plane landed in Memphis. Like a bad poker player, I showed every card in the hand my heart, which was bursting like the Grinch's heart when he discovered the true meaning of Christmas, held to a woman who had never shown anything historically other than she knew how to trash that heart. The lessons of 1977, Elwood, and Bubba dissipated like fog on a sunny morning. The Eagles, the Miami Dolphins, and the cocaine Cowboys weren't even a blip on my radar yet and by the time THEY appeared, I would be so severely addicted to the crack they would merely serve as an incentive to take another hit.

After three weeks of this soul baring, one morning I sent what I deemed to be a particularly brilliant piece of prose, one which drew spiritual circles around our doomed relationship like a Picasso painting. I even sold out my friend Jesus by referring to Him as the Intimate Stranger, a man who could walk up to anyone, any person on earth and KNOW their heart, KNOW their needs, comfort them, and love them like He had been with them for years, for a lifetime. From this tenuous cliff hanging, I drew a circle back to Lila and I, leaving Jesus scratching his head at my lostness and the ridiculous sublimity of my analogy. Pastor Wilt and I have had many conversations about twisting, not the Chubby Checker variety, but the type of twisting many of us Christians do when we try to distort what God has actually instructed us to fit our own fleshly path. When it came to Lila, I was twistin' again...like I did last summer...you know, that summer of 1977.

Lila wrote back that she didn't know how to respond, no one had ever professed such things to her before. She proclaimed how awesome it was that we both just wanted happiness for each other and we were finding it together. I mean, seriously, how much responsibility actually should fall on her when her supposedly enlightened lover boy is explaining how when God said blue and I said green, God really meant green.

Lila was maybe even following her heart, while I knew better. I had already learned that through my futile pursuit of my marriage to Grace. As Pastor Wilt has said many, many times, "the heart is the problem." Following the heart is why men commit murder, why husbands and wives leave their partners of 20 and 30 years in pursuit of the "destiny" calling them by virtue of a pretty or handsome face. The trick is to LEAD with your heart. That's what my friend Jesus wanted. Lead, don't follow. Lead.

Admit it, you think I am as insane reading this as I do writing it. It's sort of like taking an old horse and throwing out all the track records cause you just KNOW this time he's gonna pull out that win. It doesn't matter that he's lost 50 races in a row. This is the one.

In September of 2013, the cold reality of those days in 1977 were as far away from my Lila clouded mind as the Siberian winter from a Gulf Coast sunset. I labored every morning over those emails like a coal miner on a double shift, sometimes spending 2-3 hours so I could deliver another literary masterpiece to Lila's inbox before she rose with the California sun. I pitched woo like Sandy Koufax in a World Series, articulating thespian like sentences of longing and lust, occasionally lapsing into song, crooning Al Green's "God Blessed Our Love" over the phone to Lila because I was so sure He did. Memphis loomed, Memphis, Tennessee. In Memphis, I would close the deal.

Chapter 14

God Blessed Our Love

I've never been a big anniversary person, not like some people. You know the ones I mean. They celebrate everything from one week to 100 years. Why the roses? Well, it's been four weeks today since I first looked at you and wished you would talk to me and remember? The next day, you did! You DID talk to me! Uh oh, that means another sleeve of those baby Almond Joys will be heading your way tomorrow too.

I was beyond puzzled then, I was positively bamboozled, when September 29, 2014 rolled around and these awful nostalgic feelings began gnawing me from the inside out like a tapeworm. Remember tapeworms? My head was as crowded as a Staten Island subway car at rush hour, filled with thoughts of Al Green, Elvis, BB King's, Ducks marching, and all things Beale Street, all things Memphis. I just couldn't shake it, couldn't shake her. I've asked person after person the question, "Haven't you ever had someone in your life you just couldn't get over?" Nope. Then when I realized that virtually all the friends I had asked were women, I decided to float the question to a few males. As I expected, I didn't get the immediate head-shaking denial that women tended to give me, instead I got this glassy eyed staring into space, but oh so yearningly look.

That must have been the look that was on my face that morning. No matter what I tried to picture, all I could see was Lila and I sitting in those pews that Sunday morning. No, not THIS Sunday morning, THAT Sunday morning! September 29, 2014 was a Monday. I mean September 29, 2013. That's the day Lila and I were in Memphis, that's the day we met our personal Memphis chauffeur John Samuel, the cab driver, and that's the day he snaked his way down the freeway and into what looked like a super normal middle class neighborhood on the south side of Memphis to drop us at Full Gospel Tabernacle

Church to experience the musical and oratory stylings of Reverend Al Green.

Lila and I had both arrived the night before. Memphis had been my idea. Well, actually Nashville was my idea, but it was all booked up, so Memphis was default second place. For the second time in my life, I had put together a trip itinerary, the first being during the marriage to Sophia when I had completely booked and planned our New England Bed and Breakfast tour. Somehow in suggesting Memphis, I had managed to find the one relevant city in the entire United States that Lila didn't already know like the back of her suntanned hand. But Al Green had been her idea, her gift to me, a salute to the fact that the time between Lila's late August trip back to Charlottesville for the football game and culminating in our trip to Memphis would stand as the "golden era of the second coming" of one Lila Wylde into my little life. From the night at the Charlottesville mall through the perfect four days we spent in Memphis, it was a different Lila that I saw, one that I had never experienced before. Open, even tender at times, caring, even though on the underside she was negotiating me away from the promise I had made to God to keep it in my pants until the divorce papers with Grace were signed. A technicality, but it was technicalities that sneaked back in the back door after they had left for the evening strictly to bite you in the ass!

> *"Sing to the LORD a new song; Sing to the LORD, all the earth. Sing to the LORD, bless His name; Proclaim good tidings of His salvation from day to day"* **Psalms 96:12**

On September 29th, 2014, I was remembering those wooden pews, and how Lila and I had stood up and clapped along to the Reverend's sermon/gospel. Honestly, he was such a master it was tough to discern the preaching from the singing, but eventually, it all became a piece, flowing together seamlessly, message, medium, messenger, all a piece flowing together like three tributaries that just reached the river. Driven by a soul band that was masquerading as a gospel band...or perhaps it was the other way around. It didn't matter. I was being haunted by those memories a year later. I turn to look at my friend Jesus. "I thought you were gonna stop this sort of thing."

"I can't stop anything, it's your own free will that runs your mind. I can suggest, instruct, and be here with you, but I can't change your mind. You're in charge 100%. It takes discipline."

> *"Finally, brothers and sisters, whatever is true, whatever is noble, whatever is right, whatever is pure, whatever is lovely, whatever is admirable—if anything is excellent or praiseworthy—think about such things"* **Philippians 4: 8**

That sounds so easy. Simple. Just think good thoughts. You know how to do that, right? It seems even my Lord and Blessed Savior understood the problem here. I could do that. I could think good thoughts, it was just those thoughts were on this morning all about Lila, Al Green, and those four perfect, well, almost perfect, days. There was one little teeny weeny imperfection. One little small red flag was being waved by an invisible little guy wearing what almost looked like a leprechaun suit. We'll get to it before we leave Memphis. As usual, those thoughts of Lila made me want to spring into action, say something, do something, make some attempt to advance my cause, the eventual capture of Lila's cold, cold heart. Sing it, Hank...you know she has one, made of ice. It was this desire to do something, to do anything, that had left me with a backlog of maybe 30 unsent emails to Lila written between that February 2014 morning when I left LA and that September 2014 morning when I was remembering the Memphis trip, all with my heart poured right out in them. Good Lord! So I wrote an email that day, one I tweaked several times over the "one year since Memphis" anniversary days. I wrote brilliant stuff about how much I missed our friendship, how those days in the late 70s when we just hung out together as best friends were the best days of our long relationship, how I hoped we could get back to that, at least. It was brilliant, heart rending stuff. Stuff that is still sitting in the can.

Doubt that Lila would even be aware of these anniversaries, if she was, she wouldn't care. If she cared and called, I wouldn't be able to talk. I couldn't control my mind anymore than I apparently could my libido, but I have learned at least one thing that makes life go smoother. Go ahead and trust God with everything. If nothing else, it absolves you of any responsibility to take action. Trusting God is the absolute best way to feel good about doing nothing. I have also discovered that I have a real talent for doing nothing. It's so easy. So it is via this route of trusting God that emails remain in the can. I just keep adding to it, or writing another one, also unsent. Still, maybe one day......

September 28, 2013: Wake Up My Soul

Dad gave me a ride to the Charlottesville Airport and dropped me off around 8:30 am on Saturday September 28, 2013. As I grabbed my bag and rolled it towards the door, I heard his have a safe trip and have fun declaration from his vehicle as I turned to wave goodbye. I'd have to say that I was definitely feeling that God was on my side as I worked my way through airport security and towards the gate to board the prop jet that would take me to Charlotte for my connection to Memphis. I had the row to myself so I was able to slip over to the window seat and drink in the beautiful Virginia countryside from a God's eye view.

After all, I could feel God release me from the burden of the hope that I had harbored for my marriage to Grace that Friday in August of 2013 before Lila came for lunch. There was no question of that release, one of the clearest heavenly originated messages that I had ever received. That pain ended that day while Richie Furay was singing, waking up my soul. Then Lila came back into my life, and got that ring off, of every part of me. Obviously, she was God's reward, right? Right? Jimmy Buffett once said there is a thin line between Saturday night and Sunday morning. Seems to me that works in our dealings with our Heavenly Father as well. Reward. Temptation. Thin line. It is so thin you might miss it altogether unless you accidentally cross over it. And how would you know if you did? Unless it was too late. It was.

> *"For the wisdom of this world is foolishness before God For it is written, "He is THE ONE WHO CATCHES THE WISE IN THEIR CRAFTINESS"* **1 Corinthians 3:19**

The magic that was going to be my Memphis trip with Lila started as soon as the 737 lifted off the runway in Charlotte. The stewardess who took up the resident aisle seat beside me was a Christian girl and in the window seat beside me was Cathy, a professor from Little Rock State and a huge music fan who was able to fill me in completely on the local Memphis music scene, who to look for, what clubs would be great outside the ones I already knew.

In return, I listened to her concerns about her husband's relationship with their daughters and tried to get Cathy to reconsider Jesus, which she left saying she was going to do. When Cathy passed by me in the terminal and offered me a ride downtown to The Peabody, I took her up on it right away, a point that later caused much contention with Lila regarding my overly trusting attitude of female strangers. On the two hour flight, I had also filled Cathy in on the purpose and circumstances surrounding my trip, so I got out with hardy best wishes from her a block from the Peabody. Everybody loves a happy ending, which I had total confidence about at that point. Happy ever after with Lila and a great big nanny, nanny boo boo to Grace!! See, once you start pumping that pride, getting that rightness, that smugness, that's when God sort of starts enjoying the little joke He's about to play on you. He still loves you, just giving you a teeny dose of your own medicine.

Lila's plane almost got stuck overnight in Dallas, but eventually she made it to the Peabody around 11:00 that night. I met her at the front desk and we quickly retreated to our room and ordered Lila some alcohol from room service. Within 20 minutes, we were naked in that big, comfy bed. About an hour later, with the fruit of say, 30 late night phone sex calls finally consummated, we emerged dressed and ready to take on Beale Street Saturday night. We found it a little more than we could handle.

The blues were nowhere to be found after midnight Saturday on Beale Street. Instead, there were lines of much younger than us people having IDs checked, opening their jackets and pocketbooks, and being patted down for weapons. The music was loud Top 40. Still, once we waited through the line, we felt a little obligated to party some, so party we did, Lila downing Chardonnay like she had been stranded in a wine desert for months and me enjoying my non-alcoholic beer. I have to say, it was amazing watching the copious amounts of alcohol that Lila could imbibe and still remain vertical, at least until she wanted to get horizontal. It's a good thing she's collecting a small fortune yearly in alimony cause she is certainly no cheap date.

God bless her though, she is generous to a fault and I mean fault. I will never forget watching her hand a "homeless" guy a $20 bill outside the Staples Center in LA. The only problem was that he was dressed better than me.

We survived Beale Street Saturday night, woke up early the next morning for a room service breakfast and got dressed in our best clothes for what would turn out to be the unexpected and delightful highlight of our three day, four night trip, a visit to the Full Gospel Tabernacle Church to hear the musical and spiritual sermonizing stylings of the Right Reverend Al Green. Yes, that Al Green. "Let's Stay Together" because "I'm Still In Love With You" Al Green.

Before Al Green, we met John Samuel, the cab driver we adopted as our official Memphis chauffeur. John was a "character", which it turned out all Memphis cab drivers were, including a random dude we got one day when John couldn't drive who fancied himself the actual Dude, as in the Jeff Bridges character in "The Big Lebowski". Remember The Big Lebowksi, the Cab, and the Eagles? Already, God was jumping up and down in the background, photo bombing my reality and screaming, "Hey, I'm walkin' heeeah, I'm making a circle heeeah, pay attention, ya darned fool!" Nope not me, not Rick, not when Lila is on the same planet.

John Samuel was no poser. He was a failed studio musician and practicing alcoholic who not only had stories to tell, but he had backstreets to tour with stories to match about legendary musicians. Turns out that John had played with the likes of Steve Cropper and Donald "Duck" Dunn before the old demon alcohol had rendered this studio musician a studio clown. John took an immediate shine to Lila and I, proclaiming us worthy of his behind the scenes tour of Memphis, even with special rates, a tour which we set aside for next time, our next trip to Memphis.

John knew Memphis like the back of his hand, but he had never been to the Full Gospel Tabernacle before, so he was as surprised as we were to find ourselves in a typical middle class suburban neighborhood when suddenly out of nowhere appeared the Full Gospel Tabernacle sign. When John let us off and the Reverend Al was emerging from his Volvo at the same time, he immediately declared that he was bringing his girlfriend to this church next Sunday! Hallelujah and thank you, Jesus! I did save a soul. Nope. Later, at Lila's suggestion, I would text John Samuel to ask about if he and his girlfriend actually made it to church the following story. John would relate a fairly convoluted story about alcohol, the old devil, and his breakup. A character.

Whatever one expected on entering the Full Gospel Tabernacle, it was the modesty of the chapel that struck you, along with its relative sparseness of customers i.e. souls to save. Lila and I took a post in the middle set of pews about two thirds of the way back, joining a relatively small group of mostly Caucasian tourists there to observe and participate in the Lord's Good News via the auspices of Reverend Al. The congregation itself was relatively small, less than 50, and primarily African American. Women dressed to the absolute nines with matching hats and fascinators, with purple and red being the dominant colors. That congregation nearly doubled in size when the choir came out. Off to the right of the pulpit sat the band, including a full drum set, bass, guitar, and one of the absolute nicest and largest classic Hammond B-3 organs I had ever laid eyes on. Interestingly enough, it was being played by a brother who was almost three times as large as the instrument itself...albeit one with a talent almost 10 times larger. He could make that B-3 sing!!

Once the choir started up, it contained not one, not two, but maybe five Aretha Franklins. It was almost scary to think these were the "amateur" singers in Memphis and just that fact plus his stories lifted pre-alcoholic John Samuel up several notches on my personal musical scoreboard. It was about 15 minutes into the service when the Reverend Al appeared through the side door, fully robed, to take his seat right in front of the choir, a seat that definitely resembled a wooden throne, very intricately carved dark wood with red velvet seat and back cushions. Al just sat there for a long time, looking like one of those NFL players they show on TV during the national anthem. Game face on, a slight occasional toe tapping, mostly just waiting for his magic moment.

When it came, Al rose slowly, not so much standing as uncurling. The choir was still singing when Al got up to standing position, shaking his head in approval while lifting his robed arms skyward. When he got to the pulpit, he turned sideways with the trademark Al Green shoulder rhythm roll, turning his head to look directly at the congregation with that killer Al Green smile. As the choir finished, The Reverend jumped right in, sans music, singing/talking, riffing off God's word.

"Oh yeah," he sang, "Love and happiness," back to talking, "welcome to the house of the Lord!!! The home of Love and Happiness!! May His peace find us all for evah-more!! Hallelujah!"

And so it went for almost two amazing hours, a celebration of God's love mixed together with Reverend Al's take on almost everything under the sun, plus music of all types. Country song snippets, rock song snippets, soul, gospel, an incredibly rich melting pot of the cultural, the personal, and the spiritual. Every now and then the guitar player or that giant of an organ player would snake in underneath Al's diatribes, twinkling or picking out the tiniest of grooves and Al would direct you from the word he was talking and reading into a full-blown song. Al roamed the church as he sang, making eye contact fearlessly with even the confused looking German tourist sitting in the back row. Vas is dis? Every now and then one of those women in the front, moved by the spirit, would jump up, raising their hands, and hat covered heads to the sky, dancing in the pews, aisles, and wherever else the Holy Spirit directed their beautifully high heeled feet. We spent most of the two hours standing, dancing, and clapping along as Reverend Al channeled Jesus in song, sermon, and prayer unabashedly.

Power: Jesus Will Fix It

Once the riffing was done, it was sermon proper time. The word was drawn from Psalms 21, a short chapter with only 13 verses, a celebration of David's trust and faith as well as God's goodness. For the most part, it was all good news from Reverend Al with one little "spare the rod, spoil the child" side road that had Lila up in arms briefly. I'm not sure her kids were spoiled, but they wore strictly Brooks Brothers clothing and had credit cards since they were 18. They seemed to be great sons and already designated for worldly success, so my hope became that when they were successful they keep in sight that while life may have been handed to them on a slightly silver platter, there are others in the world who can barely get a cafeteria platter. Lila may have turned out to be a flighty lover, but there was never any question that she was anything other than a rock solid mom.

Al's final act was to call forth those in need of prayer. Several parishioners lined up in front of him at the side of the stage. Each request elicited a unique response, sometimes an appeal to God to fix or at least make the problem understandable, but occasionally a mere declaration "Here is what God put in my heart for you", and Al bursting into a song relevant to the person's situation. I can't think of a better way to spend three hours.

As we waited on John Samuel to pick us up, Lila, the open and upfront personality, struck up a conversation with one of the dressed up women who asked where we were from. Lila fielded the question and started a conversation.

"He's from Virginia," Lila said, nodding towards me, "and I'm from LA."

"Did y'all enjoy the service? Did you know the Reverend's music before?"

Lila chimed back, "Oh yes, he's a DJ and I've been listening to Al's old music for the last couple of weeks." And then she had to ask the Lilaesque question. "That Reverend Al also was hot when he was young, huh?"

I saw the dressed up woman's demeanor change as she leaned to Lila and whispered in her ear. A second later, she was, like John Samuel, offering us to come on down to the Peabody and show us a personal tour of Memphis. Lila took her number just as our taxi showed up.

It turned out that the woman told Lila that it was rumored that she and Reverend Al were lovers. We had a laugh about that as John Samuel drove us back downtown, and wondered how many unsuspecting tourists had been descended upon by that woman and scammed by that woman and her private tour of Memphis.

Part of my pre-trip research was to get the scoop on the best Memphis Barbecue joints, so on this beautiful Sunday afternoon, John Samuel dropped us near Central BBQ, adjacent to the Lorraine Hotel, which forever lives in infamy as the spot where Martin Luther King was murdered. It's not the best part of the city, but truthfully, once you get out of the museums, downtown, and Beale Street, it's hard to find a good part of Memphis. Lila was a barbecue lover and connoisseur.

She designed the barbecue at Central Worthy, so there we sat, satiating ourselves with pork, Memphis barbecue sauce, beer, and pro football. A short walk through a dicey area got us to the trolley stop, then after a couple of turns around the same block we figured out where the Peabody was and went up to our room where we continued to satiate ourselves as well as watching pro football. As much as I love football, the idea of having sex while football is on TV...well..it just never ever occurred to me. Maybe when your ex-husband is a major TV sports executive, I don't know. Perhaps that's just what happens when a woman's divorce therapist is a sports psychologist by trade. One man's Marvin Gaye is another man's Michael Strahan, that sort of thing. Lila's man, Dr. Allouette, was the team psychologist for the Seattle Seahawks and could take at least partial credit for the team's first Super Bowl win, which would come the following February.

For the next three nights, we would hit Beale Street every night, searching for the blues and a little Stax soul. We found the blues at Blues Hall, Rum Boogie Cafe, and the Beale Street Tap Room. Blues Hall, in particular, was about as authentic as it comes. Dirty, dank, with no seating, stage so crooked it looks like a small mountain range. As the week wore on, the blues got better, and deeper, starting Sunday night with Dr. Feelgood and his blues band.

The good doctor wore two slings full of harps, a variety of sizes, keys, etc. He looked like Clint Eastwood in one of those spaghetti westerns, except for the fact he was about five foot, three inches, black, and 75 years old. Still, as he pulled out weapon after weapon from those slings, each tone getting richer, more melodic. His band looked like practicing heroin addicts, but they could play the blues like banshees. They were the STILLEST rockin' band ever, barely moving as they nailed note after note. Let's face it, when you have to have a 75 year old front man...

By Tuesday night, we were down with the smooth sounds of Earl The Pearl. OK, not so smooth, just the right degree of roughness. Earl might actually have been five years younger than Dr. Feelgood and he played guitar, a mean sitting guitar. We actually found a little soul at BB King's, which became our favorite hangout due to the excellent ribs, the constant music, and a saucy young bartender named Abby who took a shine to us when we hit the bar the afternoon of our Graceland trip. Lila, dressed in a jean jacket and funky red sneakers, went out to the street and befriended a 13 year old street acrobat, causing Abby to proclaim Lila as "jazzy"...and cool.

Ribs? Oh yeah, remember Lila was a connoisseur of barbecue. As such, she felt obligated to try the short ribs at virtually any restaurant that offered them, anytime of the night we were there. I watched her eat ribs, by hand, lick her fingers, and drink wine for three straight nights. She had this finger dancing thing she did. Eat the ribs, lick the fingers, drink the wine, then suddenly her hands would move back and forth to the beat of the music. Soon, the first finger of each hand would be pointing and going back and forth to the beat. Then it wouldn't be too long before Lila would look at me in a certain sleepy-eyed way and that little magic tongue of hers would come literally darting between her pursed lips, moving from one side of her mouth to the other. That was my sign it was time to walk back to the hotel. Whoopie time!!!!

September 30, 2013: Graceland

Driving I-40 between Nashville and Memphis is like driving any other interstate, at least it was in May of 2012 when I drove it. When the Music Road signs started appearing, for me there was a little time displacement that occurred. I remember turning on the radio and searching deep to find the stations that were playing the real stuff, not Top 40 country, classic rock, pop Top 40 nor any of the other canned genres of music. Suddenly you're back in the late 1940s, or early 1950s. That must have been around the time a young Elvis Presley, situated between the white country, bluegrass sounds of Nashville and the decidedly black sounds of blues and soul that were emulating from Memphis, was also listening. Elvis is also brought up with a deep love of the hymns and church songs that permeate his personal culture. It's easy to picture him switching stations between Hank Williams and Memphis Slim, taking it all in and creating his very own musical American melting pot naturally, without calculation. Take those sounds of country heartbreak, boastful blues, and uplifting gospel and inject them into a ridiculously good looking, coordinated hip gyrating white boy with a voice like an angel and you've got an American Icon like no other.

It seems a little cheesy that Graceland is on Elvis Presley Boulevard, at least until you see it and realize that Graceland IS Elvis Presley Boulevard. At first glance, Graceland seems a little like any other tourist trap, a virtual mall of Elvis related shops and restaurants across the street, the mansion surrounded by a steel bar and brick fence with, of course, the famous "musical scales" fence opening and closing as the buses enter the property. I've been to Graceland twice, once on a solo trip with the eventual destination of Oxford, Mississippi and Darin's graduation from Ole Miss, once with Lila, who turned out to be the perfect person to visit Graceland with. Lila's mother, a huge Elvis fan, had actually taken a seven year old Lila to see Elvis. Not in concert, at the Marion Train Station when the King's train went through on the way to Charlotte. Lila told me how they strained to glimpse him as he waved through the window at all the gathered fans.

Apparently, Elvis even hopped off for a minute to greet fans and sign autographs, but getting anywhere close was arduous at best, so they only saw the very tip top of the King of Rock n' Roll's greased-up pompadour in the distance. Lila read an Elvis biography by Greil Marcus called "Mystery Train" before the trip, so she knew a few Elvis facts that even I didn't know. Sports psychologist for a therapist. Everything sort of becomes a competition, you know. Truthfully, though, that was one of the things I loved about Lila. She constantly kept you on your toes, even as she occasionally stomped on them.

The first thing you notice about Graceland is that despite a constant flurry of activities, shops, buses going around, tourists, and Elvis music everywhere, despite all that it is a very peaceful place. In a way, it's like a constant ongoing wake for Elvis. Especially when you have those headsets, they give you for the audio tour with Lisa Marie talking in your ear. Another thing is that even though it's called a mansion, it doesn't exactly resemble any traditional concept you might have.

Heck, the Jungle Room alone establishes that 100% shag carpet covered, ceiling and all, cheesy green and yellow stuffed plastic chairs. Kmart style luxury. The decor, the stories Lisa tells, the golf carts they rode around the property, even the cookbook with its primo fried peanut butter and banana sandwich recipe, everything screamed white trash made good. Touring Graceland, you actually wonder a few times if that's where the idea for the Beverly Hillbillies came from. The car collection...I mean, two Stutz Bearcats...the jets...any type of vehicle that could be dreamed up. Before the King ended up face down on those bathroom tiles in 1977, Elvis had them all. The man knew how to rebel against a poverty stricken upbringing like no one before or since. Through it all is Elvis music, rockabilly, country, hymns, and pop, an incredible amalgamation of American music. If you made that drive down I-40, as I had in my first trip to Graceland, your mind starts connecting the dots and the man's accomplishment hits you right between the eyes. It wasn't like this before Elvis, even music was segregated before the King. Walking through Graceland, you're transported back to the 1960s or early 1970s, but once you sense what Elvis actually did, you are way back in the world of the 1950s.

As if to remain true to the ongoing Elvis wake concept, the last stop is the family cemetery. Elvis, his Dad Vernon, his mom Gladys, his grandmother, and even his stillborn twin brother Garon, all lay in their eternal rest beside the King, constantly primping for millions of photos and movies being filmed daily. The cemetery is the only place in Graceland where you actually fight a crowd.

Reflecting on Elvis' actual life, how disconcerting it must have been to him being born into and growing up in that innocent world, then experiencing the juxtapositional lifestyle he found himself in from the time his music hit it big until he departed the planet on August 16, 1977. Here was a guy whose first recording "My Happiness" was a cheap acetate made for $4 to give his mother Gladys as a birthday present, who sang "Can't Help Falling In Love" to a grandmother in Blue Hawaii. A church singer, a good Christian boy shoved by fame into a world of sin, and temptresses, a world where nothing he desired was beyond his reach. It must have been such a relief to him when he met 15 year old Priscilla, he may have even saw the possibility of restoring innocence. But it wasn't to be. Instead, the same world that swallowed him up chewed up his marriage and spit out poor Priscilla like a bad seed. I thought about Grace at 19, her innocence and her ultimate infidelity. Was she hoping for some restoration of that lost innocence when she stalked me at that reunion in 1999? Was I? Elvis after Priscilla was never really the same. He just gave in, long before he gave out. The Elvis of "Love Me Tender" was swallowed up by the Elvis of "Suspicious Minds". I thought about Lila and I, our long relationship, friendship, and occasional romance would certainly belong to more to the realm of the Elvis of "Suspicious Minds." That notion would be rearing its ugly head soon enough, but when we visited Graceland, not a red flag was in sight.

October 1, 2013: Suspicious Minds

On the final day of our trip, Lila and I visited the Stax Museum as well as Sun Studios. While nothing was to compare to the sublime experiences that Reverend Al and Graceland had provided us, at Stax we explored the Memphis Soul Sound of Otis Redding, Booker T. and the MG's, Eddie Floyd, and Isaac Hayes amongst many artists who had taken the blues of the likes of Albert King and given it a unique Memphis soul spin to create the Stax Sound, precursor and influencer of the coming Motown Sound. It was a studio converted to a museum, complete with videos, original outfits, studio stacks displayed, and a fun ride. At Sun Studios, it was very cool to be given a photo opportunity with the same mic that Elvis had used, a fact that allowed us to overlook a pretty young lady that was possibly the world's worst tour guide.

The Peabody was a great hotel, although we never saw the famous duck walk. Doubt that it would have been more entertaining than the pip voiced Southern gentleman who introduced the walk twice a day, plus it was fun to miss just to hear Lila say in that southwest Virginia accent, "We missed the fuckin' ducks!" Lila could cuss like a sailor and was extremely creative in the use of the F word. Amazingly so.

Lila and I spent any spare time in the room, consummating that fruit of late night phone sex that I was talking about. Phone sex had never been a part of my repertoire until Grace and I met again, she in Southeast Florida and I in Virginia. The key to great phone sex is your ability to be uninhibited. You have to be confident enough to say something that you believe will totally shock your partner. Nine times out of ten not only is it NOT going to shock them, but rather it will drive them to higher and higher levels of perversity trying to create their own shock moment. That's when you're driving the BMW of phone sex. Both parties see how far they can go. It takes imagination...and a nice voice helps. I had been in radio and was a highly experienced as well as accomplished phone sex participant. If only there was a way for a male to make a living at it.

Beginning in early September of 2013 and up to our late September trip, the time period of the second (or third) coming of Lila, she and I spoke nightly, sometimes with phone sex, sometimes not. We emailed daily, flowing romantic emails from me to her every morning, occasionally romantic responses from her, it was a golden month, the best month ever in the history of my relationship(s) with Lila. To read my emails and her responses, you would be sure these are two people on the same track. A Mystery Train straight to happiness, bliss, my personal reward for all the rain that Grace had brought down on my life. Remember what I said about God giving us everything we ever want before he drops the hammer on us? I was being set up for the fall. More appropriately setting myself up for the fall.

What about that one red flag? That little teeny tiny one? Well, that appeared one afternoon during one of our private moments when Lila, in a full orgasmic frenzy, made the out-loud inquiry of "What's the next person gonna do?" Next person? This is not exactly the sort of confidence building exclamation once expects a woman to make in the middle of an orgasm, you know? At least there was no Eagles music playing.

October 2, 2013: Hello Mr. O'Grady

On Wednesday morning, we shared a cab to the airport, had breakfast and said our goodbyes. As we ate, I began to notice the distance in Lila's eyes. I saw it, but I didn't want to, so I ignored it, of course. If I had paid closer attention, I might have realized the look on her face that Wednesday morning in 2013 as being very similar to a look she carried around most of the late autumn of 1973.

When I got to my gate, I texted her. "Is it OK to say that I miss you already?" She texted back right away, "corny but ok." As I look up from the text, over in the corner I see a leprechaun sized figure sitting there. I look around at everyone else in the boarding area to be sure that I am, in fact, hallucinating. Since no one else appears to be disturbed by seeing a tiny little Irish guy with a scraggly red beard sitting there grinning, I assume I am. Meanwhile, the imaginary leprechaun is smiling mischievously in the corner and looks straight at me, then begins waving the tiniest of red flags back and forth. Faintly, I can hear the little bastard singing *Hotel California*.

Chapter 15

Thieves in The Temple

For some stupid reason, it never occurred to me that my first view of California, specifically LA, would be through a tiny 737 window and partially blocked by a jet's wing. Duh! In fact, the view would actually come from the tiny window on the other side of the aisle from my seat, thanks to the sleeping lady beside me who had her shade pulled all the way down. Doesn't she realize I'm a friggin' tourist?

Being the music fanatic that I am, I had a vision, a vision of LA, of my personal entry into what I considered a Mecca that spurned glorious visions of Laurel Canyon, Joni Mitchell, Crosby, Stills, Nash, and even the Eagles... OK, maybe not so glorious of the Eagles! I pictured myself driving through the desert, perhaps stopping to spend a quick night at The Joshua Tree Inn, where one of my biggest musical heroes, Gram Parsons, staged his departure from the planet. Maybe even stay in old Gram's room, the notorious Room 8, where I would certainly be visited again by his forever 26-year-old apparition. The next morning, I would arise and head down that desert highway to the end of the line. As the desert ends, I emerge from the tiny two-lane desert highway to the freeways and sprawl that is Los Angeles, laid out before me like a vision of Babylon rising from the sand of the desert and standing mercilessly between me and the blue Pacific. I had the merciless part correct anyway. Mercy was nowhere to be found in the City of Angels. Pity, yes, mercy, uh-uh.

My dream, my vision, of LA was nowhere to be found that Sunday morning when I strained my eyes to see through the tiny windows of that 737. It all happened so fast that we were on the ground before I realized that a piece of my own mythic history had been peeled away like the first strip of a banana skin. It was only the beginning.

But wait, I'm jumping ahead of myself here. What about Memphis? What about the imaginary leprechaun waving the tiny red flag?

Early October 2013: After The Thrill Is Gone

In the days that followed Memphis, the distance between Lila and myself turned out to be far more than the 2,500 geographical miles that separated us. Heck, that was nothing. I could leapfrog that distance with the sound of my voice, with my ability to weave words sexually or non-sexually. All those days of watching Oral Roberts and soapbox preaching in my grandmother's living room paid off. The fact that old Oral turned out to be a charlatan didn't escape me either, especially in that rearview mirror.

Turns out that imaginary leprechaun packed up all his little red flags and hopped on that plane back to Charlottesville with me. After speaking almost constantly for over a month and spending four nearly perfect days together in Memphis, I didn't hear a peep from Lila the entire first day after we got on our respective flights to opposing coasts. Finally, around 1:30 am, with my brain and heart imploding, I picked up the phone and punched in the 310 area code. It was a sleepy-voiced Lila on the other end of the line. I heard myself talking, not sure if I was in control of my words or not.

"Hi. I hadn't heard from you, I just wanted to be sure you made it home OK". Liar. That's not what you're thinking. Inside you're saying why the hell haven't you called me? We talked every night for over a month, and we just spent four perfect intimate days together. What is frigging up?

"Sorry, I fell asleep. I'm fine." Then silence. Dead silence, killing me silence.

"OK, well I'll let you get back to sleep, I was just worried." More lies.

"OK, thanks, good night." They say the world will not end with a bang, but rather with the proverbial whimper. As I was to discover an unfortunate multitude of times in the days ahead, that's the way it would be with me and Lila. Or perhaps I was looking for the bang, but all she had to offer was the whimper. That's probably more like it.

I was busy driving ahead, looking through the front windshield to my destination, which I didn't even clearly recognize as neediness, pitiful neediness. If I had bothered to check the rearview, I would certainly have noticed that leprechaun running behind me, frantically waving that red flag.

"Even fools are thought wise if they keep silent, and discerning if they hold their tongues." **Proverbs 17:28**

As the next day passed, like the dutiful puppy dog that I was, the tradition of the morning email soldered on while Lila remained silent on all fronts, as if ignoring me would chase that elephant right out of the room. I'm guessing spending 27 years with a man who intimidates you so much that when you plot your escape, you have to sneak out like a thief in broad daylight doesn't exactly hone your communication skills. I, on the other hand, had no such problem and thus I poured my soul into those morning masterpieces, even though my internal radar was pegging into the red zone. Lila owned me, but she hadn't broken me down yet, so I came up with a plan to extricate the truth from her with laser-like precision and lo and behold, it actually worked.

We flew back to our respective coasts on Wednesday, but even though we talked by telephone Thursday night, it was painfully obvious that something was completely amiss between Lila and myself. In the rearview, it probably would be more akin to something amiss between Lila and herself. By Friday morning, very EARLY Friday morning, like around 4 am, I was composing an email that struck dead to the heart of the matter, delineating the changes in Lila's demeanor since Memphis and concluding with the tone of reconciliation and resignation that she had her life, I had mine, let's love each other without expectation or explanation and see where that leaves us. Sure, like I could handle that when it came to Lila. I even noted in conclusion that I had preemptively checked some late October flights and would be willing to hop on one if the owner of my heart so designed.

I took Dad to the doctor that morning. Lila, upon reading that email, called immediately and, as I sat in my van after the appointment, declared that it was the saddest email she had ever read. She explained she wasn't leaving me in a lurch, a statement so nebulous that it had me googling it later that day. The love of my life was nothing if not obtuse. In the conversation that followed, she told me that she just didn't want to be the sole source of my happiness, even proposing that I search *match.com* for supplementary sources. Yeah, I know. If I didn't, there were plenty of female friends around me who would later clue me into the facts, Jack.

Guess what, Rick! When she tells you to date other people, she's just not that into you. As I said, when someone actually tells you who they are, BELIEVE them. Lila was telling me straight up, this is who I am, this is how it will be, I was rejecting the truth like a FedEx package I wouldn't sign for. The leprechaun is no longer in the rearview mirror, the little S.O.B. She is sitting right in the seat beside me whacking me in the head with that little red flag. Then Lila followed up with the most telling comment so far in this round when she noted my sensitivity to the changes in her demeanor by saying, "I guess I'd better not cheat on you cause you would know right away." Nice comment to be making to a man who just shook the five monkeys out of his ex-wife's tree. My friends, you don't even have to touch the stupid stick. The leprechaun drops the red flag, instead picking up a two by four to whack me in the head with. What is wrong with you, man? I bounce up grinning from ear to ear like one of those weighted Bozo the Clown punching dummies from the 1950s.

'How much better it is to get wisdom than gold! And to get understanding is to be chosen above silver.' **Proverbs 16:16**

By Saturday afternoon, Lila was warming up, even coddling up to the idea of my butt in an airplane seat en route to LAX in late October, texting me at a wedding I was working at a beautiful venue near Montpelier Estate in Orange County, Virginia. By Sunday night, I had not only that flight lined up, but also another one which would take me to LA in late November for the purpose of us spending Thanksgiving together, not cooking a turkey, but rather lounging by the pool at Lila's favorite luxurious desert resort in Palm Desert, California. In route, we planned the stop at Joshua Tree where I would finally get to spend the night in the room Gram Parsons rented the night he decided to depart our earthly companionship in 1973. The 40-year thing was smacking me in the head along with the leprechaun, but somehow I still felt like a baseball team that had gone into the bottom of the ninth down 9 to zip, only to rally for an incredulous 10-9 win. What a trip from that dreary Friday morning to that glorious Sunday night which found not one, but two, planned trips to LA in my bat bag.

Hi, I'm false hope. Can I introduce you to my good friend, false sense of security? As I get off the phone that Sunday night, the imaginary leprechaun has tossed his red flags down and is instead sitting in the corner head in outstretched hands shaking it back and forth in complete disbelief. Even he knew that I was hopeless at this point. Lila had dangled the carrot like a piñata at a birthday party and I wanted that candy, all of it.

In the three weeks that followed and led up to that Sunday morning in late October when I boarded a Virgin America flight from Dulles to LAX, we, or more conclusively I, followed the formula of heartfelt morning emails in combination with late-night phone sex calls. Someone along the line, the two began to intermingle, the sex crept into the emails, the phone sex got more elaborate, and chocolate cheesecake became a sex toy. Where was I headed here? Pretty sure even God was throwing up His hands at that point... you want to go off without me, go ahead, see where that leaves you.

The imaginary leprechaun hung out a while longer, but eventually even he would pick up all his red flags and walk off into the sunset whistling.. Was that "Hotel California?" In a virtual plethora of danger signs that appeared on my personal highway to Los Angeles, California, two incidents stood out like sore thumbs on a Mexican gardener.

The first occurred on Friday morning, a week before I would head to LA. Lila called on the way to, I don't know, maybe Pilates? Heck, it could've been yoga, a massage, or perhaps one of the multitude of tennis matches she played every week. Lila had a plethora of activities that could have been straight out of the script of "Bob & Carol & Ted & Alice" to fill her week. It would be long after I took that awful cab ride to LAX in February 2014 that it would hit me that those activities took precedence over me, even though it would have been clear as a bell to my flag waving leprechaun were he around. By that time, Mr. O'Grady (even imaginary leprechauns deserve names) would be well down the road, having thrown up his hands, like God, at my peculiar brand of self-obsessed stupidity. OK, make it Lila obsessed stupidity.

Lila was her usual good morning world self when she called, excitedly telling me about the crew of Latino ladies cleaning her house that morning. These women cleaned her ex-husband's place every week, then one day later showed up at Lila's place. Apparently, her ex was so boring there was no gossip to share about him. With Lila, they seemed to want to create gossip. As Lila rattled on happily that morning, she interjected one thing that definitely made my ears perk up.

"They've decided I need a boyfriend." I'll let you decide for yourself, my friends, if that particular comment is an appropriate one to make to a man you have actually called your boyfriend, especially one who is about to embark on a journey of over 5,000 air miles for the express purpose of spending time with the woman making the comment. The boyfriend thing had been a point of contention, but it was actually Lila who continued to invoke the term. I just followed along like the obedient puppy dog I was. The truth, painfully obvious, is that I would have gone along with whatever this woman called me merely in the hope of spending a little precious time with her. I couldn't help myself... as had happened so many times before with Lila, my brain took leave of my body and my mouth took charge of itself.

"And I don't suppose you mentioned that you already HAVE a boyfriend?" My ears and the other parts of my consciousness exclaimed a collective "Oh no" the minute those twelve words escaped my mouth. Wouldn't it be great if reality was like a DVR? I could have just backed it up, chopped out that sentence, and reacted silently, the best possible choice.

Unfortunately, that was not a possibility. It was out there now and I would have no choice but to follow down the path. Where it led was to a discussion of PDAs, another term that sent me to Google. What is this? Do they speak a different language in Cali? Lila began to explain that Manhattan Beach, Hermosa Beach, and the ritzy areas of LA, were actually like a small towns. Everybody knew everybody else's business and was into it. I was expressly forbidden on that call to make any PDAs on my upcoming trip. For those of you, my friends, who are as clueless as me to Millennial Speak, it's **P**ublic **D**isplays of **A**ffection. Like Cornwallis at Yorktown, I reluctantly agreed to the terms.

The second telling incident occurred Thursday night, actually the Friday morning before I would board that 737 on Sunday. Lila had told me she was going out with some of her girlfriends that night to the Hermosa Beach Pier.

While the Pier is a wooden structure that extends out into the ocean exactly as you would picture, it also extends back to Beach Drive, the main drag of the Hermosa Beach social scene, which is a plentiful scene to say the least. The part of the Pier between Beach Drive and the Strand, which we easterners would refer to as a boardwalk, is primarily lined with t-shirt shops, surf shops, and, of course, bars. As for the girlfriends, well, that's another story altogether. I have my own thoughts about girlfriend culture, especially the girlfriend culture in this part of LA. Divorced, well-moneyed, usually from alimony, these women plaster Facebook with pictures of themselves and their happy smiling children. What happens to those children while the girlfriends incessantly play tennis, sip Margaritas at the country club, and attend any of a variety of girlfriend social affairs, usually catered and certainly liquored, is somewhat of a mystery to me. I just imagine that babysitting is big business there.

So it was about 2:30 am when my phone rang that morning, night, whatever you call that time of day. I used to call it God time, but the Lord was taking a break from my shenanigans, so I guess at this point it was Lila time. It was my home phone, but the 310 area code and number told me exactly who it was. I picked up to hear that sweet, but spicy southern accent with a slight slur.

"I've been a baaaad girl. I'm drunk and I've been dancing." I mean, seriously, what do you say to that, especially when you are getting on a flight three days later to see this woman? She proceeded to tell me the tale of the evening, which involved a multitude of Margaritas that eventually evolved into Tequila shots, several bars, lots of dancing, a man wearing roller skates and shorts (you picture it, I know what I'm seeing!), and another man who tried to, quoting, "stick his dick in my butt" on the dance floor. Holy Smokes! After this tale of debauchery was fully woven into my fragile consciousness, Lila offered her usual words of comfort.

"We need some real men out here.... men like you!" We? OK, I admit I contemplated the possibility, if only for a second. I probably don't have to tell you this road led to some pretty extensive phone sex. Goodbye, Holy Spirit, hello, holy crap!

Sunday October 27, 2013: California Feelin'

I know what you're thinking. Heck, I'm even thinking it reading what I just wrote. So you didn't go anyway, did you? Come on, you KNOW the answer. Lila OWNS me. I justified, brothers and sisters. I packed up my bag and turned to false hope saying, "Come on, you're going with me, we can beat this thing." Sure.

I even became concerned when the driver Lila had lined up for me showed up an hour late that Sunday morning. John Lennon said it best, "nothing's gonna change my world." In Luke 9:51, the Bible says Jesus was fixed on Jerusalem when His time came. I was fixed on Lila, on LA. Nothing, nobody, was going to change my path. Jesus knew what was waiting for Him in Jerusalem. Rick Trax didn't have a clue. Not that it would have stopped me.

I got to the gate in Dulles early, plenty of time for a cup of coffee. Once I got on the plane, I dutifully called Lila at 5 am LA time to let her know. Hey, she told me to, no way I would ever disobey Lila, right? God? Yes. Lila? Never. She ruled me. I'm being kind to myself here.

Truth be told, I didn't give a whet of thought to the fact that my entry into LA was totally askew. I was so fixed on Lila. I texted her as soon as we hit the ground in LAX. Ever the teaser, she texted back, 'guess I'd better get up.' She told me to head towards the ground transportation, which I did, dragging my bag along behind me. When I emerged from the tunnel, I was surprised to see her smiling face waiting for me. I rushed up to give her a greeting kiss, then remembered the no PDA rule. Seriously whipped, folks. Once we got to the car, Lila announced that we were headed to her church, the Agape International Spiritual Center. They called it that because they couldn't think of a more pretentious name. Lila had said that we might go there first. Actually, it was a choice between church, breakfast, or sex. Naturally, I choose sex, but apparently I lost.

The Spiritual Center of the Universe was located in a pretty normal looking middle class LA neighborhood. To be fair, Lila had sent me a link weeks earlier from a Doctor Oz show that the church leader, Reverend Michael, had appeared on. So if you're keeping score, in this corner, we've got Lila, her divorce attorney from Good Morning America, her therapist from the Seattle Seahawks, and her pastor from The Doctor Oz show. In the opposite corner there's Rick. He was once on local radio in the 253rd largest market in the whole USA. All that was missing from the picture were the Eagles.

12 Jesus entered the temple courts and drove out all who were buying and selling there. He overturned the tables of the money changers and the benches of those selling doves. 13 "It is written," he said to them, "My house will be called a house of prayer,' but you are making it 'a den of robbers.' " **Matthew 21:12-13**

The solicitations started as soon as we got out of the car and continued as we walked our way to the line to the "sanctuary," a term that I use very loosely here. There were vendors everywhere, and those 10 x 10 pop-up tents abounded. Banquet tables filled with literature and donation boxes. Music, stages, everywhere you turned there was a hand outstretched waiting to be filled with cash. The angry Jesus described in the passage above would have had a donnybrook outside of Agape. I mean, you couldn't help but think about it. I started looking around. Are Bob & Carol & Ted & Alice here somewhere?

Eventually, we were ushered into the large sanctuary, ahead of everyone else due to my visitor status, a status which was designated by a wristband that was like those ones that say, yes, I am old enough to drink! Once we were seated, I started looking around at the congregation. The meek, supposed inheritors of the earth, were nowhere to be found. Neither were the poor nor the children. The service started with a smooth-voiced gentleman who sat at the front of the stage for 30 minutes leading not a prayer, but a meditation. The general theme was that we were all one with the universe, a theme I don't exactly remember being in my Southern Baptist handbook.

After that came the choir, the dancers, the music and the spectacle made it feel like you might be on the set of "Hair" circa 1969. Bob? Carol? Ted? Alice?

"Watch out for false prophets. They come to you in sheep's clothing, but inwardly they are ferocious wolves. **Matthew 7:15**

All this hoopla led up to the spectacular entrance of the one and only Reverend Michael to an amazing uproar from the congregation! I mean, we're talking mega rock star entrance, my friends. President Obama would've been jealous.

The good Reverend emerged from the wings wearing a white tunic. Tall, although not by Pastor Wilt standards, fit, handsome, and dreadlocked, Michael raised his arms and hands with double peace signs that would have put Tricky Dick Nixon himself to shame and drank in the tumultuous ovation before launching into what, I don't know. It wasn't exactly a sermon. More like a group therapy session. Or perhaps a pep rally of the soul. Think Joel Osteen without God.

Oh yeah, God. He was nowhere to be found in the words Reverend Michael spoke, more like exhorted, from that stage. Jesus? Not in sight. According to Reverend Michael, the power is all in you. Self-propelling spiritual fulfillment. Prosperity is heavenly bliss. It was quite the spectacle indeed. According to Lila, Reverend Michael must have mentioned Jesus at least once as whatever he said caused her oldest son, a devout Catholic, to walk out of Agape during an Easter service. Lila declined to share exactly what the Reverend said. It must have been awful!

When it was over, Lila asked me the magic question, "Was there anything that bothered you about it?" God gives me one more chance as I hear that voice in my head, "Stand up for me... tell her!" Once again, my brain left the room to take a powder. My mouth takes over of its own accord.

"Nope, didn't have a problem with anything." Pretty sure I heard the sound of running water as the Heavenly Father washed His hands of me for now.

Hermosa Beach: Don't Get Above Your Raising

After we left Agape that day, we headed in the general direction of Lila's new Hermosa Beach digs. In retrospect, the immediate vibe, the aura that was to hang over the entire four-day visit was set that morning. In retrospect, I didn't even need the rearview mirror. It was all happening right in front of me, I was simply in a complete state of denial.

The route took us down Vista Del Mar Boulevard alongside the Pacific, past the power plant, the trailer campgrounds, and a never-ending series of ocean-side parking lots that were mostly empty except for the occasional surfer packing away his board for the day. As we entered Manhattan Beach proper, the road turned into Highland Avenue. More like high falootin' avenue as I got my first true glimpse of the multitude of social statuses that stood between Lila and I. One look at the shops that lined the streets, the cars parked along them, and the few people who were already milling around on this early Sunday afternoon were enough to let me know that I wasn't in Kansas anymore.

Our first stop was outside a small grocery store. Lila told me to wait in the car. No PDA, I remembered. But parking almost a block down the street, so no one could possibly see the shadowy man in the boots and jeans, was an extra layer of security. In that ever-present rearview mirror, I can now see it for what it was. I was being kept under total wraps. 'Twas a little more than no PDA. I was in the no-view zone. I must have sensed something because as Lila walked back to the car carrying a grocery bag, I didn't get out to help with the bag nor open the door for her, actions that were completely out of character with my mannered Southern upbringing and demeanor. Excuse me, sir, could you please step to the back of the bus?

One more stop before we get to Lila's place, a stop at a small seafood shop right on Beach Avenue in Hermosa. Here, I was allowed to disembark the vehicle and actually enter the store. Much to Lila's surprise, we immediately ran into a woman she knew from her second home, the Manhattan Country Club. I clearly remember Lila having that deer in the headlights look as she physically distanced herself from me. Him? Who's he? I thought he was with you. Pretty sure that wherever that imaginary leprechaun was then, he was drinking with his leprechaun buddies and raising a toast to my blind obliviousness.

From there it was on to Lila's... I don't know, what do you call those cracker boxes? Beach homes? Townhouses? We pulled into her bottom-floor garage and I carried my bag up to Lila's second-floor bedroom, then we walked up to the third floor, a wonderful huge open room with a giant flat-screen TV on the wall above the electric fireplace, a dining area, and an open kitchen large enough to have an island with stools in the middle of it. The appliances were all stainless steel. Outside of that, the theme of the entire place was a deep brown mahogany wood. It was everywhere, inside and out. It was a beautiful place, but it did strike me at some point that with all that wood, it was a pretty manly-looking place. The third floor patio was the piece de resistance. The complete front end of the townhouse was glass doors opening to this patio, a superb vantage point to watch the beautiful sunsets over the blue Pacific, which peeked over the flat rooftops of the neighborhood. Heck, I was ready to move in.

Lila and I walked down to a little Greek restaurant off Beach Avenue for lunch, then came back for sex, then walked down to the Strand, came back and had sex. That night, she took me to the Magic and Comedy Club down the street where Jay Leno, still hosting The Tonight Show, did a comedy set every Sunday night, finishing up by trying out some of the material he would be using on that week's show. We had dinner, Lila imbibed multiple glasses of wine, saw the show, and then went back to her place and had sex. I think you're pretty much seeing the pattern of this little visit.

Lila did her best to entertain me, taking me to scenic Palos Verdes, to the opening game of the Lakers season, walking around on Sunset Boulevard, to the amazingly entertaining freak show that is Venice Beach, all the hot spots. I saw the Hollywood sign and rode through the Hills... Beverly that is. I spied the Chateau Marmont, where my musical hero and occasional hallucinatory buddy Gram Parsons spent so much of his time in LA.

Even then, despite my denseness and virtual blindness when it came to this woman, I sensed some underlying conflict. Don't ask me how it's possible to feel distance from someone you're having intimate relations with several times a day, but that's what I felt. Everything went as smoothly as the ocean on a calm day, but underneath those calm waters, even though you couldn't see them, you just knew there were some sharks circling around. This distance manifested itself in a number of ways and, frankly, in the rearview again, despite the stranglehold she had over my heart, I felt some underlying resentment myself at the fact that Lila seemed to look down on my semi-tourist status. I mean, come on, man, I'm a music person, a rock music person, yet this woman made me feel like I should be castigated for being excited about seeing one of my mythic musical destinations.

The real Lila that I hung with for those four days was a far cry from the one that was so fired up when we talked about me visiting LA that first night at the Sky Bar in Charlottesville. That Lila excitedly exclaimed, "We can go to all the music places, Rick!" That's my Lila. She runs hot, she runs cold, but mostly she just runs, especially from me. You have to wonder how this woman could be such a competitive athlete, yet shrink away so quickly when the pressure is on in the stadium of interpersonal relationships. Maybe the famous Dr. Alouette could answer that one. Maybe Lila just couldn't handle the pressure after 27 years with a control freak. I don't know, self-perpetrated victim that I am.

The no PDA rule was actually quite understandable. As I said, this Manhattan Beach, Hermosa area, for all its sophistication, might as well have been Mayberry. Every Aunt Bea in town knew all your business, so her contention that if her sons, who grew up there, were going to find out she had a boyfriend, they should find out from her, was easy to understand. I had to cut her a break on that one. Old college friend visiting from the East Coast, first time in LA, pretty easy to explain. Old college boyfriend walking down the street hand in hand or arm in arm, that was another matter. She gets a pass on that. On some of the other stuff, not so much, especially in that ever-present rearview.

Palos Verde: Don't Think Twice (It's Alright)

The day Lila took me to Palos Verde, we went to a Restaurant called Nelson's that was part of Terranea Resort, a huge, luxurious, wasn't everything luxurious in Lila's world. Terranea was a sprawling complex that dominated a whole batch of the rolling oceanside terrain that was Palos Verdes. Nelson's overlooked the cliffs, featured open-air fireplaces and stunning views, and was allegedly the best whale-watching spot in South Bay. Naturally, the food was delicious and outrageously expensive. We sat outside on one of the porches and ordered our food and drinks. After the waiter left, Lila "gave me permission" to take some pictures, just as a day later she would allow me to take a picture of her at the Fisherman's Wharf in Torrance.

I'll never forget the eerie similarities. Lila looked at me from behind her sunglasses at the outdoor table at Nelson's after the waiter left and she ascertained we were alone. It was almost a stern look, although very matter of fact, almost peering over the edge of her shades. "You can take some pictures now."

The next day at the Fisherman's Wharf, we were randomly walking along the wharf when she stopped and walked over to the handrail, pulled herself together and leaned against the rail. "OK, you can take my picture now."

After Nelson's, Lila took me for a cruise on Pálos Verde Drive South. With the Pacific on one side, the winding two-lane highway snaked through the hills of Palos Verde in a familiar fashion.

"You probably recognize this road, Rick. They have filmed lots of TV shows and movies up here." It struck me how many car chase scenes and just general driving scenes I had seen with the backdrop of these hills, the windy road, the drop off to the ocean.

"I'm taking you to see an outdoor church."

"Cool." One of the things that has always frustrated me about Lila is that she GETS me. She knows how to float my boat and seemed always to delight in my happiness when she came up with a plan that pleased me. If it wasn't for the fact she breaks up with me every other minute and treats me pretty crappy when she does…

The Wayfarer's Chapel was not technically completely outdoors. It actually was enclosed in glass, arch-shaped with rows of beautiful rich wood pews, spotless, and landscaped perfectly. The Chapel, the grounds, and the sublime architectural design felt like a little shaded Nirvana, a perfect spot for meditation or prayer. As Lila and I walked back to her SUV, we passed a huge truck with TV equipment around it and "REVENGE" on ABC plastered all over it. Leaning against the back of the truck, toking on a joint is GP's ghost, wearing a grin that says "what do you expect? It's LA!"

All of the previous incidents, however, paled in comparison to the events of the evening of Wednesday, October 30th, the night before I flew back east. It was my last day in LA so Lila had offered me a smorgasbord of potential activities from which I had chosen to cruise around LA and sightsee. Lila played tour guide, an activity she would later say she deplored. She took me downtown to the Sunset Strip, through the Hills of Beverly, and eventually to the human circus that is Venice Beach. All the while, I sensed that Lila's emotional distance was increasing. Naturally, I ignored it, so it didn't stop us from an enthusiastic roll in the hay before we showered to head out in Hermosa Beach.

It was the evening of the sixth and final game of the 2013 World Series between the Boston Red Sox and the St. Louis Cardinals. The Red Sox led the Series 3-2 going into the evening. Lila had no vested interest in either team, although since the Cardinals had beat her precious Dodgers in the National League Series, she leaned their way. She also just didn't care for the Boston teams, any of them. I had made the mistake of confessing that I was once a Red Sox fan. We decided to head down to an Irish Pub on Hermosa Avenue, Mickey McColgan's, to eat, drink (well, Lila was drinking... a lot!), and watch the game.

The trouble that was going to take place that evening was hinted at as we walked down to the pub when I contested one of Lila's self-improvement suggestions. God knows what it was, and I can't remember, there were so many of them. All I remember was her comment to "Trust me, Rick, I'm your friend, I wouldn't lead you wrong." The friend's emphasis was so strong that I realized she was trying to make that point, although I probably didn't want to admit it to myself. As we watched the game, which the Red Sox won 6-1, wrapping up the series, and as Lila drank more and more, she subsequently became more and more contentious and confrontational about the stupid friggin' baseball game, upset that I claimed no vested interest in who won, which was true. Lila continued to beat that horse senseless all night until the poor animal was staggering around the room like a frat boy at a Saturday night party. The badgering continued when we got back to her house with her eventually uttering one of the classic Lila statements, a statement that just makes me cringe to this day if someone says it. "Own it!" She was talking about being a Red Sox fan, which I refused to own because I wasn't. The conversation bordered on being, no, it WAS ridiculous. Me being mentally and verbally whipped by a semi-drunk woman merely because I expressed no strong ties to any particular sports team. I was beginning to understand why the house was so masculine.

Pretty sure if Mr. O'Grady had been there, he would be smacking Lila with the red flags, just to shut her up. I have to give her credit, though, she knew which head I was thinking with and eventually came over to put herself across my lap and her tongue down my throat.

Then she gave me that same teasing darting tongue come to me look as she had in Memphis and smiled. "Everything's alright." She emphasized the point by pulling up her shirt and pulling my head to her erect nipples. I mean, come on!! End of conversation, end of conflict, goodnight, Vienna.

The next morning, we were up early to get me to my 7:30 am flight out of LAX. Here are another couple of mental notes I made here. First that Lila sat on the small couch across from me, dead in the middle, so I couldn't sit beside her. The other was when I went to give her a goodbye kiss at LAX. We spent four intimate days and nights together, weren't going to see each other for at least a month and she barely pecked me back. She implored me to get out of the vehicle because they "don't like us to park here too long."

Why didn't I call bullshit? Because it was Lila, and, you know, we wouldn't want to take a chance on pissing off Lila, would we?

See, I actually AM aware of what was happening, and I just didn't want to admit it to myself. Or perhaps I was thinking it would change, it was only temporary, and she would come around. She would, but only so she could go away again... and again.

I probably don't even have to tell you the silence that ensued on my first few days back east. It was deader than Bonnie and Clyde. I played my cool this time and kept up the emails. I did a wedding that next Saturday, November 2nd, and got home around 1:30 am. It was just after 2 am the phone rang. She was inebriated pretty well to the max. She had been to The Hermosa Beach Yacht Club, a true dive right down the street from her house. The berating that I had taken just a few days before put on a fresh suit and came after me again with a whole new set of tactics. One particular set of comments stood out like a sore thumb.

"I've been down at that dive bar, the Yacht Club. It was awesome!"

"Great! Glad you had fun."

"I just met like 30 guys."

"And we are telling me this why?"

"That's what was going on... You don't even want to KNOW what I did last night."

So it went. Sick as it is, this led to phone sex. Now I know how all those medieval kings got poisoned. How can you not when the poison tastes just like honey?

November 3, 2013: The First Breakup

By the next day, November 3rd, even my Lila twisted mind realized we couldn't continue down this toxic path. I wasn't completely lost in the desert yet, but my camel was pretty damn sick. I texted Lila in the afternoon.

'Want to talk?'

'I guess so.'

I called right away and was shocked when the first words out of Lila's mouth were, "Tell me what you're thinking." A complete idiot would have taken a second to think about that, but I was more like a devoted puppy dog.

"I'm still here 100%. I'll do whatever I can to make this work." I should have regretted those words the minute they came out of my mouth, the fact that I didn't is simply further proof of my absolute lostness at that moment. I could have sworn I saw Mr.O'Grady parading by the window waving red flags. And over by the kitchen door, it looked like the ghost of Gram threw up his hands in disgust and then swigged down half a bottle in one gulp. I had time to see all this because of Lila's silence on the other end of the line. After a deep breath and matter of fact chuckle, she spoke.

"Rick. I can't have a boyfriend. I just got out of prison after almost 30 years. I at least owe it to myself to date a few people. You'll take this relationship as far as it can go, I can see it in your eyes, I can't do that." We batted the ball back and forth for a while with me finally asking, "If you knew what you were going to do, why did you even bother to ask me what I was thinking?"

After a second she answered, "I wanted to see what you would say." Damn!!! Really? Over the next few minutes, Lila pulled out all the cliches attendant to breaking up. There's no easy way to do this, you deserve better, you name it, she said it. The encyclopedia of breaking circa age 16. Then we hung up. I think I may have called her right back to tell her I didn't ever want her out of my life, because that's a really smart thing to say to a woman who has just kicked you in the teeth.

I stood there speechless in my townhouse living room, not that there was anyone to talk to, at least other than the three cats. At that moment, even that conversation would make more sense than the one I just had. I thought to myself, OK, that's it... Game over.

Really? Come on, you've read this far, you know better.

Chapter 16

Sitting In Limbo/The Late Show

'Stand up in the presence of the aged, show respect for the elderly and revere your God. I am the Lord. **Leviticus 19:32**

Before Lila ever made that late Saturday night call about the 30 guys, before she dropped the bomb on me that Sunday afternoon in very early November, God cast the die that would be my hand for the next year and into the future. Upon landing in Dulles after a completely miserable six hours flying cross-country on a Thursday that was Halloween 2013, I had two messages on my phone. As I strolled through the gate and down the causeway to the shuttle which would carry me to the main terminal, I punched the access code in. I didn't recognize either number. 910 area code? Where in the heck is that? It was one of my parents neighbors. Dad was unable to get out of his chair. Low blood sugar was the culprit. The neighbors had taken him to the hospital with dangerously low counts.

The driver Lila had graciously lined up for me took me straight to my townhouse, where I dodged and ducked the still wandering ghosts and goblins in search of candy and treats long enough to deposit my bag inside, grab the keys to my van, and scurry down the road en route to the Martha Jefferson Hospital on the far east side of Charlottesville atop Pantops Mountain, a location that I would be spending so much time at for the next year that it would become the second home I never wanted.

As it turned out, this would be the easiest round with Dad, sort of like a pre-game warmup. My mother stayed in the hospital with him, he was out in less than a week and able to go home, with no rehab and no assisted living. That was coming in the next round, all of it. By this time next year, I would know more about the state of our medical system for the elderly than the Surgeon General. God was just giving me a preview. Or a warning.

Early November 2013: Sitting In Limbo

Oddly enough, I wasn't completely annihilated by that Sunday afternoon conversation with Lila. Much to my surprise, the sky didn't fall, and the sun didn't stop shining. OK, the birds weren't exactly singing. Lila and I had talked every night for over two months, not just talked, we had pretty much lived together by telephone, happily co-inhabiting that spot in the ether that was between LA and the right coast for hours each day. Well, except for that brief burp when we returned to our respective coasts after the perfection that was Memphis. Beyond our sexual chemistry, apparently so potent that I'm not even sure 30,000 miles could have disrupted it, we shared stories of our lives and families.

OK, rear view mirror time again. In retrospect, each of us gained a little something, perhaps not equally. Lila picked up a pair of sympathetic and understanding ears to the tales of her years behind the prison that was her marriage to a man who by all counts was a classic narcissist. I gained a wind beneath my wings as Lila pushed me in the direction of building and rebuilding the relationships with my parents and children after years of foundering on the rocks that were my one-sided marriage to Grace. The fixer and the thinker. A woman of action and a man of contemplation.

It was the Tuesday after the Sunday Shakedown when my will finally came crumbling down like the walls of Jericho and I sent Lila the text that had been on lined up on my fingertips since Sunday night like Usain Bolt at the starting blocks of the 100-meter dash.

'Can we talk again?'

It was every bit of about ten seconds later when I heard the lilting New Orleans style melody that was Lila's ring in my pocket. It was no small irony that the ring was called The Big Easy.

"Well, that didn't take long!" I exclaimed.

"Is your Dad OK?"

Only be careful, and watch yourselves closely so that you do not forget the things your eyes have seen or let them fade from your heart as long as you live. Teach them to your children and to their children after them. **Deuteronomy 4:9**

Even through my fourth year at UVA, my folks remained involved with my friends, all of whom actually quite affectionately referred to them as Ollie and Bernie. I'm not sure I exactly realized what a blessing that was until Mom and Dad both got down and those same friends, who hadn't seen them in years, inquired in every conversation, how are Ollie and Bernie? It took that long for me to grasp what a blessedly normal family we had, to understand that normalcy was not the RULE in familial relations, that it was in fact as rare as a Dodo Bird at the North Pole. It was only years later when my sister would quip that she had looked around quite a bit in the garden of parental love, that I would realize that our folks were among the brightest of flowers.

It was truly a gift that as I moved through the four, OK, four and a half, years at UVA, my folks remained involved, occasionally throwing picnics, grilling burgers for all my friends, and welcoming them into our family home. The only thing we had to bring was our own beer. Lila had been to a few of those picnics. Even when she pulled out the classic "let's see other people" in college, I kept Lila close. Let's be honest, I just assumed that it would work out. In fact, when Lila and I were an item on Cupid's menu in the autumn of 1973, we would frequently "visit" my mother on weekday mornings, usually right before she would have to take off for work. Sure, Mom, I'll lock up behind us, we'll be leaving right after you...and a brief retreat back to my room and a "rest" on the single twin bed there.

Lila would reckon years later that Mom knew exactly what we were up to. She did, but she was so happy to have her son beyond the clutches of Grace that would have overlooked anything short of a blatant orgy. Anyone but Grace at that point for Mom, so Lila got a free hall pass that she never even knew she possessed. Honestly, so much water had passed under the bridge my mushy brain resided in that I had forgotten those twin bed mornings until Lila reminded me. One thing is for sure, I couldn't blame the stock I arose from for my late life problems. It was solid. I was and am what a buddy of mine would later refer to as a first generation fuck-up!

Even a fool, when he keeps silent, is considered wise;

When he closes his lips, he is considered prudent. **Proverbs 17:28**

I spent the first 10 minutes of that Tuesday night conversation assuring Lila that Dad was recovering. That was easy. Then came the time to lift the veil of the purpose behind my call. I didn't know how to tap dance around it, so I just blurted it out.

"I miss you, Lila. I miss talking to you. I miss sharing my life with you. If friends are all it can be, that's what I'll take, I just don't want you to slip from my life again." The strange thing is that from everything I had been through over the last year, everything that had happened attendant to Grace pulling the rug out from under me to the monkeys tumbling from the tree, the words coming out of my mouth felt natural. I completely recognized the guy saying those words. Over the last year, I had gotten to know him. I liked him.

"Well, can I tell you something? I miss talking to you too." Lila had a few moments of crystalline clarity during this conversation. In the rearview, I would have perhaps been wiser to work with and expand those moments rather than ignore them, which was what I did. It's a funny thing about fear. It's not what we do, but what we don't do that fuels it, that fans the flames into a full blown forest fire. Especially if it's fear of the truth. That's what I had. The erstwhile confident love of my life disappeared and I perhaps gained a glimpse behind the veil of Lila's heart. Who knows, you know? Will the real Lila please stand up?

She didn't know what she was doing. That's pretty much a direct quote, followed up by the confession that she had gone to dinner with somebody she didn't even know the night before. We could talk, she and I, but she would insist we slow way down, say to a crawl. Me crawling around Lila was certainly no problem. I had been doing it for years, in a multitude of directions both to and away from her.

Oddly enough, I was at peace before, during, and after this call. I like to think it was my friend Jesus, perhaps pleased that even after being run over by the freight train that Grace had unleashed, even after having any semblance of trust that remained violated by Lila's constant and ongoing flakiness about our little affair, I was still stepping forward in love, as I liked to call it. I was willing to turn the control over to Him, willing to let go of the worry. I knew that only when we try to control events and people do things really start going haywire. I was happy with hanging up with no questions answered outside of the supposition that Lila would still be in my life. God could figure everything else out from there. I can't remember if I told Lila as such, but for me it apparently passed through one ear and out the other like a strong wind through an open barn.

The next time I would call Lila would be two days later on Thursday night. By that time, she would be cool, stand-offish, and intensely impersonal. I hung up from THAT call thinking the ball was completely in her court and there was no shot clock. That was OK, I could live with that.

November 6, 2013: The Long Run

Meanwhile, life after Grace, and now it seemed after Lila, marched on. In the day bookended by those two Lila calls, I went to a beautiful spot west of Charlottesville called the Old Trail Golf Club for a wedding professionals half-day workshop. For whatever reason, November ended up being the nicest month of the autumn of 2013. Comfortably warm and sunny with the Virginia fall colors shining in the light like the rhinestones on Elvis' white jumpsuit, which, by the way, Lila and I saw at Graceland. Such was Wednesday, November 6th when the event took place in the tiny ballroom of Old Trail. That was when a very attractive, very Italian looking woman with glossed-looking jet-black hair walked up to my front row table and asked to sit down proclaiming, "We've met before. Can I sit here?" I don't really know who you are lady, but the last time I checked I wasn't turning down any nice-looking women who asked to sit by me despite my ongoing residence in the Lala land known as Lila's web. Marie Ferrari not only sat down, but eventually she and I took seats at a table on the sunny patio outside the ballroom to share the post-workshop lunch with the awesome fall colors of the Blue Ridge forming the perfect portrait for midday scenery. Energetic, intelligent, and effervescent, Marie kept the conversation lively. She was entertaining, self-effacing, and highly engaging to the point that it was only in the ever present rearview that I even noticed her personality was similar to Lila's. Instead, I stupidly began to think, maybe this is the next woman like God was lining up candidates like suits on a rolling rack. What about this one? Do you like her? Something shorter, darker? How about this?

Marie, for her part, would be none too thrilled to hear the comparison except for the fact that like Lila, she struck a chord in my soul that guaranteed she and I would be friends for life. As for me, if my lack of self-awareness is not clear to you, my friends, at this point, then come on down to the muddy pit of confusion and wallow around in it with me. I stated early on in this narrative that God has a sense of humor. Well, He must have been up there wryly smiling as I frantically searched for love for my life like a kid looking for the prize in a box of Crackerjacks. I've spent a lot of time talking about how hard it is to distinguish false hope when it parades around as real hope, and there is something almost evil about confusion when it dresses up as clarity. That's when the emperor really has no clothes, that's when he's parading around showing off his new outfit while anyone with a virtual lick of common sense is sneaking away at the first chance to let their snickers emerge into outright laughter.

At the age of 61, I was quite apparently picturing myself as I don't know what, maybe some sort of late-life Romeo. This is one that when viewed in the rearview mirror, stimulates the desire to back up and run over myself. God was on my side, sure, but He wasn't above letting the devil play round with me a little for the purpose of humbling me in the long run (good Lord, that's an Eagles song, see what I mean... irony abounds in this self-righteous scenario).

1 Jesus, full of the Holy Spirit, left the Jordan and was led by the Spirit into the wilderness, where for forty days he was tempted by the devil. 2 He ate nothing during those days, and at the end of them he was hungry. **Luke 4:1-2**

In the actor's workshops that I took, the term frequently tossed about was that you had to be "in the moment". When I performed in the one play that all those six years of workshops led to, I learned the application of that in real life. It wasn't enough to know YOUR lines, even to know your cues, you had to be THERE. Not only there, but aware. You had to know everybody's lines. You had to live that story... every night, five nights a week.

If I had been in the moment in that November, if I had really been aware, been as close to God as I claimed to be, the significance of the number 40 would not have eluded me. The truth is that my will had already taken over, and my desire to control had already taken the wheel away from God, I just didn't know it. The real truth is that even if I had known it, I would have found a way to deny it. I would have called a meeting of the board. False Hope, Fear of Truth, come on in, take a seat, fellows. We're here to take a vote on who is in control, me or God. Who thinks God is in control? Two hands would have shot up right away. Well, that's it, no further vote is necessary. Obviously, God is in control, the board voted.

If the significance of 40 had been in front of me, I would have made the connection that it had been exactly 40 years since the autumn of 1973 when Lila and I first connected. If I had truly been in the moment, I would have further connected the dots and understood that over and over again in the Bible the number 40 is used to signify a time of God's testing, of trials, of tribulations. Jesus was in the desert for 40 days, Moses was on the mountain for 40 days and nights, and the Israelites wandered in the desert for 40 years, it goes on and on like those endless reruns of The 70's Show.

That would have been some nice awareness to have in my hip pocket when Lila started contacting me again that next weekend by text and finally by telephone on Sunday night. A bell would've gone off in my head when she said, "I miss you, I'm not sure why." Perhaps I would have come to some conclusions and taken False Hope's driving privileges away. Wait a minute, this woman wondered aloud in the middle of an orgasm how the next man would satisfy her, and she told me to see other people, she started a fight with me over a baseball game I could have given a rat's rump about, she gleefully told me about meeting men, she unconscionably had me cancel a plane ticket to LA, the freakin' list goes on and on. And now you, Mr. False Hope, are telling me to trust her, give it one more shot, that this is destiny? Hockey puck, hand over those keys now!! That's probably what SHOULD have happened.

If that had happened, then when the phone rang that Monday night, the conversation would have been utterly different. Heck, if that had happened, the phone may have never rang on that Monday night. But it did.

9 Two are better than one because they have a good return for their labor. 10 For if either of them falls, the one will lift up his companion. But woe to the one who falls when there is not another to lift him up. **Ecclesiastes 4:9-10**

It was November 11th.11/11. I can still hear my daughter Amelia saying it when the clock turns, "It's 11:11, Dad, make a wish." Now I had seen the perpetually cool Lila unhinged once. That was back in 1977, when she stood toe to toe with Elwood in the living room of my apartment, chastising him, pointing her finger at him, and eventually bitch slapping him. It was all over the drug deal gone south that he and his buddy had gotten myself and my roommate involved in, the one that nearly got my roomie offed by that Connecticut based mafioso when the "speed" he sold the guy tested out to be basically cold powder laced with caffeine. That was a very controlled unhinging, similar to a SWAT team kicking the door open.

The Lila that spoke when I answered the phone that November evening was nothing like that. That Lila wasn't coming unhinged, she was having a meltdown.

"Rick, you're a psychology major. Can you tell me why I'm so fucked up?" Now I didn't have a clue about the Eagles, the Dolphins, the hit men, or the drug dealers, but even without that, I had met Lila's serial cheating father, who was the perennial snake oil salesman, on one occasion. He didn't like me, it was ironic that a month after that December 1973 meeting, she was telling me that we should "see other people", another term firmly in the top 10 things 16-year-olds say when breaking up. I had pretty much met, or knew the scoop on every man that had been in the boyfriend parade between 1973 and 1978. Trust me when I tell you Elwood was the high point in a series of spectacular lowlights. To say these guys were flawed is putting it mildly. A new car with a scratch on the door is flawed. These guys were train wrecks and Lila was the track, creating an endless series of he cheated on me, so I cheated on him scenarios that plunged all participants into the murky ocean of darkness, distrust, and faithlessness.

While Lila was the one having the meltdown on that call, I was the one who melted. At the first sound of her confusion, her tears, my heart melted like a candle on a picnic table in the sun in 90-degree heat. It wasn't like she purposed that, her anguish was quite genuine, it was just that she owned that pile of muscle and blood that resided in my chest and her tears set it pumping like a steam engine going uphill. I ruminated on these men, the men that had proceeded to become the narcissistic control freak she ended up spending 30 years with, the ones who not only confirmed her sagging self-esteem, but kicked it over and over as she wallowed in it.

Of course, what I tossed aside was my own rumination, my own damage, both self and Grace inflicted. This was my Lila and she finally seemed to need me. I just wanted to rise to the occasion and I stood up completely oblivious to the fact that somewhere behind me were Grace and those five monkeys, gleefully tugging at the tail of my coat as I tried to move forward. Whoa there, buddy, where do you think you're going without us? It was like a patient in the middle of a heart attack performing surgery to remove a cancerous tumor. Like two sick people, make one healthy relationship. Sure!

As I sped forward, the front windshield view was quite clear at the moment. There was Lila, the one permanent resident of my heart and soul, writhing in pain. All I had to do was get to her and revive her. In the rear view, it's clear that if I had just left God in charge he would have taken care of the revival. After all, it was His speciality. In the rearview, I can see myself gripping the reins in a most unhealthy manner with the declaration that I was the one polished gem in the bag of stones that Lila carried around as the men of her past. Rick trying to control, Rick trying to be tangible, Rick turning to God and going, no, I got this, you can take a seat by the bench. Man!!!

I listened as Lila poured her heart out like holy water going through a sieve. "Why do I make these awful choices, Rick? What's wrong with me?" This was a Lila I had not experienced before.

"Honestly, Lila, really none of them were very great guys."

"You're a great guy!"

"Well......"

"And look what I did to you!"

Funny, after all those years of waiting for Lila to take down those walls and invite me into her heart, when she finally did my selfish side took over without me even knowing it was in the room and I totally missed all the collateral damage from the blow that Grace and the monkey tumble had delivered to my fragile ego. I completely missed the neediness that was behind my attempts to subtly control and direct the situation.

What I did do right was be there, and listen, perhaps too sympathetically, but I was still under the Love banner that had been raised under my friend Jesus' tutelage during the fall from Grace. Sadly, when Lila cried "I'm sorry", it was like music to my ears when it should have been a call to action. Some kind, any kind of action. I threw out the lifeline, but still tried to pull the victim into the boat of my choosing, my needs. Eventually, the conversation progressed to the point where Lila uttered, "One more thing... I love you." That was it. The pinball machine in my heart went on tilt!

"I love you too... and I always will."

"You WILL? Do you promise? Even if you meet the girl of your dreams, you'll still be my friend?"

Here's where a simple heartfelt yes would suffice, but False Hope and it's little brother Fear of the Truth decided to speak for me and inform Lila that I would never, ever meet anyone like her! Three hours after it started, the therapy session was over. Satisfied, still calm and cool, I totally zoned out to the fact that I was trying to control every single part of the session, I turned in. How pleasing was it to my ego to get up in the middle of the night (hey, I was 61, and sleeping straight through the night wasn't even on the radar screen anymore!) and read an email from Lila on the front of my iPad screen.

'Hi. Hope you are sleeping like a baby with the cats. No joke, I swear. Thank you for being an amazing friend. When I said I love you, I do. Lila '

Late November 2013: Woman Comes And Goes

And so the dance continued, Lila leading the orchestra and me following along. Anywhere. Anytime. She was my singer, and I was her song, sure, but she changed the arrangements anytime it suited her. I don't even think she meant to. She just followed her heart wherever it led her and I chased along much like I followed her to her dorm that first night when we met back in 1973. Cancel my flight? Sure. Wait while you decide if you actually want to see me as opposed to making me a permanent voice on the end of your phone line? Sure, whatever. Go to the desert on the trip which we planned to take together and have me living it vicariously through the telephone line? Not a problem. I'll do that.

I did give up the biblical emails, I am sure there's some rearview significance to that. The nightly phone calls continued, sometimes for hours, sometimes for minutes, sometimes sacred, occasionally profane, that is, if you considered two hours of solid phone sex profane. Heck, at the time I considered it sublime, apparently oblivious to the fact that I was doing the work and she was having the fun. OK, it wasn't really work.

As November rolled on, Lila's Thanksgiving trip to Palm Desert approached like a dust storm in the Sahara. I was playing so many roles I felt like Sally Field in that TV movie *Sybil*. Lover, best friend, therapist, psychologist, and even relationship coach. Oh yeah, that last one was a killer. Nothing like hearing the woman you love tell you about her obsessions with the handyman, the neighbor, and the Fabio look alike that runs the Italian bakery. Somewhere my little leprechaun, Mr. O'Grady, is wearing a Rat Pack tuxedo and singing *What Kind Of Fool Am I* while snickering uncontrollably.

In Lila's defense, she was being pretty honest or at least trying to. On one occasion, I bemoaned the fact that the evening of the rival football game between Virginia and Virginia Tech was going to be cold, with temperatures projected into the mid-30's by game time. Lila had a simple solution, stated matter of factly.

"Find a hot woman to take along."

Of course, her defense leaves me with none. I told you I was looking at other men, I told you to see other women. Heck, not even Perry Mason could've gotten an acquittal in this case. BAM! Down comes the gavel. Guilty of, I don't know, what? Self-delusion? False hope? Downright stupidity? I promise you I am capable of normal logical reasoning. I actually have a college degree. It's just this one thing that I suffer total blindness about. The captain of the Titanic only missed one iceberg. It just so happens it was a big one. I only have one flaw. OK, two if you count Grace's blindness in there, it's just that it's a fatal flaw.

The week after the football game, Lila took me with her vicariously as she drove into the desert for Thanksgiving. Of course, what she didn't take was any remorse for the fact that less than three weeks earlier she had virtually forced me to cancel my Virgin America flight to accompany her. Again, in the rearview mirror, the Grace experience certainly conditioned me to a total lack of remorse from the women in my life. Damn, did I just accidentally kick you in the nuts again? Whoopsie daisy! You see, I had made the decision somewhere along the line, sometime in the middle of Grace Heartbreak Time, to ALWAYS err on the side of love. I took C.S. Lewis to heart. I was determined not to "wrap it carefully round with hobbies and little luxuries; avoid all entanglements. Lock it up safe in the casket or coffin of your selfishness." I would take my chances. I STILL would. This is one case, the only case, where I would turn around and smack my leprechaun buddy with his own red flag. For all my blindness, I knew there was only one way to draw my friend Jesus back to me when I got lost in the wilderness. Err on the side of love... always... without question.

20. Walk with the wise and become wise, for a companion of fools suffers harm. **Proverbs 13:20**

Once Lila actually arrived, she took me with her everywhere. Well, maybe not everywhere, but she spent a lot of time on the phone with me while she laid around the pool and she did call me from the hot tub once. That was some very interesting phone sex. I actually had to take into account exactly how long I could hold my breath underwater. I finally realized what the hell, it's phone sex. I can hold my breath as long as I need to. Lila took me to the bar with her a couple of times, but only a couple. She spent so much time wishing I was there that I finally reminded her that I would have been if she hadn't made me cancel my ticket. Oh yeah. That. Whoopsie daisy! Of course, I know you. My friends would be disappointed in me if I didn't admit that I also self-flagellated over the timing of the ticket cancellation. This is all my fault. Why didn't I wait a few days? I should have known she would change her mind, what's wrong with me?

Over the course of Lila's five days in the desert, one particular event stood out. As always, it was an event which was so much clearer in that rearview. Lila had told me about a woman, the sister of one of her LA friends, who she was supposed to meet up with in the desert. She bemoaned the fact that this woman wanted them to go to a popular hookup spot called The Nest, where she apparently hoped to run into her ex. Yeah, I know, really? Do you want to go to a hookup spot to see the man who has already professed to NOT want to hookup with you? For the purpose of what? Watching him hookup with somebody else? Actually, perhaps this woman should have been meeting up with me. She certainly seemed my match in terms of utterly stupid logic and misplaced hope. Lila, for her part, didn't want to go there, saying she hadn't gone to the desert for that sort of thing, it would be different if I were there...la la la, la la la.

I, of course, simply said don't go, well aware that the likelihood that my missive would be ignored was in the 98 percent range. And, of course, I was correct.

At first, Lila texted me incessantly after going into The Nest. 'This is the weirdest place I've ever seen. I'm fighting off men.'

'Help.' She described a meat market scene that sounded much like the beach bar that Grace and Darla had taken me to that Sunday night in Deerfield Beach. I imagined the men were a little upscaled, less open collar next chains, more pulled up collar Izod, but I'm sure the concept and purpose were the same, a bunch of horny old people with sizable wads of cash.

Finally Lila texted me 'Ice has been broken, I just danced.' I shot back something completely flippant, less Lila should know I was semi-consumed with a jealous bone. I had learned almost 40 years ago that any admission of potential jealousy to Lila was the psychological equivalent of pouring gasoline on a fire to douse it!

My flippantness earned another reply from Lila, an apparent attempt to see if I was still paying attention.

'Only The Lonely Roy Orbison'

'Great song,' I replied.

Then after that… silence, dead silence. Suddenly my heart, my spirits, and my hopes took on the shape of a deflated beach ball. As I heard the air rushing out of the ball, it sounded remarkably like monkeys tumbling from a tree. Not a word, a text, an email, or a peep of any kind for the entire night. Make that the entire sleepless night. Not a wink. Finally the next day, just as I was getting to my weekly kibitz with my new friend Marie Ferrari, I got a text from Lila explaining that she was sorry she didn't call because her cell battery was dead and she accidentally hooked it up backwards. When we talked later she explained how she had left and taken a cab home at 11:00 from what she described as a very weird scene. As we already know, the synaptic reactions in my Lila obsessed mind just didn't connect correctly when she was anywhere near the thought pattern. This was my excuse for believing a woman who had described the craziness that was her life in Miami when she described what was by all accounts a normal middle aged hookup spot as strange.

Note that since then, I have tried and tried to hook my iPhone up backwards and, apparently, I'm not smart enough to do it on purpose, a mistake that Lila made by accident. No assumptions, just observations, my friends, the most astute of which was my own willingness to accept whatever Lila said as truth without question, well, except for the ones that kept me awake all night. Those remained unspoken because, as we have noted on multiple occasions, the mere thought of incurring Lila's disdain by holding her accountable struck fear deep in my soul. What escaped me completely in that front windshield was the fact while staying awake all night because Lila didn't stay in touch didn't say a thing about her that she hadn't already proclaimed both in words and actions since that first weekend in Charlottesville in September, it spoke volumes about my own insecurities, not to mention that my old friend False Hope was now wearing a shiny new suit and was calling itself Toxicity.

Chapter 17

Flaw

5 Keep your lives free from the love of money and be content with what you have, because God has said, "Never will I leave you; never will I forsake you." 6 So we say with confidence, "The Lord is my helper; I will not be afraid. What can mere mortals do to me?" **Hebrews 13:5-6**

As November passed into December and the nightly phone marathons continued, Toxicity sat over in a small corner of the room like an uninvited party guest eating all the hors d'oeuvres and drinking all the liquor without anyone noticing. Every now and then, my leprechaun friend would show up waving a tiny red flag, such as the time Lila told me about her 35 year old handyman laying on her bathroom floor while she had impure thoughts about him. I can still hear that sweet Southern accent.

"Wouldn't THAT be a nice early Christmas present?"

Ever the comforter, Lila assuaged my concerns by telling me that if she was really going to do something she shouldn't be doing, she wouldn't tell me a thing about it. Ever the trusting fool, I completely failed to make any connection between that comment and her dead battery in the desert. Not that it meant anything, it was just that Lila seemed convinced, or at least sought to convince me that I would lose interest in her if she wasn't "bad". I played along like the good puppy that I was, but the truth was that nothing would have made me happier than a tamed Lila opening up her heart to me. We could then save the bad girl for the bedroom where she belonged.

There was also the night when she called me after going to a friend's traditional Christmas party, describing how she could tell how all the husbands were lusting after her with a "you can tell they want you" stance, all while she occasionally retired with the two young guys that were her son's friends to take straight Tequila shots (she counted five). Needless to say this led to... wait a minute, why am I even telling you, you know the drill at this point.

Sometime during this time frame, Lila first told me about the Miami days, not the Eagles, but she did make mention of a former Miami Dolphin snorting cocaine off her bare arm in addition to a plethora of other lovers and one-night stands during that era. At this point, my leprechaun has again sauntered off into the sunset while Toxicity is in the corner drunk as a skunk from my liquor.

Lila hosted her entire family over the actual holiday, which led to a mountain of phone calls, many in late night when her 81 year old mother turned in and her 20 something sons were out on the town, or more appropriately, the Pier. Remember the Pier? She seemed to be using me as some sort of safe harbor from the storms that her familial relationships seemed to bring upon her, as if I was her personal Tahiti and the family was Captain Bligh. She loved them, but all together they seemed to overwhelm her. I happily served any lowly spot she awarded me with. Meanwhile, Toxicity has awoken from its slumber and is now raiding the fridge and the liquor cabinet. Yep, she owned me. Maybe she didn't even want to, she would perhaps have rather traded me in on a newer model, but she owned me.

Then, sometime a few days after Christmas, Lila's family was gone. It was December 26th when she packed her mother and her youngest son on flights back to the cold East Coast. She called me on the way home from the airport. The change in her demeanor was immediate, the distancing from my affections was obvious. Imagine a warm winter day, a shirt-sleeve kind of winter day. Suddenly, a cold front moves in and what was once a breeze immediately evolves into a wind, an arctic one at that. It wasn't the words she said, it was the ones she didn't. It was the timbre of her voice, the sharpness of the words that were once rounded, soft, and inviting. Actually, the conversation didn't change much, aside from a noticeable decline, making that a virtual elimination of the sexual innuendos that Lila and I had been bandying back and forth like one of her tennis balls for almost two weeks. I don't know, friends, I had known this woman for over 40 years, I was well aware of her idiosyncrasies, her sometimes inexplicable need for space, her inescapable need to play the bad girl... then the good girl. This was different. We had talked about me visiting her in January. Heck, it seemed to me like a great time to be in LA, while everyone on the east coast was freezing their patooties off.

Maybe once the last remnant of her family cleared the runway at LAX, she started to feel the pressure. Honestly, I was still pretty cool and accepting at this point, willing to work with whatever Lila offered me, which wasn't much over those last few days of December of 2013. People in her life who had names before became "a friend of mine". Social gatherings that were once described in detail became immediately nebulous and were hinted at with implications there was something more going on. Girlfriends with husbands and names suddenly evolved into "some people coming over to cook burgers and watch football". Friends became "company". Lila became an armadillo drawing itself into its hard shell, protecting itself against the threat, which was apparently me.

Slowly, but surely... well, not too slowly, it only took about three days... my cool began to crumble like a graham cracker being made into pie crust. As I started to sink into the quicksand of my own confusion, I noticed my little leprechaun buddy sitting in the corner, shivering as he pulls his collar up from the cold. He's not waving that little red flag. It's in his tiny hand, but I'm guessing he's thinking I'm not worth the effort at this point. He's humming a poppy tune I slightly recognize, but can't name, a slightly obscure Matchbox 20 semi-hit called *She's So Mean*. The significance, which I was completely blind to at the time, would become crystal clear by the end of the next month, January of the year 2014.

December 2013: One Fatal Flaw

Encouraged by Lila, I had planned a trip to Florida to celebrate the New Year of 2014. Let's be honest and this is really, really sad. I took that trip because I wanted to please Lila. I wanted to show her that I could do my own thing. I don't need you honey, I can do my own thing, you don't own me. What a sick, make that lovesick puppy I was. Slowly but surely, I was letting go of my trust in my friend Jesus, trying to take control and in the process, of course, actually spiraling out of control.

In the rear view, this trip was actually the beginning of the end of this round with Lila, although it would take another month, a mountain of phone calls, and another trip to LA for the entire drama to play itself out. Perhaps drama is not the right word, more like Shakespearean tragedy. When I took acting workshops on a regular basis, one thing I noted was there was no question, no mystery, about the way things were headed. It was more of a psychological study of the characters, characters who were oblivious to the impending doom they were about to crash head-on into. Yet to those in the audience, that disaster was about to occur was glaringly obvious. Such it was with the interactions between Lila and myself between Christmas and that miserable early February flight back to the east coast. If only my leprechaun had stayed along for the ride and smacked me in the head. "Coulda had a V-8!!!"

I remember that flight to Tampa on December 30th. My thoughts, in reality, were consumed by the fact that Lila, despite my virtual begging of her to call me the night before the flight, she had not returned my texts or calls. Here, my friends, is where I confess the depth of my illness. I got on the flight thinking she would feel horrible if the flight went down. That would teach her a lesson, once and for all. WHAT??? I wish I was kidding, but that thought actually passed through my obsessed brain. Really, Rick? Sadly, yes indeed. It did. Heck, Dr. Phil wouldn't be able to cover the depths of my mind's sickness over this woman, even in a two-part episode. It would require an entire mini-series.

Here I was on a flight to Florida with the ultimate destination of Orlando for New Year's Eve, where I would welcome the year 2014 being entertained by one of my favorite musicians, Todd Rundgren, in the company of 500 or so people who were into his music at the same level as me, many of whom were already friends of mine, and all I could think about was a woman a coast away who couldn't offer me the courtesy of a phone call I vicariously got on my knees and begged her for.

Actually, as usual, Lila did toss me a bone the next day. It was around 4:00 pm when the text bell on my phone went off. 'Sorry I couldn't call last night. My company didn't leave until late. Have fun on ur trip.' Oh, OK, that explains it. I completely waxed the fact that my final text to her before another sleepless night asked her to give me a quick call no matter how late it was. It totally eluded me that the nature and verbiage of her text was basically saying have a great time, but let's not talk. In fact, when we talked about the trip a week or so previous and I made reference to the fact that I wished she could be with me, Lila had again pulled out the classic line, "Take a hot date."

Irresistible force, immovable object. Me, Lila. I had been around her enough to discern her silence, her distance. Understand, not accept. My mind had a very clear grasp of what was happening when these distant, silent periods occurred. My brain kept sending telegrams to my legs with just three words. Run, Forrest, run!!

It was my heart that kept dragging me back. The heart is the most deceptive of all organs. No matter how many times my mind would say that's it, let's get out of here, my heart would just grab its hand and drag it back. No, things have changed, let's go back there. Everything is cool!!

December 30, 2013: Future

Once you've seen Disney World and Universal, Orlando has to be the most boring vacation spot in Florida. In my two days there, I found myself either walking pointlessly along International Drive by the endless landscape of chain hotels and chain restaurants or wandering aimlessly around Pointe Orlando, the shopping area which housed BB King's, the site of Todd's New Year's Eve show, as well as variety of, you got it, chain stores.

By the day of New Year's Eve, the aimlessness was being broken up by a multitude of appearances by the University of Wisconsin marching band, football team, and a variety of red clad fans who all sounded like they walked straight off the set of *Fargo*. SOOO, you're thinkin' we'll win, eh? In contrast, were the fans of the opposing team in the 2014 Citrus Bowl, the University of South Carolina with their Scarlett O'Hara like uppity southern accents. OK, in retrospect, I have to admit the contrast was pretty damn funny.

These people were everywhere, filling bars and restaurants. Every time you turned a corner, there was another site to behold. The restrained southerners of the Gamecock nation sipping mint juleps and watching the over the top cheerleading antics of the Badger faithful with bewilderment. What the hail are them people doing, Rufus? Every now and then, I would randomly run into one of my fellow Todd fans, designated so by their insistence on spending the entire two days wearing something that bore Todd's name, picture, or some slogan recognizable only to Utopians, as the Todd fans call themselves. It was like a runway fashion show for rock concert vendors.

Oh yeah, Todd. My connection to him went all the way back to 1970, around the time I first hooked up with Grace. His hit was *We Gotta Get You A Woman*, which to this day reminds me of my college breakup with Grace. In March of 1974, Lila, against her will, joined me at a Rundgren concert at the beautiful Mosque in Richmond,

Virginia. Wearing a skin-tight Wizard suit, the bone-skinny Todd accompanied himself on reel-to-reel recorder for the first half of the show, doing the more pop stuff. It wasn't the greatest hit, but I had already been warned about Todd's onstage unpredictability. Then Todd took a break, during which Lila made no pretense of her annoyance at even being there.

Todd came out for the second half with his six-man space rock band Utopia, who preceded to join him in a series of meandering 15-minute pieces that resembled nothing if not Jon McLaughlin's Mahavisnu Orchestra. Lila had come along on the promise of an evening of pop music. Uh oh! I then exasperated matters by occasionally dozing off due to the combination of bourbon and marijuana that I had used in preparation for enjoying my first TR show.

Lila's elbow smacked me so much every time I dozed off that I awoke the next morning to find my right arm covered with tiny bruises until the early 80's. I didn't blame her. Drag her all the way to Richmond to a show she didn't want to go to, where instead of cheerful pop, she is tortured by seemingly aimless synthesized never-ending fusion based pieces like *City In My Head*, the Utopian anthem, then falls asleep while she suffers the torture alone? Who could blame her for punching me? In fact if my leprechaun buddy was there, he would certainly have joined in the fray. What are you thinking, man???

I can still hear her angry toned sweet Southern accent whispering in my ear. "Wake up, don't you dare fall asleep while I sit here and listen to this crap." Reflecting back, I'm sure the evening helped to hammer a pretty solid final nail into the coffin bearing our once promising relationship in that autumn of 1973.

The concert was in March of 1974 so Lila and I were already well into our "seeing other people" phase. Still, as bad as I remember things being, I distinctly remember them being worse after the show.

After that, I still bought all the albums, but left my Todd obsession behind after that show until around 2008. That's when a buddy of mine hooked me into a group of hard-core Todd fans centered around an internet radio broadcast called Rundgren Radio... talk radio for Todd fans. Seriously, I can't make this crap up. The net result was that I ended up attending a couple of premiere shows in Akron during my marriage to Grace. She was invited but declined both times, declaring when she left me that I spent all my money on Todd Rundgren's shows. She meant instead of traveling overseas with her, although I'm pretty sure the hotel rooms would have been fairly crowded with Me, Grace, and her Italian ex-fiancé Guido in there. Now here it was New Year's Eve 2013 and I was in Orlando for a Todd show encouraged by Lila, who would within a month be dropping her third or fourth breakup bomb on me preemptively! Suffice it to say, ladies, that if you are ever dating me and I even mention Todd Rundgren, you just as well start dictating the Dear John letter.

Friendship is born at that moment when one person says to another: 'What! You too? I thought I was the only one. — C.S. Lewis

In Orlando, I was connecting with a bunch of people with a deep appreciation of Todd's music like myself. This was my third event with this group of hardcore. I already had some friends, but by now I knew the ropes, so striking up with folks was relatively easy. There definitely were some over the top people. Check the previous paragraph about the fashion show here, but the vast majority were as nice a group of human beings as you'd ever want to mingle with. Great folks from all over the country, my buddy Byron and his equally wonderful wife Jill, the beautiful and kind Kayla, who actually lived in Boca Raton with her family but was kind enough not only not to like it, but to share her feelings over the shallowness of the Southeast Florida culture.

Beautiful? Yep, that's right. Todd's music attracted people who were smart, well-spoken, open-minded, spiritual, and generally liberal. How else could you follow a guy whose only consistency was inconsistency, a musician who could seemingly write an impossibly addictive pop hook at will, yet choose on a whim to explore every genre from fusion to opera to hard rock to acapella to electronic hip hop, even Bossa Nova, and back again, all thematically woven with human themes both personal and altruistic? Todd's shows were equal parts sublime inspiration and sloppy frustration. We all said it wasn't an official Todd show until he forgot a lyric, an instrumental part, or made a truly awful choice in cover songs. Yet we all loved him, unconditionally. Women, in particular, connect with Todd. Of course, they are all in love with him... for his brain! Women of all shapes, sizes, and social statuses, the one common factor is that they are all very smart. Many are indeed very beautiful, many not so much, many are married to men willing to stay behind while their wives trek off to hang out with fellow hard core fans and, for some, it becomes a family affair.

Helen Elliot was smart, not too awfully attractive, from Atlanta by way of going to UVA and loving Charlottesville, knowing almost as many local musicians as me. She was also an anomaly in the world of healthy-eating liberal female Todd fans. She was a chain-smoking, bourbon-guzzling photographer and videographer who not only didn't seem to know where the edge was, but was also totally oblivious to falling off of it. I met her the first night in Orlando during an open mic night that was basically an excuse for all the Todd fans to gather in a large and open room in the back of BB Kings, which was located on the upper deck of Pointe Orlando, accessible only by a long line of steps that was difficult to negotiate dead sober and an equally challenging escalator.

As I was sitting at a table with some new friends, they noticed the girl at the next table taking pictures of us and called her over. It was Helen. With squinty eyes, round wire rimmed glasses, and shoulder length frizzy reddish hair, she resembled a live version of Peppermint Patty from the Charlie Brown comics. Hilariously, once she opened her mouth, she even sounded like the cartoon character. I was expecting her to call me Chuck any minute. She sat with us for the remainder of the evening. Her conversation started somewhere near the top of the mountain but tumbled down the hill rapidly as she guzzled bourbon on the rocks. She also disappeared about every three minutes to step outside and smoke another cigarette or three.

The host for the evening was an affable gentleman from South Carolina only known as Dolph. In between the brave souls willing to embarrass themselves in front of the crowd, Dolph kept us entertained with a rousing group of singalong classics, everything from Jimmy Buffett to Neil Diamond. Todd's bass player, Kasim Sulton, came up and did a brief acoustic set, the highlight of the evening. Eventually, the Todd house DJ took over and people filled the floor dancing and singing to songs that while great, had about as much beat as a dripping faucet. It was hilarious!

As the evening drew to a close, I took note of the fact that poor Helen Elliott was having serious trouble simply negotiating her chair away from the table to stand up. I mean, number one, I am southern, number two... well, the Jesus way was my way, at least I thought it was, so I offered her a helping hand, arm, and as it finally turned out body to help shore up her slumping drunk bones. As she talked, I actually understood about every third or fourth word. Who needs nouns?

"Helen, where are you staying? I'm gonna walk you home." Like I had a choice. She was capable, at this point, of about one step before tumbling head first.

"Wha?" she turned towards me, thankfully grabbing my arm to steady herself. "Mish otel dere." Her head was bobbling back and forth like one of those back window bobbly head doggies, but she did manage to get an arm up and point in the general direction of the street.

Getting Helen down that escalator to ground level was no mean feat unto itself. The only thing that worked was me standing on the step below to keep her from falling forward and down the escalator. It was difficult covering all the flanks, however, so once we hit the ground and started walking, Helen quickly took a sideways dive, almost breaking through a Victoria's Secret show window, which is a damn hard way to slip into something more comfortable. I had no choice but to wrap my arms completely around poor Helen, occasionally just dragging her feet behind. No, she's fine, officer. Really!

This comedy of errors continued as we negotiated our way across International Drive's four lanes, through several parking lots and, eventually on an elevator to the second floor of Helen's motel. Naturally, I had to use the key to get her in, no way she was doing anything that required even basic coordination. It just wasn't happening. After I got the door open, I was plotting my escape when after stepping briefly inside Helen reappeared at the room door sans the Peppermint Patty glasses.. Uh oh! Danger Will Robinson!

She was able to plant one weakly delivered kiss on my lips and state her intention that I sleep with her the next night before I got away. Heck, I would have agreed to anything at that point that would have gotten me back on that elevator. I did have a distinct weight advantage, however, much easier to use that advantage with an opponent sporting a blood alcohol level of maybe .25!! Whew!!!

The next evening was New Year's Eve and the 500 hard-core Todd fans filled the entirety of BB King's. After an opening set by the Pat Travers Band, our common hero came on the stage with a varied set of tunes from all parts of his storied career, sending half of the completely drunk Toddheads into a screaming frenzy leading up to a sloppy performance of "Auld Lang Syne". Todd continued the show after the obligatory kisses, which thankfully the very pretty lady who stood by me for the show had more dignity than to take part in.

As the show ended and people began filing out, I saw Helen, who had actually been in pretty good shape for most of the evening, leaning against the bar. OK, being held up by the bar. Her Peppermint Patty glasses were as crooked as a roulette wheel in Vegas. In fact, she was the visual epitome of the term 'disheveled'. Oh crap, here we go again.

I nearly left but then Jesus tugged me on the arm, so I went back in and retrieved the drunk elephant in the room. The trip back to Helen's room was a virtual carbon copy of the previous evening's journey, with the singular exception being that on this night Helen was way too gone to even walk into the room so I had no choice but to take her over to her bed, where she... well, I don't have to tell you, my friends, you know what happened. In between escape attempts, Helen told me that she was coming out of a 35-year marriage and hadn't had sex in seven years. Oh man!!! You talk about a pressure cooker.

When I looked up the entire imaginary leprechaun population of Ireland was marching through my mind, all carrying red flags. Finally, I was able to make my physical escape, which is not easy with a pair of female legs wrapped around your knee cap like a vice. Jesus wasn't going to let me off that easy though. I had to stand there a few minutes longer, telling Helen it wasn't her, she didn't want her first time in seven years to be in a hotel room with a man she likely would never see again, it should be more special than that, she deserved better. OK, that last one was from the 16 year old greatest hits of break-up lines, but it had to be said. Miraculously, Helen, even in her sublimely inebriated state, seemed to understand. She thanked me for, well, being me, as she released me from her final hug and I left the room. Whew again! I had dodged ANOTHER bullet. In fact, sadly, that dodged bullet would take on cosmic significance when about six months later, the chain smoking Peppermint Patty lookalike Helen would be diagnosed with Lung Cancer. Occasionally, some of God's greatest gifts are the things we DON'T get! Thankfully, Helen is still present on the planet as of this writing.

Once I returned to the room that night, the prospect of the two-hour morning drive to Orlando loomed and I was again alone with my thoughts of Lila. Here it was New Year's Eve and the woman I truly loved was a coast away. It may as have been another galaxy. After not speaking with her for six days, the longest period since the early November breakup, after the Helen experience, the distance between Lila and I that night was filled with more pain than a visit to a Marine dentist. Purposefully unsentimental, Lila had answered my heartfelt if calculated 'thinking of you and wishing I was with you...Happy New Year' text with a decidedly brief 'Happy New Year' after about an hour. My fitful sleep was disturbed around 5:30 am and I never really recovered. That struck me later when I would tell Lila I almost called her at the New Year and she responded that she wouldn't have heard as she was at a party at her country club with over 700 people and that she had stayed out until 2:30, exactly 5:30 east coast time. I'm not really sure where my leprechaun would have stood on the coincidental nature of these events, but I'm guessing it would have involved some red flags.

January 1, 2014: The Last Ride

Unable to sleep, I got myself up, checked out of my hotel and hit the road in the direction of Sarasota and my sister's house around 7:30, having completely put the joy of hanging out with my Todd buddies behind me so I could subsequently torture myself with thoughts of the missing Lila, the distant lover, as Marvin Gaye would call it. It was among the most self-inflicted miserable two hours of my life. I was so stupidly miserable that I even pulled into a rest stop to write an email to Lila. Thank God I didn't save it to remind myself of what a miserable wimp I was that morning. It was sort of goodbye, but would you like to come to my pity party approach? I deleted it before I pulled out of the parking lot, instead sending a pleasant text saying that I was on my way to my sister's. Once I got there, Lila eventually sent a text saying she was taking down the tree. Over the next few days, I hung out with my sister and her family, watching football, playing board games, and visiting Siesta Key in Sarasota, a favorite area replete with shops, restaurants, and bars. I had a nice time, but after the excitement that the craziness of Orlando offered, the family scene seemed a little tame. Probably partially due to the dark cloud that seemed to be hanging over everything. It's pretty sad that I couldn't make myself happy enough to forget about Lila and simply enjoy the time with my family. At the time, I wasn't able to beam in on the fact that my poor soul was as damaged as the Titanic's hull and I was destined to sink. I had given up all semblance of my friend Jesus and was clearly struggling to maintain control of myself.

Of course, the harder I strained to gain control, the more I lost it. I could feel it, and Lila, slipping away from me. Lila and I stayed in touch by text and by phone, but the distance was obvious and disheartening. For my sick, twisted heart, the fruit of almost 40 years of yearning and longing, fruit which had seemed like it was going to re-bloom during November and most of December, now appeared to be dying on the vine. Bye bye love. Bye bye happiness. Hello loneliness. The Drama King was in the house.

Even the weather reflected my mood. I was in Florida in January when temperatures were usually in the 70's, beautiful and perfect. Not this January. Instead we had highs in the mid 50's, and nighttime lows in the 40's. By the time I got on the plane back to Virginia that following Tuesday morning, temperatures were in the mid-30s and my mood was way below zero with snow in my brain and ice in my heart. By the time we touched down in Charlottesville late that afternoon, a cold rain was falling and local temperatures were in the 20's. My dad picked me up just outside the baggage area door and dropped me off in front of the townhouse. I went inside and felt lonely at home for the first time in months, the first time since the struggles over my impending divorce from Grace had awakened me at 4:00 am every morning in the dead of winter. Even my leprechaun wasn't waving any flags. He was just holding out a fresh bottle of Irish Whiskey and a shot glass. Time to start drinkin' again, me laddie. Naturally, the cats had spread dry food all over the floor and crapped in the hallway. I was home.

Chapter 18

Waiting In Vain

The original plan with Lila had been for me to get to LA in January so we could consummate our over-extended phone sex relationship again. The cold, which had followed me around like death since my late October trip to LA, continued to stalk me and set in like day-old concrete in early January. Temperatures plunged into the teens and my mood plunged into the sub-arctic. One thing was sure. No way was I trusting my buddy Jesus to be in control anymore. He had walked far away and gotten behind His door again. He knew I would be knocking again. I would be seeking. The time would come when He was my only choice.

Not those first weeks of January though. By then, I was firmly, regrettably, taking charge of my own destiny. The only trust in God I owned were those words on the change in my pocket. I let the charade of LA DI DA phone calls go on for maybe a week after my return from Florida before I finally broke down. My tortured brain was hearing the words of one of my Beatle heroes, just gimme some truth. And since truth wasn't exactly knocking on my door, I decided to take the bull by the balls and seek it out proactively. I sort of forgot that one of the problems with that approach is that the bull can still drag you in the dirt behind him. Then all you have is whole friggin' stadium full of flag waving leprechauns laughing their butts off at your utter stupidity. You grabbed a bull by the balls!! You dumb ass!

Pretty sure it was a Tuesday night when I decided it was time to pull that truth out of Lila. Something about Tuesdays. Then again, maybe it was like pulling my white socks all the way up to the bottom of my football pants, which I did when I played in high school, giving the impression that I was wearing a very tight pair of white deck pants with cleats. The fact that I thought that brought me good luck just proves that I was already OCD long before the days of Grace and Lila.

Once Lila picked up, I didn't waste a second, likely fearful my nerves would leave like sports fans after a blowout.

"OK, Lila, what's going on?" For the second time in my life, I wasn't sure who was inhabiting my body as I spoke.

To Lila's credit, she didn't obliquely dodge the question for even a second. No what are you talking about? No what do you mean? She launched like a destroyer making a preemptive strike. It was almost as if she had been waiting for the question. I'll say it here. When you're in a relationship, telephone or otherwise, with someone who is almost 3000 miles away and they are not saying what you want to hear, your mind starts shuffling blame like the cards in a Canasta game. Who has her thinking this way? Is it Dr. Alouette? One of her friends? Who can I talk to? Come on out, you sneaky bitch!

The truth is that it wouldn't have mattered anyway. It was Lila I was talking to, her voice, her sentences, her decisions whatever they were. Whether another person had laid a smorgasbord of options in front of her or not, she was the one who had made the choice, the decision. I had known Lila intimately for over 40 years. She was no one's puppet, except for maybe that allegedly narcissistic bastard of a husband that she had for almost 30 of those years. In retrospect, that was much more a mother thing than a wife thing though. She allowed him to keep her locked up for the sake of her sons. I really had understood that from that first lunch at the Timberwood when we met again. The problem is that while I clearly understand these things now, I was virtually clueless that night on the phone. As Lila explained how she needed to work on herself for herself, she needed to take this journey to freedom on her own, all my small mind, pretty damaged in its own right, comprehended was 'she's doing it again'. It's hard to escape the clutches of our own selfishness anytime, for me it was impossible during the course of that call, especially with my best advisor Jesus locked away behind a door that I had closed.

26 "In your anger do not sin": Do not let the sun go down while you are still angry, 27 and do not give the devil a foothold. **Ephesians 4:26-27**

The brother of selfishness is the need to control, and that brother was fighting for his older sibling that night. There are times when the best person to sell to is a salesman. This wasn't one of those times. Lila's perception of my neediness ("Oh, you are going to miss your January trip and you're feeling sorry for yourself") pushed that neediness over the brink into desperation and I took the stance of an undefeated basketball coach struggling to accept the fact that his team is now 10 points down with only 10 seconds left. This can't be happening! As I struggled to come to terms with what was going down, every single word that came out of my mouth came out wrong. The harder I tried the more I failed. It wasn't too long before Lila had enough and hurried off the phone, saying all she wanted to do was lie in the bed and read her book. I continued to grasp for straws, remembering the old never go to bed mad trick that I had used on Darin so many times in his youth. While he laid in bed pouting over life, his dad or just the universe's mistreatment of him, I would sneak in continually asking for a smile or a kiss, citing the awful consequences of going to bed mad. As Lila shooed me off the phone, I reasoned this would work, I would just shame her into making up before we said goodnight. See what I mean? Desperate, no downright stupid, logic... or illogic.

Lila actually picked up the call and I jumped right in. "Lila, I love you, I just can't go to bed knowing we're mad at each other."

"Well, I can!" Click.

The Next Day: It Wouldn't Have Made Any Difference

After the click that night, I decided I just couldn't be miserable anymore. I had tramped through Orlando, been to a great New Years Eve show, driven around Sarasota, been with my sister's family, all tempered not by anything Lila was doing a coast away, but rather by my own consternation at what she was not doing. I had frustrated most of the imaginary leprechauns in Ireland, driven the apparition of Gram Parsons to wandering around the afterlife looking for smack, even caused Jesus to walk away and slam the door, and finally, driven Lila to hang up the phone on me when she detected my manipulative neediness. The next morning I put the clamps on myself. In one those rare attacks of actual discernment and wisdom that had very occasionally visited me on my journey, I willed myself to accept that the next move, or non-move, was Lila's. I had called her, apologized, been hung up on. Weak and manipulative as that apology was, it was also sincere. I would let it stand. I walked through the following day resisting the urge to text, call, email, restate how sorry I was. It was almost like I was beginning to get a grip on the depth of my own illness. What I didn't have was a clue to the depth of Lila's. Here was the formula that eluded me: take two damaged beings, beings whose souls had been lost in the emotional wilderness for years, add some unrequited love, unintended manipulation, unrecognized neediness, a dash of sexual obsessiveness, and finally mix in a little past history and viola'! You have conflicted, confused, and convoluted emotional relationship of catastrophic proportions that can potentially infect dozens of people who spin through the orbit of the two individuals in question with any sort of regularity. Look this up under toxicity in the psychiatric cookbook of borderline mental illnesses.

Fortunately, the extended infections didn't happen in the case of Lila and I. Grace and I, well, that's another matter altogether. We infected everything close to us.

Lila called me the afternoon after she clicked me, acting as if nothing out of the ordinary ever took place. WTF? I hang up on people everyday. You mean you don't? I made a quick decision that obliviousness was my new best friend when she called. That friendship would serve me well until I deserted it in the last two days of the late January trip to LA that began our little story here. The click was never mentioned again. I'll say one thing and you can take for what you want, my friends. In my entire life, over 60 years, only two people have ever clicked on me. The first was Grace.

"Patience does not mean to passively endure. It means to be farsighted enough to trust the end result of a process. What does patience mean? It means to look at the thorn and see the rose, to look at the night and see the dawn. Impatience means to be so shortsighted as to not be able to see the outcome. The lovers of God never run out of patience, for they know that time is needed for the crescent moon to become full."

— Elif Shafak, The Forty Rules of Love

In the days ahead, Lila and I fell back into daily conversation, led by her initially, but later the puppy dog followed where its mistress led. Despite the fact that my friend Jesus was firmly behind that locked door, I did my very best to employ a patience strategy when it came to Lila's struggles to understand herself, her marriage, where the desolation of that 30 years left her standing. As she kept journals and we talked nightly, I even asked one time if I should step away. Perhaps it would be easier on her if we didn't talk, I suggested. She countered with her need for a good friend, someone she could talk to. I, of course, complied, and here is where the lines between motivation and action blur a little. In agreeing, I was committing to an act of friendship, deep friendship, but my motivation? It was clearly romantic love. I'll do this, but in the hopes that you'll do that. In the rear view, I perhaps could have done both of us more good by stepping away, but I was bent on my path and, in my own way, again in the rear view, I was as lost in the chains of my past as poor Lila was. We were like two trains headed in the opposite direction on the same track. Destined for a collision no one could see coming until it was too late. An inevitable crash, to say the least.

I did a pretty good job of being Lila's therapist for the first few weeks of January, while her real therapist was busy getting the Seattle Seahawks, the eventual Super Bowl champions, ready for their run. One might even say that me and Mr. O'Grady, the imaginary flag waving leprechaun, were behind the scenes contributors to the victory. I'm not exactly sure about the therapeutic validity of sessions that normally ended with an hour or so of phone sex, but I'll leave that up to The American Association of Psychiatrists to determine. They can do it when they strip the license that I don't have. You mean a BA in Psychology doesn't qualify me to treat patients? I did not know that.

Whatever listening skills I possessed that had not been honed previously, they certainly got their workout in these phone calls as we covered every aspect of Lila's life that she was willing to share, every man, every drug, every screwed up situation a young woman between the ages of say 23 and 27 could put herself into en route to a train wreck of a marriage with an apparently completely narcissistic, angry, controlling megalomaniac. We actually never got around much to the narcissist, as Lila reviewed relationships with man after man, some casual, some serious, for the most part, with rare exception, all deranged in their own unique way. When, on occasion, usually after a story involving copious numbers of men, drugs, and highly questionable situations, Lila would exclaim, "and that's just the tip of the iceberg", I would press forward like Lewis and Clark at the Continental Divide, despite the fact that Mr. O'Grady was standing in the corner waving flags like an Air Marshall on the runway at Laguardia.

The bodies of these men, apparent casualties of Lila's battle with the low self esteem that had been her serial cheating father's legacy, were strewn from Southwest Virginia to Charlottesville (where my own unmarked grave lay) to Palm Beach, Fort Pierce, and Miami back north to Charlotte and finally to New York City where destiny presented the narcissistic yin to her lowly esteemed yang to capsize the next 30 years of her life. God didn't let Lila drown, though. He eventually tossed her a lifeline in the form of her two sons. This became her mission. When I would visit her in LA, I became, frankly, envious of her relationship with them as they called her daily for guidance in their lives. To her great credit, Lila never said bad word one to her sons about the narcissist once she unlocked the cell and set herself free. She didn't need to, he would do himself in wallowing in the pit of his selfishness. Much like Grace, I admire much about Lila, even as I wiped her footprints off the side of my head.

Our calls went on through the first two weeks of the new year of 2014, until the fateful Friday night of January 17. That's when we had the call that would alter MY destiny.

"These things I have spoken to you, so that in Me you may have peace. In the world you have tribulation, but take courage; I have overcome the world." **John 16:33**

My friend Marie had turned me on to the burgeoning Charlottesville jazz scene, which was, oddly enough, made up mostly of people that I already knew from my years in the wedding business. Many of these folks were actually world class musicians who spent their time in the little burg of Charlottesville by choice, something I never understood. Perhaps it's tough to see the value of a place when you grow up there and watch it evolve from an All-American small town to a bohemian bastion of liberalism. These cats could easily make a living gigging in New York, LA, or any of the other American Meccas, but their choice was Charlottesville and a life of teaching music lessons, further perpetrating the seemingly endless stream of top notch musicians emerging from the little town known as The Hook.

I was at one of those shows that Friday night in January before Lila called. I got back to my townhouse around 10:45 or so as I recall. It was close to 11:30 when the phone rang. Lila and I talked almost every night, but I immediately noticed a different tone in her voice, somewhere between sweetness and desperation. She skirted by the small talk quicker than a pickpocket scoots by a cop, immediately getting the point of her call. Her sweet southern accent beckoned my heart.

"Rick, my heart misses you. I miss you. Do you think you could come out here and we could just hang out for a few days like two old friends, just do normal stuff, watch TV, go out to eat, just be together. We could do things... or we could do nothing. We can go to the beach, ride bikes, just live life." Honestly, I THINK that's what she said, something like that, anyway. The truth is that my brain tilted around the time I heard the words 'come out here' and I became as focused as one of those zombies in The Walking Dead. Come out, yes! See you, yes! My eyes glassed over, my periphery vision ceased to exist. I may as well have had my arms straight out. See Lila. Go to LA. Self control? What's that? Never heard of it.

While Lila was talking about who knows what, I was online propagating the money stashed in my Virgin America account from the canceled November flight towards the upcoming late January flight. By the time Lila asked if I wanted her to pay for my flight, I had already secured said flight.

10 days! I was going to stay 10 days. In the rear view mirror, it's easy to see. That's a LONG time. I didn't care. My brain was off on a Caribbean vacation somewhere, leaving my heart in charge, which was tantamount to leaving the inmates in charge of the asylum. Mr O'Grady is jumping up and down around me waving red flags like a cheerleader shakes pom-poms. 10 DAYS!! Are you crazy? Why yes, thank you.

The conversation quickly turned to ways to fill the 10 days. Visions of desert trips, seeing college friends, smoking pot for old times sake, all implanted by Lila, filled my imagination. This was when the talk to turned to LA itself and, of course, the Eagles, the Dolphins, the hit men, and the Cocaine Cowboys.

The Ghost of GP is now in the downstairs bathroom desperately searching for heroin. Mr. O'Grady is now back at the pub turning up pints with the other leprechauns, having a good laugh on me. Do y' believe this guy? What a blitherin' fool? They are laughing and singing pub songs while I'm following along on Lila's stories without the slightest semblance of care when, in fact, it should have sounded like a 20 alarm fire in my brain. I missed the obvious, such as the fact it was exactly 40 years since January of 1974, when Lila had first pulled out the 'let's see other people' line. Apparently, I preferred to wallow in the obliviousness of a true, but completely blind heart. Never you mind, said my heart, everything will be fine. Just hand me my sunglasses and cane. Still keeping a stupid score? Go ahead, my friends, mark me down.

Quick side note; the next morning I called Lila to ask if she was sure she wanted me to come. Instead of a comforting "absolutely," she instead replied, "why? Do you not think you should?" Mr. O'Grady must have been some where sleeping off last night's party, otherwise he would have certainly smacked me with that red flag about then. What's wrong with ya, ya moron? Can't ya hear her tellin' ya she not ready? Not that I would've listened. I was fixed on Lila, fixed on LA, bent on my path to certain heartbreak and emotional disaster.

As Lila and I talked over the next two weeks, the trip "evolved." It was pretty simple in retrospect. When Lila was drinking a little, she offered more options than Domino's does toppings. We could do this, we could do that. All just seeds, apparently tossed on rocky soil. The dead sober Lila focused more on me. When was the last time I just sat on the beach for a day? Why don't I own a bathing suit? What's wrong with me that I just can't sit and relax? I should have sensed where this was all leading. Heck, all I wanted to do was get the small talk out of the way so we could get to phone sex and build up to the physical consummation of all those conversations when I hit the ground in LA. I know, I know. Wrong head thinking!

The truth was that I despised swimming, maybe it was a lingering bad taste from the 13 grand Grace had sunk into her backyard pool while I was doing the financial bellyflop into bankruptcy, maybe it was the thought of my oldest, Darin, torturing me mercilessly when we went to the neighborhood pool together, perhaps it was the absolutely terrifying vision of Grace's potbellied ex-fiancé Guido parading around in Speedos. Whatever it was, the thought of diving into water merely for the sake of getting wet made my skin crawl. I mean, come on, isn't that what plant sprayers are for? As for spending hour after hour lying in the hot sun soaking up rays, that particular desire had deserted me sometime in my late 20's and in my current alcohol and drug free state, even the idea of faking it and listening to some music had about as much appeal as watching paint dry.

Did I share any of these thoughts with Lila? Of course not. We wouldn't want a little truth to stand in the way of maybe a million to one shot that I could actually make make her love me the way I loved her and miraculously work out the vast oceans of difference between us, emotionally, socially, financially. I was just going to wave my wand and use my charm, my sexual prowess, to slash through all that red tape and then march into Lila's life and heart like Sherman marching to Atlanta. Mr. O'Grady was in the pub most of that final two weeks, using his red flags for the dartboard. May as well get some use out of them, I sure as hell wasn't paying any attention.

So the last weekend of January of 2014, I traipsed up to Vienna, Virginia on Saturday afternoon to my old college buddy Tom Strait's place, where I could leave my van for the entire 10 days. I left the three cats to their own devices, stocking them up with water, food, and, of course, the all important kitty litter, confident in their comfort and the fact that when I returned to the house two weeks later, their tiny little minds would perceive that wherever I was all day, now I was finally home to give them fresh food. Tom and I spent the afternoon watching basketball at his country club in Vienna and the evening going to a movie which his wife Jane lined us up tickets and seats for. We all socialized some before turning in, me with a quick call to Lila. I was as excited as Ralphie with his Red Ryder range rifle on Christmas morning! Somewhere back in the far corner, deep left field, sat My. O'Grady waving one teeny tiny little red flag, the one which shot up when Lila suggested Tom and Jane hop on the plane with me and come on out. That's when Tom pointed out that ticket would only be about $2,000 each and suggested that normal working people don't do things like that! I was too busy playing with my new

Red Ryder to pay attention, unaware that I was about to shoot my eye out!

Chapter 19

She's So Mean

Sunday January 26, 2014: It Never Rains In Southern California

It was cloudy when I flew into LA. LA, where it never rains. LA, where there's NEVER a cloud in the sky. The same LA that Brian Wilson is still writing musical paeans to after over 50 years of recording. LA in Southern California where it never rains, but as the song reminded us, it does pour. It pours. I landed on Sunday. In seven days it would pour, right down on me!

Lila wasn't waiting at the end of the causeway this time, she picked me up right outside the automatic doors under the Virgin America sign. That yellow sundress? Oh yeah, you remember that. It was the perfect amount of tight yet loose. Lila wore it so naturally it seemed almost innocent, but it couldn't be. There was that neon sign blinking constantly from the place where the material sunk between her legs, loosely, revealingly. One thing some women don't understand about some women is that they just HAVE it! They have it so much it transcends any single thing of the multiplicities of reasons they can come up with as to why you wouldn't want the one who HAS it. She's overweight. Her hair's too blonde. She's too tan. She looks like this. She acts like that. Not a single one of those things matter the tiniest bit when a woman has IT. Nothing will stop you. No matter how many times they seemingly cruise you under their boot heels they HAVE it. They have it so good you'll crawl through glass to get out from under that heel just so you can worship at their feet again. For me that was, and is, Lila. In eight days, she would sink me to the lowest low in my over 60 years on the planet, virtually crushing a hope that had existed in my heart for over 40 years! She would treat me in ways that seemed impossibly tortuous and completely unnecessary, making me feel like not only less of a man, but less of a human being in the process. Yet I tell you now, my friends, and even you, Mr. O'Grady, that if she walked through the door of this room I am writing this in right now and held her arms out, I would do it all again... even knowing how it will end. Lila HAS it!!

"Everything in the world is about sex except sex. Sex is about power."

— Oscar Wilde

As in my first trip to LA, consummation of all those phone calls was delayed. This time Reverend Michael didn't have a thing to do with it. Instead it was this tiny little Greek restaurant that set a block off the beach at the corner of Hermosa Beach Drive and, I don't know, maybe 5th Street. It was tiny and had two modes, either open air completely or shut down like a clam. That Sunday afternoon when we had lunch was the only time It was open in the whole 10 days I was there. The food was absolutely delicious, but what the owners actually did for a living, well who knows? That day we walked from Lila's three story on Manhattan Avenue, about two blocks off the beach or more appropriately, off The Strand. The Strand is not really a boardwalk, although that would be the appropriate easterner's reference point for description. It was more like a one lane street with no traffic that ran the length of the beach from Hermosa Beach to the beginning of Manhattan Beach. Separated from the actual beach by a three foot concrete wall on the beach side, The Strand was lined with top dollar beach homes, usually extending up to a second, sometimes a third floor. With horizontal real estate at such a premium and the homes literally crammed right next to each other, home improvements ran vertical and normally each of these beach side palaces had a patio or a porch which looked out to the beach, many with fire pits. Each home was different and certainly worth a minor fortune. So this was what happened to the rich and famous after Robin Leach left them!

Lila's three-story had a third floor patio veranda which featured a nightly view of the stunning sunsets over The Pacific. Being in these places reminded me of the California-based TV shows of the 60's.

Remember the Mod Squad? No? Oh man, I do. The veranda was covered with lounges and enough padded furniture to host a small party just out there. The patio doors stretched the width of the house and opened to allow the ocean breezes to invade the living room. More couches, including one that Lila and I had broken in properly during the final evening of my ill-fated late October trip, and a spacious kitchen in the backside with a 20-foot island that could seat maybe 15 comfortably for breakfast.

On the living room wall above the electric fireplace with glass beads hung, maybe a 60-inch television. For those inclined to find bliss in the material comforts of life, the search for nirvana was over. Down the first flight of steps lay the true nirvana, Lila's bedroom with a huge walk-in closet, adjoining bathroom with a huge walk-in shower, double sinks, and a free-standing tub with gold fixtures beside it, we'll hear more about that tub later. Then out in the main room was the central focus of the bedroom, a fairly luxurious king-size bed that would also become the main focal point of the 10 days.

Once lunch was out of the way that Sunday that I flew in, we wasted no time in reposing to that bed where we consummated three months worth of phone sex calls. Perhaps began to consummate is the more appropriate term, as I'm not sure we actually could have ever caught up. But we sure tried. Again and again. We put every ounce of effort we had into it for seven straight nights and the better part of most of the days as well. While my sexual desire for Grace had fallen off during the waning years of our marriage as she dallied with divorce and conducted her clandestine search for the next candidate, my desire for Lila knew no such boundaries. She just couldn't treat me bad enough to stop me from wanting her. If you drew a graph line of that desire from the time I met her when I was 21 to the LA trip when I was 62, it would be a straight line that actually may have risen significantly as I aged. Even when I denied her that one time back in the mid-1970s, it was more to do with a sudden attack of self control than a lack of sexual lustiness for the still sweet southern accent that now more overtly conveyed the delights held inside that surprisingly spicy pecan pie of a woman. As I said Lila HAD it, at least for me. She owned me, lock, stock, and barrel. And she knew it.

After that first consummatory experience, she waved what should have been the first red flag of the trip, but naturally, I paid exactly zip attention. She announced to me that not only my luggage, but my showers and other bathroom related activities were to be relegated to her youngest son's room next door. When I went in to drop my bag, I noticed the two t-shirts and THREE bathing suits lying on the bed. That's a helluva lot of beachwear for a gringo who doesn't even like the beach. I didn't even notice Mr. O'Grady standing behind the bed, slowly waving his little flag as he hummed *Hotel California*. Thought nothing of it. Lila wants my stuff in the other room, no problem. All I cared was that I was in the right room when the action started, which it would on an alarmingly frequent basis. Which head was thinking? Rear view mirror.

Monday, January 27, 2014: Rich Girl

The next morning was our actual first venture together. We went to Lila's club, the Manhattan Country Club, for her to play a morning tennis match. The sign out front pompously announced it as THE CLUB. It was all about the tennis with a seemingly endless vista of courts once you stepped out onto the back veranda. Lila quickly introduced me around as her friend Rick, although she had obviously shared more information with some of those friends than with others. The immediate thing that occurred to me, as Mr. O'Grady was wont to point out, is that these ladies were more like the people I was usually working for than socializing with. Lila introduced me to the bartender at the pool bar and told him to give me whatever I wanted short of lobster, which, naturally, prompted me to say, "Got any lobster?"

By way of saying that there was no place for me to watch, Lila made it clear that I was relegated to the pool area until after the match. I grabbed a cup of coffee and sat down to do some work with my iPad by the pool, taking note of the fact that not only could I see the court they were playing on from my spot at the pool, but I could also clearly see that the court next door was empty with plenty of room for me to sit and watch. Yet still, I got the need not to have a leering boyfriend watching even as that third-wheel feeling was creeping into my consciousness. That feeling grew by leaps and bounds as I became the only male sitting around the cocktail table once the match was over. Not only was I out of the conversation, I didn't have a clue what most of it was about. Only one of Lila's friends, a nice Swedish lady named Maryann, displayed even the remotest interest in conversing with me. I was clearly out of my element. Lila's friend Debbie, the only other person who knew the whole story about the Eagles, the Dolphins, the hit men, and the Cocaine Cowboys, was there. Lila had described this woman as her true soul mate, so much like her that if they could have sex, they would just get married. She never said word one directly to me, but the feeling I got from her was extremely familiar, a feeling I now recognize as exactly like the one I had 40 years earlier when I met Lila's father for the only time in my life. It wasn't that she didn't like me. Hell, I doubt she even gave me enough thought to know. I wasn't what she had in mind. I could sense her controlling impulses emulating from across the table, thankful I wasn't the target of them. She was controlling this interaction without saying a word or even tossing a glance. Her silence was as clear as the Gettysburg Address. Wow!!! What had I stepped into? Mr. O'Grady has given up completely. He's not even waving his flag, just leaning back against the wall turning up his bottle of Irish Whiskey!

Everything was a competition with Lila. That afternoon we played a great little par three golf course next to her club. I beat her by one stroke which earned me the right of first request in our nightly session that evening. Of course, there were no real losers in that competition. The sex just got better and more intense as the week went along. While Lila erased the bad memories of 30 years of bad viagra and scotch driven sex with that narcissistic megalomanic, I exercised the demons of the supreme kicking my gonads had taken at the feet of Grace and the monkeys. The intensity reached a peak on Thursday night with no less than five couplings ranging anywhere from 30 to 60 minutes per session, these between the hours of midnight and 7:00am. I mean, seriously. We were officially in our senior years. OK, Lila had a few months to go, but, nonetheless, we outdid most of our output in the 70s over the course of these seven nights.

"Ask the Lord your God for a sign, whether in the deepest depths or in the highest heights." Isaiah 7:11

In the throes of such passionate intensity, even Mr. O'Grady would have forgiven me for missing the danger signs that were popping up along the side of the road like fields of clover. It was Wednesday morning when Lila and I went down to Tammy's, a little organic (hey, it's LA) restaurant just around the corner from her place on Hermosa Beach Drive that specialized in breakfast. Tammy, who was a very attractive and sweet lady in her own right, offered comfy booths and a pretty amazing array of omelets. As we sat there on that morning, I spied a look in Lila's eyes that I recognized not only from the Memphis Airport but also from late 1973. That distant look, you know, the one where someone is looking at you but somehow you sense they're looking through and past you at some approaching disaster on the horizon. I HATE that look!!

Emboldened by the sexual splendor of the previous three days, I leaped into the great unknown.

"What's wrong?" There it was. I put it out there.

"I have something to tell you."

"Well... fire away. Is it bad?"

"No, it's not awful, but it might piss you off." My mind reeled. There's no way she could have had the time or the energy to sneak out and be with another man. We had just had some extremely satisfying sex only three or four hours previous. WTF?

"Well, just tell me."

"There's no way I can go to my book club and make it back to pick you up for my tennis match." I actually felt relief. I wasn't being kicked out of LA, at least not yet. I look over at Mr. O'Grady and he's just shaking his head in disgust. It's OK, I say, I'll just hang around here and do my own thing. I mean, after all, I have THREE friggin' bathing suits, I can put on a fashion show walking to the beach in my spare time. Lila looks relieved and expresses as such. Afterwards, we trek back to her place where she hooks me up with a beach chair with a built-in cooler, sunscreen, the works. Then she's off to book club.

I know, I know, this is all pretty clear to you, my friends, but you have the benefit of the rear view, eh? My nose was pressed up against the front windshield so tightly at the time that I was virtually devoid of even peripheral vision. Not excusing, just saying. It's pretty damn clear now. First of all, it's a BOOK CLUB. For heaven's sake, just skip the last 15 minutes and go pick up the man who has just flown almost 3,000 miles to see you!! Second of all, it's a BOOK CLUB, skip the stupid thing and spend your time with the man who has just flown almost 3,000 miles to see you! And then third of all, what stupid idiot listens to that and says, oh, it's OK, I'll just spend my day staring at an empty beach and watching the waves roll in. That's what I flew 3,000 miles to do. For God's sake, man, grow a pair and tell her to drop you off somewhere to rent a car so you can drive out the hour out to Joshua Tree and see the one LA based sight you've been wanting to see for over 40 years!!! Tell her to have a great day and you'll be back when you get back. See, I'm not a complete idiot, I was just suffering from temporary blindness. It only lasted 40 years.

It's not like I didn't see some of LA, it's just that it was exclusively Lila's vision that I saw. We had an In-N-Out burger. We got Korean foot massages (it's best you don't ask). I spent lots of time relaxing. After all, it was MY vacation. Lila was just living her life. Beginning to see the disconnect, my friends?

On Thursday evening before the Super Bowl of sex, Lila and I took off walking to Chart House, a stellar restaurant right on the beach in Redondo, sitting at a table right in the complete glass front of the place where we got the spectacular view of watching the waves crash right towards us and under the restaurant. There we ate high end steaks, I drank non-alcoholic beer and Lila finished an entire bottle of wine. Now I should put it out there that since then, I have finally figured out the amount of emotional affection that Lila is willing to commit to me is pretty much directly proportional to the amount of alcohol she has imbibed during the time frame examined, but that particular evening I had not yet received the benefit of such clarity. As she drank, for whatever reason, Lila began to head down the path to emotional confirmation of our relationship, concurrently admitting that she was so damaged she didn't know what she was capable of while simultaneously stating to me, in a fairly drunken slur, "you know I love you, Rick. And I would never fuck you over." That statement would have passed completely meaningless to me were it not for the fact that just over 48 hours later, she would "fuck me over" to the extreme, at least that's what it seemed like to me. And if he gets a vote, Mr. O'Grady agrees, I might add.

Is there more? Of course, I could go on endlessly, but honestly friends, how many smoke signals do you have to see before you realize you're in Indian territory? For those of you who haven't skipped ahead, who began this little story with that awful February morning that I flew out of LA, who have been patiently waiting to see what the hell could have turned all this sexual and emotional bliss into the disaster that you read about in Chapter one, your patience is about to be rewarded, but I warn you. Before you read on, set your sights on the old adage applied to the end of the world throughout time, my friends. The adage that it will end not with a bang, but rather with a whimper.

February 1-2, 2014: Super Bowl Weekend

There was really nothing extraordinary about that final Saturday morning of my extended LA trip, at least not in context of what had transpired in the previous six days. I had resigned myself to my fate of mostly hanging around the unreal world, beautiful as it was, of Hermosa and Manhattan Beach, the lifestyles of the rich and famous, not to mention the infamous, which included Jordan Belfort, the renowned wolf of Wall Street and a member of Lila's club. At that point, days walking up and down the Strand, sitting on the beach waiting for Lila to return had become the norm, the standard. Meanwhile, when she was available, we took long bike rides, watched sunsets, and visited Happy Hour at the Irish Pub on the Hermosa Beach Pier, Hennessey's Tavern, which Mr. O'Grady had taken quite a shine to. Thus, it was no surprise to find myself resigned to a day of Strand walking and beach sitting that morning as Lila prepare to play her tennis match. The order of the day for me was the same as more than half of he previous days. Hurry up and wait... for Lila. I even asserted myself when she text me that she was home by spending an additional hour diddling at the shops on the Pier.

When I finally completed the 13 block walk back to Lila's and traipsed up the three flights of steps to the living room, she was sitting on the couch reading. After a little conversation, she offered me a choice. We could go back to the Chart House for Happy Hour and free hors-d'oeuvres or we could repose ourselves in the giant tub with the gold fixtures downstairs for a bubble bath. Uhh... well, needless to say that was a no brainer. We spent about 30 minutes in that bubble bath before retiring to the giant luxurious king sized bed in the next room with something called lemon Thai oil for what could best be described as a full body sexual experience. By full body, I mean full body, from the tips of the toes to the top of the head with frequent station stops along the journey. Add the oil and not only do you get the picture, but no road map is required to see where all these paths led to. At one point, we took a brief break to nourish ourselves, but aside from that brief break, we became even more intimate with each other, if that seems possible, over the course of what seemed like hours and hours. As the darkness took over and it became obvious that where we were was where we were going to be for the remainder of the evening, we lay there naked, dozing and waking up to partake of each other occasionally. Lila asked me to go and get her some water in the glass she already had. I put on my warm ups and grabbed her glass. As I rounded the bed to get my own glass I cracked my shin on the oak frame that jutted out from under the comforter, exclaiming loudly in pain. Lila asked if I was OK. I said I would be fine but as I went to leave the room I felt something distinctively wet on my leg against the warm ups and reached down to feel what was most certainly blood fairly gushing down the front of my lower leg. I retreated to the bathroom only to find, to my horror, blood dripping down my leg, completely over my foot and out onto Lila's white tile floor. Lila hopped up and tried to apply pressure to my leg. Since I was a daily baby aspirin imbiber due to the family history of heart issues, the blood was thin and highly resistant to clotting. I eventually took a wash rag and just held it against my leg. The bleeding didn't stop but was soaked up for the most part by the wash rag. As I sat down on the bench at the foot of the bed, Lila frantically scrambled to clean up the blood, which had spilled everywhere, including the dark wood floor in the main room. It seemed to clean up easily, but was no doubt laborious. We conversed as she cleaned up and that's when I sensed the change in her mood. Not only was the distance back, but it seemed to have a companion making its first appearance, a companion best described as a touch of anger. Lila mentioned that the incident was sort of a "buzz kill". Heck, I wasn't worried about a buzz kill. I could bring this back from the dead. When I finally stopped the bleeding and laid back down, Lila already had on what could best be described as conservative pajamas and had her iPad on her lap playing Words With Friends.

Come on, you've read enough now to know that I couldn't leave well enough alone. I fell into a pit of unconfident neediness trying to desperately pull Lila off the edge of despair and unhappiness, asking what was wrong so many times I began to sound like a broken record. The net result was that Lila spent the night on her side and I was certainly relegated to mine. The next morning she hopped up and headed to the bathroom, shutting the door not only on me but also on any hope of morning makeup sex.

That was it. That was the whimper. We never recovered, never pulled completely back from the edge of the abyss that I had unknowingly driven us over the edge to. Oh, there were conversations, we talked about how it was over and forgotten, but you know when the promise of forgiving and forgetting is a rouse. Lila's friends came over to watch the Super Bowl, but nothing, I mean nothing, was ever the same. That night as I sat down beside her on the couch and put my hand on her thigh, my arm around her, she pulled away, coldly. I was like a wounded animal, staggering, disoriented, lost. I did some passive aggressive things, at least according to her, but they were born not out of a need to control, but rather of a desperate need to understand. A snow storm was impending on the east coast and the airline emailed me offering up charge amnesty for early flights back east ahead of the storm. I asked Lila if she preferred that I just take off the next day, prompting her anger to the surface as she declared, "you're homesick". I assured her I wasn't and that I would rather be there with her than anywhere in the world, a desperate statement which just served to fuel her anger. It was beyond pitiful, it was downright embarrassing. I was a man grasping for a life raft but instead sinking further and deeper under the water. As we retired for the evening, Lila made it clear that touching her was verboten, scooting all the way over to her side with her back to me. I finished the evening with some inane statement about respecting her need for space to which she angrily replied, "well, I need it now!" That was her final word of the night. I should know, because for the second night in a row I was sleepless.

Monday February 3, 2014: The Last Day

When I was playing various sports, I remember a few times we entered the fourth quarter, the last inning, or whatever increment was relevant, with a seemingly insurmountable lead only to lose it incredibly and end up at the wrong end of the score. It was always like it was happening beyond your control, like you were a mere observer to your own destruction. Whatever you tried, whatever you did, it just led you further down the path to self-defeat. It was the absolute most horrible feeling in the world.

The next morning I made one more feeble, useless attempt to retrieve the situation with Lila when we woke. I made the ridiculous statement, "Lila, I love you and you know there is nothing I would ever do to hurt you." After I said that she made one of those sure, buddy laughs as she bounded from the bed to the bathroom and shut the door. As I lay there, even Mr. O'Grady wasn't waving any flags anymore. He was just packing them up along with the water cooler and everything else on the bench in preparation for the inevitable head hung walk to the locker room. To her credit, Lila did her best to respect the final day of my visit. She offered me numerous options, many of which involved more Strand walking and beach sitting. I made clear that since it was my last day, I would prefer to spend the entire day with her. Yeah, I know, the smart money would already be on that plane back east cutting your losses but when it came to Lila, well, you know, you've read this far. I'm guessing the early Christians getting ready to enter the Roman colosseum to arm wrestle lions likely felt similar to the way I did at that point. I wandered aimlessly around Manhattan Beach while Lila went to the dentist, pretending everything was OK and buying Lila some roses at a grocery store, which only seemed to make her feel worse. The skies were clear and sunny but a dark cloud hung directly over me. Lila suggested we go to a local mall where we eventually sat down to share a burrito. This was where she did what she had wanted to do since Saturday.

"Well, what's next?" The question caught me by surprise, even flirted with a sense of hope, false as it was.

"What do you mean, for us?"

"Yes." False hope strutted around. Not over yet, she's talking about the next step. I played, saying she could come visit me or we could meet in New York, the other thing we had discussed. Lila launched her final drive.

"I'm still not sure there's a future for us." Really? "No, as a matter of fact, I'm sure there's not. It's not there for me."

Damn!!! Game, set, match! There it was. The words that had been trying to wrestle their way out for two days finally were hanging out there. She followed up with a final crushing blow just in case I had some life left in me.

"When this happened the last time I thought there was something wrong with me, but no, I'm OK." Well then, I guess that lets us know who is the one with something wrong with them, doesn't it honey? There were other words, but they don't matter. Nothing did. I became the romantic equivalent of that team that had entered the fourth quarter with a seemingly insurmountable lead only to now find itself running the clock out just to get back to the locker room and lick your wounds. Why had she bothered to ask? Just to see what I would say. Why ask if you knew what you were going to say? On and on, blah, blah, blah. None of it mattered. It was over.

The formalities remained. We walked down to the Pier and Hennessy's with Lila pulling out all the cliches, and emptying the bench. You deserve better than this, Rick. This will be a good stepping stone for both of us, Rick. I have a good feeling about you, Rick. On and on. Fuck you!!

At Hennessy's, we toasted our friendship for life and when we went to an Italian restaurant that Lila insisted on taking me to despite the fact that I was about as hungry as a chemotherapy patient, she continued the drinking and did the usual rope a dope. Would you ever consider moving to California, Rick? We could be neighbors, Rick! As we walked home... well, I walked, Lila sort of stumbled, I actually began to contemplate whether I could get one more tumble in the hay before leaving. Glad it didn't work. Anger sex has never really been my thing. I shoot myself in the foot as usual anyway by asking jokingly whether she was going to make me sleep in another room. Anger welled in her again.

"Yep, I think I will, think I'll put you in Jarod's room."

"Come on, Lila, I was just kidding, I don't want to sleep in there." As we walked down for the night. I walked into her room.

"What are you doing? We talked about this. You're gonna sleep in Jarod's room!"

Again, I reiterated my desire to sleep with her, but soon tucked my tail between my legs and headed to the bedroom where my suitcase had resided for the length of my stay. I heard the door shut and checked back in the hallway to be sure it was Lila's bedroom door. It was.

I felt horrible. About LA, about Lila, about the whole trip, but mostly about me. Who screws things up this bad? Furthermore, what had I done? I mean, I had a few ideas but nothing definitive. I finally lay down on the bed that was noticeably less comfortable than Lila's. For one second the thought passed through my head that she had gotten herself a better bed than her kid. I laid there in the dark with negative self-analysis flowing threw my brain like a category three hurricane, prepared for my third sleepless night in a row. It was after 4:00am before I even noticed how cold I was.

Chapter 20
Heartbreak Time 2

As I have aged, one thing I have noticed is that the lowest of lows don't look nearly so low until until you actually stare back at the depth of the pit you were wallowing in. Damn, I was down THERE! Gracious! Sort of like the clarity in the rearview mirror thing except more painful. I guess we just develop some deflection mechanisms that keep us from being fully able to wonderfully wallow in our misery such as when we are young.

After six fairly miserable hours on the Virgin America jet that brought me back to the east coast that February day, I was ready to be deflected. I tried to make the best of things. I mean, I had a whole row to myself. That's something to celebrate on today's usually crowded flights, right? I had free internet, allowing me to surf the web at will for the vast majority of the six hours. Of course, I spent the majority of the googling phrases that started with the words "what to do when your girlfriend......". There was the cool little menu on the touchscreen on back of the seat in front of me. I could and did order an overpriced sandwich which actually resembled one of those prepared ones you get off the refrigerated rack at the neighborhood Seven Eleven, only at triple the price. You could even watch TV on the touchscreen. We all know how great daytime TV is after the noon hour, that is unless you wanted to watch ESPN's constant ongoing analysis of one of the most lopsided Super Bowls in history! The thing was, no matter which of these endlessly fascinating activities I sunk my mind into, I just couldn't shake the thoughts of those last two days that culminated in the lonely night in the cold bed in the separate room and the cab ride in the dark morning with the Eagles playing. Over and over in my tortured brain, every little detail, every scene replayed and I analyzed. Oh man, did I analyze them!!!

If only I hadn't done this, said this, thought that, not done that. On and on the movie played, over and over. I applied stop motion so much that it looked like an instant replay marathon. On every replay of every scene, I beat myself up a little more and more. Finally I was slumped in the corner of the ring, still struggling to rise to my feet just one more time, being egged on by Mr. O'Grady and my flag-waving fan club of imaginary leprechauns.

One deflection occurred when my good buddy Tom Strait picked me up at Dulles. No way was I going to let him see the despair which was overtaking my sorry spirit at that point. I had actually called Tom the day before as I wandered aimlessly around downtown Manhattan Beach, so he had a clue what was happening. As we drove the 20 minute drive back to his Vienna home and passed the Wolftrap, a concert venue favorite, I delineated the sad details of the nasty vision that had played in my brain over and over during the six hour flight.

Tom, always the optimist, quickly assessed the situation and exclaimed, "it just sounds like she doesn't know what she wants. Just give her time, give her space, and she'll figure it out." My good old buddy false hope, having absorbed the knockout punch of that night in a separate room followed by the right cross of the lonely Eagle music-filled ride to the airport, had been laying flat on his back on the canvas. With Tom's words, he opened his eyes and rolled over, raising himself onto his elbows. "Just play your cool and give it a while, she'll come around." False hope grabs the ropes and pulls himself to his knees, finally to a full stand and retreats to his corner as the bell rings ending the round. Yes! I survived. I'm still in the fight.

Once we got to dinner with Tom's wife, Jane, and I relayed my sad tale to her, I became filled with optimism as we ate our dinner that evening. Jane told her story of the girlfriend culture of Chicago that she was lost in and how Tom overcame merely through the power of communication, eventually asking the key question, "are you happy?" Send some flowers, said Jane. Yep, that's it, what had me thinking this was over just because I was tossed to the curb and then kicked incessantly? That's no reason to give up hope, right? This was going to be a lot easier than I thought. What the hell was I thinking? Piece of cake. Send flowers, make a few calls, send a few texts, you're golden. One little teeny weeny miscalculation. Jane was in her 20's when this happened, and Lila is in her 50's as we speak. Jane had never been married. Lila had been a virtual prisoner of war for 30 years under the thumb of the narcissistic megalomanic she called a husband. Other than that, they may as well have been twin sisters.

As we sat at dinner, that night, it was Jane who introduced a word that would come to haunt me many times over the coming months into my personal lexicon. NEED. As I talked about Lila and what happened in LA, what had happened over the course of the last five months, a flash of cognitive recognition came over Jane's face and she leaned forward ever so slightly, "I see... you NEED her."

It was like a truckload of bricks was dumped on me. Vision of flag-waving leprechauns played in my brain. Need? Me? Need? Oh no, no, no, no, no! Not me! Holy crap! Was it that obvious? No way. I don't need anyone. Oh man, was I in trouble! See, this is where the smart money would have folded up the tents, put them in the wagons, and moved ahead. And I thought about that for about five minutes. Then false hope whispered in my ear that everything was okay and the next thing I knew, I was on my iPad ordering up roses for Lila. They got a huge reaction. A text back that next night saying 'thank u 4 the flowers.' Damn! She doesn't even care enough to spell out a three-letter word. This was the beginning of sort of a final descent, a five-month dance with false hope, a slow dance to painful awareness.

8 We are hard pressed on every side, but not crushed; perplexed, but not in despair; 9 persecuted, but not abandoned; struck down, but not destroyed. **2 Corinthians 4:8-9**

Dreary as my townhouse had been on that early January day when I returned from Florida, that was practically tropical compared to the dank, dark, and depressive atmosphere I walked into the early

February morning after driving from Tom and Jane's home in Vienna. Or perhaps that was just the color and condition of my soul. The memories of those last two days in LA played over and over again like a bad movie for the entire two-and-a-half-hour drive. A Groundhog Day of heartbreak. What if I hadn't done this? What if I hadn't said that? Stupid, stupid, stupid!! I had met the enemy and he was me. How dumb to crack my leg on the bed. If only I hadn't done that everything would have been cool, I would've been able to keep the spell going. I totally missed the point that even without the bloody leg, totally aside from the night in the son's room, even without the forced cab ride, sooner or later, I was going to be exactly where I found myself. Heartbroken, bewildered, and wondering where the truck that hit me was. It was gonna happen, and it was just a matter of how and when. I missed the point that it had nothing to do with me and everything to do with Lila. Whether I helped her bring it down or not, it was coming down like the Walls of Jericho, like the Alamo, bound to fall.

Fortunately, or perhaps not so fortunately, I was well practiced at sitting around my townhouse nursing a broken heart by that time. All those months of pining for Grace paid off..... pretty sad, but that was it in a nutshell. Didn't make it any easier. Lila, for her part, had her money, her friends, her LA lifestyle, and a trip to Cabo planned for the week after she jettisoned me. Money doesn't solve life's problems, but it sure does make it easier to put them on hold for a while. It's a little bit tougher to be miserable when you're sitting in a lounge chair on the beach watching a Mexican sunset while sipping Margaritas through a straw than sitting on a cat fur-covered couch in Virginia drinking Beck's non-alcoholic while wrapped in a blanket watching Seinfeld reruns. Ever the puppy dog, I even texted Lila the basketball scores while she lay by the pool sipping said drink. Good doggie!!!

2. When you pass through deep waters, I will be with you; your troubles will not overwhelm you. When you pass through fire, you will not be burned; the hard trials that come will not hurt you. **Isaiah 43:2**

It's hard enough to even figure out who you really are, much less gather the courage to be who you are. By the time Lila crushed me, I had spent the better part of almost two years studying Jesus, coming to grips with the fact that he was FULLY a man, made of flesh and blood, subject to the same weaknesses, temptations, and pain that we all are. Yet He somehow transcended, virtually inventing the principles of unconditional love in the process. The journey through understanding, attempting to understand that, had carried me miles and miles. The remnants of that journey, even though I had deserted it, had carried me through the first four months of my renewed relationship with Lila. Yet when it all crumbled and Lila sent me packing in the cab that dark LA morning, I sought solace everywhere but in the arms of my friend Jesus, the arms that had carried me so far, at least until I got down and tried to walk on my own without Him. It's like admitting to parents that you were wrong, that they were right. Who wants to suffer that humiliation? Better to hide behind false realities, and couch the real you in a shell of tough guy coolness. Of course, the point missed is that all that coolness is actually self-defeating, especially when it doesn't ring true. You miss that Jesus walked around with a perpetually broken heart. Who better to comfort you in yours?

I turned my Lila project over to my buddy Tom for the next month or so after my return. Oh, occasionally I would step out and be the real me, such as when I sent Lila a Valentine's card that was waiting upon her return from Cabo. That generated a surprise call from her followed, oddly enough, by an email apology that she called. Other than that, I worked with Tom to craft myself as the cool, aloof tough guy that we presumed would impress Lila. Tom was doing his best to help, I just didn't have a lot of material to work with. It was, for the most part, a miserable failure. I was simply horrible at projecting the image that Tommy felt would cause Lila to step up to the window and say, maybe I should try that on again. When I vacillated between that image and the real me, which was something akin to a jellyfish, only a little MORE than spineless, the result was eternally embarrassing even in the rearview mirror. No matter how many times you look back, all you see is a wreck, a completely preventable one.

Then in the middle of all this, God must have decided there was no way I could pull myself out of it, so He gave me the slap in the face I needed. Snap out of it, will ya? Pay attention! You gotta life heaah, ya know!!!

The slap took place on Tuesday, March 4th, exactly one month to the day after my slightly less than amicable ejection from LaLa land and the home of Lila. Around nine that evening, I got a call from my father asking if I would come over to their house and pick my mom up off the floor as she had fallen. Dad could no longer help her without hurting himself. His fluctuating blood sugar levels determined his strength at any given time. It was low that night, so before I headed home, I stocked him up with candy bars and peanut butter crackers. I was sleeping fitfully at best when my phone rang at 3:00 am. While the sight of my parent's number on the caller ID struck terror in my heart, the sound of my mother's panicked voice drove me into action. It's funny, I don't even remember hopping in my van that morning, or driving over, but I clearly remember the sight of my father lying face down on the floor. That was the beginning of the real journey. That's when God had enough of my wandering and willfulness. That's when He expressed His very real sovereignty over my life. Here's what I have for you! Just try and switch your focus back to the City of Angels, your own selfishness, your deceptive heart. I'll just smack you again. And He would, over and over again during the next year. My path was undeniable. The path He had chosen for me.

The sight of Dad lying on that floor and my grim realization that my 185 pounds was not going to be able to move his 250 pounds a single inch was beyond sobering. After struggling to try for a couple of hours, I finally had to give up and call 911, a thought Dad hated because he knew what it meant. It meant emergency room, it meant hospital, it probably meant rehab, and mostly it meant he couldn't be there to take care of my mother, which had fully become his mission of his later years. He was diagnosed with a separated shoulder and they also discovered a toe that was about to fall off of its own volition. Both of our paths were set, not to mention entangled, as they had been for every sport I played in my youth. Here we were, together again, this time with the roles reversed. Al least, I knew that, it would take Dad a while to figure it out. When you're an ex-cop and coach whose used to running things, it ain't easy to let go of the reins. It was a lesson in grace for me, not one I took to easily.

As projected, Dad went from hospital to rehab, where it became obvious things were NOT going to be the same again for him. Mom stayed at home a while and I would sleep there, but soon enough I was moving her, first to my house and then, when I realized I couldn't be there to take care of her and we were basically an accident waiting to happen, to an assisted living facility near my house. It didn't take me long to realize that life was not going to be the same for me anymore either. What was shocking to me was how easily people forget the elderly once they're tucked away. Oh, there was a multitude of supporters in the short run, from the grandkids to the church folks to the immediate family, but slowly and surely they all fell away.

They became "too busy". Oh, they're still THERE!! I'll have to try and get by to see them sometime. This is no indictment, it's actually a pity, mainly because these folks in these nursing homes and other facilities had real value, value beyond their obvious experiences. Standing here now, I can honestly and truly say, my friends, that these events precipitated what would be a golden era of my time on this planet!!

March 2014: It Ain't Over 'Til It's Over

So what about Lila, you may ask? What else happened? Did it end there? You know better than that, right? Of course it didn't end. It never ends with Lila. You might think it ends, she might even tell you it ends, but it doesn't end. It never ends. You might take a little 40 year two marriage break, but it's not over, not even then. It's never over with Lila!

What happened next was the first key to understanding what was locked behind the door that I will call the 'mysteries of Lila'. After the way I was unceremoniously ejected from LA, it would be easy enough simply to dismiss Lila as a bitch. In fact, I'm pretty sure if you told the story to 10 people, at least seven or eight of them would agree would that assessment. But that just wasn't true. Lila was highly thought by friends old and new, I had personally known her for 40 years. She was feisty and didn't take a lot of crap for sure, but she wasn't mean, she wasn't a bitch. Grace, maybe. Lila, no way.

The minute that Lila got word of my plight with my parents, she sprung into action, first via a Facebook message, then by email, and finally, via a phone call. What could she do? How was I? Was I okay? Lila was a fixer and now I finally had something to fix. She was resplendent with advice, her best instincts kicking into gear.

I wish I could say that I took the high road, that I soldiered froward bravely with grace. I really wish I could say that, but it wouldn't be true. In fact, it would be an outright lie. Instead, I took the occasion to plot and plan ways I could use the sad situation to maneuver my way back into Lila's good graces and her heart. I'm sorry. I know. I'm a lousy hero. You deserve better. You can revel karmically in my utter failure. Lila and I talked a few times, and even had some phone sex. OK the phone sex might have been a mistake from a pure manipulation standpoint. After that, Lila declared me still horny, thus OK. There went all my pity points, right down the tubes. There's no sympathy for a lustful man. No pity fucks were in my future. Meanwhile, Lila had her life, her party! That continued. She headed out to Party town in the desert with a friend. I was taking notes on each of our calls and when Lila made the ridiculous suggestion that I give my mother a bubble bath, after I stopped laughing I took serious note of Lila's comments that a great Bubble bath is like pure Nirvana. My mission was clear. I would find the nicest bubble bath I could and send it to Lila. See what I mean? Thought processes are just not registering correctly. The synaptic train had jumped the tracks a little.

So through Amazon I found what looked like an amazing bubble bath. I mean, seriously, the world is crumbling around me, parents are sick, kids are estranged, business is struggling, and what do I worry about? Sending a bottle of bubble bath to a woman a coast away who not only shows no real interest in even being in my vicinity, but drew rather severe emphasis on that fact by her acrimonious treatment of me on the occasion of my sacking from her personal Hotel California. So while Lila was in the desert, partying, certainly thinking of me every second, I was busy sending her a bubble bath to seal her heart to mine. Somewhere in Ireland, Mr. O'Grady is buying the entire bar a round and toasting to the incredible unbelievable stupidity of this American guy he knows... "And while she's out partying, dancing, and chasing around, this fool is buying her bubble bath...oh hahaha...can we toast any higher to this blooming idiot!"

Remember what I said about God wanting me to pay attention? It was a couple of days after Lila returned from the desert when I finally called her. The tracking told me the bubble bath had been delivered a day or so previous to the call. I fished around for 25 minutes before finally just blurting it out.

"Do you get a package from me?"

Lila turned suddenly nebulous, "what was it?"

She definitely exploded when I told her bubble bath, it just was a very different explosion than the one that I had foreseen. Lila had returned to find the package on her front porch bubbling over like a Hawaiian volcano. Apparently, it had set there for a day so the mess had set in. Really? I mean really? The most expensive bottle of stupid bubble bath that I could find was not only gonna get broken in delivery, but was going to make such a mess that not only would the recipient never receive the gift, but would alternately receive the gift of having to clean up a huge soapy mess instead. See what I mean? When God wants your full attention there's not a lot you can do. How about instead of her not only not receiving your gift, how about I use that gift as an instrument to create in her anger about the gift? How does that work for you, my bad son? From my prospective it was pretty simple. My world had turned into one HUGE crap sandwich and I was being asked to take a gigantic bite!!

I gave it a couple of days before I called again. Lila was none too happy with the prospect of cleaning up that bubble bath, which she referred to as a $40 mess requiring $250 of cleanup. I was on the ropes before the brief conversation, which took place on, I believe, March 29th. I was already back pedaling when I stupidly mentioned that next time I would deliver and demonstrate the bubble bath in person.

"Good luck with that," said Lila sarcastically, which then led to my descent into a passive aggressive statement that was like lighting the fuse that was coming out of Lila's head. Those words, OWN IT, came tumbling out again, followed by these..." and I have to go." Click!!!!!

Spring 2014: Sound Of Silence

Yes, she did. Again!!! She clicked me. I remember staring blankly at the phone for what felt like an hour, like I could do something different than what had just happened. God couldn't have been a lot more clear. OK, the bubble bath broke, your brilliant plan shattered into pieces, and now she's clicked on you after a less than five-minute phone conversation. What are you missing here, buddy? It must have worked because, frankly, I could not think of a remotely appropriate or suitably subtle comeback, I had no choice but to let it go. For three weeks, I was silent as a mouse, with no texts, no calls, no emails, not even a Facebook like. Oh, I thought about her incessantly, that's my MO, but I played my cards right next to my vest. I finally broke down around Easter, sending two dozen yellow roses which got me back the heart rendering text, 'thank u 4 the flowers.' Touching!

I held my cards for another two weeks, then in early May, I got an email one evening late:

Hi Rick

I just wanted to say that I'm sorry we haven't been able to talk. I hope your parents are doing well. Hope we can talk soon.

Lila

Whatever Lila wants, Lila gets, so by the next night she called, she was coming to DC for her son's graduation. At one point, she had even mentioned me going to that graduation with her. What do I do? For months afterwards, I would be haunted by Lila coming out of her hiding to contact me a week before that trip. Was I supposed to invite her down? Invite myself up?

The double click kick in the heart had me wary so no invitation was issued. My cards stayed close, even when Lila drunk called me that first night in DC, high on Gin and Xanax. When I wrote her a quick email cautioning her about mixing the two and she responded by telling me she had been mixing drugs and alcohol since I was a child, even I sensed a callousness there that I could not deny. The trip passed with no more calls from Lila, although she did post numerous pictures of herself, her family, and the graduate. Of course, she looked great and the inclusion of her family served to reinforce my own sense of isolation from the events and I spent five distraught days knowing a woman I apparently loved so much I was willing to make a complete spectacle of myself over was a mere 100 miles away. It was so completely torturous that I felt an incredible sense of relief just knowing her return flight had lifted off the ground and was en route to LA. Though it was completely out of character for me, I actually made a decision. Never more would I put myself through that again. The next time Lila came east, I would ask the question and then deal with the answer, whatever it was.

That chance was to come up at a surprisingly quick intersection. I had called Lila numerous times, on her birthday, on her return from a wine country girls' weekend, quite a bit. One of those times, she had actually skipped past the Miami story and retrod back to her days of growing up in Southwest Virginia, along the way telling me about every man she had been with there and including stories of Danny the druggie who had snaked her affections from me after my fourth year of college. Truth be told there likely wasn't a lot of snaking, he was loaded with drugs of all types, so it was more like a pied piper effect. Still, the stories about Danny struck a chord with me as I noticed changes in Lila's demeanor with me. She became a little more distant, a little less familiar, and had no interest in phone sex. That was when I started thinking about the road map that God had given me from the start. The 40 year parallels! Maybe there was a man, perhaps men, there was something, that explained a lot.

Pretty sad thought process, especially when you realize it is emanating from a 62 year old noggin!

When Lila told me around mid-June that she was coming back to DC in two weeks, I wasted no time asking her to come see me. She said the room and the flights were booked, and she couldn't make changes, which I knew was poppycock. Then I called her one final Sunday night just ahead of her trip to DC. There was a tone that I hadn't heard before and Lila fairly rushed me off the phone that night. It sounded like a goodbye to me. Maybe it was just my self-preservation instinct finally kicking in, but I hung up that night with some resignation. Oh, I contacted Lila a couple of more times, including when she was in DC, just in case I could help, but I could finally see the proverbial handwriting on the wall, the handwriting that had been there for months.

When I texted Lila a Happy Fourth of July the next week and heard nothing back, I just accepted. I bought in. Finally. It might not ever be over for me, but perhaps if I at least acknowledge it is for her, I can begin to move forward some. That was my thought, my concept. I had been clicked, downgraded, and forced into strange beds, taxi cabs, and situations. I might not ever be able to let it go, but dammit, I can face it. At least enjoy my broken heart and all the inspiration that entails. Yep, there were no two ways around it. That conversation sounded like goodbye, like Harry Carey giving the final box scores and signing off for the day. My brain began to grasp what my broken heart was saying. It's over man. Mr O'Grady's waving the WHITE flag over there. If only my heart was like a telephone. I could click.

Chapter 21

The Heart Of The Matter

You see, in the final analysis, it is between you and your God;

It was never between you and them anyway.

...Mother Teresa of Calcutta

Once you accept the inevitable, then you have to deal with it. You have to feel that emptiness that goes along with looking your phone and realizing she won't be calling anymore, those emails won't be coming in, you can stop checking your texts. She's gone. Then you have to accept that you have to accept. That means no more plotting and then making the call, text, or email that will turn it all around, no chance of completing the Hail Mary pass of love cause you aren't gonna throw it anymore. You're just going to kneel down and let the clock run out then walk off the field with your helmet in your hand and your head hung low.

There's no neatness, no easy, well defined, cutoff point, not even the proverbial bang, rather a never ending series of progressively weaker whimpering sounds that eventually end with you face down on the ground with your arm behind your back, almost crying a barely audible "uncle."

The first couple of weeks after accepting the end of Lila were pretty despondent, to say the least. At first, I was in disbelief there were no calls, no texts, that someone I had known as a friend and lover for 40 years could let it go that seemingly easy. I kept expecting, there was a LOT of hand wrenching and teeth gnashing and my love, my feeling for Lila took the persona of a dying patient fighting it until finally, peacefully, that dying breath leaves its body.

So how does it all end? Where is the punctuation point? Well, when I started writing this, I assumed that it would have a happy ending. A ride off into the sunset finish. I would finally be declaring the past dead via the auspices of me somehow meeting the right "one," the one who could drag me away from the past once and for all. She would be the light that shone on the muddled mess that I made of my life, family, and relationships. All the clouds would evaporate, all the rain in my heart would cease and I would fully walk into the light of the future with realization that it is not behind me anywhere trying to catch up, but rather I was behind it and trying to catch up. I was so sure that was gonna be it. Perpetually heartbroken protagonist finally meets the woman who can heal him once and for all. That's what I expected anyway. But that's not what happened. And to be truthful, I'm so dense I'm not sure that I would recognize her if she showed up.

Honestly, nothing well defined happened, but rather a series of hazy, nearly formless scenarios that served to put me in touch with myself, perhaps more appropriately my weaknesses. Self realization doesn't exactly rise like that bright Florida sun did above those beaches in Boca Raton. It's more like the rays that break up a cloudy morning in the mountains. Slowly, but surely, the light dawns.

Oh, there were plenty of concerns to go around. The situation with my parents was ongoing, fluid, and could take over my life at any given moment to at least some degree, as it often would over the next year. There was my estrangement from my sons, especially Joe, the youngest one, the one damaged most from the marriage with Grace. Marie Ferrari and I had a long talk about Joe and she told me in her matter of fact way, "Just send him a postcard saying you're sorry and let him know how important he is to you."

Marie turned out to be quite wise. It was about three weeks later when Joe called me, explaining that he was never upset with me, expressing his appreciation for the card and the apology within. As for Lila's men, that was all theory and assumption on my part. I never actually saw evidence, but I trust my sixth sense when it comes to her and I have usually been right. Ultimately, it doesn't matter.

34 "A new command I give you: Love one another. As I have loved you, so you must love one another. 35 By this everyone will know that you are my disciples, if you love one another." John 13:34-35

Now my walk with Jesus hasn't been exactly a straight line. You know that poem about the footprints in the sand? Where the guy ask Jesus why for portion of his journey, there is only one set of footprints in sand? Jesus tells the guy, "that was when I was carrying you." Well, it's pretty much that way for me except that in addition to the single set of footprints there is also occasionally a large wide spot where Jesus would not have been carrying, but rather dragging my carcass towards the RIGHT THING, probably with some heel tracks where I tried to dig in and halt the progress our Lord and Savior was virtually forcing me to make.

"Excuse me...Jesus...what that big wide swath in the sand with the occasional trench on either side?"

"Why, my son, those are the places where your WILL to do the wrong thing was so strong that I had to put you down and drag you by the nap of your neck!"

I think about that day when Grace called me from Charlotte and He was whispering in my ear, that night with Lila at the Sky-bar when He whispered in my ear...non-stop! I was getting dragged a lot for the last 15 years. Jesus just couldn't drag me away fast enough to keep me from getting kicked. Maybe I was supposed to get kicked. Either way, it's pretty clear that I am covered in bruises and have a virtual butt load of sand on my rear end.

August 2014: Another Reunion

I thought attending the Lane High school all classes reunion in August of 2014 would be a safe bet. Grace surely wouldn't show up, she never cared at all about the reunions except for the one she snared me at. Lila was almost 3,000 miles away, the likelihood of any Eagles music playing was beyond remote, not a single old girlfriend in sight, Samantha, my cheerleader true love, was the only un-married one from my high school years and she was no where to be found. It seemed safe, like a great way to make some halting steps towards a new start. Stay to myself, soldier forward, onward to a new life. Things started out spectacularly when I had a conversation right away with Jackie Glasgow. Jackie and I had gone to grade school together as well as high school. Lived in the same neighborhood, maybe even had a few classes together. And the most beautiful thing about it? In all those years, neither one of us could remember ever having a word between us. It was perfect. Someone you knew, but you had never known. We talked, danced. I gave her my number. She left early. I was on a roll.

After Jackie left, I struck up conversations all around the room. I was well on my way to success with my goal of no old relationships revisited, just a good night with no complications. I was obliviously wallowing in my expected success when I noticed a familiar face out of the corner of my eye, turning me around to look full on for the only time of the night.

Oddly enough, it wasn't Grace that I saw first, it was Mark. Her boyfriend. Yep, the same boyfriend I caught her having coffee with in Florida, the same one she insisted on showing me pictures of when we had coffee.

One thing getting back on the Jesus train had done for me is show me that my job is merely to forgive. Any judgement, any assessment of sin, of wrongdoing was one hundred percent under the auspices of our Lord and Savior. Still, what to do. The available choices were pretty obvious. The right choice. Not so much.

I could:

A. Rush up to the happy couple and proclaim my everlasting happiness at their everlasting happiness. Uh, no, I don't think so.

B. Casually say hello, acting cool and uncaring...eight years of acting workshops and even I am not that good.

C. Ignore them completely and pretend they don't exist... BINGO!!!!

I must guiltily admit that I turned a few times to catch a glimpse and track their movement in the room. A few times I caught Grace looking my way, but our eyes turned away from each other, much like the positive poles of two magnets repel each other. Grace and Mark wandered and danced around the auditorium for about an hour before leaving, the brevity of their stay leaving me scratching my head in bewilderment over the purpose of their appearance. The thing is that I wasn't exactly upset, in fact if I had to quantify and label my feelings, I'd have to say pity was the dominating emotional mood. I actually felt bad for Grace and her need for what? Protection? Security? Ultimately, it didn't matter. While Grace's appearance at the reunion made for great drama and gave me a story to tell for the next few days, it was meaningless. Conversation fodder.

What did come out the reunion and held meaning was Jackie Glasgow. It was three days later when Jackie emailed me. We went out on a few dates over a couple of months until we finally settled into a very close friendship. It was much like my friendship with Marie, but Jackie was nothing like Lila. At least not now. She had been in the past, but no more. Jackie had spent eight years in an abusive marriage with a guy I played football with in high school. It was physically abusive. Jackie had been knocked down, knocked out, and threatened with her own mortality by this angry monster. She had lived in fear of him for years after the marriage. Jackie had also spent her time hurting back, mostly random guys she used for sex and whatever else she needed from them. For almost ten years, she cut through a swathe of men, twisting their emotions and sometimes just flat out using and abusing them. As she described it, it was all she could do. She wasn't capable of anything else. Finally, after years of this, Jackie had gotten some help, not a sports psychologist, but a psychotherapist who dug deep and put Jackie in touch with the part of herself that not only allowed her to be abused but also caused her to go out and abuse.

Jackie taught me that abuse was abuse, fear was fear, and convinced me that the 30 years Lila had been through was in its own way as bad as having a guy three times your size beat the immortal crap out of you on a weekly basis. It was a truly fascinating curtain to look behind and gave me a completely new and different filter through which to see Lila's actions, her treatment of me at times. Jackie was the correction that Jesus sent my way. Fear is so very much more complex than we ever give it credit for. Like a subtle charlatan, it controls us in way we can't even begin to recognize. Of course, just as Jackie no longer excused herself because of the fear factor, she was not inclined to extend total understanding and grant Lila a total pardon. She clarified that while she knew the results of her own actions, she was governed during those years by a selfishness that was a necessary counter action to what she had been put through. By this, she concluded that Lila likewise knew the games she was playing with my heart, but played them anyway because it suited her need, a need which had gone unmet for almost 30 years.

As for myself, I reflected on the stories Lila had shared with me, stories of her life and her marriage. I was the witness. The problem was that I was a witness with a vested interest in the verdict. Perhaps I was a victim as well.

September 2014: Heartbreak Time 3

It's not supposed to be this way. No, no, no, no, no!! There's not supposed to be a THIRD heartbreak time! This crap is supposed be over. New life. New me. New everything. You're not supposed to spend nine months suffering when your girlfriend you saw only a total of four times in a five month period breaks up with you. That Hall and Oates song is not supposed to play in your head ad nauseam. Nooooo!!

It really started the first of September 2014, almost four weeks before the Memphis Memories would drop me to my knees. What I didn't know was that while I was down there on my knees the knockout punch was headed directly to my face.

Back to September 1st, it was almost 2:00 AM when I turned up the hill to my townhouse and heard the text bell on my phone go off. I was returning from working a wedding in D.C. After I pulled in, I looked and felt a sense of shock, perhaps relief as I gazed at the screen:

"Lila Wylde..Text message...Did u go to the game?"

At 2:00 AM? That's 11:00 PM Cali time, late for even her. I had not heard a peep from Lila since texting her on July 4th. Two months of dead silence broken by a text at two o'clock in the morning? Really? Why? To ask if I had gone to the football game? Somehow the discipline of not contacting Lila had left residue in my heart fogged brain of almost something resembling common sense. I choose option C. Answer in the morning. The craziness that had surrounded Lila's second appearance in my life made it almost impossible not to over analyze damn near everything that happened and involved her. After all, this woman told me I wouldn't like her if she wasn't bad, had detailed a vast majority of her sexual exploits, called me a month after breaking up with me to have phone sex, then declared me "OK" on the issue of taking care of my parents because I was still horny. What? Am I crazy for thinking this is crazy behavior or am I crazy for not running like the wind?

The texting amounted to about three or four texts each, all about the college football game. Then she dropped it, again leaving me in bewilderment. I know what you're thinking. That's where you seem to live permanently, buddy. Point well taken.

The problem with that path is that once you go down it, you're immediately lost and you don't know it. First she starts the conversation, then she drops it. Why? Why even start? The next week I pack up a gift, a tennis visor, a UVA tennis visor. It's a gift that's been laying around the house for weeks, actually months, that I had purchased right after the last time Lila and I spoke, which had been back in June. My thoughts, erroneous, of course, are why not just remove all vestiges of Lila completely? I don't need this crap hanging around in my life. Out with old, in with the new, that sort of thing, you know? If only it was that simple. It could be, you know, if only we could get these damn pesky people out of our lives.

When I go to the packaging store, I quiz the clerk on two things. When will it get there and will it have a return address on it? Friday and yes. I think back to all the flowers I tried to assault Lila's heart with after she broke it off in February. Each bunch of roses elicited a text back, usually just "thank u 4 the flowers." Even those get overanalyzed by my sick mind. You mean I didn't even deserve her spelling out "for." Three little letters. I'm not even worth spelling out three little letters? This what one of the "loves of my life" has now reduced her affections to? See what I mean? A sick mind. Diseased to the freakin' core.

Friday passes, then the weekend. No texts from Lila. No email. Nothing! So this is where we are now, not even worth a shortened text as a thank you? Oddly enough, I feel almost a sense of relief. At least now I know. Better to know where you stand than to step into quicksand. Again! So I was feeling that sense of relief when the following Tuesday night rolled around. I was exhausted that night, sacked out on my couch in front of the TV. Zombified I believe is the word. Then at 12:40am I heard a familiar ring, one I hadn't heard for months. I picked up the phone from the coffee table to confirm it was Lila calling. Something inside me screamed "don't answer". Surprise and Lila never worked very well over the phone, except that night back in November of 2013 when she poured her heart out for almost three hours. After a minute, it's over...she's gone. Then about two minutes later the voicemail ring goes off. Lila never leaves messages. She always knew that I would call her back. Why now? See? Sick, sick man with a sick, sick mind.

"Hey...it's Lila. I just wanted to thank you for the visor. It's very cool...and I'll wear it tomorrow. Thank you. Bye." I notice she struggling a little for breath, like it took everything she had to make that call. Again, why do I notice? Why the hell does it matter? I spend the entire night and part of the next morning struggling with whether to call her back or not. Finally, I text her. "Sorry I missed ur call. Was out like a light. Hope the visor brings you luck today. Talk soon." I put it out there and she replies....nothing. No more words. Again, the sick mind goes into overdrive. Why didn't she text back? Am I supposed to call her? What does she expect? Sick, diseased. Whatever it is, it's eating me up. One step forward, twenty steps backward. Dammit!!! She has me again.

October 2014: Woman Comes And Goes Again

If only that was the end of it, but noooo! After marching towards mental health steadily in the days that passed between July 4 and September 1, the synaptic reactions of that sick mind go from a straight line advancing steadily forward to something resembling those little plastic electric football players going around in circles, running into each other. Calm to chaos. All it took was one little contact from Lila to send everything haywire, totally haywire.

Then it gets worse a few weeks later when she announces via Facebook that she is headed east in late October. Suddenly I go into total meltdown mode. Tilt!!!! Questions that border on ridiculous invade my mind. When she called about the visor was she looking to talk about her trip east, fishing to see if I would issue the invitation to come see me? Was the public announcement of the trip a way of letting me know? Should I call her? I mean, seriously, what am I, voluntarily insane? What sane person thinks like that? It's WAAAY beyond OCD. At least I have sense enough to realize that I am insane.

After a day or so of obsessing..well, obsessively, I realize that I need help. I run the whole thing by my group of predominantly female friends, the ones who have been begging me to give up on the Lila thing for months. They know poison when they see it. Everything they tell me makes 100 percent perfect sense. She knows where you are, she knows you'd want to see her. Wait on her. She'll contact you if she wants to see you. Finally, the killer nail in the coffin, to a woman, they all said, "trust me, I'm a woman." That is pretty much impossible to argue with, but, as we know, when it comes to Lila, for me the suspension of belief is as easy as slicing lemon meringue pie with a butcher knife.

I keep wondering why God won't just fix it and take Lila out of my mind. Come on, Jesus, I know you're here somewhere. Take me away from this mess. I don't care where it is, just give me some freakin' relief from this obsession so I can move on to the more manageable tasks of life, like taking care of my parents, fixing my estranged relationship with my kids, the stuff that actually matters.

5 Trust in the Lord with all your heart and lean not on your own understanding;

6 in all your ways submit to him and he will make your paths straight Proverbs 3: 5-6

So I fall back to my default counselor, the world's tallest preacher, my buddy Pastor Wilt. To my surprise, he agrees to meet with me right away. I'm not sure if I sounded that desperate or if Wilt just needs some entertainment to break up his day, but a couple of days after Lila's trip announcement, I find myself sitting across from him around the coffee chat table he keeps in his office. As usual, he listens patently while I detail the mess of relationships and confusion that represent

Grace, Lila, and all the other torn and broken textures of my personal reality. For the hundredth or so time. I mean, really, Pastor Wilt should be sainted on the basis of his tolerance of just me, no less the other lost sheep in his flock.

As we talk...OK, as I mostly talk and the good Pastor listens, he finally stops me, saying, "Rick, it sounds like you think all these things are things YOU can fix." That statement stops me dead in my tracks. Time to listen. Wilt likens my situation to a football team that has been banged up. They need a bye week to heal up before the next game. God wants me to take a break, heal, I'm broken and just trying too hard to fix everything on my own. He uses the same analogy for winning teams that he used in Sunday's message. Winning teams adapt to the future, losing teams long for the past. I am oh so clearly a losing team at this point. That's the issue. The pastor points out to me that Lila had other things to take my place. Money, travel, girlfriends, tennis, worldly things I didn't possess. Broken as I am, I have nothing comparable, so I spend my precious time trying to fix things that are God's concerns. Each day has enough trouble of its own, who amongst can add a single moment to their life by worrying about the morrow? That's what my friend Jesus asked. We can't fix everything. Sometimes we have to just apply the duct tape and pray, "Father, I just hope this holds." After that, we have to let it go. Let go, let God, that's the ticket. Trust Him. Trust His plan. You can't always get what you want.

"You really loved these women." Those words resonated with me more than anything else that Wilt had said that day. I really loved these women. I just couldn't shake that. I thought back to first Heartbreak Time and how sure I was that if I just loved Grace the way Jesus had taught me it would work out, how many times I had played these same games with myself that I was now playing, except it was Lila instead of Grace. Same script, with different actors. Getting over Grace was hard. It had taken forever and really didn't end until she showed up at the reunion with Mark in tow. That had shut the door, not to Grace. I still held the love for her, but the love didn't hold me prisoner. In fact, it set me free. I thought about my friend Jesus and the journey He had been at times literally dragging me along on, the journey into the very nature of love as He defined it. I even thought about my mother and "The Station", a poem she had sent me no less than three times, usually during critical points in my messy life. Pardon me, self made messy life. Let's give credit where credit is due.

THE STATION
By Robert J. Hastings

TUCKED AWAY in our subconscious minds is an idyllic vision. We see ourselves on a long, long trip that almost spans the continent. We're traveling by passenger train, and out the windows we drink in the passing scene of cars on nearby highways, of children waving at a crossing, of cattle grazing on a distant hillside, of smoke pouring from a power plant, of row upon row of corn and wheat, of flatlands and valleys, of mountains and rolling hillsides, of city skylines and village halls, of biting winter and blazing summer and cavorting spring and docile fall.

But uppermost in our minds is the final destination. On a certain day at a certain hour we will pull into the station. There will be bands playing and flags waving. And once we get there so many wonderful dreams will come true. So many wishes will be fulfilled and so many pieces of our lives finally will be neatly fitted together like a completed jigsaw puzzle. How restlessly we pace the aisles, damming the minutes for loitering, waiting, waiting, waiting for the station.

However, sooner or later we must realize there is no one station, no one place to arrive at once and for all. The true joy of life is the trip. The station is only a dream. It constantly outdistances us.

When we get to the station that will be it!" we cry. Translated it means, "When I'm 18 that will be it! When I buy a new 450 SL Mercedes Benz, that will be it! When I put the last kid through college that will be it! When I have paid off the mortgage that will be it! When I win a promotion that will be it! When I reach the age of retirement that will be it! I shall live happily ever after!"

Unfortunately, once we get "it," then "it" disappears. The station somehow hides itself at the end of an endless track.

"Relish the moment" is a good motto, especially when coupled with Psalm 118:24: "This is the day which the Lord hath made, we will rejoice and be glad in it." It isn't the burdens of today that drive men mad. Rather, it is regret over yesterday or fear of tomorrow. Regret and fear are twin thieves who would rob us of today.

So, stop pacing the aisles and counting the miles. Instead, climb more mountains, eat more ice cream, go barefoot more often, swim more rivers, watch more sunsets, laugh more and cry less. Life must be lived as we go along. The station will come soon enough.

One Sunday in October of 2014, I had risen early as it seemed a good day to go to the gospel church I had attended on occasion. As I dressed, it hit that the inspection sticker on my work van, the only vehicle currently accessible to me, was four months out of date. Sunday mornings are slow for cops. I mean, how stupid would it be to get a ticket for going to church? I resigned myself to coffee and my little Southern Baptist church. That's where I was when the door knock came.

It was Joe, who came to do my yard work. "Why are you doing here so early?" I asked. 3:00 PM had been the instructed time. I thought about Marie's words. Focus on Joe, forget the circumstances, focus on him. Give him his time, and his respect. I resigned myself to the fact that church, which I sorely needed, might not be in the cards on this Sunday morning. Joe knocked out the work in about an hour, got paid, gave me a hug, and pulled away. I check the time. Still time to get there.

As I walked through the front door of the tiny chapel, everyone was standing and singing. What I don't know, as between the greeters and my desire to find a seat that would allow me to suffer my pain in solitude and peace, I drifted into a fog that only lifted when I fell into the seat. When I came to, Harry, the assistant pastor and music minister, was speaking in preface to the tune I Surrender All.

"When we sing this song, really think about it. Have you truly surrendered all to Jesus? Because if you truly have surrendered all to the Lord, you are a slave. We all are. You should be saying "Master, what would YOU have me do?" Oh man. Smack me upside the head!

Thus began a virtual landslide of heavenly instructive lessons. I almost dreaded the appearance of my friend Pastor Wilt in the pulpit and, sure enough, when the world's tallest preacher started he proceeded to continue the smacking that I was taking from the Good Lord's ruler.

Straight away, Wilt showed a video, looking to make his point about the challenges of truly following Jesus. I recognize it right away as the video Lila's son Jamie shared on her Facebook page as a Mother's Day tribute, all about some fake job that paid nothing where you worked 24 hours a day, 365 days a year, without break or vacation. REALLY? What are you trying to say here, God? That she is a good mother? Heck, I already knew that. Who would even want to take that away from her? She was a GREAT mother. Finest kind. The woman lived for her sons. And tennis. And great sex, probably in that order.

Wilt begins his message about the choice we make, the price of following Jesus, truly following Jesus, Jesus is right there beside me. Sitting in the pew leaning over with His arm around my shoulder, whispering in my ear as He had so many times. "You're either going to be with me or not." Above the whispers of my Lord and Savior, slightly beyond my focus on the voice in my ear, I hear Wilt's soft voice drifting in from the pulpit, which seems a million miles away, like an airplane overhead. A drone you can barely discern but as the sound grows closer, slowly moving from the back on your mind fully into your awareness, your brain grasps it and declares "that's an airplane." Jesus slowly sits back in the seat and the only voice I hear is Wilt's.

"It's a choice beloved, a choice you have to make every day, a conscious choice. Jesus said in order to follow Him, in order to reap the benefits of following Him, we MUST take up our cross daily every day." Wilt is speaking directly to me as he has so many times before. In the pet store. In his office. In our many, many personal encounters. Like Jesus, the innocent but all knowing Lamb. A contradiction from the ways of the world, the people of the world, the LA world of Lila, the money culture Grace worshipped while giving lip service to her faith. Faith, my friends, is like a wise child. It is sometimes just too simple. How can we trust it? After all, we can't touch it. It doesn't have a smooth, tanned body like Lila. No stunning physical beauty like Grace. Just a promise. Peace. Usually not even a deep and lasting peace as the world comes knocking at our door, wanting back in, shouting how can you not love me? We've had so much fun together!!

Wilt's soft voice, the voice of Love, again rises above the din.

"It's not even an easy choice...sometimes it's like wearing around a pair of shoes that are too big....it's a struggle to keep them on your feet...to keep walking ahead. That is the flesh...that is the world...that's why we slip sometimes, even when we don't know it".

Wilt's voice tones down like a trucker gearing down for a steep ride up the mountain. Now he's almost whispering. "Make the choice... choose Jesus." The truck drops back another gear. "He is waiting for you. He loves you. He wants you happy. Choose Him....trust Him...He will hold you up every time." One more gear down as Wilt speaks his final word. "Every time......every time."

As Wilt and the truck cross over the peak to the downhill side, the verses from God's word that offer comfort in our daily decisions, Jesus sits back up in the seat. He smiles and puts both His hands on my head, blessing me, almost anointing me. I snap back a little and look around me. Don't these people see Jesus, the Lord and Savior, sitting here? Can't they see his hands on my head?

I smile and giggle a little to myself. Like a massage therapist, Jesus presses his fingers against the side of my forehead and it all starts swirling around like a kaleidoscope. Movies in my mind. Grace walking into that reunion, her voice on the phone with God whispering in my ear, Joe's amazing courage in that trip to the wolves den at the age of 10, his love of his father, the night at the Sky Bar with Lila, the doomed trips to LA. Heck, even the Eagles. It's all circling around.

The words Wilt had spoken now come from Jesus. "It's a choice. Be with Me or be with them." You can't have it both ways. They had been MY choices. I chose to follow Grace. I chose to leave Joe. I chose to give in to Lila. I chose. It wasn't them. IT WAS ME!

Forgiveness

Forgiveness has three parts. First, forgive yourself. We make mistakes. Second, ASK for forgiveness of those around you who were harmed by those mistakes. Third, forgive those who may have hurt you and then WALK AWAY!

I think I have had some success with the first two parts of forgiveness. With part two, reaching out to those around me, I think a lot of success. As for forgiving myself, I mostly do, but there are times I slip. I question myself, but deep inside I know it's just the devil...workin' those old details.

Part three. Well that's the bear, isn't it? When I looked at that, the forgiving part is actually not as hard as it sounds, you know? WALK AWAY. That's the real heart of the matter, right? Without that, we may find ourselves lingering on hope, sitting on the edge of anticipation of something changing until we fall into the pit of self-pity. Perhaps lost forever to ourselves, our past, our desires, and whatever demon is chasing us. Right?

I snap to again. Jesus is gone...but still there, just changed from sitting beside me to being everywhere, infesting that tiny church with Love. And wisdom. Wisdom. The toughest part of Love. Wisdom. That's where choices must live, in the house of wisdom. The house of wisdom, where bad choices are like bad children. Never scolded. Never judged, just gently nudged in a new direction by Love.

Harry has his guitar on again and he's strumming I Surrender All...the ONLY song I would sing on this Sunday. Jesus returns long enough to nudge me. And I smile. OK, OK, I get it. I finally get it. This time I am there. Completely. Singing at the top of my lungs. As the tears well up in my eyes, I slip my Ray-bans on and suddenly there's Elwood Blues in the back of the church, singing praises and turning his poor soul and pain back over to the REAL first love of his life. Jesus! Jesus paid it all. Jesus will fix it.

My mind returns to that oh so brief period of true peace between my revelation in December of 2012 and Lila's appearance In August of the next year to that November morning when I was so broken from Lila's first sacking of my affections and I met Marie.

It won't be easy. There are gonna be choices. Every day. Every hour. Remember, your shoes don't fit. They might fall off. But they will fit. Walk in them. Don't give up on them just because they slip off a few times. Eventually your feet will grow into them and when they do, your footprint will get larger and larger.

7 The righteous man walks in his integrity; his children are blessed after him...Proverbs 20:7

The song ends, the closing prayer is spoken and I just stand there. Drinking in a deep, deep gulp of the moment. Contemplating the journey ahead in full realization that my future is no longer behind me. That I have to make a choice. A conscious choice. Perhaps daily.

As I look into that ocean of thought, I see the rough seas that will be ahead sometimes. My ship will be tossed and turned, there will be times when I will want to abandon ship, but I can't. I'll just have to keep my hands on the stern and sail ahead through the storms.

I reflect on a moment that morning when Joe came. I was up in the shower and suddenly thoughts of some of the GOOD things that are part of Lila's legacy start popping into my brain. Always looking for the positive when it came to Lila. This time was different though. This time I was already trying to process where things are, putting the yoga mind twist on it, slowly turning to see it behind me yet with the realization of the benefits of the twist, of the legacy. I remember thinking that one day Memphis would be in time a really good memory bank, but there was no hurry. Let time do it's job. LET Jesus fix it. Permanently.

The next day Grace texts me in the early morning. May I visit the kitties? Instead of the usual struggle between doing the nice, Christian thing and doing what may be best for me, there is a clarity there. It's OK. It's OK to heal. It's OK to walk away. They belong to Him...just like me. He doesn't need me. I need Him. He can take care of them. He doesn't need my help. My help can be a hindrance. I text her back that I don't think so, no further explanation. It doesn't feel so bad to think I won't see her, like I am lifting the anchor that bound me into the port of the past. The sails rise and I sail out of that harbor. My eyes are straight ahead and when I do glance back, my mind makes a choice to turn my gaze back to the horizon.

Snapping back into reality once again, I glance down at my feet. You can't ALWAYS get what you want. I can feel my shoes getting tighter.

Chapter 22

All You Need Is Love

December 2014

If I have the gift of prophecy and can fathom all mysteries and all knowledge, and if I have a faith that can move mountains, but do not have love, I am nothing. 1 Corinthians 13:2

Let's face it...the holidays are a bitch. I mean, THE holidays, not like Valentine's Day, the Fourth of July, or God forbid, Halloween. Those are easy, wussy holidays. Pick up some flowers, maybe a bottle of wine, fireworks, a scary...or goofy...costume. Just do something. There's nothing else attached. No expectations...consequently no letdowns, no disappointments. Comparing these allegedly special days to THE HOLIDAYS is like comparing the Dallas Cowboys to a Junior College team. THE HOLIDAYS are not for the squeamish or weak of heart. They require chutzpah.

My kids used to make fun of the fact that I ran the movie "A Christmas Story" on the living room TV for almost the entire 24 hours that is on between Christmas Eve and Christmas Day. Usually the sound was off, but we watched the entire movie at least once all the way through with sound. Besides offering one of best screen dad performances of all time by the perpetually underrated Darren McGavin, Peter Billingsly's Ralphie character almost perfectly encapsulates the insanity that begins to assault us all on Thanksgiving Day like the first wave at D-Day and doesn't stop until the inevitable letdown that is January 2nd of whatever year you pick, dragging even the most jaded minds into its path, sometimes kicking and screaming all the way. Then January 2nd comes, the day after....everything! The Germans are reeling, we've won the battle, but the truth of the matter is that even once we pull all the casualties off the beach, it's a mess...just like it was on June 7th.

Every year we pull our hair out wondering who started all this insanity only to eventually look in the mirror and realize that it is us, we who are our own worst enemy. What is it? The shopping, the cooking, the weather, the tree, Santa (no it can't be Santa), the Christmas music? Too much, too much, too much!!! Pressure, way too much pressure, pressure to be generous, pressure to have fun, pressure to feel happy! Who the heck can hold up under all those expectations? No wonder suicides are rampant and we have to invent terms like "post-holiday syndrome". The unbelievable pressure to enjoy the holidays just builds to a symphonic crescendo that reaches its seasonal high point around December 24th before teetering into eventual dead silence on the aforementioned January 2nd. Then the real depression sets in.

All You Need Is Love

When the 2014 holidays rolled around, my life was in its usual unsettled state. Both parents having issues: mom in assisted living, dad in the hospital (twice!), kids estranged, hadn't seen my granddaughter in six months, broke, business on the rocks, unsure whether I can ever come up with December rent. The usual stuff. Nary is a sign of Grace or Lila on even the broadest horizon. Sure I had gotten a few random texts from Lila around Thanksgiving, even two phone calls which she portrayed as "pocket dials"...or more appropriately, "purse dials" (the phone was in my purse and randomly dialed you...twice...in four minutes...not at all certain why). I even received a text from her late on Thanksgiving night saying she hoped I had a great Thanksgiving. Grace had made her presence known by issuing a "happy birthday" text...a week late. OK, make it eight days late. She can't be expected to remember, we were only married a mere 13 years ago.

I began to adopt the idea that for the first time ever, there would be no Christmas presents for my three kids (who I probably won't see anyway), there would be no family dinner, no tree, and none of the other holiday trappings. I made jokes about how I would be celebrating this year by driving around to look at the lights that everyone else had put up. Talk about no fuss, no muss. That was me coming into the 2014 holidays. Expectations were under control, no money to overspend, and I was able to blow off the fact I probably wouldn't see my kids by virtue of the fact the holidays I would be able to spend with my aging parents were diminishing. Thus it was easy, even noble, to brush aside the need for traditional holiday gatherings for the purpose of serving the higher good of making my folks last few holidays on the planet as pleasant as possible.

Then, as often happens when God decides to intercede in your life, "stuff" happens. Suddenly a friend hands over $350 worth of bar trivia gigs and now the kids ARE having a Christmas. Next thing you know you're standing in Target looking at the card rack, the Christmas music is playing over the house system, and all the clerks are wearing either Santa caps or those dumb-looking reindeer antlers. You begin to ponder, "Well, maybe I could send Christmas cards, that won't cost that much...should I send one to Grace? To Lila?" Your arms are now fully detached from your body and without any direction from your brain, they are randomly shuffling through cards, occasionally tossing one into the shopping basket that has somehow found its way to your arm, even though you have no memory of picking it up. Then, finally, you find yourself standing at a cash register you never planned on being at with a basket filled with items you never planned on purchasing, looking at a freckle faced red haired kid wearing a red Target vest and smiling..."Will that be cash or credit?"

You've been completely had, sucked into Christmas like loose dirt on a wood floor being vacuumed by a Hoover. You're giddy, the whole world looks rosy, the birds are singing...HALLELUJAH!! It's Christmas!

13 And now these three remain: faith, hope and love. But the greatest of these is love. 1 Corinthians 13:13

My poor father made his contribution to keeping me on track during the 2014 Holiday season in a most untimely fashion. He spent the week after Thanksgiving and the next in the hospital for fluid around his heart. By the time I got him home, it was almost mid-December. Then on the Sunday before Christmas, December 21st, he broke his hip, guaranteeing that both he and I would spend a good portion of our Christmas in the hospital. It turned out to be a blessing. The other side of obligation is unavailability and the time I spent with him made me unavailable to all the various Holiday elves spreading expectations like fertilizer spiked with manure.

You probably have questions, though, yes? What about the cards, Rick? Did you send one to Grace? To Lila? You already know the answer is yes, right? Grace was sent a standard card with a high emphasis on wishing Chaz, my stepson, a Merry Christmas. Lila? Well, you probably know the answer there too, right? Yep, I went all out. I didn't intend too. I was all about downplaying, but in retrospect....... I mean, it was Lila, the woman who, let's admit it, owns me. You don't have to do a thing. I actually just whacked myself with the stupid stick for you!

It was a funny card, two dogs standing in deep snow, one a Lab with only his feet and legs snowbound, the other a Dachshund with his poor little belly dragging the top of the snow. While the Lab quips, "My feet are freezing," the little hot dog shoots back, "I wish that was my ONLY problem." I know, I know. Really? You call that downplaying? No ma'am, I call that an attempt. A failed one. Then, of course, I sent both cards without any expectations, nary a one...right!

Holiday expectations, once they get their evil little claws into you are like distant relatives that refuse to leave. You can put them away in a closet, lock them in, but they still find a way to sneak back into your consciousness. Despite my admonition not to, my brain began to contemplate Lila's reaction to the card, whether I'd get one from her, a text, an email, maybe a phone call, the holy grail of Lila contacts. Fortunately for me, the issues with my parents kept me from being able to focus too much on anything other than running back and forth between the hospital and the assisted living place.

Needless to say, no contact ever came. The fact I even remotely hoped for it spoke volumes to me about my lingering feelings for Lila.

Happy New Year: Love, Love, Love

See, that's the other thing that happens...during the holidays, that is. You begin to examine. How can you not when every little thing that happens within a gnat's wing of you drips with either sticky gooey sweetness or unbearable disappointment? In my case, I began again to examine that which I have spent the last two years of my life examining, turning inside out like a two-way jacket and upside down like an empty bucket with something stuck. I began to examine the nature of love itself. Why love? What is love? How many kinds of love are there? Are they all really love? Is Love the strongest force in the universe? Yes! That one I knew the answer to. The others, not so sure.

My love for my parents, my kids, and other relatives is pretty easy to characterize. Love for friends, OK? They are not going to make you forget their "idiosyncrasies," but nothing complex. Love that makes you do tough things, like visit a friend's widow as she puts their business in order, perhaps angry that it wasn't take care of to start with, that love is a little tougher. Jesus love, well that's the gold standard, isn't it? That the love that gives a man the ability to hang in a cross dying and proclaim, "Father, forgive them....." It's at once the simplest and most complex love that ever existed. Like God's love, boundless, beyond reason, beyond anything other than the power of itself, that love is pretty impossible for we humans. But we have to try.

These were the contemplations that were on my mind as I came down with New Year's Eve illness and realized I'd be missing the party. They dominated my mind the first few days of the New Year, eventually finding their way back to the two suspects who called love into question in the first place...Grace and Lila. Grace was easy. At this point, I even felt sorry for her new boyfriend. She and I had never really been friends close. It was either lovers or nothing. I could be there for her if she ever needed me out of love, but not romantic love.

Lila then, well, that situation was a little more complex. She and I had been friends, and had professed to remain so, I had made a love promise to a crying Lila that November night in 2013 that I would still be her friend even if I met the girl of my dreams, who I, of course, immediately told Lila she was. I wouldn't want to hold anything back from Lila, you know, she's so trustworthy. Then there was the fact that I flat-out just liked Lila. Despite everything, I liked her.

You're being an idiot, I told myself, overanalyzing texts, Facebook posts, and stalking her Facebook activity. Why can't you just accept her as a friend and let everything else go, Rick? Would you rather have a funny friend that you like or a lost lover that you can't stand? Accept the facts and accept her. Swallow your pride and don't give a crap what anyone else says. That's what I was telling myself the first Saturday night of the New Year around midnight when the text bell on my iPhone went off.

"Hi. Happy New Year. I've been thinking about you a lot. Hope you are doing great! I really miss talking with you. I don't know how you feel about that. If you ever want to chat, I'd like that. I just want to hear how you are. I reread all our emails last night and I feel badly that I just threw all that emotion away. Even tho I really really really wasn't ready for a relationship I do very much think about you and care about you. I only want the best for you! So at any rate, please just send me a quick text letting me know that you're happy Lila."

Chapter 23

Aftermath: The Return Of The Grievous Angel

The Future

It was a day that turned out to be about 15 degrees warmer than its counterpart of February 4, 2014, the day I flew back east from LAX into Dulles. The 55-degree ground temperature when we lifted off the runway at Dulles at 4:30 PM felt relatively balmy by comparison. On that day in 2014, I had landed in Dulles about an hour previous to the time we took off today. I remembered it being a damp, dark day. A day which pretty much matched my mood. This day also matched my mood. Sort of neutral, but not too dark. Hopeful anticipation might be the term applicable. As I took my seat by the window about halfway back on the Virgin America jet and waited for the plane to fill, I was delighted when I realized that I had the row to myself.

I smiled as the 737 lifted off the runway and I heard the screeching mechanical sound of landing gear disengaging as we passed over the suburban Northern Virginia neighborhoods sprawling around Dulles, drinking in the view of the barren trees and brown grass that was winter on the east coast. I smiled a lot through the entire six-hour flight, lost deep in my thought and the gospel mix playing in my ear via the ear jacks of my iPhone. I watched the flight tracker on the back of the seat in front of me, taking careful note of our location at all times, slipping over to the window as we passed over the Rockies, and the Grand Canyon, seeing these clearly for the first time. America from forty thousand feet.

I think my personal California dreaming started back in my teenage years, in the 1960s. I don't remember the music of the Beach Boys selling me on the Golden State, but the influence of the Beach Party movies and TV shows like the Mod Squad loomed. My vision was a golden land of sunshine, carefree living, and social equality. I don't remember the cynicism of "Hotel California" ever being remotely part of that vision, at least not until I had actually visited the beach communities and experienced the soullessness that hid behind all of the random spiritual searching and apparently endless supply of financial wherewithal of that world. There was my dream of becoming an actor in the mid-1970s, interrupted by meeting Sophia and her calm, settling influence over any wanderlust. In many ways, I had maintained that naive view of the state for most of my life. In many ways, my visits to Lila had only reinforced these visions, but the cynicism of the Eagles vision had snuck in the back door of my consciousness. I knew in my heart there was more to LA than those wealthy beachside communities, that there was a soul and a reality there somewhere. You just had to know where to look.

Gram Parsons had, in many ways, been swallowed by that world. A Southern boy from a wealthy, but troubled background, a trust fund baby with an insatiable appetite for illegal substances of all manner, GP had also been a Southern Baptist like myself. He was defined very well by his famous Nudie jacket, now hanging in the Country Music Hall Of Fame. That jacket featured naked women, marijuana leaves, prescription pills, windowpane acid, and, oh so ironically, a shining cross on the back, a Christian cross, the cross Jesus had hung on to pay for all of our sins. I guess old Gram felt that since Jesus had paid, he may as well partake. By all accounts, although he was unreliable to a fault, he never completely lost that Southern sweetness, and although he had a huge appetite for the drugs, and the LA lifestyle, the poor boy just didn't have the constitution to hang with the likes of Keith Richards. Life and money just came too easily to him. Still, I have to think part of him yearned for that peace found in a gospel song, although he just couldn't tune the world out in the process. Perhaps the desert at Joshua Tree offered some sense of that to him, yet eventually that's where he died, in the now infamous Room 8 of the Joshua Tree Inn. As for my story intertwining with his, I find no small irony in the fact that when he made that final and fateful trip to the desert, he was not accompanied by any rock n' roll concubine but rather by an old high school sweetheart, Margaret Fisher, from his days in the prestigious Bolles School in Jacksonville, Florida, someone he had known since he was fourteen. Do all naive Southern boys reach back into their past when their future seems to be failing them or do they just have a strong sense of loyalty to the people they love in their life?

Up until I went there to see Lila, Gram was my reference point for LA, thus California. Gram and Brian Wilson, who continues to paint sunny and perhaps slightly naive portraits of the City of Angels in his post-Beach Boys career. It wasn't until Lila that I even considered the jaded point of view presented in Hotel California, but that point of view held validity. It was all LA, all California. The city was like a woman. To fully appreciate her beauty, you had to learn to equally appreciate her idiosyncrasies, not to mention accept her occasional forays into the dark side. It was like being in love with an extremely complicated woman. That's what LA had eventually evolved into for me after my sacking from the city by Lila.

Oh yeah, Lila! Did I think of her on that flight, over the course of that six hours? Funny thing, something I'm not sure you'll understand, but I'm betting you might. Lila never passed through my mind, yet Lila was always on my mind. She never left. That was the lesson my friend Jesus had taught and left for me. Love had no requirements. Love, without condition, without expectation, was a gift from above. I was blessed with love for Lila. Whether or not Lila felt blessed with love for me was inconsequential, as was whether that love was ever consummated in any normal manner. Love, God's type of love, that agape love, is the rock that my friend Jesus told us to build our houses on. We are all builders, like it or not. The house is there. It's a shelter built on rock, the door is there for knocking. That's all we can do. Love... and build the house.

I did think about all those Leprechauns, about my buddy Mr. O'Grady. I missed Mr. O'Grady, but I guess since there weren't too many red flags to wave Mr. OG was out of a job. Too bad, cause an imaginary flag-waving leprechaun is a pretty damn handy thing to have around if you are an aspiring writer. So I found a way to keep Mr. O'Grady busy. He could wave red flags for my blog, and my record reviews. You know, one red flag, sorta bad, two red flags, pretty awful, three red flags, run, Forrest, run! Pretty good, huh?

My meandering brain is called to order by the voice of the pilot over the intercom telling us we will be landing in 15 minutes. I perk up and glue myself to the window. I put aside thoughts of anything but the moment and pressed my face to the glass, watching the Santa Monica Mountains loom in front of, then beside, then behind us as we cruised over the sprawling suburb that is Los Angeles below. Weird the way the smog forms a thin coating over the city even on the clearest of days. LA doesn't look that much like a city from above. The mosh mash of various architectural styles makes it look more like 25 to 30 miles of pure suburbs. Without a doubt, one of the more fascinating cities in the world from an architectural standpoint. As the 737 settled in and approached LAX, we passed over the freeways and neighborhoods surrounding it, finally touching down on the runway on a perfect LA day. In fact, the sun was just starting to go down as we pulled to the gate.

I quickly grabbed my bag from the overheard and my laptop case from under the seat below and disembarked. Once in the terminal, I find my way to the next floor down, past the baggage claims and outside to wait for the shuttle to take me to my rental. It strikes me for the first time how different it feels not having Lila pick me up, briefly thinking it would be nice to have her smiling face and a big hug waiting for me. That thought leaves me quickly as I board the shuttle and I refocus on the moment before me. As I arrive at the rental counter, pull out the appropriate identification, credit card, and whatever is needed to rent a Kia Sportage, the real terror strikes me as I realize there is no Lila to drive like a maniac through the legendary LA traffic, that this time I am all on my own. The young Asian girl at the counter asked me where I was headed and I actually had to stop and think about it for a second. Then I smile as I take the keys from her, "Joshua Tree".

"It's beautiful there, I love it. Have you ever been there before?"

"Nope, the first time. I was supposed to go... twice... but somehow I never made it."

"Well, I'm glad you're finally getting there. Are you staying there?"

"Yep, at The Joshua Tree Inn. Room 8."

"Well, enjoy it." She gives me a slightly strange look, undoubtedly wondering how and why I might know EXACTLY what room I will be in.

Outside, I locate my silver SUV with California plates, open up the back, toss my bag and laptop case behind the seat and the storage area. As I get in and turn the key, I take a deep breath, contemplating the drive through LA traffic to the freedom. GPS, don't let me down now!

Once behind the wheel, I find my way to South Sepulveda Boulevard, which quickly takes me to the ramp for Interstate 105 East and I merge onto the endless flow of traffic. I find the negotiating of the highway surprisingly easy. Just like Lila and Grace both said, you have to drive to the level of aggression around you. The GPS on my iPhone performs admirably and I am well prepared by the time I see the exit for Interstate 605 North almost 20 miles later. LA seems virtually endless as the sun sets and darkness overtakes the city. I had warned the Innkeeper that I wouldn't be in until almost ten. From there it's on another 10 miles to the Pomona Freeway. I finally make it to Interstate 10 East, the primary freeway that leads to destinations in the desert west of LA. Then finally about 20 miles later, I see the exit, the sign saying Yucca Valley and take it.

I'm there. The road sign says Route 62 East, Twenty Nine Palms Highway. I smile broadly at the realization that this is the highway that will lead me directly to my destination. Finally I'm alone on the highway, a two-lane highway so I pull the Kia over to the shoulder, being careful not to get too far off the road into the sand. I cut the car off, get out into the total darkness and look up at the largest sky with the most stars I have ever seen in my life. I notice the pleasant chill of the desert air and grab my Sin City jacket. As I stand there, I revel for a moment in the fact that it was probably a night exactly like this when a very drunk Phil Kaufman carried the stolen body of a very dead Gram Parsons to torch it in the legendary, but damn near comic incident portrayed in the independent film Grand Theft Parsons. Poor old Gram. Not only was he dead for the most famous thing that ever happened to him during his lifetime... well, right after his lifetime, but he had been dead long enough perhaps for rigor mortis to even set in. I'm looking forward to seeing him again.

My room reservation awaits. I get back in the Kia, start the engine and turn on the lights again as I pull out onto the dark desert highway, checking to see if my iPhone is properly hooked up to play music over the Sportage system. The stress of LA traffic behind me, it's time to enjoy the drive. I find the iTunes icon and locate the mix I had made weeks ago specifically for this drive, pressing play as I drive ahead in the dark and starry desert night. As the familiar high pitched voice of Randy Meisner comes over the speakers, I smile as I think to myself, I'm on the highway, I've seen the sign, but I'm not taking it to the limit this time.

The desert sky is huge through the front windshield. Out of the corner of my right eye, I see a shooting star and follow it all the way to the ground somewhere up ahead.

"Hello, Gram." I knew he'd be waiting for me in Room 8, probably having a couple of ghostly cocktails waiting for me. As the mix switches to the next track, I focus on the road ahead, laugh out loud, and start singing at the top of my voice!

Billboards and truck stops pass by the grievous angel

And now I know just what I have to do

(Gram Parsons, Thomas Brown)

"Return of The Grievous Angel" as performed by Gram Parsons and Emmylou Harris

The Soundtrack

The original manuscript of Love Blind was called You Can't Always Get What You Want. It was a brilliantly created stream of consciousness piece with the story BRILLIANTLY integrated with hundreds of song lyrics driving the story. To publish it would probably have only cost a few million dollars in royalty rights. This list is provided chapter by chapter:

PROLOGUE
You Can't Always Get What You Want-Stones

CHAPTER 1
Hotel California-Eagles
Rivers Of Babylon- Melodians
Do It For Love- Hall & Oates
Take It To The Limit-Eagles

CHAPTER 2
We Gotta Get You A Woman-Todd Rundgren
Groovin'-The Rascals

CHAPTER 3
Sweeter Memories-Todd Rundgren

CHAPTER 4
I Met A Little Girl- Marvin Gaye
Come Get To This- Marvin Gaye
In My Hour Of Darkness- Gram Parsons
Hot Fun In The Summertime- Sly & The Family Stone
My Old School- Steely Dan

CHAPTER 5
Be Young, Be Foolish, Be Happy- The Tams
Big Yellow Taxi- Joni Mitchell
Killer Queen- Queen
Me And Mrs. Jones- Billy Paul
Cocaine- Jackson Browne

CHAPTER 6
Family Affair- Sly & The Family Stone
Papa Was Rolling Stone- Temptations
Daddy Don't You Walk So Fast- Wayne Newton
Remember When- Alan Jackson

CHAPTER 7
Sweet Blindness- Laura Nyro
Life In The Fast Lane- Eagles

CHAPTER 8
Two Lonely Old People- Paul McCartney
In The Name Of Love- U2

CHAPTER 9
For What It's Worth- Buffalo Springfield
Three Little Birds- BobMarley

CHAPTER 10
At The Dark End Of The Street- Flying Burrito Brothers
A Well Respected Man- The Kinks

CHAPTER 11
Got My Mind Set On You- George Harrison
Money Honey- The Drifters
Monkey Man- Stones
I'll Tumble For Ya-Culture Club

CHAPTER 12
The Power- Al Green
Peace That Passes All Understanding- Richie Furay

CHAPTER 13
Christine's Tune (aka Devil In Disguise)- Flying Burrito Brothers

CHAPTER 14
Open Up My Window- Christopher Cross

CHAPTER 15
God Blessed Our Love- Al Green
Wake Up My Soul- Richie Furay
Jesus Will Fix It- Al Green
Graceland- Paul Simon
Suspicious Minds- Elvis Presley

CHAPTER 16
Thieves In The Temple- Prince
After The Thrill Is Gone- Eagles
California Feeling'- Brian Wilson
Don't Get Above Your Raising- Ricky Skaggs
Don't Think Twice (It's All Right)- Bob Dylan

CHAPTER 17
Sitting In Limbo- Jimmy Cliff
The Long Run- Eagles
The Woman Comes And Goes- Hall & Oates

CHAPTER 18
Flaw- Todd Rundgren
Future- Todd Rundgren
The Last Ride- Todd Rundgren

CHAPTER 19
Waiting In Vain- Bob Marley
It Wouldn't Have Made Any Difference- Todd Rundgren

CHAPTER 20
It Never Rains In Southern California- Albert Hammond
Rich Girl- Hall & Oates

CHAPTER 21
It Ain't Over 'Til It's Over- Lenny Kravitz
Sounds Of Silence- Simon & Garfunkel

CHAPTER 22

The Heart Of The Matter- Don Henley

CHAPTER 23

All You Need Is Love- Beatles

AFTERMATH
The Return Of The Grievous Angel- Gram Parsons

Made in the USA
Coppell, TX
14 November 2023